Sean Patrick O'Mordha

₪

Incident
at
Beaver Creek

Incident at Beaver Creek

ISBN: 9780982984239

Cover Design © Bill H. and Ephraim D. Moore

This is a work of fiction. With the exception of familiar geographical locations within the states of New Mexico and Arizona, all names, characters, places and incidents are the product of the author's imagination or are used fictitiously. Any resemblance to actual persons, living or dead, businesses, companies, or events is entirely coincidental or used according to trademark and copyright law. In particular, the Antigua Pueblo Indian tribe is entirely fictitious, and religious ceremonies described are based on generalities gathered from public sources. The Pueblos do not share details of their religious ceremonies, therefore the author has used literary license to create ceremonies for this book. They are not actual Pueblo religious ceremonies.

Produced in the United States

Celtic Publications
Sparks, Nevada

For other stories by

Sean Patrick O'Mordha

Visit

oldguey.webs.com

celticpublications.xipherzero.net

and

smashwords.com

Dedicated to

Jayne Furness Moore, Ph.D., RN
(Dr. Mommy)

For her support, knowledge, encouragement,
and kindness without which this story
would have remained
just an idea.

Special Thanks To

Danny Blanton
and
Gary Prazen

Of Original Creations, Inc.
Helper, Utah
for use of the picture of their statue,
Kokopelli

original-creations.com

and to

Bill and Ephraim Moore

for the cover design and map

Portion of the Sacred Mountain township

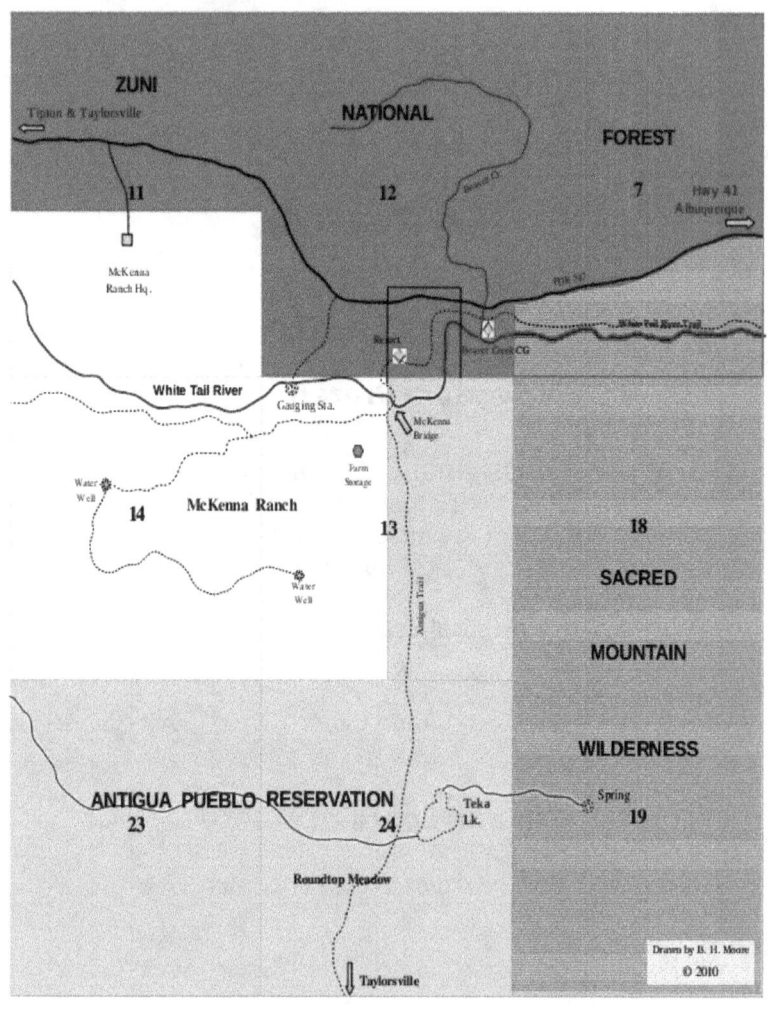

Incident at Beaver Creek

Chapter 1

The winter snows were melted except from the perpetual cap atop Turquoise Mountain, a sprawling, rugged, tree-covered volcano rising a mile above the desert floor. It and its legends beckoned exploring, and therein lay the problem. From a distance, the mountain appeared as a dark blue jewel inviting adventure, but those who understood, the mountain could be an unforgiving place to the imprudent. To the region's Native Americans it was a sacred place, home to the turquoise and black gods, and those who came had better show due respect to them, not to mention the rugged terrain and volatile weather. The mountain gods claimed one victim in April, and for the second time before the middle of May Jake received an unwanted radio call from Curt Hayden perched atop Jay's

Roost fire tower as he was about to leave the Arroyo Forest Service field station office.

"Mr. Bershinsky, Ray Hume just radioed to say that he found the missing hiker's vehicle."

"What missing hikers?"

"Apparently a couple college kids took off for a weekender in the Cebolleta Wilderness and didn't show up for classes this morning."

It came as no surprise. He'd be the last person Sheriff Barker would call for help. "Where is Ray?"

"Bandelier trailhead. He was wondering if you could bring him up a horse and track in with him?"

"Sure. I'll be there in about an hour and a half."

The drive to the trailhead wouldn't take long, about forty minutes. Latching the green horse trailer to his rig, and loading up an extra saddle and equipment was easy enough. Rounding up two horses lazily grazing as far from the barn as one could get in the elongated pasture would take some time.

Walking part way up the half-mile long meadow, he issued a shrill whistle to get his Arabian stallion's attention. Shaking a pan of oats enticed the other horses to follow the leader in a thundering race to be first in line. It worked like charm as the herd of four circled around him giving Mōhf the space he expected. Laying a halter on one of the Quarter horses, he swung onto the gray's back and took the two back to the barn. The stallion needed neither bridle nor saddle as he responded to leg commands. Of course, the two horses were reluctant to leave the oats behind, but satisfied to find a nice helping waiting in the trailer.

Jake's wife, Katelyn, came out of the house with a brown grocery bag and large thermos. "I made sandwiches and drink. I'll bring up a hot meal if you plan to stay up there the night," she said, standing on her bare toes to give him a kiss. "Be careful."

Wheeling into the trailhead parking lot, Jake spotted the warden's dark green Ford pickup parked behind an older, weather-beaten Toyota pickup in need of a wash job.

"Where's search and rescue based?" Jake asked.

"On the east side by the Obsidian Cliffs. Don't ask. There wasn't any indication the kids were over there except through someone's crystal ball. That's why I headed this way looking for their vehicle so to know where to start."

The New Mexico Game and Fish Department hired Hume as a game warden straight out of college three years ago. First working the north-central New Mexico region, he accepted a transfer placing him in Jake's area in February. They'd spent some time together as Jake showed the twenty-seven year old around, and from that encounter, Jake could see he'd be an asset to area.

"I guess they know what they're doing. Deputy Putnam shot through here just after I called you. Frankly, I wouldn't want to ride a dirt bike on some of those trails."

"You say what?"

"Putnam. He rode down here, saw the car, and headed back up the mountain."

"He's riding a dirt bike in the wilderness."

Hume knew better, flashed a grin while nodding his head, yes. The third week on the job he encountered Deputy Sheriff Bertram Putnam and wasn't impressed.

Turning their heads along the road, the two watched a Sheriff's pickup approach. Parking so not to block the road, Deputy Bradley got out and waived.

"Hello, gentlemen. Have you seen Deputy Putnam?"

"He passed through here about two hours ago," Hume answered.

"He radioed and said his bike broke down. Ran out of gas more likely. Wants to be picked up here."

"Glad to hear that," Jake said as he leaned back against Hume's truck and keyed the radio microphone attached to his collar. "Jay's Roost this is Bershinsky. Curt, ask the Forest Supervisor if he gave the Sheriff's office permission to use motorized vehicles in the Cebolleta Wilderness for a search and rescue stuff."

He already knew the answer before Curt radioed back, "When I asked, it sounded like the Super blew a fuse on that one. To translate, he said, no."

"Thank you. Bershinsky out."

"I'd say your timing is pretty good," Hume said, nodding toward a lanky officer in a florescent yellow-green vest pushing a motorcycle through the trail barricade.

"Load that piece of crap on the truck," Putnam said to Bradley, ignoring Jake. The two never got along since junior high school. Jack figured it was the crowd he hung with. Of course, getting his nose wiped in a fight then penalized for instigating trouble didn't help their relationship.

"See anything?" Bradley asked as he slid the loading ramp into position.

"No," Putnam snarled.

"I didn't know we could use motorized vehicles in a wilderness," Hume said, acting ignorant.

"Can, if we got a search and rescue or stuff like that, kid." He flashed a nervous glance at Jake.

"Oh, I wouldn't go so far to say that," Jake said trying to sound polite as his blood pressure began creeping up. "Practically takes an act of Congress to have that happen, and they're busy campaigning this week."

"You were gone a long time and now stuck out here in the sticks, Bershinsky, so you don't know how things work in Fredericks County these days. Let me enlighten you. Sheriff Barker is the chief law enforcement officer in these parts, and he's in charge of all search and rescue stuff. That gives him the authority to go anywhere in this county to enforce the laws or protect the citizens."

"No argument there, Deputy Putnam. He has concurrent jurisdiction so he can do just that, but there is a little thing that puts a dent in his carte blanche. He has to adhere to Federal laws like everyone else. It takes special permission from the Forest Supervisor or the Regional Forester to authorize violation of Congress' intent about prohibiting motorized vehicles in a wilderness."

"Look, Mr. Forest Ranger, you don't tell me or the Sheriff how to do our jobs," Putnam countered, wagging his finger in Jake's face like an old maid, school marm at an errant student.

"As long as you are in my jurisdiction you will obey the law just like everyone else," Jake answered with forced calm, but firmly, wanting to reach out and snap the wagging finger off and stuff it up the man's long nose.

"Yeah? Sounds like you're tryin' to interfere with a duly sworn law enforcement officer of this county acting in the performance of his official duties?"

"Nope. If you have reasonable grounds to believe someone is in this wilderness and needs medical attention, and can't be extracted by other means, then permission can be given to violate the wishes of Congress. So far, you haven't indicated any such condition. It appears you have been having a grand time tearing up the trails with no results."

"Well, I'm going back in there, on a motorized bike, and just what are you going to do about it, Mr. Green Jeans?" Putnam replied, placing his hand over the butt of his sidearm. "Right now you're interfering with a duly appointed law enforcement officer. Back off with that Federal crap or you're apt to land in the county clink."

Jake's eyes narrowed. Putnam had always been a little

nuts, and putting a gun within his reach was dangerous, but Jake wasn't intimidated.

"Planning on using that thing?" Jake asked.

"I'll use whatever I need to get you out of my way so I can do my job."

"Like at Culver Crossing?" Jake said, referring to the altercation he and Henry Riley had with Putnam, several friends, and Clyde Barker, now the Sheriff, when they were teenagers. Putnam had come at Jake with a baseball bat. That's why Putnam's nose was now a little off center. The deputy saw the look in Jake's eyes. There was no anger, no fear, just something that reminded of how the forest cop had behaved when a teenager. From past experience, and the ranger's Army reputation, Putnam felt pressure building in his urinary track.

"Step aside. I got a machine to fix so I can get back to lookin' for them kids."

"Let me make this perfectly clear. Bottom line Putnam, I catch you riding a motorized vehicle in that or any wilderness without prior approval, you will find yourself explaining it to a Federal judge." Jake's voice was low, even, and colder than the top of Turquoise Mountain.

Putnam glanced toward the other officers. With a snort, he brushed passed Jake and said to Bradley, "I'm driving."

Jake leaned back against the warden's truck and watched the deputy turn his vehicle around, a relatively easy maneuver if executed properly. It wasn't for him as he jackknifed the trailer putting a dent in the truck's fender.

After he left Hume exhaled a deep breath. "A bit of touch and go there."

"Not really. He makes the same mistake every time. Has to get in a guy's face. Don't ever get that close to a dangerous person until you have complete control."

"Are you dangerous?"

Jake chuckled. "Let's find those kids."

As Hume backed the horses out and put on saddles, Jake used a Slim Jim to open the Toyota's door. There was a scrap of paper on the seat.

"Using a motorbike might be a good idea to cover a lot of territory," Hume said.

"Yeah, except you could practically drive over a lost person and never hear them call out."

They rode into the area along the main trail about a half hour before Jake veered onto a small, side trail.

"You think they went this way?" Hume asked.

"I found was a grocery receipt in the car. Judging by what they bought they aren't campers. Heavy stuff, but one item was sunscreen. Two bottles. Cocochino Falls is about a mile down this trail, a favorite spot for the skinny dippers from the college. Also, there are two sets of footprints heading in, but not coming out."

Hume looked at the ground. He didn't see anything except dirt and rock. As the trail circled around a volcanic dome, he could see a small lake through the trees below. Jake gave out a shrill whistle that ricocheted around the rocks.

To his amazement, a voice answered back. "Help. We're down here."

Cocochino Creek tumbled down a boulder-strewn hillside into a small lake before continuing on. At its edge, two hikers huddled in a small spot of sunlight trying to keep warm. Surrounding them were shredded blankets, backpacks, foodstuffs, and equipment. The camp looked as if hit by a F5 tornado.

"This how your rooms look back home?" Jake said as he stepped off Mohf.

"A bear raided our camp while we were swimming. We

yelled, but it just stood up and growled at us," one of the young men said as he stood up.

"I think it wanted to eat us," the other said, remaining seated.

"But we swam to the other side to get away because bears can't swim," said the first.

"That made it really mad so it tore up everything we had. It even ate our shoes."

"Yeah, the damn thing just lay here eating everything we had and playing with all our stuff."

"We had to stay the whole night on the other side before it left," the hiker on the ground said.

"How'd you keep warm?" Ray asked.

"There's a small cave on the other side," the standing hiker said."

"It was cold, but not like being out in the open."

"We had to huddle together."

"Two rules when lost in the forest. Hug a tree to be found, and hug a friend to keep warm," Jake said. He retrieved blankets and Katelyn's sandwiches from the horses. "What kind of bear was it?"

"Black," the seated one said, inhaling half a sandwich into his mouth.

"No, it was Brown."

"It was black."

"It looked black because it was in the shadows."

"Did it have a hump on its neck?" Ray asked.

"Yes."

"No."

The two lawmen looked at each other. For all these city kids knew, the critter could have been a raccoon except for the obvious track. Ray looked at it.

"Not a grizzly, but a fairly large Black. I'd say about three to four hundred pounds."

Jake glanced over his shoulder. "Osoquenada."

"It has a name?" the hiker on ground asked.

"An old acquaintance," Jake said.

Hume looked at Jake. "You think it was him?" Jake just nodded, yes. "Well, you guys were safe enough. He likes people. That makes him a royal pain with his antics in campgrounds, but pretty harmless."

"We tried to walk out yesterday, but saw that monster at the top," the boy who hadn't risen said.

"It was sitting on the trail waiting for us, so we ran back here."

"That's when I sprained my ankle."

"You couldn't have asked for a better visitor, actually," Jake explained. "He must have realized you guys were in trouble and was standing guard so cougars and such wouldn't bother you. I spotted him leaving as we rode up. By the way, Osoquenada means Bear-That-Likes-Water. Darn good swimmer."

The young men fell totally silent.

Hume checked the injury. "What's your name?"

"Paul Evarts."

"Ankle's pretty swollen and discolored, Paul. I'm going to splint it so we don't cause any more damage."

"What about you? What's your name?" Jake asked the other boy.

"Jack Perkins. I'm okay. After seeing that thing was waiting for us, I was too scared to go out by myself and I didn't want to leave Paul alone. If no one showed, we figured to try getting out tomorrow."

"Good idea," Jake said, looking about the camp. The bear hadn't left anything untouched. Retrieving a black, plastic garbage bag from his saddlebags, Jake handed it to Perkins. "Gather up the trash and we'll pack it out. Jack can ride behind you, Ray. I'll double up with Paul . . . and you don't complain," he wagged a finger at his horse who snorted.

"What are we going to do when we get back? We don't have any clothes," Paul said.

"We'll go to the Arroyo Ranger Station. I've got some sweats you can borrow; in the meantime, let me show you how to make a loincloth out of these rags."

When the party topped the ridge, Jake radioed Jay's Roost. "Let the Sheriff know the boys have been found. They're okay. We're taking them to the station. Also, let my wife know there'll be a couple visitors for dinner, and have someone from the Cosa Peluda rescue unit meet us there. One of the boys has a bad ankle needing some attention."

A little while later Curt radioed back. "Mat and Roy from town will be up in a couple hours unless it's an emergency. They are transporting a patient to Albuquerque, otherwise to call Tipton."

"That's fine. It's not something we can't deal with until they get there, just a badly sprained ankle. I gave him ibuprofen, which will help. Osoquenada ate all their marijuana."

"Oh, great. Now we have a happy, crazy bear on the loose. Mrs. Bershinsky says she has extra plates set. Your mother is there to help. It's beef stew and cornbread night." As Paul's stomach complained loudly Curt added, "Can I come?"

"Sure. Might as well," Jake laughed.

"How about me?" Ray called out from behind.

"Tell Katelyn to add a place for the game warden, too."

"Will there be enough food?" Paul said.

Jake laughed. "Oh, yes. My wife always has enough to go around."

"The other good news is that the Sheriff is sending someone to get the names and addresses of the hikers. He's going to send them a bill for the search and rescue," Curt added.

"Oh, man!" Paul groaned.

"Like he's going to get blood from a turnip?" Jake muttered with a laugh in Paul's ear. Then to Curt, "Tell the Sheriff not to waste the gas. No fault of their own, they were treed by a bear. I'll send him a copy of my report. If he wants to send the bear a bill, good luck. He's a deadbeat."

₪

Incident at Beaver Creek

Chapter
2

The Chivato District's Law Enforcement Officer used any excuse to ride his gray through the forest. Too often, it involved looking for lost people like the two college boys a week earlier, but there were days like the present that involved checking trails for winter damage before the influx of summer hikers. Little did Jake realize that each step Mohf took forward brought him closer to a collision between the present and his past. For the moment, he enjoyed the blissful silence as a gentle breeze whispered softly through the trees, carrying the sweet aroma of pine scent, and providing a gentle, cool caress to buffer the warm sun. The hooves of his Arabian striking the ground in the metered beat of a walking gait, the creak of saddle leather, the rhythmic rocking chair sway, no voices, no sounds of war, this was exactly why he joined the Forest

Service eight years ago after retiring from the Army. There were other reasons, of course, but riding his own horse in the backcountry the first days of summer was at the top of job perks.

Spotting a black bear sow with two cubs traversing a hillside a half mile off brought back the memory of the college kids and their encounter. Something akin to live Yogi Bear, he and Osoquenada already exchanged words more than once this season about behavior more dangerous to the bear than to people, but that wasn't entirely his fault.

Apparently abandoned, the cub was rescued by a lonely, old lady who lived on one of the private ranch enclaves within the Forest boundary. When she died, Osoquenada began searching for human companionship and the food he enjoyed most. Forest visitors didn't understand his peculiar behavior and either freaked out or complicated the situation through shoddy camping techniques or outright feeding him.

Jake chuckled to himself over Katelyn's expression when he escorted the two all but naked hikers into the house for a trip through the shower and into sweats. The EMT's arrived as dinner was being set. Re-splinting the ankle, there wasn't much else they could do so they all sat for a solid meal. The injured hiker wasn't feeling much discomfort after a couple painkillers so their trip back to town and to the hospital for X-rays wasn't all that bad.

Of course, Sheriff Baker still tried billing them for the search and rescue operation, but a preemptory call to the US Attorney's office snipped that short. Baker was steamed, then had to answer to the wilderness trespass. The man had a seismic run in with the US Attorney, but something about two bored US Marshals looking for an excuse to "play" squelched Barker's volatility. Thinking of how the attorney could humble the arrogant Sheriff erected a blissful memory of thirty-six years before until a strained radio call shattered it.

"Jake, this is Carrie. I've got a situation at Beaver Creek Campground. Can you meet me here?" Carrie Nichols was one of Jake's seasonal compliance officers, steady as granite for someone in her early twenties. The tone in her voice told him the call was serious. That she called it a "situation" implied she wasn't going to mention it for all the Forest personnel to hear.

"I can be there in about an hour," he said.

That was the downside of being a forest cop. Backup could be a long time coming. Pulling down the front brim of his gray Stetson, he pressed his heels to Mohf's flanks. That was all the signal needed for the Arabian to shift gears. Normally preferring an easy walk, Mohf was enjoying the cool smell of spring in the air tickling a frisky nature. Breaking into a distance-eating lope through the conifer canyon was perfectly fine, especially if there was a reward at the end.

As the back of the campground drew close, Jake could see a number of sites already filled with tents and trailers. Beaver Creek was a popular spot for fishermen intent on snagging a hungry spring trout. At this moment, however, campers were huddled in small clusters, most with arms folded across their chest or hands stuck in jean pockets, talking in hushed voices while staring toward the river.

A nervous silence hung over the camp like a thick fog giving the beat of the gray's hooves to sound like the distant rumble of thunder. Eying the three-rail, pole fence ahead, Mohf instinctively paced himself. As heads turned in their direction, horse and rider sailed effortlessly over the fence and continued toward the river without breaking stride, arriving forty minutes after the initial call to find Carrie seated at a tree shaded picnic table on the edge of the riverside parking area. A ten-year-old boy hovered close to a man seated with her, watching with wide-eye awe as the ranger reined in his horse, stepping from the stirrup as the animal came to a sliding stop. Carrie met Jake half way.

Keeping her voice low while speaking she said, "Mr. Andrus was teaching his son to fly fish when the boy spotted a body stuck on the upside of that island. Hard to see from here, even with binoculars. He was standing in the river about thirty feet from where it's caught in the debris."

Jake walked to the muddy, rock-strewn edge of the river, the clear water gently lapping ashore. The White Tail River finished its run through a narrow canyon at this point, spreading out some one hundred-fifty feet wide. The lack of snow in the high country caused the flow to be much less for this time of year. Hopefully, the July monsoon would replenish the moisture or there would be a continuation of the drought and the increased chance of serious fires.

The small rock and debris island lay fifty feet from shore diverting the main current to this side of the river. Using binoculars, he barely discerned the arm and leg of a human body embedded on its side in the conglomeration of broken branches knitted together by the current.

Fireguards, Mike Dale and Bill Muir were just exiting their truck in the parking lot as Jake returned to where Mohf was ripping off mouthfuls of grass from one of many clumps. "Gonna need a long rope," he called out while beginning to unbutton his shirt.

"Whata we got?" Mike shouted back.

"Body wedged on the upside of that island."

"The water's cold," Mike said as he walked over to Jake.

"Yeah." Jake wasn't looking forward to the swim.

"So, I'll go. Don't give me that look, boss. I'm not

patronizing. I don't wanna see you gimping around 'cause the water aggravated your arthritis."

Jake didn't disagree. Riding rodeo broncs as a kid and twenty years in the Army, two tours in Vietnam, the aftermath of injuries were beginning to surface with age. Still, he had a mentality that continually put him in the forefront of difficult situations despite the pain.

"Flip you for it," Jake said, pulling out a quarter.

"Okay, but Carrie tosses," Mike said.

"Don't trust me?"

"With my life, but we both know how to manipulate a toss."

Jake called tails as Carrie flipped it into the air. Catching it, she turned it over the back of her left hand. Mike smiled and unbuttoned his shirt while Bill retrieved a hundred foot climbing rope from their truck, obviously grateful it was his partner and not him. By the time he returned, Mike was down to his boxers so he'd have dry clothes when finished. Carrie smiled. He was a lot like her brother, also known not to be self-conscious or bashful. Perhaps growing up the youngest and only boy in a family of girls tends to do that. No privacy. Then, perhaps, was the four months spent in a military hospital recovering from a battle wound. No privacy there, either.

Jake smiled as well, about something else. Mike sported a colored mermaid tattooed on his upper left arm, a kid in the military rite of passage thing. Jake had a bear standing next to a rabbit tattooed on his right arm. Very few people knew about it; Katelyn, the kids, and the men in his Army unit knew. He had it done by a good artist just before leaving Japan and returning to Nam after recuperating from wounds the first time. It had meaningful significance to him and the men in his platoon, a powerful talisman that got them all home safely.

Slipping the noose over his head and hooking it under his left armpit, Mike stepped into the water twenty yards upstream. Each step brought the water higher on his legs until he was knee deep. The muffled expletives escaping his lips needed no explanation. Carrie was glad he at least had sense enough to keep the campers from hearing most of them, but sympathized. The water was still frigid coming from the last snows high on the Sacred Mountains. As it reached his thigh he'd come to where the current had gouged a channel. With a gasp, he uttered a pitiful howl, and dove in, using long arms to propel forward the last twenty feet as the current carried him downstream.

Landing mid-island, he pulled himself ashore and rested a moment, shaking off the energy-sapping cold, glad for a warm sun to help. This was Mike's first job upon leaving the Army to begin work on a Criminal Justice degree. At twenty-six, he was proving to be a good hand. Smart, people-skilled, and in good, physical shape from continuing rehab, Jake enjoyed bringing him up to speed with the way the Forest Service did things. The old guard didn't like cops in the Service. Under the usual procedures, Mike's chances of being hired were slim except for being wounded in the last days of the Persian Gulf War in 1991, and was recommended by his hometown Congressman whose district encompassed much of the Zuni National Forest. That gave him some clout to land the job, and caused the good old boys to tread lightly. Jake watched as his protégé gingerly picked his way across the debris barefooted until reaching the upstream end and look over the edge.

"Wedged in a bit," Mike called out over the movement of water before trying to untangle tree limbs from body. Jake watched, knowing the young man wasn't bashful about asking for help, secretly hoping he wouldn't. Lying on the ground, Mike slipped the rope from off his body to work it around the corpse. The boy who made the discovery hovered near the picnic table with his dad, watching as intently as if on the set of *The Fresh Prince of Bel-Air*.

"Would you bring my horse over here, son?" Jake called out.

The twelve year-old horse had wandered near the picnic table to graze, an enticement to any boy. Small compared to the fifteen-hand animal, the size difference didn't seem to intimidate the boy who had already reached out to pet the gray's neck. Having lived around Jake's children, Mohf sponged up the attention while acting aloof and not missing a blade of grass. Jake rolled his eyes knowing Mohf to be a con artist, having maneuvered close to the table to receive the attention when there were thicker patches of grass elsewhere. Having the boy bring the Arabian really wasn't necessary. A whistle would have summoned him, but Jake knew boys and what they needed to feel a part of the approaching adult world.

"Your son ever ride a horse, Mr. Andrus?" Jake asked, while securing one end of the rope to the pommel.

"We have friends who own horses. He rides theirs once in a while . . ."

"Good enough. What's your name, son?"

"Albert."

"Sure could use your help, Al. Mind getting aboard and giving me a hand?"

The boy looked expectantly at his father who nodded permission, broke into a huge grin, and easily jump into the stirrup.

"When I give the signal, pull back on the reins gentle like, and say back. He's got a good reverse gear."

Led to the edge of the river, Mohf performed his ritual, dainty dance until finding a relatively dry spot of ground to stand on to get a drink. A phobia about water was one of the animal's quirks, and it was embarrassing. Jake tried to ignore the antics while waiting for Mike to finish securing a line on the body when a branch he'd been leaning on snapped with the sound of a .22 bullet, sending the young man tumbling into the water. Both Jake and Bill were about to leap into the river as Mike struggled to keep from being pinned against the debris. Thankfully, the current wasn't strong due to the reduced flow, but still had enough power to hold a person against the debris underwater long enough they could drown. Muir was up to his knees in the water when a hand rose up out of the water, latching onto another thick branch followed by a head as Mike pulled himself up until safely above the water's surface. A waive indicated he was okay before continuing to secure the rope. At least now, he was able to use both hands. Seconds later a circling wave indicated it was time.

Jake motioned for Al to back Mohf. As the line went taut, the body and a large clump of limbs broke free to float down stream. Mike swam to shore behind the debris as Bill hurried to where the grizzly catch came ashore downstream, dragging it onto land. Meanwhile, Carrie had retrieved a wool blanket from the first aid kit in her truck and wrapped it around Mike's shoulders as he stumbled out of the water. Long hair plastered over his eyes he stood shivering. Jake checked him out.

"Lovely shade of blue. Got any coffee in your truck?"

Unable to mouth an answer with a jaw shuddering uncontrollably, he nodded, yes.

"Carrie, go fetch some. Not a becoming color. Stay in the sun, Mike." He then went to where Mohf and Al waited and removed the rope. "If you want to stay on him that'd be fine. Walk him around a bit so he don't get stiff. We had a pretty hard ride over here, just kinda stay clear of the body. He doesn't like dead things."

That was another of Mohf's quirks, but he also didn't want the boy having nightmares by pursuing natural, morbid curiosity. A dead body was not always a pleasant sight especially under these conditions. Seeing something like that from a distance would mediate the experience.

Walking to where the corpse lay on the bank, he looked down. "Darrel Windpipe," he said, after rolling the body onto its back. "Went to school with his dad, James." Jake then removed the portable radio from his belt, switched to a private enforcement channel, and keyed the microphone on his collar. "Herbert this is Bershinsky." He was calling the assistant War Chief of the Antigua Pueblo and head of police in Taylorsville.

"Hey, Jake. What's up?"

"When did Darrel Windpipe get out of the Navy?"

"Showed up a week ago. Was here a couple days then left in his old truck. Haven't seen him since. Got word yesterday afternoon he jumped ship. The Navy's listing him AWOL. Why are you asking?"

"We just fished his body out of the White Tail at Beaver Creek," Jake said, continuing a visual of the body.

There was a long pause before the chief answered. "Drowning?"

"Not sure, Ken. Some things don't look right. I'll have the Tipton unit bring him over to the Taylorsville hospital for an autopsy. Give Doc Gardner a heads up."

"Okay and I'll notify the family. James really doesn't need this on top of everything else."

"Better let the Navy know, too. I'll call you tonight with my report."

While Mike dressed in dry cloths, Carrie used the blanket to cover the body. "How long is that family planning to stay?" Jake asked her.

"Paid for a couple days," Carrie said as the two walked over to Mr. Andrus who was sitting at the table while Al continued having a blast walking Mohf in figure eights and other maneuvers, discovering how responsive he was.

"He's a pretty good rider," Carrie said.

"Yeah. Wish I could afford a horse of his own," the father said as his son reined Mohf up to where they were standing.

"Thanks for calling us," Jake said, being sure the boy heard as well. "Appears to be a drowning. Gotta be careful in these rivers. If the currents and undertows don't get you, the cold will. Hypothermia can take a person down pretty quick. You can see what it did to my officer in that short time. You've been a big help and we sure appreciate that, Al. Carrie will refund your camp fee. Least we can do for your help. Stay as long as you like. It's on the house." Jake chuckled to himself. The recreation department was going to love that.

Tipton, a small lumber town turned summer home site, lay sandwiched between the Reservation and Forest twelve miles to the west. A volunteer service, the rescue unit arrived a half hour later. With the body placed in a black, body bag, the paramedics were in the process of loading it into the truck when a siren pierced the forest solitude. Jake rolled his eyes. Deputy Putnam. The guy hardly ever went anywhere that he didn't use lights and siren.

Entering the parking lot, the white pickup with a brown, diagonal strip along each side came to a gravel-spraying stop. The boy was still exercising Mohf who didn't flinch but merely turned his head momentarily to look at the new arrival with an annoyed glare. As the dust cloud barely began to clear, a string bean of a man stepped out, hitched up his gun belt, and swaggered to the ambulance.

"Who authorized the body to be transported?" he said.

"I did," Jake said, as everyone secretly laughed at the Barney Fife impersonator.

"You got no right."

"Arrest me," Jake said. His tone was unsettlingly jovial as he turned and walked away. He just couldn't take the man seriously.

"Hey, I'm not done talking to you," Deputy Putnam called out. "I said, I'm not done talking to you, half-breed," he repeated, placing a hand on Jake's shoulder.

Jake might be old in Mike's eyes, but he didn't feel it at forty-six, and his reflexes were still catlike as he spun around to come nose to nose with the deputy. Putnam jumped backward, tripping on his own size twelve feet to fall backward onto his butt, gripping the butt of his Smith and Wesson.

"Putnam, you are an embarrassment," Jake said, shaking his head, and walking to where the boy was putting the horse through another series of figure eights. "Thanks again for your help, Al. That man's family will be real grateful someone found him, and don't worry too much about what happened today. Accidents happen. I know Mohf here's enjoyed his time with you," he said as the boy jumped to the ground.

Swinging effortlessly into the saddle without using the stirrups, he rode to where Putnam stood brushing the dust off his light brown pants. Leaning over so only the deputy could hear he said, "This is out of your jurisdiction Putnam. That body over there is a Native American. He died on Federal lands. If there's any notion of foul play, he was active military so the Navy crime folk will investigate." Jake straightened, smiled, touched the brim of his Stetson with two fingers, wheeled Mohf about, and rode off, the horses' long tail flicking up, causing the deputy to lean back to avoid being swat, and almost falling again.

Putnam felt humiliated. It was his own doing. Reaching for his weapon had been reflexive. He wasn't entirely stupid, however. When he reached for his gun, Carrie laid a hand on her weapon. It was not a good situation and he quickly backed off. He didn't know the two firemen and didn't appreciate their smirks. He'd keep an eye on them whenever they left the forest.

Turning to Carrie he said, "So what happened?"

Carrie wanted so much to say, "You fell down," but refrained. "Appears to be a drowning. Name's Darrel Windpipe. Mr. Bershinsky knows the family. The reservation police have been notified." She said, conveniently forgetting to mention the AWOL. Putnam put on a show of being satisfied, smiled strangely, and without looking at the body, left. Carrie shook her head, completing her assessment that the man was obviously short more than a couple IQ points.

An hour before dinner, Jake settled behind his desk to begin working up a report about the Beaver Creek incident. Once the District Ranger's home, a large room at one end served as the main office. Basically abandoned when the Ranger and staff moved to Cosa Peluda in the seventies, the large, log house sat more or less vacant until Jake moved in when coming to work. It was highly convenient, eliminating the thirty-five mile trip from town every day, maximizing work time, family time, and being away from too many people.

Carrie's report was already on the desk, kept warm by Malachi, the family's black and white Manx. The cat rarely went outside unless accompanied by one of his people. Something had frighten him when he came to live with them three years earlier and he wasn't about to have another such encounter alone again. Despite being an occasional nuisance, he kept the mouse population to zero inside while his counterpart, a yellow tabby, long ensconced on the compound, patrolled the outside. The two often sat on opposite sides of the kitchen or office screen door to stare at each other, never displaying animosity toward one another, it was a strange relationship.

Normally Malachi curled up in Jake's wood, office chair or jumped onto it when someone wanted to use it, refusing to move until all but sat on. Assuming the seat before the cat could move to it, Jake smiled at the small victory and pulled the report from under the cat. Flashing an evil glare, Malachi shifted into a more comfortable ball and draped one paw over his eyes.

After reading the handwritten document, Jake began calling up a blank report form on the computer screen when Ken Herbert strolled into the office. Unlike Jake who was forty-six and battling a paunch, the Antigua's Chief of Police was a finger over six feet and hard as a Pro Football halfback. Sixteen years Jake's junior, he was an oddity among Pueblos, being a college grad.

"Just getting started on the report," Jake said. "How's James and Mary doing?"

"They're taking it pretty hard, especially James."

Jake stepped to a topographical map of the forest and surrounding areas that dominated one wall of the office. "The north fork of the river might have enough water to carry a body, but he would have had to come around to this side of the river to access it. No one's seen his truck. The south fork is too low right now. I'm thinking he must have gone in the water somewhere in the canyon. Carrie checked the roads on this side and didn't see anything. The only access to the river from the res side would be on foot or horseback," Jake said, tracing his finger along the river's course.

"No one saw Darrel with a horse."

"Only a couple places could get him close. It'd still be a hike," Jake said, stabbing a finger at the two locations.

"I'll scout them out tomorrow," Ken said.

"Any idea what was bothering him to go AWOL?"

"Nada. James was pretty tight lipped when I talked to him about it yesterday."

"Doesn't know or isn't telling?"

"Hard to say. He put a lot of store in that boy. Was real proud of him. Real proud. We all were. The Navy's sending out investigators."

"Hope I don't have to babysit some city boys," Jake mumbled while reaching to answer the phone. "I've got a lot of stuff on my plate right now before the Fourth of July camper invasion."

Ken listened as Matt Douglass, the Forest Service Special Agent headquartered in Santa Fe, received a narrative summary on the telephone. He was Jake's immediate supervisor. A few minutes after hanging up, Katelyn, stuck her head of auburn-colored hair through the open office door. "Dinner's on, Jake. You, too, Ken."

חנ

Incident at Beaver Creek

Chapter
3

Charles Todd rose through the ranks to become the Zuni National Forest Supervisor in 1986. When superiors and the local Congressmen occasionally teased him about the lack of hair he'd smile and chuckle politely at their inane jokes, but that was a sensitive issue. A genetics class in high school had been like a crystal ball. He had a beautiful head of hair then, thick, golden brown, Afro style. From that class he realized it was doomed. His maternal grandfather looked like a bowling ball by fifty. He started to shed like a dog in the spring by the time he was twenty-five. By twenty-eight, all that remained was a wreath, which he grew extra-long to vainly comb over the top at least to cover some of the shine. Whenever he went outside and there was a wind, the strands invariably took off making him look like the Flying Nun. Now at fifty-nine there wasn't even that. Everyone knew he was bald and appearing with a hairpiece would have made things worse. Besides, they made him look like a dork. Staring across the desk at the two young Navy investigators with full heads of hair, he was secretly jealous.

He filled the agents in with what little information he had and descended to small talk until hearing Bershinsky's voice in the hallway. Jake wasn't much for driving the nearly one hundred-fifty miles into Santa Fe where the Supervisor's office was located, but his boss, Matt Douglass, asked him to hand deliver a copy of his report about the drowning to the Forest Supervisor and talk to him about it.

He no sooner stepped to the receptionist's desk than she said, "The Supervisor is expecting you. Go straight in." Connie was a no-nonsense person, unhappy with her job, unhappy about the prospect of retirement, and unhappy with life in general. Several co-workers suggested she needed a man in her life, but Jake knew there had been one and that was a lot of the reason for the sour attitude. She and Jake got along well enough to have a cup of coffee at break time if he was about, but she was definitely off kilter today.

"Jake, these gentlemen are Special Agents from the Navy's Criminal Investigation Service in San Diego, Lawrence Davidson, and Frank Hayes. They're here regarding the drowning victim."

"Red eye flight?" Jake said, shaking hands. Davidson smiled weakly to indicate, yes.

A youthful, Oriental face clouded his age. Jake guessed him to be in his early thirties, part Japanese, as he later learned. Hayes was Spanish Harlem, a Nuyorican – New York City Puerto Rican by ancestry, but not by culture. A couple years younger than Davidson, Marine was plastered all over him, from haircut to spit-shined shoes. Both wore slacks and sport coats, white shirts, matching navy blue ties, as one would expect of a government agent. Except on Sundays for church and appearing in court, Jake shed the tie nonsense faster than Superman stepping into a phone booth, preferring the low key, casual look, even in the Army, and especially since retirement.

"Flew in two hours, fifteen minutes ago," Hayes said.

"Douglass wanted me to personally deliver the drowning report."

"Thank you. I read the one you sent on the computer," Todd said, handing the envelope to Davidson. "Sheriff Barker called this morning, Jake. Pretty upset you had the body moved and wouldn't let his man investigate," the Supervisor continued, twirling a pencil with his fingers. A nervous type, he would bounce a knee up and down when seated, or play with some object like now.

"I didn't want him screwing up what is obviously a Federal case," Jake replied, still standing.

"I understand you had the body transported to the reservation?" Davidson said.

"Yes. Taylorsville Hospital. It's a good facility, so's Doc Gardner. Has forensics training so he's capable as anyone at performing an autopsy. He'll get it done and release the body in a timely manner."

"The Pueblos have a superstitious thing about burying their dead as fast as possible," Todd said.

"They want the person's spirit to move on and not hang around to cause trouble," Jake said.

"Your report says the victim was naked," Hayes said.

"Not unusual in alcohol overdose cases among the Indians," Todd said.

"I see you noted injuries on the body," Davidson said. "Abrasions to both ankles and wrists, and considerable bruising to the body."

"That could be the result of being washing down the river and going over the waterfall," Todd put in. Jake wished the man would stick to forestry.

"No," Jake said flatly, cutting him off. "The bruising occurred before he went for a swim."

"Sounds like you are ruling out accident or suicide," Hayes said.

Jake shrugged. "The chest wound kinda does that."

"But your initial report described it as a puncture wound," Todd cut back in.

"Yeah," Jake answered. "According to Ken Herbert, he's head of the Antigua Pueblo police, the victim left his home on the res driving a '67 International pickup. An antique. He spent his money restoring it instead of on booze. He's checking out a couple places where it might be parked on the res side, which should give us an idea where the boy got into trouble. It's a remote and hard area to access, though. That's about where we're at."

"You're cutting Sheriff Barker out of the loop?" the Supervisor said.

"Yes," Jake answered as Davidson was about to say something.

"I see. I know you and Sheriff Barker have been at odds since you were kids. Is this more of the same crap I've put up with since I got here?"

"I'm alright with that," Davidson said. "As Officer Bershinsky said, the death occurred on Federal lands to an active member of the Armed Services. Further investigation will be under my direction."

"Good. I need to see the US Attorney, and then get back to the District. I'm guessing the SUV with smoky windows parked outside is yours. It's about a three-hour drive to Taylorsville. Straight forward once you pick up US-

550. Takes off the 25 at Bernalillo, but it's not especially well marked. Construction. The secretary out front can give you a map so you don't get lost. I asked our radio tech to set up a two-way for your use. She'll get you in touch with him. The channels are marked on the back. You'll want to use channel three. It's the enforcement channel we use. Only my people and the Jay's Roost fire tower hear it. Channel 4 connects to the res. I gave them a heads up so to expect your calls. They speak passable English," Jake said, turning and walking out. The agents saw the sly smile and wink Jake made, but not Todd.

The Supervisor frowned as he watched the lawman leave, and then said, "The Pueblo speak good English. It's comments like that and his general attitude that riles me sometimes. If I was his boss he'd take some lessons on diplomacy."

"Who is his boss?" Hayes asked, realizing the Forest cop had a hand on Todd's chain and knew how to yank it.

"Matt Douglass, Special Agent for Region 3. These law enforcement types were supervised by District Rangers until a couple years ago when they were put under the Regional Agent, answerable only to him. Jake handles the Chivato District. It's the largest area on the Zuni with a heavy recreation use. It's like having a loose cannon. I've got no control on any of them. About five years ago, one of our district staff pulled a stupid stunt, cut firewood for personal use in a closed area. Jake cited him instead of taking the problem to the District Ranger. The guy nearly lost his job. It could have been handled it a lot differently."

"Yeah, cover it up with a hand slap," Hayes and Davidson both thought to themselves.

"Don't get me wrong. Jake's a good lawman. Retired military. A Colonel. That's part of the problem. No offense, but you can't handle everyone like they were soldiers. My people are foresters and biologists. Most have never been in the military, but that aside, he knows his business. An added plus is that he has an in with the Indians around here. I just wish he'd learn diplomacy instead of being such a straight arrow."

"So, where do I find his boss, Douglass?"

"His office is at the other end of this hall, but he's not there. On some kind of joint operation at Gallup. I have no idea when he'll be back."

~ ~ ~ ~

After Jake left to entertain the US Attorney with a report concerning another matter, the agents picked up maps and the radio before driving to Taylorsville. Somewhat centered among five different Pueblo groups, the hospital was part of a consolidation of facilities and services to improve management of their limited dollars. Doc Gardner, the chief, and for now, the only full time physician, was in surgery when they arrived. A young girl in a bright, peppermint-striped dress and sweeter-looking smile escorted them to the dining room where they huddled at a table, sipping coffee while reviewing the contents of a brown file folder bearing the Navy seal.

"I'm surprised this kid just cut out. From all the comments in his record, he liked Navy life," Hayes said. "According to his C.O., he was well liked and worked hard. Was up for promotion, but things changed when he got a letter a month back. Became distracted and introverted. Said that there was some kind of trouble at home and asked for a leave."

"Should have been granted a hardship leave if there was a serious problem," Donaldson said. "Looks to have been denied."

"It must have been serious if he felt it necessary to jump ship when they put in at Seattle on a quick turnaround," Davidson said.

"I wonder what the problem was?"

"Darrel was pretty family oriented," a police officer said as he joined them. "Hi, I'm Ken Herbert."

The Pueblo War Chief's responsibilities were primarily to protect the land and people. Now in his eighties, he delegated most of that responsibility to Herbert. The police chief was not at all, what the agents expected. Native Americans the NCIS officers encountered so far were average height tending toward stocky. Herbert stood slightly over six foot. Regular workouts kept him as trim and hard as Hayes. The khakis uniform bore an ironed, military crease overlaid with the traditional Pueblo kilt. The long ponytail and light blue headband were traditional as well. He carried himself easily, but with an authority that setting him apart.

"It sure would be helpful if we knew what was in that letter," Hayes said, "Do you have any idea what the problem was?"

"I am working on that, but hunting cougar with a switch would be a lot easier. My guess it involved his younger brother."

"What about Officer Bershinsky, the guy who found the body?"

"Jake? Good hand."

"Is he Indian, I mean Pueblo?" Hayes asked.

"Half white, half Pueblo. Raven Clan. You'd never know it, but he carries a lot of weight among our people, not just because of what he is, but who he is. To the younger kids, he's something of a legend, someone the elders tell stories about. To my generation and older he's a respected friend and relative."

"I understand he's retired military?" Hayes said.

"Twenty years. Well, looks like Doc Gardner's coming," Ken said, indicating a young looking man in blue surgical scrubs.

A cooperative effort of the Caucasian and Pueblo communities built a new hospital in Taylorsville. In some ways, it had been a carrot to appease Indian activists, one in particular, with substantial contributions from special interest groups, matched by Federal Health and Human Services funds. Finding staff was a problem, delaying the opening until two young doctors came as part of a Federally funded education loan program. It was obvious they wouldn't stay, but a permanent change was in the works.

A year after the hospital opened, James Begay, a Navajo, graduated from Stanford Medical School in Palo Alto south of San Francisco. Two hundred fifty miles away in Reno, Nevada, the Director of Nursing Programs for Truckee Meadows Community College was actively recruiting Native Americans into their program as a way to improve health care on reservations. Permanency came when Dr. Jim and two Nevada graduates arrived as summer was about to settle a blanket of pre-monsoon heat over the region, and the two original doctors left. Dr. Jason Ryan arrived a few months later on the loan payback program, married a girl from the neighboring town of Cuba a year later, and stayed. Jake got to know them and the nurses pretty well when he was fourteen, thanks to a shattered leg when thrown from a horse. Gardner was Doc Jason's son.

After introductions, the doctor didn't waste time, going straight to the issue. "I'd say you boys have a problem. Darrel didn't drown. The lack of water in his lungs indicates he was dead before entering the river. I did find some whiskey in his lungs, though. Also in his stomach, but a blood alcohol came back normal. If I were to wager a guess, he didn't ingest it willingly. There are abrasions on his wrists and ankles that appear to be rope burns. In addition, a number of bruises and abrasions on the legs, arms, torso, and head are not consistent with banging around on rocks while in the water or going over the waterfall a couple miles above where they found him. When I opened him up, I found sufficient evidence of internal damage that he was beaten. A knife entering below the sternum penetrated the heart. That was the puncture wound. It was about two inches at the hilt and ten inches long. It's going to be difficult to determine the approximate time of death because of the cold water he was in. Maybe the state lab will have something."

"I might be of some help there," Ken said. "Darrel was last seen three days ago."

"That's helpful. I did find something interesting," Doc Gardner said, holding up a small, clear plastic, evidence bag. The three lawmen looked at the long, brown, tooth-pick-like thing inside.

"What is it?" Davidson said.

"Looks like a wood sliver," Ken said.

"That's my guess. It was embedded in Darrel's back, just under the skin."

"Kind of dark," Hayes commented, holding the bag at different angles.

"Old wood," Ken said.

₪

Incident at Beaver Creek

Chapter 4

Wobbling more than walking, Curt Hayden's mind was a sponge squeezed dry as he left his Media Technology final exam. Feeling dazed, he walked zombie-like from the classroom building to the student center next door where he slumped into a lounge chair. With the first year at the University of New Mexico done, the "now what" began weighing in. He needed a soda. Reaching into his pockets the fingers came up empty.

"Hey, Curt," his name rang out across the commons. Looking around he spotted Flo and Steph, two girls he'd met at the LDS Church Institute last fall. They hung out a lot during the year. He dated Steph a couple times, if going to free meals and dances at the Institute constituted a date.

"Hi," he said, getting up from the lounge chair in which he had collapsed.

"Tests all done?" Steph asked.

"Yeah, thank goodness."

"How'd it go?"

"It was murder, but I think I did okay."

"What are you going to do now," Flo asked.

"I dunno. Find a job for the summer, I guess."

"Good luck. Not much out there with the way things are right now," Steph said. That was the kind of encouragement he needed.

"Are you going to Friday Forum? It's the last one until fall."

Curt enjoyed Friday Forum. The religious oriented talks were short and to the point followed by free food. Of course he would go. From the Student Union to the Institute was a fairly straight shot of about six city blocks. It didn't seem that far walking with the girls. Within a half block of their destination he could smell the burgers cooking, reminding him breakfast had been a long time ago. The student committee decided to hold the forum outside to take advantage of the spring weather.

Sitting on the grass listening to the speaker, his mind wandered ahead. With term over, he was about to be turfed from the dorm with nowhere to stay. The possibility of camping out for the summer in his old car seemed more likely than ever. There was no motivation to drive 800 miles home and listen as his old man belittled him about being penniless. It had been his dad's plan that Curt join the family business. Crawling around on some roof nailing down shingles the rest of his life never appealed to him, although there was nothing wrong with that. It was honest work, but he wanted to do something more than smash his thumb with a hammer. His old man just couldn't understand. When offered a baseball scholarship, Curt jumped on it. He saw his future being in the new field of digital communications, a job for "nerds," his old man summarized, adding a few off colored remarks spiced with references to San Francisco which made no sense to Curt.

"Hi, Curt," Brother Maxwell, the Institute Director, said, stepping alongside as Curt left the serving line with a plate crowding the sideboards with food. "So what's in store for you this summer?"

"I dunno. Get a job, I guess."

"Not going home?"

"No." The answer was more sharp than intended. Besides, having no motivation to drive home, he didn't have two nickels to rub together for the gas, and he wasn't about to ask his old man.

"Have you found anything, yet?"

"Haven't had time to look." The truth was Curt tended to procrastination, which often led to pending disasters, like now.

"Could be tough from what I'm hearing." Another encouraging remark. "Would you be interested in spending the summer stuck in a fire tower out in the middle of the mountains? Pay's pretty good." The word "pay" was highly motivating at the moment peeking the young man's interest. "My neighbor works for the Forest Service and told me this morning the person they hired for the job suddenly backed out."

Curt's departure was almost instantaneous. After clearing his plate, he stuffed a couple dogs in his sports jacket pocket, just in case. Being desperate, he didn't pay much attention to the rules of appearance to apply for the job. Penny loafers with no socks, denim trousers, T-shirt under a thrift store sports coat, and three-day stubble, he looked better suited standing at an intersection holding a homeless, give money sign.

Completing the application, the secretary told him to

sit in the reception area and wait for an interview. She was sharp and rude. He felt as out of place as a deer standing at that same give money intersection. Everyone passing by was either neatly dressed or in uniform. They glanced in his direction and smiled, not a "Hi," kind of smile, but one of those, "You've got to be kidding," kind.

The receptionist kept flashing scowls in his direction until a younger women wearing a light lavender pants suit took over. Her smile was kind of a sympathetic flirtation and he was about to try striking up a conversation when a man in a Forest Service uniform walked in. Something about him dominated the room. The way he held himself, the way he walked, the starched crisp uniform with military creases, the gun on his belt, his presence demanded attention.

"Mr. Bershinsky, this gentleman is applying for the Jays Roost position," the receptionist said.

"Really?" the officer said with a smile Curt interpreted as, "You've got to be kidding," but that was because he was feeling so self-conscious. "My name's Jake Bershinsky," he said, stretching out to shake hands. It was a firm handshake, really firm, not crushing, but something that let you know he was no lightweight. "Let's talk," he said, receiving the application from the girl and motioning for Curt to follow.

As the two entered a conference room with a long, oak table surrounded by a lot of cushioned chairs, Curt was trying to figure the man out. A number of the forest types in uniform had beards of various kinds. He was clean-shaven. Others were bald to hair just over the ears. His was long enough to have a ponytail tied in back. His complexion was dark amber, but his facial features didn't suggest either Native American or Hispanic. Maybe Asian.

"Have a seat, Mr. Hayden." Curt sat on the edge of a

chair while Jake sat in another a few feet away and began going over the hurried application. He knew this was a waste of time. He should never have tried for the job.

"I'm sorry, sir, but I haven't any experience for something like this," Curt said, deciding to throw in the towel and leave as gracefully as a squirrel dodging cars.

"Relax, son. Let me see, vision 20/20, don't drink, don't smoke, clean record . . . speeding tickets don't count. You like to read. Eagle Scout." Curt had thought some of the questions on the application were strange. "Mormon. Didn't go on a mission?"

"I didn't have the money. I got a baseball scholarship. It was the only option other than slinging hamburgers the rest of my life."

"Don't like roofing?"

"No, sir."

"What are you intending to get a college degree in?"

"Science Technology Security." Jake's left eyebrow arched up. Curt wasn't sure if that was from surprise or being impressed.

"When can you start?"

"Today."

"Fill out these forms for Uncle Sam. I'll be back in a few minutes and we'll talk about the job. Oh, and they allow eating in here, if you're still hungry," he said and pointing casually at Curt's coat pocket leaving him to wonder how his new boss knew about the dogs. "Sodas are in that cooler over there. Free."

When Jake returned to check over the forms, he said, "How soon can you pack your stuff and be back here?"

"An hour."

Curt almost got another speeding ticket as he returned to the dorm, haphazardly jammed his clothes into plastic garbage bags, and tossed them into the back seat. Steph caught up as he was returning to the dorm room for a second load and helped, agreeing to return his textbooks, and let Brother Maxwell hold onto the money. He was back to the Forest Service office in fifty-five minutes.

"Do you know where Abiquiu Reservoir is located?

"Yes, sir."

"If you head that way, take State 96 to Cosa Peluda that way you can avoid all that road construction south of here. You'll see the Forest Service office. Ask for directions to Arroyo Station. It's a hundred-twenty-seven miles."

"Oh," Curt said, his enthusiasm faded like the sun behind a cloud.

"Here," Jake said, handing him a twenty-dollar bill. "Will that get you there?"

"Yes, but . . ."

"An advance on your paycheck. Don't worry about groceries. The Service takes care of that. A job perk."

Not daring to push the antiquated Ford Capri more than fifty, he arrived at the station three hours later. Stepping into the office, he was nervous enough his knees quivered. Jake stood talking to another man in a Forest Service uniform at least forty years older than Curt. A boy, all of eleven, occupied a swivel chair nearby, rotating back and forth, milking an obnoxious squeak.

"Come in, Curt. This is Alan Frye, one of our fireguards. He'll take you to Jays Roost tomorrow and get you situated. He's been doing this a lot of years. And the noisemaker is my oldest son, Henry. He'll show you to your room for the night. The woman you meet passing through the kitchen is my wife, Katelyn."

Mrs. Bershinsky, a perky redhead, was plagued by an errant lock of hair dangling over the left eye, which she blew aside while kneading bread dough. It continually returned to dangle like a worm off the end of a hook.

Knead, knead, blow . . . kneed, knead, blow. She had a good rhythm and a big smile.

Once settled in a room, which meant tossing a duffle on the floor, Henry gave him a tour of the facility, strutting like a Banty Rooster. Of course, the tour included the barn. Curt had never been this close to horses as a gray unexpectedly stuck his head out the top half of a Dutch door. He was amazed how silky soft the big proboscis felt. Tossing its head, Curt thought it didn't want his nose rubbed.

"Scratch under his jaw," Henry said.

Curt was afraid the horse would fall through the door as it reacted by raising his head and leaning against the heavy bottom half of a door. Not only did the horse become his friend at that moment, so did Henry. After having dinner with the Bershinsky's, Mrs. Bershinsky became Curt's best friend, too, and he willingly helped Henry with dishes—a lifetime first.

Following Alan's green, dual wheel fire truck into the mountains the next morning, Curt needed little imagination to see the resemblance of Sombrero Mountain to a hat as it's flanks rose above the surrounding terrain. A little over one million years ago, the whole region was a mass of volcanic activity until something happened to trigger a horrendous explosion displacing fifty cubic miles of rock and creating the Valles Caldera, a sink fifteen miles in diameter. Volcanic activity continued building many of the peaks now dominating the skyline. One was Sombrero Mountain that lifted skyward as a steady stream of lava rolled down its sides to spread out for miles in all directions. Although considered "dead," every now and then a tremor rattled the unwary's nerves. Because of its dominating height, President Roosevelt's Civilian Conservation Corps, or CCC, erected a fire tower on top in

1933. There weren't many obstructions as the perch projected above the hundred foot Lodgepole pines.

Each summer since construction, someone climbed the one hundred-eight-four wood steps every day to scout for fires. There was a lot to learn and a lot to do as Curt settled into the new job, not as lonely as people might think. By noon each day, he climbed to the glass-enclosed loft. Except for a couple quick, round trips to use the latrine, he remained until at least ten at night when he came down and walked along the graveled path ten yards to a CCC log cabin where he bunked.

During that time in the air, there were always visitors stopping, curious vacationers, and other Service employees taking a break, and climbing up for the spectacular view. The job was to watch for signs of smoke by day and the golden glow of fire at night. During lightning storms, he sat on a wood stool with glass insulators on the bottom, plotting ground strikes. For the next twenty-four hours, he kept a wary eye on those locations. If the roving fireguards weren't busy, he sent them to look at specific spots. He also coordinated with a flyover the afternoon following heavy lightning activity, which checked the deep ravines he couldn't see into. This became Curt's life, envisioning more summers to come as he planned to continue through a Master's degree.

Jay's Roost not only afforded a commanding view, but also the best radio reception. Until the radio tech installed an automatic relay just before beginning this third year, Curt served as the primary radio contact point. With the new equipment, Forest personnel could talk with one another from practically any location directly relieving him of that relaying job, but he continued to monitor the frequencies for the game wardens and local ranchers in case of an emergency. He also had the frequencies for the reservation police, the local Sheriff's office, and State Police.

From this vantage, he listened to what was going on at Beaver Creek Campground. The next evening scattered thunder showers popped all along the White Tail River late into the night, normal for the mountains. Using binoculars to scan the area south and slightly west on Taylor Flats, his heart skipped a beat as a yellow light flickered, seeming to move along the ground.

ﬡ

Incident at Beaver Creek

Chapter
5

Stretched out beneath an old Ponderosa, head resting on Katelyn's lap, eyes closed, Jake listened to the light moan of the wind among the pine needles mingle with the playful giggles of their children. The warm, spring sun bathed the grass and scattered piñon and juniper sloping down to the village a mile away. Flitting from branch to branch, a grayish-blue Pinion Jay busily collected nuts. The clang of the church bell echoing through the valley furrowed his brow. That was wrong. That bell only sounded on Sundays and for emergencies. At that moment, an elbow jabbed his ribs.

"Why does she always have to nail that one rib?" he thought.

Jake tried to hold on to the dream, but the bell and Katelyn's persistent elbow poked him back to reality. It wasn't the church bell, but the raucous clang of the telephone.

"Sorry to wake you, Mr. Bershinsky," a nervous voice said. "This is Curt at Jay's Roost. I really debated calling you, but, well, I was taking a final look before quitting and saw what looks like a light on Taylor Flats."

"Fire?" Jake said, his speech slurred by sleep.

"I don't think so, sir. It appears to be moving along the ground."

"UFO?" Despite what some folk thought, Jake did have a sense of humor, even when half asleep.

"I know it sounds crazy, but I'm sure someone is driving a vehicle out there. I last saw it near the old mine."

"What time is it?" Fighting through the cobwebs of sleep, he couldn't focus on the bedside clock.

"One-forty."

"Okay. So long as it's not a fire, I'll check it out first thing in the morning. Call if you see anything else." Running off into the night to chase a vehicle was impractical

"What is it?" Katelyn groaned as he hung up the phone.

"A UFO over by Eagle's Nest. I'll go talk with them tomorrow," he said, snuggling beneath the covers and wrapping an arm over his wife. She scooted closer. When what he had said dawned on her, Jake was asleep.

~ ~ ~ ~

Eighteen years earlier, Congress incorporated Taylor Flats, a huge, rolling, meadow dotted with small islands of stunted spruce and fir, into the Sacred Mountain Wilderness, closing it to motorized vehicles. The remnant of an old wagon road snaked across the meadow, the deep ruts a permanent scar carved into the ground as miners hauled props in for the Sebastian Mine overlooking the river. Hikers and late fall hunters continued using one rut of the trail as they sought the stunning, raw beauty of the White Tail River separating the meadowlands on the north from the sheer Tertiary cliffs of the Sacred Mountains on the south.

When the five-thirty alarm rang, Jake quietly slipped out of bed and donned his uniform. Moving was difficult. He ached. Arthritis began creeping in from the things he did when younger. Popping four Ibuprofen became something of a morning ritual, especially whenever a storm approached. Boots in hand, he tried traversing the pinewood floor and stairs down to the kitchen as quietly as possible, but the boards still creaked and popped. In the early morning silence, the sound seemed amplified. Even Malachi's padded dash to the kitchen carried an audible thump.

Still trying to shake sleep from his mind, he poured a glass of milk, using it to wash down a donut from Katelyn's baking efforts the previous evening. Malachi sat next to his bowl and meowed.

"Sh-h. Here, beggar," he said, giving the cat some milk, too. "Don't suppose you want a donut? Good. You're getting too fat as it is."

Pulling on the cowboy boots, he slipped a couple more donuts unto his coat pocket before going into the office. Removing a revolver from the gun safe, he slipped six bullets into the cylinder and locked it into the holster on his belt. Hesitating a moment to look at the collection, he removed a Winchester Model 94 rifle before relocking the door. From a locked drawer in the base he removed a box of shells and loaded the rifle, putting the remaining rounds in one side of the saddlebags slung over a spare office chair.

Cold, crisp air splashed over Jake's face as he stepped off the porch and began walking toward the horse barn. In the pre-dawn darkness, a restful silence hung over the Arroyo Station broken only by the crunch of pine needles beneath his boots and birds beginning their morning chirping. Presently the ever so slight sound of movement drifted upon the breeze, followed by a soft nicker, as he reached the corrals to be met by the warm muzzle of his Arabian stallion. Jake was somewhat of a rarity among Forest Service employees in that he used his own horse. The two had been together since Mohf was a shaky legged colt twelve years ago. An instant bond formed when the newborn hesitantly walked up to nuzzle the man sitting quietly on a bale of straw.

Gradually developing into a powerful stallion with all the inherent interests, Mohf was also very gentle, especially around children. Although one of the family, man and horse were a team, each relying on the other, despite occasional differences of opinion.

Loaded into the two-horse trailer, Mohf was too busy devouring the pan of oats to be concerned with the sometimes bumpy ride to the Sebastian Mine trail head, no more than a wide spot on the side of Forest Development Road 547. There was just enough room to park four cars or two trucks with horse trailers bumper to bumper. Usage didn't warrant a larger area except during the fall hunting season. At that time, vehicles could park across the road in a small clearing.

FDR 517 marked the northern boundary of the wilderness, cordoned off along the right-of-way by a zigzag, split rail fence, boulders, or thick forest growth. The only way for a vehicle to access the area was through a locked gate left over from pre-wilderness days. Before taking Mohf from the green trailer, Jake inspected the ground around the gate and parking area.

"The earth is a book with many stories," his teacher had said as the two studied a set of different animal tracks when he was a kid. "Now, nephew, what story do you read?"

₪

Incident at Beaver Creek

Chapter
6

Lawrence Davidson was a city kid until joining the Navy and spending life aboard ship and a tour of duty on Iraq's desert ocean. The closest he'd come to this kind of nature had been at the San Diego Zoo. Frank Hayes was from the sky scrapper jungle of New York City. What he knew were the squirrels of Central Park, so both were like wide-eyed kids in a sweets shop as they drove to Taylorsville. Before returning to Kirtland AFB in Albuquerque where they were staying at the base hotel, they decided to follow the forest map to Beaver Creek and take a look at where the body had been found. There wouldn't be any further clues, but it gave them a feel for the territory. Following a pretty straightforward map, they pulled into the Arroyo Station from the back way where they found the ranger fueling his pickup.

"Good afternoon, Colonel," Davidson said.

"Howdy. Enjoying the fresh air?"

"Yes, sir."

"You can drop the formalities, gentlemen. That's was another life. So, you learn anything new?"

"No, Sir . . . I mean Mr. Bershin . . ."

"Jake works."

"Not much more than included in your report. Here's a copy of the autopsy. It might help if we knew where the murder occurred."

Jake was more at ease and willing to help as he unfolded a map and spread it over the hood of his green Ford F-150. The two watched, listening closely as he traced the White Tail's course on the map.

"I'd say Darrel's body would have had to enter no further than six miles upstream from the campground."

"How's that?" Davidson said.

"The White Tail branches into a north and south fork sixteen miles upstream from Beaver Creek. We didn't get the usual snowfall this year and it's pretty much all melted now. The monsoon season hasn't started, so water levels are low. To access the north folk he would have to drive around to this side of the mountain. The District has a lot of activity going on in areas along the river and no one has reported seeing his truck. To access the south fork would be one heck of a hike through some really rugged country. Besides, the channel is more rocky and a body'd get hung up. That would have been a free lunch for bears, coyotes and other varmints. That didn't happen. My guess is he entered the water and began moving downstream fairly soon after death. Just below where the two branches converge the terrain narrows into a canyon. The river becomes deeper and swifter with no real obstructions. A body would be transported pretty quick."

"So, we just need to find a place in that canyon where he would have been killed and dumped in the river," Donaldson said.

Jake closed his eyes mentally trying to visualize that stretch of river. He hadn't been that way in years. The only access from the north side was across Taylor Flats, and a trail following the river upstream from where Beaver Creek dumped into the river. He looked at the map again. There was a lot of detail, but on a horribly small scale, something like a Congressional bill, a little of everything for everybody and nearly impossible to sort out hidden pork without a magnifying glass. His finger pointed to where they were standing.

"There are only a couple ways to access this stretch of canyon from the south side. One is three miles upstream from Beaver Creek. It's an ancient trail the Antiguas have used for as long as man remembers to access Chochuschuvio Falls." The name slipped off Jake's tongue with ease.

"The what?" Davidson said.

"Chochuschuvio. It means white tailed deer. Guess that's what it looked like to the grandfathers when they first saw it, the white south end of a deer heading north. There's a clay deposit there they've used for centuries for their pottery. Pretty good fishing, too."

"I understand you are Indian," Hayes, who had been quiet, said.

"Yeah. The other access point is a narrow canyon that drops down to the river across from the Sebastian Mine. The mining company built a road through it to haul out the ore, but it's been totally washed out, so the closest a person can drive to the river is seven miles, then it's shank's mare."

"Shank's mare?" Hayes said.

"On foot," Jake explained. He was silently impressed

they had been able to navigate on the forest so far.

That encounter had been yesterday. As Jake drove toward the Sebastian Mine trailhead to follow up on Curt's report, he knew the NCIS agents scheduled a day on the reservation to interview folks and find out more about the deceased. He secretly wished them luck. Most everyone was related in some way and protective of their privacy with strangers. At least the reservation roads were decently marked so they shouldn't get lost. Of course, that wasn't any guarantee. Sometimes he had trouble after a few years absence and flash floods moved things around.

As the sun crept over the ragged horizon, he pulled into the trailhead parking lot. The first thing was to scout around the boulders forming part of the barricade. Five years earlier some teens in a Jeep attempted to winch a boulder out of the way so they could drive to the river for a secret and undisturbed beer, sex, and pot orgy. The winch broke. Unable to loosen the cable before one of his compliance officers drove up, they got caught like a hungry trout. The judge was none too kind and filleted their wallets pretty good. The boulders didn't appear tampered with this time. He inspected the ten-inch posts buried in the ground, staggered to allow passage of person or horse, but not a vehicle wider than thirty inches. Each was tight with no indication of ATV tire marks running between them. He was about to check a metal gate off to one side which once permitted fire vehicle entry, when the NCIS agents pulled up in their Ford Explorer four by four.

"Good morning," Davidson called out cheerfully.

"Morning. You're up early," Jake said as he continued to the gate to inspect the weathered bronze, Forest Service padlock.

"Wanted to get an early start. The kid up in the lookout tower said you'd be here. He tried calling to let you know we were coming."

Jake reached for the radio on his belt. An inward groan wasn't audible. He'd forgotten to turn it on. Resuming the inspection, he looked at the ground around the gate, letting a faint smile slip across his lips. Squatting, he ran an open hand a fraction of an inch above the ground. Davidson and Hayes looked over his shoulder.

"Had a report of a vehicle in the wilderness last night," Jake said as he stood up, his body still stiff from the approaching storm, but no longer hurting. "This is the trail I told you about yesterday. Runs up to the old mine. That split in the mountain is where they hauled the ore out. Got time for a short hike?"

Davidson was wearing black, denim trousers, a long sleeve, plaid, wool shirt, boots, and agency cap. Hayes was slightly different, sporting a solid red T-shirt with a Marine Corp logo over the left breast overlaid by a lightweight, dark blue jacket. He sported black tennis shoes. Hayes looked to be in slightly better condition physically.

Not especially concerned that the two wouldn't be up to a hike, Jake headed across the Flats looking for evidence of a vehicle trespass. Davidson was used to slow, methodical searches not at an Indy 500 clip on foot. A half mile in Jake stopped to squat. Picking up a long, green, pine needle, he rolled it around in his fingers thoughtfully before sticking the sharp end into his mouth and proceeding on. A hundred yards further, he stopped again and squat.

"Yup. Tire track. Fresh," he said while gazing toward the cliffs.

Hayes looked at the spot, but didn't see anything more than a small black smudge on a melon-sized rock mostly buried in the ground.

Without further comment Jake headed back to the trail head, veering left just short of the gate to look at a large clump of brush encircling two conifers, like a chicken's wings protecting her brood. Even the citified agents could see someone had stepped down the tall grass. Davidson and Hayes watched as Jake disappeared into the brush, emerging several seconds later holding a small pine branch.

Removing the green needle bundle from his mouth he said, "This is a leaf from a Ponderosa Pine. Still fresh." He showed them the sticky sap opposite the end he had been chewing on. "Baby branch here is off the papa tossed in the bushes." The agents easily saw the needles matched. "No Ponderosa in this area. All cut down for mine props years ago. The nearest is about three miles. Whoever it was used papa branch hidden in the bushes to wipe their trail. Got a hunch this isn't the first time and probably won't be the last . . . until they're caught. Time to ride." Jake walked to the trailer.

"You going alone?"

"That's how we generally work out here. Besides, whoever was in here is long gone."

"How can you be sure, Tonto?" Hayes said.

Jake stopped to stare at him.

"Sorry. I didn't mean . . .," Hayes sputtered as his cheeks darkened.

"I take that as a compliment, Kemo Sabe." His smile relieved the agent of further embarrassment. "Actually, the tire track talked to me," Jake said, as he backed Mohf out of the trailer.

₪

Incident at Beaver Creek

Chapter 7

Feeling more confident the agents would not get lost, Jake waived as they continued toward Taylorsville, and saddled Mohf for the trip to the old mine. With the moist, early morning air surrounding them like a blanket, Jake let the stallion pick his own way along the trail as he read the ground and nibbled a donut.

The slanting sunlight cast a shadow to help with the fine print. At one point, he dismounted, picked up another pine needle bundle, stuck it in his mouth, and fingered the dusty trough carved by the old wagons. After checking the saddle's cinch, he remounted to continue on.

"Is that you, Mr. Bershinsky?" Curt Hayden's voice said over the portable radio on Jake's belt.

It was 9:30. "Yup."

Jay's Roost tower was eight miles due north of the trailhead with a clear view of his location. Curt was, if anything, conscientious. From the lofty position the young man had a dominating view of much of Jakes' district— over 400,000 acres of multiuse Federal lands. To facilitate the summer work, the Forest Service employed a number of seasonal employees for timber, recreation, wildlife, and engineering projects, allowed to work one hundred-eighty days, but most returned to school by Labor Day or soon thereafter.

His budget allowed for two, roving, initial attack fire trucks, each with a two-person crew, Curt to man the fire tower, and six compliance officers who patrolled the campgrounds and roads. Because they attended school in Santa Fe or Albuquerque, or lived in the area, they could work weekends through hunting season. They fell under Jake's supervision because of their enforcement responsibilities, except for Curt who was considered a dispatcher.

"Have you found anything, yet?" Curt said, using the enforcement frequency.

"Haven't made contact with your UFO, yet." Jake liked teasing the "kids" as he referred to those he worked closely with. Following a silence he said, "You saw right. There was a vehicle in here last night. They tried erasing their tracks by dragging a Ponderosa branch. Not especially effective. Drove too fast. I'm going to nose around the mine to see what was so important for somebody to drive in."

The Forest Service used a generic padlock on just about everything. Whoever passed through the gate had a key, which meant nothing. Too many of them were floating around after all these years.

As the sun rose higher, chasing the silvery dew from

the meadow, Jake took a deep, satisfied breath. Every day was different, doing what he enjoyed most since childhood —being outdoors, hiking, riding horseback alone in the wilderness, and being paid for it. And on days off it was doing the same things with family, except whenever he had Sundays off, then Katelyn hauled them all to church.

A steep-sided ridge extended along the north side of the river running east from Beaver Creek and terminating at the meadow as a broken, rock outcrop. From there eastward the ground was relatively flat, making a precarious plunge to the river. The mining company must have had a decent trail for the wagons to negotiate, but a landslide wiped it out. What existed now were a series of switchbacks created by hikers and hunters over the years down the face of the decline to the river and maintained by wildlife using the route to water.

Directly across the river, Sacred Mountain rose nearly vertical out of talus debris to create the jagged Eagle's Nest Peak. A tall spire geologist call a hoodoo, set out from the cliff face, rising up like giant smoke stack. Considerable controversy continued surrounding the origin of the anomaly because it did not fit, giving credence to the Pueblo stories, which Jake figured were more correct about its origins.

According to stories hundreds of years old, a huge Eagle's nest has always capped the tower. At this point, a gorge split Sacred Mountain as if cleaved with a hatchet, running from the river up a steep grade to the upper plateau seven miles south. In this, geologists were probably accurate, tending to be an explanation as bland as the rocks they studied. Jake preferred the Antigua's version. It was a lot more colorful.

It was also at this point the narrow gorge confining the river pulled back to form a wider area so the water ran more shallow and a bit slower. Except during high run off, the river was only eighteen inches deep at this point allowing easy passage from one side to the other.

With arrogant disdain, the gold mongers ignored and plowed over objections from the Antiguas and other Pueblos. The only thing sacred to them was the shiny metal. With a small army of trigger-happy guards at their command, they built a road through the gorge to connect the mine with a smelter in Taylorsville twenty-five miles distant. That abandoned eyesore once again became a bone of contention the year before as non-residents wanted to make it an historical site, a monument to the memory of greed and arrogance.

The mine itself penetrated the north side hill fifty feet above the river. Mine tailings excavated from the earth's bowels eventually created a large, flat area extending from the mine portal to the river.

Letting Mohf forage along the edge of the sterile plateau, Jake poked around the old entrance sealed by a heavy, rusted, iron gate. There was a fairly new Master lock attached to the closure chain that appeared to be Forest Service issue, but not one he was readily familiar with.

Keying the radio's transmitter button, he said, "Van this is Bershinsky." Van was the District's Engineer responsible for monitoring mining operations and reclamation of abandoned projects. There was no reply. He tried again. After a few moments of silence, a voice came on the radio that sounded as if a speaking in a tin barrel. Jake didn't like the reply. It was the radio tech.

"Jake, this is McAfee. Sorry, I'm working on the repeater. It'll be down for a while. Van had to take his wife to the hospital late yesterday. He'll probably be off the rest of the week." Van's wife had MS.

"Is there any way to check with Engineering to see if

Van put a new lock on the Sebastian Mine tunnel gate?"

"Hang on a minute. I'll open your enforcement channel."

After more silence, Curt answered. "Mac told me what you wanted. I got them on the phone, Mr. Bershinsky." Despite the close relationship developed over the past three years, Curt could never seem to address Jake except by his last name. "They say he was replacing some, but don't know if he got to that one yet. The log is locked in his desk. He definitely won't be back until Monday. Had to take his wife to Phoenix."

During this exchange, Jake walked out to the edge of the tailing mound overlooking the river to stare at the alluvial fan spread out in front of him on the other side, then up the gorge from which the intruding material had been flushed down. Signing off the radio, he closed his eyes. As a cool breeze and warm sun mingled on his face like sweet and sour sauce, he thought back to a special time during his childhood. He and Henry Riley—his best and only friend in those days—had come to Eagle's Nest on a spirit quest. That was a sweet time in his life, but whenever he thought of those days, it resurrected the bitterest memory as well. Opening his eyes before that memory fully returned to haunt him, he glimpsed a pinpoint of light near the top of the gorge, flashing intermittently like an airport beacon.

Retrieving binoculars from the saddlebags, he tried to identify the source of the light. It appeared to be sunlight reflecting off glass. Although not part of the wilderness, access to that area was closed off because it led to an especially sacred spot on the reservation. Yet, it appeared someone might have parked a vehicle up there. He radioed the tower.

"Curt, I just spotted a possible vehicle on the res side

of the wilderness, near the upper mouth of Cuchillo Cortar Gorge. Notify the res police. Might be the one they're looking for. I'm going across to investigate. It will take me a couple hours to get up there."

Turning to gather up his horse, Jake noticed a shell casing on the ground partially hidden by a flat, hand-sized rock. Picking it up, he rolled the shiny brass cylinder between his thumb and first two fingers. It was new, "Winchester 243" stamped on the end of the casing around the primer. A small game load. Looking again, he spotted several more just over the edge as the tailings fell steeply toward the river. He'd have to rappel down to retrieve them. He'd do that later, if necessary.

Slipping it into his pocket Jake said, "Well, old friend, time to wear off some of that grain you've been storing around the middle."

卐

Incident at Beaver Creek

Chapter 8

Davidson nearly missed the opportunity to work in NCIS. He'd taken Navy ROTC classes in high school because of a girl he was trying to impress. His dad was a used car salesman and that income sort of kept a roof over their heads, food on the table, and clothes on their backs, but affording college was out of the question. His ROTC advisor took a personal interest in the skinny kid, convinced him of the need for college, and then helped him earn a ROTC scholarship. He graduated from the University of Southern California with a degree in criminal justice and a commission, but the Navy owned his soul for at least six years. He thought it a fair swap.

Opting to specialize, he accepted a Warrant Officer 2 commission rather than a general officer's commission. Following a stint at the US Army Military Police School at

Ft. Leonard Wood, he spent much of the next eight years at sea or at overseas shore stations. During a tour in Kuwait, he was promoted to the rank of Chief Warrant Officer, CWO-3 and recruited into NCIS. Mostly a civilian agency, he retained his active status. The investigative challenges were something he lapped up like a thirsty dog at a water hose.

Donaldson loved the work, but felt the kind of Navy life he lived was not conducive to marriage, so remained a bachelor. On the other hand, Hayes married in college. Also a graduate of Ft. Leonard Wood, he was Marine. A CWO-2, he transferred to the Reserves when assigned to NCIS. Although privately considered the rookie because he was the youngest on the team, the two worked together well.

Arriving at Pueblo police headquarters, Sgt. Walter met them at the front desk. A fireplug of a woman, she looked capable of taking on a mountain lion with a matchstick. Like her boss, Sgt. Walter wore a starched and well-creased, tan uniform shirt with blue jeans, rolling her black hair into a bun on the back of her head.

"The chief isn't here. He had to drive to Albuquerque for a meeting with the Pueblo governors. Says you want to interview people about Darrel Windpipe."

"We'd like to determine if the reason he was murdered has any connection to a letter he received a month before coming home." Donaldson was sensitive not to mention the AWOL charge.

"Guess the best place to start is with his father. When will the body be released?"

"Later this morning."

"Don't expect much. James is pretty broke up. He was proud of that boy. We all were. A real good example for our young people. He brought us honor."

"Well, somebody wasn't proud enough."

From the direction they arrived, the Antigua's pueblo appeared as an assortment of flattop, adobe structures placed to take advantage of the uneven terrain and to live in harmony with the land, not bend it to their will. Their first impression was of an area of poverty. A number of abandoned buildings in various stages of ruin were scattered among occupied homes that were simple, functional, and neat. Aside from the old derelicts, what gave a negative impression was the barren, dark, rust-colored ground, so poor that given a good rain it moved like loose Jell-O.

"How come you don't tear out those places that are falling down? They look dangerous. I'd be concerned kids would play around them and get hurt," Hayes said.

"No problem. No one goes near them. Someone died there and their spirit might be hanging around. In a couple cases, the dead person is buried under the floor," she said casually.

Set atop a rise, a Catholic mission church over-shadowed the community; an impressive-looking structure built four centuries earlier with forced labor as the charitable Spanish ruthlessly tried to convert the Pueblo people to Christianity. It stood as a gleaming, white monument to European incursion and failure. The Antigua outwardly adopted features of the new religion while quietly and doggedly maintaining their ancestral beliefs. What the agents did not see from this vantage was the new school complex and condo-like homes on paved streets located on the other side of the mission hill. The Antigua may not have adopted the religion, but they had no qualms about keeping up with the Joneses.

Sgt. Walter pulled up to a particular home toward the outskirts of the older section of the community. Two small, barefoot boys in jeans and T-shirts stopped their play in the dirt at the side of the neighbor's house to stare.

"Hi, Rudy. Hi Tommy," she called out and waiving. The boys waived, but continued to stare giving Hayes the feeling of being on the animal side of the fence at a zoo.

Built in true adobe brick fashion, James Windpipe formed, laid, and joined each brick with own hands thirty-five years earlier. The walls were thick, providing warmth in winter and cool comfort in summer, although it didn't often get hot at the nearly 7,000-foot altitude, not like along the Rio Grande rift valley.

As the agents approached, Hayes noticed a two by three foot area on the wall where the plaster had fallen off exposing the bricks near the south corner. Hayes noted other areas that could use attention, and thought the whole could use a fresh coat of paint.

Dictated by tradition, the door faced east. Round poles jutting out from the wall near the roofline were not decorative ornaments as on the newer houses made with concrete blocks. These were actually the ends of the roof supports. It might have been old, but the house appeared sturdy and comfortable. A woman in a fully pleated, maroon skirt and flowered blouse, her graying hair tied back in a long ponytail, came out to meet them.

"These men are from the Navy, Mary. They come to speak with you and James," Sgt. Walter said.

The woman didn't look directly at the men, but they could tell her eyes were dull and bloodshot. She had obviously been crying. Saying nothing, she nodded and turned away, expecting them to follow her to the rear of the house where they found a man in blue jeans, plaid shirt, and cowboy boots rocking slowly in an old, wood chair beneath a pole and stick shade structure. Sgt. Walter squat next to him to be on eye level.

"James, these men are from the Navy. They're here about Darrel," she said softly.

The man lifted his head to look toward them. His expression seized Davidson's heart. He appeared so old and haggard, and frail, his eyes red and puffy.

"We are very sorry about your son, Mr. Windpipe. I'm Agent Davidson. This is Agent Hayes. We're criminal investigators for the Navy, NCIS. We've come to find who murdered your son." Davidson's voice was soft as his heart genuinely reached out to the man's pain.

A tear trickled down the well-creased, brown cheek. Jim Windpipe motioned for them to sit on a bench across from him.

"I've read your son's personnel record. Darrel was well liked by his officers and fellow seamen. I have been told they are very upset at his loss. A detachment of sailors can be here tomorrow to help with the funeral."

"A military burial?" the old man barely managed to say, his voice weak and cracking.

"Yes, if you'd like."

Mr. Windpipe nodded his head, yes.

"I understand Darrel received a letter about a month ago. It upset him, but he wouldn't speak about it, except that he had to come home. Do you know what was in that letter?"

Mr. Windpipe turned his head slightly to glance at the agent before turning away, saying nothing. Davidson picked up on the minute expression. The old man knew, but seemed unable to discuss it. He allowed a lengthy silence to pass until the old gentleman was ready to speak.

"I am responsible for my son's death."

Davidson and Hayes glanced quickly at one another, both shocked at the statement.

"What are you saying, Jim?" Sgt. Walter said.

"I wrote the letter. I told him his younger brother was having some trouble. I should have never done it. My son would still be alive." Tears began cascading down the weathered face.

Davidson waited some more. When it was obvious nothing further was coming forth, he primed the pump. "What kind of trouble?" That he had been sent here was fortunate. Not many agents would have the patience necessary for such a protracted inquiry. Fifth generation Nisei, he had been raised with elderly grandparents amid elderly Japanese. He learned to respect his elders and patience.

"Raymond has been getting drugs," Mrs. Windpipe said from where she stood next to the house, arms folded across her chest.

"What kind of drugs?" Sgt. Walter asked.

"The real bad kind," Jim said. "Cocaine. We can't handle him anymore. That's what I wrote Darrel about. I should have never done it. He came home to talk to him. Raymond wasn't here. He was in the mountains. Said he was going hunting. That was a lie. He gets his drugs in the mountains."

Hard drugs were supplanting booze among some of the younger people, but the police hadn't been able to figure out how it was coming in, despite numerous road checks and inquiries. This new information peaked Sgt. Walter's interest.

"You say Raymond's been getting drugs from the mountains?" she said. "Do you know where?"

"No. They only brag in whispers that it comes from the spirits in Sacred Mountain. That is wrong. Those spirits would not do that. Darrel went to find Raymond."

"Apparently he did," Davidson thought to himself, now having a motive for the murder. "Do you have any idea who Raymond may have contacted while in the mountains?" he said to Jim, but the question was meant for both parents.

"No."

"Where is Raymond now?"

"Don't know. He has been gone maybe a month. He does that."

The agents spent some time with the Windpipes, as they began remembering their son, a bright young man with a dream to succeed in the White man's world as an example to the Pueblo's youth. The agent told them about the reports he'd read in Darrel's folder, things they could be justly proud to remember. As they drove off Hayes put in a call to arrange for an honor guard for the funeral..

凹

Incident at Beaver Creek

Chapter 9

For a stallion, Mohf had an even, unflappable disposition with a couple quirks he always insisted on negotiating. One was dead things. He didn't like being around them. The other was water. He insisted it was fresh if he drank it. He barely tolerated the baths his family afflicted upon him so long as the water was warm. If not, he had ways to letting them know of his displeasure, like snorting, stomping, and his favorite, shaking so water flew all over them. A wet tail alongside the head got him into deep trouble. He didn't use that any more. He simply didn't like getting his feet wet, barely consenting to crossing streams when he and Jake worked the backcountry together. He really balked against water that was up to his belly and not long before had been ice. As a youngster, he stubbornly refused to put one hoof in so much as a wet spot on the ground, resorting to bucking, but Jake was annoyingly persistent and too good a rider to be unseated.

Stopping short of the bank, Mohf surveyed the water. He could see it flowing at a goodly clip, and it looked deep. Pretending to drink was a way to check the temperature. It was cold. He preferred his drinking water to be cool, not cold. Lifting his head, the other side was quite a ways off. He didn't see a need to do this and turned away to find grass, unfortunately, Jake was being narrow-minded and insisting they cross. Following some discussion, he reluctantly stepped into the White Tail, plowing across, doggedly placing each foot carefully as the current tried to sweep them away. The only acceptable thing about this, the bottom was relatively smooth gravel and no deeper than half way up the leg. He positively hated when icy water fingered his belly.

Once on solid ground, he snorted loudly, shaking his head to express displeasure, relieved the ordeal was over. The problem was that the horse was unable to contemplate that the way to the barn and a well-deserved bucket of oats was returning the way they had just come. That return did occur to Jake and knew a repeat performance would take considerably more persuasion. Hopefully, the round trip through the gorge would tire him sufficiently to forgo much argument. Convincing a highly intelligent, thousand-pound animal to do something contrary to its mind was a task the ranger didn't relish, especially at the end of a long day.

According to geologists, Cuchillo Cortar was born about the time of the Valles explosion, a super nova eruption triggering an earthquake that split the mountain from north to south in a nearly perfect straight line. Over time, runoff from the plateau above and springs within carried more silt down to the river cutting the fissure wider and deeper. When the wagon road was built to carry ore to Taylorsville, the engineers thought they had accomplished a great feat until the first monsoon down pour that following July. Maintaining the road became a nightmare as each spring snowmelt and then summer monsoons purged improvements. The Antigua smiled silently. What they could not thwart, the twin gods did. Abandoned after the mine played out, the mountain spirits quickly flushed all vestiges of their labors down the river as if someone pulled a toilet chain. Standing on the alluvial fan of coarse debris, Jake turned to face the rising pillar.

"Maseway, it is I, White Bear. I've come to investigate a strange thing that does not belong at the top by your brother."

Anyone but an Antigua would have thought the lawman had been in the sun too long, but the teachings of his youth still played a role in his life that occasionally surfaced. Looking up at the top of the massive column, he spotted a Golden Eagle perched on the edge of its nest. He could feel the piercing stare of the great bird. He waited. A sharp cry echoed off the cliff, repeating through the canyon until sounding like last chords of a fading chorus. Permission granted . . . granted . . . granted. He thought it sounded curiously mournful.

This was a special place, not just to the Antigua, but to Jake as well, holding the most special memory in his life. As horse and rider started into the narrow defile, the feeling of renewed joy felt overshadowed by something oppressing. He stopped abruptly and closed his eyes to let his spirit reach out. Was there evil here, now? No. Sorrow, great sorrow. Could this be the place where Darrel Windpipe died? Was it his spirit lingering here that Jake felt?

Proceeding slowly, trying to phantom the problem, they hadn't gone thirty yards when Jake swung out of the saddle to pick up a leather bag laying on the ground next to a boulder the size of an old Volkswagen Beetle. Hefting the bag, it was full of liquid. He checked the contents. Water. He began reading the ground more closely. A few feet beyond was a melon-sized rock with a blackish stain on it. Mohf followed as Jake walked up hill reading the story imprinted on the ground. He knew what the water container meant. He'd had one much like it when he had been here as a youth. It did not belong where it was found.

ℿ

Incident at Beaver Creek

Chapter
10

Summer evening temperatures plummet in the high country after the sun goes down, but that wasn't the reason Jake shivered like jigglers in an earthquake. Covered with no more than a kilt and blanket held tightly about the shoulders, he and Henry followed close behind Uncle Marshall along a trail running from the back of his house toward a small hill a quarter mile away.

Each of the twelve moieties making up the Antigua Pueblo had their own kiva, a sacred house about twenty feet around, each located in one of two areas. Here they conducted business and religious rites concerning their individual group. One of these groupings, known as the Turquois kivas, set at the southwest end of the community. Governed by the winter *cacique*, the true Pueblo leader, they took charge of Pueblo activities from November to March.

The second group set in the northeast, the Squash kivas. Those moieties took charge of activities from March to November under the direction of Uncle Marshall, the summer cacique. The much larger community kiva was located near the Pueblo's center with all the homes arranged around these centers in as orderly fashion as the ground allowed in keeping with their refusal to bend the land to their will, but to adapt to what had been given them.

Outside the community, some distance away, were two additional kivas. One belonged to the warrior society headed by the War Chief. He and the caciques were the only persons appoint for life, and he answered only to the caciques. The second was even more recluse, being a small structure where the caciques went alone to meditate. Whereas the warrior kiva was nestled among Aspen and Ponderosa, the cacique kiva sat on a barren hill. This was where the three headed.

When Toleshnec took charge of educating Jake and Henry, he made it seem like a game, but the intent was gradual conditioning directed toward this very day. They were to commune with the Kachinas, the spirits, and seek a personal connection with them. This event normally happened no later than when a boy turned thirteen. That should have happened last year for Jake and Henry, except for a rattlesnake.

When some cows slipped a fence to check out grazing along a highway right of way the War Chief sent the two boys to put them back. Everything was going as smoothly as recalcitrant cows allowed when the whole thing blew up in their faces. Jake vaguely remembered hearing the telltale buzz of a rattlesnake cowering under a sage bush. A millisecond later, his pony went ballistic as cows scattered in every imaginable direction like paper in a dust devil. He was a good horseman, but this caught him totally off-guard. He vaguely remembered hitting the ground, then rolling onto his hands and knees as Henry beat the snake away. That's when the pain hit, shooting up his right leg as if it were on fire. He rolled onto his back, screaming, the thought he'd been bitten flashing into his mind.

"Hold still, brother. Oh, crap!"

Hearing Henry's expletive exasperated that fear. He never cursed, not much anyway, but cut loose this time.

Jake heard his voice, but it sounded as if in the next county and strained. "What is it? What is it? Did he bite me?"

"No. Stop moving! Your leg is broke."

For whatever reason, Jake's panic diminished a bit. He was more afraid of a rattlesnake bite than a mere broken leg, although it sure hurt.

Six miles from help, Henry did his best to comfort his brother, but he had to leave to get help. He was well aware of the dangers of shock and Jake was showing definite signs as his tanned face turned a ghostly gray. He couldn't leave him like that, yet he had little choice.

"Jake, I got to get help," he said, "but I can't if you go shocky on me."

Suddenly, Jake quieted, staring off to one side, lifting his arm up as if taking someone's hand. That scared Henry even more until Jake turned to look at him. The color was closer to normal, his eyes not quite as glazed. He wasn't nearly as knotted.

"It's okay. He's here."

"Who?" Henry looked around but couldn't see anyone. He was really scared now. His brother was hallucinating.

"Angak. He's come to be with me. Ride for help."

A quiet feeling came over Henry that it was going to be all right to leave. What happened next, he would only tell Uncle Marshall in private, later. As he gathered up his pony for the ride a voice said, "Use Jake's horse. She will run on the wind for your brother."

Henry spun around to see who had suddenly come to their aid, and that's when he almost wet his pants. Kneeling next to Jake, and holding his hand, was a man with wild, raven-black hair to the waist and matching beard to his chest. Henry was familiar with stories of Angak, the healing and protective spirit from the Kachina ceremonies. His appearance was disheveled and frightening, but when their eyes made contact, Henry felt peace. Taking Jake's filly, Viento, he swung onto her back for a ride he would never forget.

"It felt as if she sprouted wings. I have never known a horse to run so fast. It seemed I had barely gotten on her back than we were at the hospital," he later told anyone who would listen.

That, of course, brought challenges to race. The filly put on a good show, but never did better than second. Still, but both boys knew what she did that sunny afternoon.

Sedated and stabilized, Jake was barely aware of people in a circle around his bed. Doc Ryan and Doc Jim were confident in their abilities, but knew enough to ask Uncle Marshall to call upon the spirits for help. Jake's mother didn't object. She wanted all the help possible, too. The best healer in the community, a man of two spirits, responded. Any outsider in the hospital might have wondered at the drumming and chanting echoing through the sterile corridors.

The resulting compound fracture of the lower, right leg and ligament damage just above the ankle required pinning the bones in place, and plastering on a cast from the hip down. Henry remained at his brother's side every day, talking, watching TV, playing card games, or just sitting silently as they often did in the mountains, content to be close to one another.

The fourth day following surgery and the morphine cleared enough for Jake to think coherently he said to Henry, "When are you leaving on your quest?"

"I'm not."

"What do mean you're not?"

"The elders spoke to me yesterday. They actually came to the hospital because I am staying here." There were two beds in the room and Henry had taken up residency in the second one. "They are concerned you might not be able to go on a quest. I told them you would go if I had to carry you, just not right away. Uncle Marshall then did something I've only seen once before. He stepped to the window and began speaking as if someone was sitting on the ledge we could not see."

"A Kachina."

"What?"

"You and the elders were standing by the door. A Kachina I'm not familiar with was sitting with his legs crossed on the windowsill. He and Uncle Marshall talked, but I couldn't hear what they said."

"When Uncle turned back to us, he said that you will go on your quest next year, and I will go with you. I guess we all knew he had been speaking to a spirit. Just, when it happens like that, it's kind of spooky."

"But, isn't the quest is supposed to be done alone?"

"Yes, but Uncle Marshall said that the soul spirits in our bodies are so close they are like one or we share the same spirit. Anyway, we will go together."

"Maybe that means I'll be crippled and you'll have to carry me like we did cousin Paul."

"Paul is a feather. You weigh like a horse. We will walk side by side."

A week following surgery, Jake went home to the Forest Service station and Henry moved in so Jake's mother could return to work. He was there not just to keep Jake company, but help him with personal matters until he was stable enough to do them himself. In the hospital that meant emptying the bedpan and learning to give sponge baths. At home, it was lending a shoulder as Jake learned to negotiate the bulk of plaster attached to his leg. It was not always pleasant work, but if their individual spirits were *like* one, they *became* one during those weeks following the accident.

Beginning the second week after Jake returned home, Doc Ryan stopped to check on his patient. He didn't have the usual confident smile.

"Jake, I spoke with an orthopedic surgeon in Albuquerque and showed him your X-rays. He wasn't very encouraging. I'll be blunt. It's a nasty break, we all knew that, and it's glued back together, but there was significant ligament damage and . . . well, I just want you to be prepared. He doesn't think you'll be able to walk the same."

"Well, he's wrong. I will walk, and run, and jump, and do all the stuff I did before, just like before." Jake's stubborn streak emerged like the sun splitting open storm clouds to bathe the land with its light.

"It will take a lot of work, and it won't be easy."

"My brother will do what it takes. If it hurts, he will cry on my shoulder. If he slacks off, I will kick his butt," Henry said.

Doc Ryan slapped Jake's good knee and laughed. "You know, I have no doubt in my mind you two will do just that. That cast will come off in about twelve weeks, and then we shall see about getting you walking again. I know some people at Stanford Medical School that might be able to help, but understand this, I know you two. Whatever we do, go slow or you will do yourself harm and prove the Albuquerque doc right. Understand?"

"Yes, sir," they answered in unison.

"Now, another matter. When's the last time you've had a bath?"

"I give him a sponge bath every day," Henry said, a bit defensively.

"Well, a good sweat bath is out until that cast is off, but how would you like to soak in a nice, hot shower?"

"I'd love it," Jake said.

"Okay," Doc Ryan said, pulling a box of black, plastic garbage bags from a sack he had brought. "Let me show you how this works." Slipping Jake's leg into a bag, he used a long, flat, wide rubber strip to close it on the thigh above the cast, making a watertight seal. "Now, that should keep the cast dry. I've got a chair you can use out in my car. Henry, go fetch it and I'll walk you through the procedure."

Doc Ryan was one of those who explained, but let the patient do the work. He supervised as Henry helped Jake to the back of the house where a large bathroom afforded a lot of room to maneuver in.

Henry started the water so it would be warm, and then helped Jake out of his boxers. He still wasn't bending very well because of a couple cracked and bruised ribs. Turning the water off, the doc's chair and an old metal, folding one for Jake to rest his leg on were set in position and Jake settled in. Leg bagged, he turned the water on.

"Oh, that feels good," Jake moaned, but there was a problem. He couldn't reach his back or his legs because of the ribs.

Henry threw off his clothes and went in. Doc Ryan shook his head and chuckled. There was no doubt these two could do anything they put their combined mind to. That was the first time Jake was physically inactive and it drove him crazy at times. His body yearned to jump and run to the point every muscle tingled, but with gentle guidance from Mom Riley, Uncle Marshall, Toleshnec, and Henry, he battled through the urges, and learned something about self-control. To help work off excess energy, his mom acquired a home gym to exercise everything from the waist up and the one good leg. His sixth grade teacher who lived a couple houses down from Mom Riley exercised his mind with a deluge of puzzles teaching thinking skills as well as the usual school stuff. She had a knack of coming up with things like that actually making school fun. He didn't attend seventh grade classes until the January term, but neither was behind. If anything, the two were ahead.

Just before sunrise, a year to the date following the accident, Toleshnec took the boys to the racetrack. Jake didn't participate in the long run a couple weeks earlier at Doc Ryan's request, although Jake felt he could do it. Doc Ryan thought running twenty-five miles might be too much, too soon and wanted him to ease into it. Jake listened.

Standing at the starting line their mentor said, "I have placed two sticks at the base of the first standing rock. That's five miles. This is not about speed, Jake, but endurance." It was a warning to pace himself. "You are now old enough to prepare yourself as Antigua have for thousands of years."

He handed each a plastic water bottle half-filled with a greenish-yellow substance. It wasn't Gatorade. They had seen other runners drink the concoction beginning four days before the big race "After you vomit, you breathe different from other people," Toleshnec said, after the boys bent over to deposit their stomachs on the ground. For a time, both wondered if they would breathe at all. "Now, rinse out your mouths with this water and return those sticks."

This was the craziest thing Toleshnec had come up with yet, but after vomiting each morning for four days, they agreed to feeling different as the miles seem to glide by, and the distance extended until both were loping cross-country at ten miles an hour. Purging wasn't an everyday occurrence, only before special occasions, so when the time approached for them to go on the quest they were not surprised when Toleshnec asked them to vomit every morning before breakfast. By this time, it wasn't necessary to use the medicine. They both acquired a feather to stick down their throats. A week later, they were called to the Raven kiva. The clan chief was there, as well as Uncles Marshall and Toleshnec, and several others.

Dressed in new cotton trousers and moccasins the two uncles had made for the boys, with a light tan kilt and matching turquoise-colored belt and head clothe to keep their long hair in place, the boys stood before the clan chief. Of average height, his shoulders were broad and powerful, bespeaking of a man who maintained the irrigation ditches. They knew him to be a stern man, but kind, as two exuberant boys learned when a practical joke misfired a couple years before. They felt fortunate as his thunderous voice set them on a better course, much more fortunate than a sixteen-year old whose misdeed several weeks earlier was serious enough to warrant whipping, a rare occurrence.

At sixteen, Walking Badger tended to being mean and defiant. Mom Riley frequently noted that he was headed for a meeting with Wapamo, the long bill spirit, just for the scornful way he treated his parents and elders. Always regarding the welfare of others lightly, his actions caused two other boys grave, physical harm, and that brought a quick verdict during a special moiety meeting.

As the Raven moiety fathers and their sons gathered in the woods near the warrior kiva, Walking Badger stood between two, stout Aspen, an arm securely tethered to each at an upward angle. He wore only a small loincloth. With a front row seat, as if a warning for them to mend their ways, Jake and Henry easily saw the smirk on the young man's face, an act of defiance as if to say, "Go ahead with your little whipping. I'll show you how tough I am."

The fathers of the injured boys would have preferred wielding the whip, but that was Wapamo's duty, to prevent any resemblance of revenge that might fracture the community. Afterward, Jake thought the punishment might have been kinder if the fathers had done it.

Everyone was present except the clan chief. An eerie silence blanketed the area. Even from squirrels who usually complained noisily about any intrusion upon their domain remained silent. When the snap of a limb sounded, everyone turned to see the frightening specter of the chief of the guard kachinas walking through the trees toward them.

Wapamo's body was naked except for moccasins and a white kilt trimmed in gray. A wide sash encircled his hips bearing the Kachina's red, white, blue, and yellow colors with black Antigua designs. The same color scheme covered all visible parts of the muscular body. However, seeing the Kachina's mask ran a cold finger of fear along Jake's backbone. The large, round face was black, appearing to be a crow with large, protruding eyes and a snarling beak. Five Eagle feathers projected equidistant around the top half from ear to ear. Black feathers covered the back of the head. Off all the whipping Kachinas, he was the most feared, and his appearance marked the seriousness of the event.

Walking Badger looked over his shoulder, and for a split moment the smirk vanished, but only for a moment. Jake and Henry looked at one another. There was no doubt who wore the mask of long bill. The powerful shoulder and arm muscles were too well known, but they also knew that while it was the Raven clan's chief, having put on the mask, he was now possessed of the powerful spirit.

The war chief greeted the Kachina respectfully and stepped aside, holding more whips. Jake wondered how many they would need. The long-billed Kachina raised his arm and brought the long, stiff blades down on the exposed back. Walking Badger's smirk didn't fade, in fact, it seemed he was about to laugh when the whip came sideways, catching him along the right rib cage. The grin evaporated as mouth dropped open and eye's bulged. When the spirit backhanded the whip across his left rib cage, the boy fought desperately to stifle a cry. The first three blows had only been a prelude. Nine more followed as Wapamo's powerful shoulder and arm muscles uncoiled, really laying into the chore. By the fifth blow Walking Badger was screaming, and crying, and thrashing hysterically. When it was over, he hung limp, his chest heaving violently with short breaths, tears streaming down his brown face, his once smooth backside from the neck to ankles crisscrossed by bloodied welts.

Punishment over, fathers lead their sons away, heads

hung in shame, but Jake, like the other boys, had to sneak a peek as they passed. That had been the first whipping in nearly thirty years, and every boy there privately swore not to be the next. If only Walking Badger had learned and mended his ways instead of ending up with a knife in his chest at eighteen.

Jake was thinking on that whipping as his bare feet cut through the icy stream before climbing the hill to the cacique kiva. This was the first stage of the ritual he and Henry were about to undergo which began with vomiting and a thorough hair washing with yucca soap.

The kiva was not much more than twelve feet in diameter, a solid, plastered adobe structure rising eight feet into the air like a short smoke stack. There were no doors or windows as in a house. A pole ladder lay on its side next to the wall. Lifted vertically, it allowed access to the roof where an entrance to the interior was located. It was here the cacique prayed, meditated, and conversed with the spirits.

Next to the kiva was a small, rectangular structure. The east-facing front was a covered, porch-like area where a sizeable quantity of Juniper and pine was stored. The boys were well acquainted with this part of the building having cut, split, and carried every piece because that was their family assignment. Respect for sacred things controlled their curiosity so that neither peeked inside either structure despite youthful temptation.

A buffalo hide covered a small door to the interior requiring a person to stoop to gain access. Uncle Marshall pulled the cover back and said, "Lay your blankets over that pole, then each of you take six pieces of wood inside and set them along the back wall."

Embers of a small fire glowed sufficiently to provide

enough light to see where they were going. The warmth quickly chased off the chill. Setting the wood down carefully, they turned to face their uncle who directed them to sit on a blanket spread out each side of the fire pit as he assumed a position facing the door with the wood in easy reach. He added more wood to the fire to increase the heat. A small opening at floor level allowed fresh air in as the smoke rose and vented out an opening at the top. This was the cacique's sweat lodge where they prepared themselves before entering the kiva to commune with the spirits.

There was a sweat lodge behind Uncle Marshall's home built of twelve, bent poles to form a dome and covered with hides. The boys used it often, preferring it to a bathtub or shower because they honestly felt cleaner and more invigorated. Few Antigua maintained a personal one, however. Jake and Henry built one at the Ranger station to use when staying there, covering it with old, wool blankets from the fire cache which were destined to be discarded. Toleshnec said it was the best way to clean the inner as well as outer body. Doing research for an English paper, Jake found a magazine article confirming that sweating not only opened the body's pores to rid it of embedded dirt, but also had the effect of flushing out bad toxins inside the body. However, this was not going to be a routine cleansing.

Uncle Marshall began a slow beat on the ceremonial drum he had brought; one Jake built after several misfire attempts. Fifteen inches around by four inches hall, he stretched a buffalo skin cover over both sides of the cottonwood core lacing wet rawhide laces that shrank as they dried creating a very taunt surface. When Uncle Marshall struck it the first time with a soft drumstick, he was delighted with the sound. Now, the sound was ominous, portending coming events.

Jake and Henry knew a few of the prayers their uncle

offered and repeated them, some vocally and some only in their minds. Others were unknown, sometimes using strange words or addressing unfamiliar spirits. As the heat radiated out from the fire, sweat began oozing out and trickle down arms and chest. After a time Uncle Marshall finished and put the drum aside and added a couple more pieces of wood to the fire.

"You can sit back further from the fire unless you want to roast." He said, lying sideways on the blanket beneath him.

Taking the lead, the boys moved back what little distance they could and stretched out as well. The heat intensified as sweat beginning to flow freely.

"My brother has spoken to you about the spirit quest so you know what remains to be done. Is there anything that concerns you?" he said in a conversational tone.

Jake could see Henry staring at him across the fire. From the first meeting each seemed to know the mind of the other. Normally Henry was the speaker and Jake the doer, but this time his brother remained silent. Jake knew what bothered him, but maybe himself more. He spoke.

"The whipping."

"You are afraid of pain?" Uncle Marshall asked gently.

"Uncle Toleshnec put us through a lot preparing for this day. My broken leg was no party. There is pain and there is pain. We have faced all kinds, but when Walking Badger was whipped . . . well, he was a really tough guy, but sometimes I still hear his screams in my head."

"Those were the cries of the evil spirits inside him. They do not like to be punished, where the good spirits will protect and comfort a person. Walking Badger was punished with yucca. They are meant to cause pain. In this ceremony, you shall feel the lash of braided corn silk. This is not punishment, but to alert you to know if there are any bad spirits inside you to be expelled. Knowing you two, I should think you will feel some of the whip."

"But we have been good," Henry said.

"Yeah, we haven't done anything bad . . . for a while," Jake added.

Uncle Marshall chuckled. "Neither of you possess a truly evil spirit. You are not mean. On the contrary, I have seen much good in both of you. For instance, last year at the race, before the accident, Jake runs his part, then takes Paul Bird That Walks upon his shoulders and starts the next part. When he reaches the halfway mark, Henry takes the boy on his shoulders to complete the race. Neither of you were good for anything for several days after that, but a boy who will never be able to run the sacred race on his own, was able to be a part of it. You have a reputation of helping when not asked, doing good toward others. You also have a reputation for devilment. For that you will perhaps feel some discomfort as that small spirit which resides within you is punished."

Jake felt a little better. A small bad spirit? Braided corn silk tassels? There would be harder things to face on this journey.

The three spent some time talking and sweating, and then Uncle Marshall sat up and began playing the drum again. The boys sat cross-legged and listened as he prayed for the spirits to guide and protect them on the journey ahead. Finished, he guided the boys outside where the cold air stabbed at them, but that was only the beginning. Walking down to a small pool behind a beaver dam, they removed their loincloths and dove in, surfacing with a lot of hissing and gasps. Uncle Marshall joined them. Feeling as if stuck with thousands of icy pins was a discomfort experienced over the years, but which he had come to enjoy —not the immediate pain, but the lasting effects that rejuvenated him to the core. He reasoned the feel of corn silk wouldn't be nearly so bad.

Wrapped in blankets again, they proceeded to the moiety kiva where a number of family members waited outside—the chief in his white, cotton shirt and trousers, light blue kilt, and moccasins, looked solemn as ever. Toleshnec and Mrs. Riley were there, as well as other men, all in traditional dress.

Uncle Marshall went up the ladder first and disappeared through the door followed by the chief, and the others. After a wait of twenty minutes, the soft sounds of the ceremonial drum lifted out into the night, and Toleshnec indicated for the boys to climb up as he followed. Jake was shivering again, but not from the cold..

ᛚ

Incident at Beaver Creek

Chapter
11

Because most religious ceremonies are sacred, the Pueblos conceal them from outsiders, sometimes even to other Native Americans, especially since the Spanish intrusion. Jake gave little thought to the fact that he might be one of the very few, if not the first White man to not just view a kiva ritual, but to be part of one considered very sacred. In his youthful mind, the Antigua had adopted him as one of their own so it must be okay.

Legs again feeling like silly putty, he inched down the pole ladder into the dark kiva behind Henry. Turning to face the gathering, his legs almost gave out completely. In the flickering firelight he saw the chief and Wapamo with the arms of professional body builder flanking Uncle Marshall.

Kachinas, the supernatural spirits, were on call to help

the Pueblos in all aspects of their lives, and over the years became a reality to Jake. When men dressed as a particular spirit, they didn't just represent that particular one, the spirit entered and became the man. The only difference between this long bill and the one who whipped Walking Badger, this one was bare footed. In his right hand was the whip with long, braided laces. They might be made of corn silk, but didn't look very soft.

On the ground, in front of them, were two circles containing sand paintings depicting other Kachinas who the boys hoped would be their protectors and help them accomplish their quest. Mrs. Riley stood to one side holding more whips. Again, Jake wondered how many they would need.

Two moiety members stepped up behind the boys and removed their blankets as Uncle Marshall continued the chanting that went on for some time until apparently feeling something that meant the time had come. Toleshnec stepped forward and escorted Henry into the left circle. As the two stood facing one another, Henry spread his feet for balance as instructed before they interlocked fingers, and their uncle lifted his arms into the air. At this point, Wapamo stepped behind Henry. Uncle Marshall continued chanting as an assistant drummed.

The first strike crossed Henry's shoulders right to left. It didn't seem too bad. Henry didn't even flinch. The second strike was a backhand over the lower back, left to right. Unlike Walking Badger who Wapamo filleted from shoulders to ankles, they were to be scourged on the back only. With the target area marked, Henry seemed all right. There must not be any serious evil spirits needing exorcised, but the Kachina was just warming up and getting in stride. The third strike came down on the right shoulder angling to the left hip. Henry flinched and Jake clearly saw red marks appear.

"So much for soft corn silk," he thought.

The fourth was a backhand from left shoulder to right hip. Henry jerked and loosed a muffled grunt. Jake knew what was coming and wanted to close his eyes, but couldn't. The Kachina took a roundhouse swing laying the whip over the right ribs, a highly sensitive area, followed by a backhand over the left rib cage. Both times Henry jerked, biting down a scream that came out as a muffled squeak. The ordeal was half over as long bill took a new whip and repeated the strokes, this time eliciting a louder squeal as the braids curled over the ribs.

Twelve strikes. It was over. Henry was breathing hard, barely able to stand as Toleshnec lowered his arms, and directed him to kneel in place. His face was ashen, eyes glazed; sweat peppered his brow, as tears trickled down his cheeks. Jake desperately wanted to kneel with his brother and hold him close, but it was his turn. Looking up, Toleshnec had moved to the right circle. Forcing legs to move, he stepped to the sacred circle. Looking down he saw Angak's face materialize in the sand painting. Jake didn't immediately recognize the Kachina next to him, yet there was something of familiarity. In an instant, the memory of Uncle Marshall speaking to someone on the windowsill at the hospital came to mind. It was this Kachina and he was smiling.

Spreading his feet for balance, careful to not step on the figures painted in the circle, he locked fingers with his uncle. As their fingers interlaced, Jake felt something slide up the inside of each foot and wrap around his ankles, like fingers. He wanted to look down, but Toleshnec lifted his arms overhead.

At that moment, Jakes eyes locked with those of his mentor. There seemed to be a light flickering in the black orbs like small flecks of gold reflecting the kiva fire. When they first met some five years before those eyes reflected the fire of hate, but something changed back then. What Jake saw now was the gleam a proud father would have for his son, and for the first time wished his real father were here.

Jake didn't even feel the whip's first blows across the shoulders and small of the back. He focused on Toleshnec's eyes, drawn deeper into those pools as if finding shelter in a dark cave. The cross lashes seemed as nothing. The strikes across the ribs drew him back some out of the safe haven, then nothing until the last two across the ribs again ended the ordeal. When Toleshnec lowered his arms, Jake knew it was safe to come out. The hands on his feet withdrew. That's when the stinging pain became noticeable, but tolerable as he knelt next to Henry who reached out to take Jake's hand and give a reassuring squeeze. All discomfort vanished.

As Wapamo climbed out of the kiva, Toleshnec knelt in front of the boys, took each by the neck with a big hand, and pressed them to his breast. Jake felt the man tremble slightly knowing he had felt every blow of the whip as well. He'd never felt closer to the man who wanted the White boy to go away.

ℵ

Incident at Beaver Creek

Chapter 12

Mom Riley stood stoically, handing the Kachina a replacement whip after each four lashings, crying silently at their pain, then from pride. However, the ceremony was far from over. They hadn't slept well the preceding night, and had been awake since early dawn. They would sleep little, if at all, until returning home however many days the quest might take.

An ointment eliminated Henry's burning pain so to sit with Jake in front on the clan chief and concentrate on further instruction. Jake received ointment, too, but didn't feel it was necessary. He had no discomfort.

While seated cross-legged, Jake's hand happened to touch his ankle. There was grit on it. Glancing down he saw dark colored sand forming a four-inch band around each ankle. He didn't need to ask. Angak, or the unknown spirit, or perhaps both had reached up to take the pain away, but why did he merit so much attention? He would talk to Uncle Marshall about it, but that would have to wait.

As the chief seemed to have no more to say, Uncle Marshall began a chanting prayer lasting for several minutes, and then stopped. During the silence the only sound was the snap of burning wood as something special, very special, was about to take place. Finally, Uncle Marshall spoke.

"Each of the Pueblo people and our neighbors tell stories of how our ancestors came to live where they do. You have heard what the Antigua say, but that story is for those who live outside of our village. You are ready to hear the true story, a story you are to keep in your hearts and not reveal outside the kiva walls."

"Once all the people lived in a sacred place called Sipapu which is inside the earth. There is light in this place, but a soft glow very different from the brightness the sun gives us. It was a good life. There was no heat, no cold. There was no thirst or hunger, but from time to time, the people fell into disagreement and argued. At one time, some felt that there was more to their lives and wanted to journey in search of it. Others were content and wanted to stay. Those who were restless left in search of this other place. This went on many times until one day he who gave life to all called the people together and asked if they were willing to leave where they lived inside the earth and go to the surface. It would be a hard life, but they were to make the earth into a garden paradise. That would take a long time, many generations.

"Those who died before the earth became this paradise would be rewarded for their work. Their name spirit would be no more, but their life spirit would be allowed to come to the Creator's paradise and live with all the family and friends they had known while alive on the earth. Many agreed, so the great creator called two brothers, Maseway and Sheoyeway, to guide them to the surface.

"Those who followed traveled for many days until coming to a ladder. Climbing to the top, they entered the world where the Sun and Moon give light. They saw that it was a beautiful, green valley, very large, surrounded by mountain peaks, some of which smoked. Maseway and Sheoyeway lead them from the valley and into the mountains. When the people looked back, they felt the ground shake and saw the valley from which they had just come suddenly sink and the door that they had climbed through disappeared. Cut off from the world underground they could not return. They had made their choice and would have to abide by that decision.

"The people wandered for a long time in search of a place to live. Maseway and Sheoyeway would not make this choice for them. From time to time, the people would disagree again and little by little, some left to find their own place. That is why the people are scattered over the land and why we don't always get along.

"Eventually, there were very few people left who still searched for a place to live. These were a special people in that they discovered that a spiritual symmetry controlled everything in this new world creating a perfect balance. There are four directions, four seasons, and four basic colors—black, blue, red, and white. However, most importantly, they learned about the four corners of balance —beauty, peace, happiness, and righteousness. By observing these things, man can live in harmony with the land and with one another.

"These people were wise, having remembered and learned from the failings of those before them. Despite what they had learned of this harmony, the people one day had a disagreement and quarreled. The people decided that a small group that understood these things more than all the others would separate and go to live in a place where they could continue the traditions and learning of their fathers and teach these as the others forgot.

"Maseway and Sheoyeway, the twin warrior gods, lead this group of people for many days through the mountains and across many mesas until they came to a great mountain that rose up from the flat ground. This, Sheoyeway said would be known as Sacred Mountain, and the people would build their homes on the other side. "But how are we to climb such a mountain?" they asked, because the it was very high and the sides straight and smooth.

"Maseway took an arrow and shot it. When the arrow struck the mountain, there was a great shaking of the earth so that the people could not stand. In that time, the mountain spread apart. When the people came to where the mountain had split, Maseway said that his brother would lead them to the place they were to build their homes. He would not go with them, but would stand guard at this sacred entrance. He then stood to one side of the trail through the mountain and rose up to become a great pillar of stone.

"Sheoyeway then lead the people up through the mountain until they came upon a mesa. It was not a very inviting place, being very hot and without water, with plants that had sharp spines, and creatures that would bite or sting. Despite looking very forbidding, at the southern end of the mesa was a beautiful valley where they built their homes, continued to live in harmony, and become the spiritual conscience of those who lived around them. With this done, Sheoyeway, returned to where the mountain split, and like his brother, took the form of a sitting rock to guard the top entrance to the sacred trail."

Jake glanced at Henry from time to time as the story unfolded. Both their mouths hung open in surprised awe. Yes, they had heard the creation stories, but not this one, and began to understand why the religious preparations.

Now Toleshnec spoke. "Long before the White man came a small child of the Raven Clan was captured by the Paiute and taken far to the north. He was too young to be a slave or sold. Their chief's daughter had lost her husband and then their child at birth. She looked upon the boy and asked to raise him to be Paiute.

"As time passed and he grew toward manhood, they forgot he was not Paiute. One day the Apache attacked his village. He was not much older than you, but he fought bravely to protect his mother, so much so the Apache became afraid and ran away. They believed only a spirit or someone possessed of a powerful spirit could fight so fiercely.

"He had not yet gone on a spirit quest, so once the people of his village knew their enemy was gone, not to return, he undertook the quest. It was then the spirits of our people came to him, and told him of his true family. He who made peace between our two peoples, and we lived in harmony for many years after his spirit body went to live in paradise.

"Not all Antigua go on a quest such as you are about to undertake, but everyone here, members of the Raven Clan, have done this. Because our clan is responsible for the leadership of the Antigua, it is necessary to be able to speak with the spirits. We can do that only with the help of a special intermediary.

"Each of us has three names. You have a name the world knows you by. You are Henry Riley. You are Jake Bershinsky. That is your name soul. I will now whisper your sacred name which belongs to your free soul, that which goes to the Land of the Dead when the time comes."

Uncle Marshall rose, stepped behind each boy, leaned over, and whispered the name into his ear. Returning to his seat, he continued.

"That name is to be kept sacred and told to no one, not even to one another," he admonished. "Your third name is that by which you will be known among the Antigua people. It is the name which shall be revealed when you have met your guardian spirit, and is the reason for this quest

"I am Grey Fox," Uncle Marshall said.

"I am Talking Warrior," Toleshnec said.

From the outer circle of men, each called out his name. "I am Yellow Hawk." It was the Antigua's governor.

"I am Walking Dog," the tribal lawyer spoke out.

"I am Black Horse." It was the Superintendent of Schools.

"I am Strong Bow," the water master said.

"I am Tall Corn." He was the Pueblo's finance officer.

"I am Iron Rod," the deep voice of the moiety chief said.

"I am Sitting Eagle." The War Chief's shape reminded Jake of a bull buffalo, big, power shoulders, and slim waist.

Yes, he knew them, important men in the community, and marveled that they would be here to see two ordinary boys off on a vision quest. In fact, he knew the governor was supposed to be attending meetings in Washington D.C., yet had delayed leaving to be here.

Uncle Marshall then spoke. "As the sun begins to rise, each of you will start cross the mesa to where Sheoyeway guards the top entrance to the sacred trail. Ask for his permission to enter. When it is given, enter and walk to where the earth joins with the water. There you will find a large, round rock. Near the top of this rock, the spirits have drawn the figure of a man. As those who have gone before you, that will be your camp. From there you will see Maseway standing guard over the sacred place high on the side of the mountain. Speak to him. Tell him who you are and why you have come. Wait for him to give his permission to step upon the prayer rock. When his shadow falls upon the rock build a ring apart from one another using rocks gathered from beneath the water. There you will begin your prayers seeking to become united with the spirit guide that will accompany you through this life.

"Do not be discouraged if when the sun warms your body nothing has happened. Sometimes the spirits wait to see if you are truly sincere and worthy. Return to your camp and prepare yourself for the next night."

They had entered the kiva several hours before midnight. The ceremony and instruction didn't seem to take very long; however, when they climbed the ladder, the last to leave and step back into the world of men, the dim light of pre-sunrise had begun.

Walking to the road, Yellow Hawk and Walking Dog met them to present each boy a pair of new moccasins. "The trail to Sheoyeway is long and the ground is hard. We have made these to protect your feet and to bring you back to us safely," they said. Jake and Henry put them on.

Sitting Eagle and Black Horse waited a little further along the road to hand each a bow and quiver of three arrows, saying, "When you have accomplished your task, you will be hungry." The boys hung these over their backs.

Tall Corn handed them each a small, leather bag containing hand-ground corn to hang around their necks. "To protect you from evil spirits," he said.

Uncle Marshall was next, handing each a hunting knife with a highly polished Elk antler handle crafted with his own hands and attached to a large, deadly sharp blade. "To protect you from evil spirit beasts," he said.

Toleshnec stepped forward and handed Jake a flute. "You have learned to play this well, nephew. Perhaps it will come in handy if the spirits want to be tricksters and delay coming. Play this and he will come, and then convince him to persuade the spirits to not play their games for long." Toleshnec referred to Kokopelli, the spirit of fertility and music who seemed to have taken a liking to Jake, visiting him several times when he played. Jake had made a flute, but the sound was not nearly as fine as this one. It was Toleshnec's favorite.

With moccasins placed on their feet, the quiver and bow slipped overhead to hang down the back, corn meal hung about the neck, sheathed knives on their belt, Jake carrying the flute, the boys continued along the dusty road that would take them to the sacred trail. Before leaving the pueblo behind, they met Mom Riley and Naoma, Uncle Marshall's wife. Mom handed each a leather pouch containing Elk jerky. It would be their only food until after receiving their vision. Naoma handed them a bulging, leather bag containing water. As Jake slipped it over his head, the water pouch felt cold next to his bare skin. Before receiving a warm blanket over their shoulders from Henry's two older sisters, each girl gave them a hug and kiss. The younger gave Jake a particularly strong hug and a secret peck on the ear, stepped back, and winked with a shy smile.

Finally, they came to Jake's mom. Placing her hands on each cheek, she kissed each of her young men on the forehead. "All I have to give is my love," she said. They both thought that was a pretty good gift.

Fully equipped, the two teens struck out for the Sacred Mountain fifteen miles distant over the arid mesa. On a small hill at the outskirts of town, others who had made the trip in their youth had come to watch, remembering their day with a faint smile.

Neither spoke as they walked the pencil-thin path across the arid plateau toward the mountain as so many had done for nearly a thousand years. Each boy secretly wondered what he was getting into despite the training and explanations, just like the thousands of others before.

"Toleshnec and I have taught what you need to know," Uncle Marshall said as they sat in the kiva. "You have learned to go long periods without food, and to camp among the wild animals with nothing but a bow, a few arrows, and knife. We have taught you about the spirits. I will now explain what to do." However, Jake knew there was a large difference between having something explained and the actual doing, and again wondered why a White boy would be accorded this privilege.

~ ~ ~ ~

According to Jakes' mom, his father's parents were from South America giving Jake's skin a natural brownish cast. After moving to New Mexico and spending so much time outdoors, it had become quite brown. Dark brown hair once neatly clipped above the ears, now hung to the shoulders, held out of his face by a bright blue cloth tied about his head. His mother never mentioned cutting it, and his grandmother in California thought he looked darling. It was easy to mistake him for Native American. The smile that often surfaced turned more than a few heads, especially on the California beaches. He seemed to attract girls as if smeared with honey.

From their first meeting he and Henry spent increasingly more time together, to the point of becoming inseparable. Unknown to Jake, after that first meeting with Toleshnec, his entire relationship with the Antigua people would change. About a month after Henry's eleventh birthday, there was a feast day to commemorate the Pueblo's Catholic saint.

Toleshnec turned to Jake and muttered, "We pick and choose what they want us to believe, just to keep them happy, deluded, but happy."

Aside from the food, among the festivities were foot races covering various distances up to twenty-five miles. Even at this early age, only a couple of the oldest boys were faster than Henry, earning him the nickname, Flying Feet. Jake hadn't planned to participate, but Henry pleaded.

Jake well remembered last year's race. Henry was in a funk for months. Something happened, but he would not speak of it for fear of being labeled a poor looser.

"See those two guys over there? They beat me last year, but if you sort of get in their way, I can beat them.

"But, isn't that cheating?"

"No, it's getting even. Last year the short guy knocked me off the trail where no one could see."

"You didn't sprain your ankle stepping on a rock?"

"Yeah, I did. The rock happened to be ten feet off the trail at the bottom of a wash where the skinny one pushed me. Just try to keep up. When we get to where the trail crosses the stream on the way back, well, that's a good place to do something."

Jake wasn't sure about the whole thing, but during the race the short one tried to impede Henry several times and that made Jake mad. The problem was that when they reached the stream Henry was a good hundred yards in front. Coming down the home stretch, Jake trotted alongside Henry.

"You're way ahead, Henry. Keep going."

Henry wasn't breathing hard, but there was an ache growing in his side, and he was sweating as if he'd just run through a waterfall. Jake didn't appear in the least bit strained. Then he heard the heavy footsteps of his competition closing from behind. Henry was losing ground, fast.

"Come on Henry, speed up."

Henry suddenly realized Jake was getting ahead of him. Reaching down, he put on a final burst of speed. The boys crossed the finish line in a tie. That's when a member of the Corn clan leaned over and remarked to Toleshnec, "I'm not surprised. Those two boys are as if one person. They even look alike."

Toleshnec startled, taking time the remainder of the day to look more closely. The two indeed had a general physical resemblance. In addition, they walked the same, talked the same, and thought the same, which sometimes was disconcerting. One had to look very closely to see small differences. Toleshnec mentioned this to his father.

"When the boy first came to us I looked into his eyes. Did I not say he was Antigua, but no one listened," Grandfather Riley said.

Shortly after that, Jake's mom, Grandfather Riley, Uncle Marshall, and Toleshnec sat together. That was followed by the latter's sudden departure for several days. Upon his return, all the moiety chiefs met with both caciques. No one discussed what was said as such meetings are privileged, but the following day the entire pueblo gathered in the community kiva to officially adopt Jake as an Antigua, specifically into the Raven Clan. No one explained why and Jake, being a kid, didn't ask. He just felt very honored, and happy, and strangely at peace.

~ ~ ~ ~

Nothing much existed on the mesa except small rocks,

scrub brush, cactus, scorpions, snakes, and lizards. Nothing at all friendly. Covering the distance took six hours beneath an increasingly harsh sun. In part, that was why they started so early, although Toleshnec had spent much time over the years preparing them to survive in the wilderness until such conditions were a mere inconvenience.

Despite this preparation, Jake was glad when the warrior god's rocky hulk hove into view like a great creature rising from a bed of conifers and Aspen. His mouth was dry as the earth they trod with barely a drop of water left in the bag, which now hung hot and limp against his side.

The mountain lurched sharply upward at this point, the gorge opening like a primordial maw revealing the river far below. From the base of Sheoyeway, water sprang forth to form a tiny stream that raced to enter the chasm. They stood at the base of the rock, hot and tired, the energy wrung from their bodies by sweat, but they wasted no time addressing the guardian.

"Sheoyeway, it is I, Henry Riley, and his brother, Jake Bershinsky. We have come on a spirit quest and seek your permission to enter upon the sacred path."

A bird chirped briefly off to one side. Other than that, there was no sound. They looked at one another. No one told them what to expect, so after a time Jake spoke up.

"Maybe we should leave an offering."

"What?"

Jake thought on it a moment then said, "The jerky."

Giving no consideration that they would be without food until the quest was over, they laid their pouches of untouched jerky on a projecting rock that could have been a foot. Jake spoke. "Sheoyeway, it is I, Jake Bershinsky, and his brother, Henry Riley. We have come to seek your permission to enter the sacred path that we may sit with your brother. We leave this food for you which is all we have."

What happened next nearly set both boys on their backsides. Jake no sooner finished speaking than a sharp, resounding "boom" rocked the mountain. They had experienced earthquakes of various proportions while camping in the mountains with Toleshnec, but the timing caught them completely off-guard.

"I take that as a yes," Henry said, recovering and smiling broadly.

Knelling at the spring, they splashed the cool water on their faces and began filling empty water bags. That's when Henry looked at his brother's back, reached up a finger, and gently touched the skin.

"Does it hurt?" he asked.

"Not really. The ointment helped. How about you?"

"It's okay. I think your marks are bigger than mine."

Jake looked at the red welts on Henry's back.

"It's hard for me to tell."

Henry moved closer so that their sides nearly touched. At least the ones on Jakes left side were larger. "Your whole back looks like that. I know the long billed one hit you much harder than me. He use more whips, too. You didn't feel them?"

"Uncle Marshall drew a painting of Angak in the circle where I stood. I felt him reach up and take hold of my ankles. At least I think it was him. There was another spirit painted in the circle, the one Uncle Marshall spoke with at the hospital. Anyway, while we were listening to the instructions I noticed sand around my ankles. And then there was Uncle Toleshnec . . . There was something in his eyes, like little fires. I think he drew the pain to himself."

"Why would they do that for you and not me?"

"I don't know. Perhaps they know you are stronger than me and I would squeal like a pig."

"Yeah, maybe. Maybe they thought you already suffered enough pain. I'm glad they helped you. It really wasn't all that bad. And maybe Little Bee's kiss helped, too."

Startled, Jake just stared at his brother and blushed.

"I saw that little peck on the ear and the smile she gave you. She likes you. Whispers your name in her sleep."

Jake's face darkened even more as Henry laughed

"We shouldn't speak so lightly in this place," he said quickly and turning away.

The ground trembled slightly.

"It would seem Sheoyeway thinks it's funny, too," Henry added as Jake walked away from his brother and the laughing god.

After cooling off and filling water bags, they entered the chasm, the near vertical walls a blessing, providing instant relief from the sun's intensifying heat. The gorge was narrow, the width of four grown men standing fingertip to fingertip, and as the trail descended, the vertical walls rose higher and the bottom increasingly darker.

"It will feel as if walking back in time," Toleshnec had said.

Jake thought it felt more like descending into the bowls of the earth. There was no evidence of the road Uncle Marshall said White men once built. The first spring was added upon by others, the water gouging a meandering channel plummeting ever downward. Rocks that had peeled from the walls littered the floor, and both secretly hoped there would not be additions as they continued onward. Eventually the giant boulder near the bottom came into sight. Upon reaching it, they looked up. Near the top was the figure of a standing man.

"How do you suppose they managed to carve that?" Henry asked.

"Perhaps standing on someone's shoulders?"

Henry had a good eye for spatial measurement. "I don't think so, Jake. It'd take at least five guys standing on top of each other to reach that high."

"A ladder?"

Henry looked across the river at the trees growing on other side. "Maybe, but I'd prefer to think the spirit gods did it."

"Me, too."

Leaving everything but loincloths, they continued down to the river where they found a convenient side pool among some rocks in which to wash the dust and sweat sticking to their bodies. The stream from the canyon emptied there so it was more comfortable than anticipated.

Sitting on boulders near the bank, they looked toward the column rising a hundred feet into the air as the sun and air-dried them. An Eagle's nest perched on top like a big hat. It appeared to be empty. On the east side of the pillar that was the second warrior god, a piece of cliff had sheared off and lay like a huge floor. Some stunted trees grew out of the space between it and the cliff face.

"It won't be long before the shadow comes upon the rock," Henry said.

They quickly turned to collecting the rocks needed to build individual prayer rings. There were many good candidates along the shore; however, the instructions were to use only those beneath the water that meant getting wet again. The sun still bearing down, it was hot. They didn't mind.

Each rock was to be no larger than a hen's egg. Finding them wasn't easy and the task took some time; selecting an appropriate rock and taking it ashore to build a ring so to be sure they had enough for the correct size.

Jake finished first and ran back to camp, returning with

their blankets so to carry them. This also gave time for the rocks to dry a bit. Toting the load flung over the shoulder, they approached the base of the hoodoo. The path they were to take lay between the pillar and cliff, a talus-strewn field difficult enough to negotiate without a blanket full of rocks continually throwing them off balance. After considerable slipping and sliding, they gained the edge of the platform. Setting the blankets on the ground, Henry was about to speak until Jake laid a hand on his arm.

"Perhaps we should prepare ourselves."

"Oh, yeah. I forgot," Henry said, looking around nervously. The oversight was understandable in his excitement, and he was grateful for Jake's attention to detail, a skill he didn't have a handle on, yet.

Working across the face of the slab, they went to the cliff base, knelt, and stuck fingers down their throats to induce vomiting. Needless, there wasn't much, but it was a necessary part of the cleansing ritual. Returning to where the blankets lay, Henry spoke.

"Maseway, it is I, Henry Riley of the Antigua Raven Clan. I have come to ask the spirits to bless me with a vision."

From high above came an echoing scream. Looking up they saw a Golden Eagle perched on the edge of the god's hat.

"I'll take that as a yes," Henry said with a smile. "Coming?"

"Uncle Marshall made it a point to say that we were going together, but should act alone. I better ask permission for myself," Jake replied. "Maseway, it is I, Jake Bershinsky of the Antigua Raven Clan. I have come to ask the spirits to bless me with a vision."

The Eagle spoke again—twice, it's voice echoing back and forth across the river making sound as if a chorus of voices answered.

Maseway's shadow began creeping onto the slab, a piece of mountain much larger than it appeared from below. After removing their moccasins, the boys stepped onto the smooth surface. Henry went to the far end while Jake took the near end, both close to the front edge. Opening his blanket, Jake quickly formed a ring with the rocks, about three feet in diameter, laid the blanket loosely over his shoulders, and stepped into the circle.

Sitting cross-legged, he took a moment to gaze out at the river below and the great meadow beyond. It was as beautiful and tranquil as Uncle Marshall had said; except for the ugly scar White men had left searching for gold on the other side. Expelling a deep breath, he began reciting the prayers to take him through the night.

Darkness gradually covered the mountain with cold. Each remained huddled beneath their blankets until the warm, morning sunlight spread over Jake's shoulders. He had dozed. He wished he hadn't. Part of the preparation was to remain awake for an extended period, but just as the sun's light grazed the horizon, keeping his eyes open become impossible. Stiff as a telephone pole, he awoke with a start, stood, and stretched. Henry approached, his face asking the question.

Jake shook his head to say, "No," and knew his brother hadn't been blessed, either.

Back at camp Jake wrapped in the blanket like a cocoon and lay on the ground. It felt as soft as a bed back home. His eyes felt as if filled with sand and closing them provided relief. It was then he thought to hear the melodious notes of a flute playing softly. He lingered to listen to Kokopelli's music. When the song ended, he opened his eyes to discover the sun had just passed its zenith. His spirit friend had lulled him to sleep. Looking over at Henry, he apparently had succumbed to the music as well.

Returning to the river, they waded further out to wash as instructed. It was frigid, but stealing himself, Jake sat, grimacing to stifle a howl of pain. Henry wasn't as successful, trying in vain to strangle the high-pitched groan creeping up his throat, but Jake heard it. He hoped the spirits didn't or they might think Henry was weak.

Returning to the rocky shelf they repeated the vomiting, removed their moccasins, and resumed their circle to pray and mediate until the sun rose a second time. Still nothing happened except their stomachs felt tighter as hunger began to beset them. Returning to camp, they repeated the routine, succumbing to the ethereal music, and resuming the vigil late that afternoon.

This night Jake played Toleshnec's flute hoping to entice the spirits. He played the ancient instrument well, the notes rebounding from the rocks as a harmony, but nothing seemed to encourage the spirits to visit.

That third morning, as the sun began to tint the horizon, Jake's stomach tightened into a knot, begging loudly for food and interfering with concentration. He prayed more fervently. He felt lightheaded, and then the world began doing strange acrobatic gyrations. Closing his eyes for a moment only made his head swim more. Opening them, his vision was blurred. That's when he thought to detect movement, not on the ground, but dangling in the air out beyond the edge of his perch. He blinked, trying to focus, but the apparition shimmered, drifting in and out of focus. From the snatches he grasped, it appeared to be a thin man, seated cross-legged in mid-air, playing a flute. Jake's eyes felt as if filled with sand. They hurt. He closed them for a moment so they would clear. When he opened them, the man was gone and the sun had risen above the horizon, but in that short time, what had seen became vividly etched on his mind.

Sitting with legs drawn to his chin, Jake contemplated the dream until Henry approached. "You've received your vision!" he said.

There was no keeping a secret from his brother. However delighted Henry was his countenance fell as quickly.

"It's alright," Jake consoled him, standing to put an arm around his brother's shoulders. "We'll stay until it comes to you as well."

"I made the spirits angry because I complained about the cold water yesterday."

"Then we shall do whatever is necessary to show them you are worthy."

After returning to camp Kokopelli's music again lulled them to sleep until awaking just after noon and returning to the river to bathe. Henry made a point to show he could stand the cold river by going in deeper water, coming out only after Jake pleaded with him.

"I've never seen a brown-skinned person look blue," he joked, but it was true.

Henry was very near to hypothermia, quaking like a lone Aspen in a high wind. Wrapped in both blankets, the sun's warmth helped him recover before returning to the table rock. Jake sat at a distance, back against the cliff face to keep him company, playing the flute, hoping to draw a spirit messenger to Henry. The fourth morning Henry approached Jake who had fallen asleep while propped against a small tree growing from the crack between the prayer rock and cliff face. The expression on his face said he had seen something, but there was a questioning look as well.

While waiting for Henry to receive his vision, Jake had

watched several Eagles, like large, black ghosts circle overhead, riding the air currents. When feeling the need, they would descend to skim the river and snag a fish, or fall upon some creature on the meadow beyond. This they carried to their nest among the crags of the mountain above them. He admired their grace, their skill, and their devotion to young. The great birds took no notice of the two-legged creatures below, except for the one directly overhead. Perched on the edge of the huge nest atop Maseway, it watched their every move. Finished, they could now obtain an Eagle feather.

"When you have received your vision, return the stones from your prayer ring to the river, and then search among the rocks below the great cliff. If the spirits are willing to bless you, you will find an Eagle's feather. You are permitted only one," Uncle Marshall had said.

As from the start, they followed instructions to the letter, gathering up the stones in their blankets and place them back in the river, a no easier task than when they hauled them up the mountain. It was all downhill, the weight of the rocks pushing them as if eager to return to the river, the talus plates acting like miniature surfboards. Returning to the prayer rock, they removed their moccasins again and stepped onto it to begin the search for a feather, but weren't having any luck.

At a rodeo the year before, a Navajo youth bragged how he scaled some rocks to retrieve a feather from the Eagle's nest, but Toleshnec warned them about doing that.

"Many years before I was born, a boy thought to show his bravery and retrieve a feather from the nest itself. The Eagle attacked, of course, as would any parent protecting their home and family. As he tried to retreat, the great bird buried her talons in his shoulders, picked him off the rock, carried him high over the river, and dropped him. Of course, the water is not deep enough to break such a fall. Some of The People were gathering clay near the river when his body passed over the waterfall. A water spirit took pity on his family and guided the body to a pool near where they were working. He did this so that the people would know not to disturb the great Eagle's nest."

From his observations, Jake understood the danger of those deadly talons if they attempted to approach, but not finding anything, the thought was tempting. After all, there were two of them. Henry decided they should continue searching further east along the cliff beyond the prayer rock, but while returning over the smooth surface to retrieve their moccasins he was surprised to see something dark lying in his path. Stopping, he stared down in amazement. It was a perfect Eagle's feather. Henry was rolling the round end between his fingers when Jake approached.

"I found one," Jake said, then looking at Henry's feather, added, "It's a bit the worse for wear, but I have a feather." Henry looked. His brother was right. It was a little broken and ruffled.

Suddenly the great Eagle's cry echoed loudly. Looking up, they saw the bird that had been keeping an eye on them the whole time, spread its wings, and take flight. As it did, something began floating down toward them. Their eyes watched in amazement as a feather, as perfect as Henry's, landed almost at Jake's feet.

Picking it up, a good feeling filled his breast and looking up he said, "Thank you, Maseway."

"The spirits really, really like you, Jake. You stay close to me all the time."

Returning to the river to bathe preparatory to returning home, Jake spotted a number of fish in a side pool, the first they had seen. Henry shot one with an arrow.

He always was better with a bow and arrow, but a wounded fish could swim away with the arrow if not tethered by a line. When Henry shot, Jake leaped into the water, snatching the shaft before it disappeared into deeper water. With great joy, they roasted the catch, their first meal in days. Breaking camp, the boys began their journey home, stopping at the spring at the top of the gorge to spend the night so as to cross the mesa early the next morning.

Breaking into a jog the last couple of miles home, a number of their friends came out to run with them, shouting, and trying to get them to reveal the vision. They would not share, not even with one another, until the clan gathered. Understanding the approaching noise, Uncle Marshall, seated beneath a shade structure whittling a piece of cedar, stood and waited for them to stop before him.

"We have done all you said and the spirits smiled upon us," Henry said, each showing their feather.

Uncle Marshall put away his knife and said, "Go to the sweat lodge. I will join you there."

With the three huddled inside, Henry's oldest sister passed in heated rocks. As the steam and heat rose, the sweat poured from Jake's body forcing the dust and sweat plastered on his skin to melt away.

Once cleansed, they exited to find the sisters waiting next to two, round, galvanized tubs, and a bowl of yucca soap. Kneeling over the tubs, the girls thoroughly washed the boys' hair after which they doused them with buckets of water eliciting anguished howls. They thought the water felt unusually cold, but were given no time to notice the few remaining pieces of ice from the local 7-Eleven the girls had used to spiked the water. The youngest sister attacked Jake's hair with vigorous rubbing to dry it, and then wrapped a new blanket over his shoulders. Henry's other sister did the same for him.

Clean, the boys slipped into a forked-stick and mud hut not far from the lodge to don new clothes made by their two uncles. Once dressed, they stepped out to sit on logs so the girls could comb their hair, braiding in a beaded rawhide on the right side before securing a cloth to keep the hair from falling into their eyes like a sheep dog. By this time, the entire pueblo knew of their return and began to gather as a drum issued the invitation for the Raven Clan and friends to come hear the report.

The community kiva was much larger than the moiety kiva, capable of holding most everyone. They loitered outside waiting for Grandfather Riley to arrive. He had been ill the night of the boy's instruction and unable to attend. To Jake he was the most fragile and ancient thing he'd ever imagined. Although the effects of his illness were evident, he insisted on attending their return.

Brown skin like old leather, heavily wrinkled, it hung loose on a skeleton that had once supported a strong, robust man. His voice was high and raspy, often faltering as he sought to mouth the words forming in his mind. A tribal elder supported him on either side as he shuffled over the uneven ground. Jake loved the old man, loved his wit, the stories he told of the ancient days and of his youth, but most of all, Jake felt the old man's love. It was Grandfather Riley who when they first met, held the boy's face in both hands to look deep into his eyes and declare him to be Antigua. To a simple child at the time, it meant nothing more than everyone in the pueblo became his friend. As he became older, Jake began to wonder.

While passing by, Grandfather stopped for a moment to look at them with dark brown eyes that appeared dim, but each knew he saw far more than ordinary men did. With a smile, he resumed the shuffling gate that took him inside. Once Grandfather Riley entered the kiva, followed by Uncle Marshall, the boys entered escorted by Toleshnec. Behind came members of the Raven Clan, followed by all the others.

The boys sat facing Grandfather Riley across a small fire. Uncle Marshall, Toleshnec, and the Raven chief sat on either side of him. Families filled in the remaining space. When the last person entered, the ceremony began. After a time Jake was asked to speak. Closing his eyes, he described the vision.

"I was sitting on a rock on the edge of a mountain meadow enjoying the warm sun and cool breeze when a red-colored bear appeared. It came straight at me. I stood. There was nowhere to run even if it were possible to outrun such a fleet-footed animal. When it was very close, the bear stopped, sniffed, barked twice, and then rose up on his hind feet. I was sure he would be the last thing I saw in this life, but all fear went away as it walked up, put a paw on each of my shoulders, and pulled me to his body in a hug. I closed my eyes ready to die, but it then turned me loose and licked my face. He had bad breath."

Jake wrinkled his nose because he could still smell the fish on its breath. "When I opened my eyes the bear had changed into a man. I thought he seemed familiar, but could not remember who it might be. The man kept his hands on my shoulders and smiled. My body felt as if filled with love and strength. The man pulled me to him once again. We hugged, and then he became a bear once more, stepped back, and returned to walking as a bear does on all fours going back the way it had come, but just before disappearing into the trees it once again stood and waived a paw. I then noticed I was standing with one foot on bare rock and the other in deep grass."

He stopped and took a deep breath. "Grandfather, I recognized the man as the one Uncle Marshall spoke with when I was in the hospital, and I saw his face in the circle with Angak before the whipping."

"He is your Kachina. It is very rare one sees the face of their spirit companion," Uncle Marshall said.

There was a long silence as those in the dimly lit room shook their heads, agreeing that this was a very good vision.

"What else did you see?" Grandfather Riley asked. The question startled Jake. It was as if the old man knew there was more.

"When the bear had gone I looked down to see that I stood with one foot on rock and, the other in grass. There was a rabbit sitting next to my left foot, on the rock side. It had a little bow and quiver of arrows attached to its back."

Grandfather's right eyebrow arched, and for a moment looked mildly surprised.

"Two spirits to accompany you through this life! This is a very powerful vision," Toleshnec said as the others nodded agreement. "Your name should be White Bear."

"You do not seem pleased," Uncle Marshall said, perceiving Jake's facial response.

"I expected something about bears. I should have anticipated something white being attached." With growth had come self-confidence, and thanks to Toleshnec's encouragement, Jake had become more outspoken.

Toleshnec was the *qaletaqua*, guardian of the people, austere in appearance, always the Native American rights activist with a profound dislike for White men. He stared at Jake for a moment before smiling very faintly.

"Forgive me, nephew. Old habits are sometimes hard to change," he said. "Perhaps something different? Say, Cinnamon Bear, or perhaps . . . Huggy Bear?"

Everyone laughed.

"The bear is indeed a powerful symbol. He was the first helper in the creation of the earth. He is physically strong, and a leader. White is the color of peace," Grandfather said. "The name White Bear would not refer to your mother's people, but to a leader with great strength and courage. That you are standing with one foot on rock and one in grass says that you have a place in two worlds— the world that is Antigua, and the world into which you were born. You can bring unity and peace to both people."

"It is an awesome vision, nephew," Toleshnec said. "Perhaps someday we will find ourselves standing side by side in the journey for equality and justice."

Although Jake agreed with Toleshnec's philosophy that the Pueblos must achieve equality, he wasn't sure if he would go so far as to stand alongside a man who so far had spent more time in jail for civil disobedience than with his family.

"What about the rabbit?" Jake asked.

"That is interesting. It would seem that you will have a rabbit as your companion. That it has a bow and arrows suggest it will also be your guardian," Grandfather said.

His voice faltered as he spoke, more than usual. Jake couldn't tell if that was because of age, or that he knew something more, but refrained from saying it. Again, the others silently nodded agreement.

The time then became Henry's to relate his vision.

"I was running, but very low to the ground. Everything was much taller than I, even the grass was taller. You know how the world looks when you lay your head on the ground. Then I stopped at a stream for a drink. In the water's reflection, I see I am a rabbit. My thirst filled, I continue running until I am above the grass, then the trees. I am flying. It's neat to look down on the world, seeing it as the Eagle. There is a great, white cloud ahead and I fly into it. I can see nothing but cloud until coming out the other side. Looking down I see a bear running across a long meadow. I follow the bear for a long time until it stops at the top of a hill and looks up at me, and waves. Again, I see a great, white cloud ahead and fly to it. Going inside once again, I am surrounded by white mist. That is all."

When Henry finished there was a long silence. Faces were grave or looked puzzled. Finally, Grandfather made the pronouncement. "Rabbit is fast, and a trickster, but brave. It is said that he stole fire and brought it to the people, and taught our ancient holy men many rituals we use today. He can jump high, even above the clouds. You shall be known as Flying Rabbit."

Henry's lips pursed slightly as if he'd just bitten into a lime.

"That White Bear saw a rabbit at his side, and that you flew for a time with a bear would suggest you are bound to one another, and shall go through this life together," Uncle Marshall concluded.

That last pronouncement made the two friends happy. Dreams were nothing new to Jake, but none had ever been as detailed or lasting in memory as his vision. It stayed, often revisiting in the waning moments of morning as when it first appeared. So did the memory of the unsettled look in the eyes of Grandfather Riley, Toleshnec, and Uncle Marshall, a haunting that would never be forgotten, either..

₪

Incident at Beaver Creek

Chapter
13

The shrill scream of an Eagle brought Jake back to the present. Eyes open, he looked around. Yes, he was very familiar with this area at the mouth of Cuchillo Cortar Gorge. A long time had passed since that important event in his life. While the outside world had morphed into something very different, here, in this sacred place, time had stood still. He sighed to himself. Mohf snorted and pawed the ground.

"Will you stop complaining? That little cold water didn't hurt you."

He looked at his horse. Mohf shook his head, snorted again, small ears cocked forward as he stared intently toward a jumble of large boulders ahead. Jake released the restraining strap on his Ruger PX38S and rested a palm lightly on the butt.

"The ground is a book. Read it."

As Toleshnec's words echoed in his mind, a lifetime of training and following instincts moved to the forefront. There was no sign of a large animal having come to water. Just above where the water bag lay, the pea-sized gravel had been disturbed. A faint furrow, small mounds as if something had pushed uphill. Squatting to look closer, he picked up a fist-sized rock, its smooth surface stained by a blackish substance. Scratching it with a fingernail flaked some off. Mohf snorted again.

Pistol drawn, Jake slowly walked uphill, following the stain trail while scanning the rocks ahead. Mohf stayed close behind on his own accord, reluctant, snorting repeatedly as if trying to dislodge something from his nose, not wanting to be left behind. The faint trail led toward the giant boulder where he and Henry, and who knows how many hundreds of Antigua boys about to become men, had camped while seeking their vision. Here, the ground was soft dirt. Near the center of the oval area was a fire pit. Holding a hand over the gray ashes, he slowly lowered it until touching. The campfire was cold. His fingers slipped into the ash. At the length of a finger, there was warmth. No moisture. Left to burn out, he estimated it to have been a couple days old.

Without moving from a squatting position, Jake looked about. Portions of the ground appeared torn up as if there had been a struggle. Near the base of the large boulder, something caught his eye. Walking carefully to it, mindful to read and not disturb the ground on the way, he spotted the imprint of a boot heel. That should not be in a spirit vision camp. Upon closer inspection, what caught his interest was the depth of the imprint. Boots generally had a heel about 1-5/8 inches in height. This was clearly taller. Placing a forefinger into the impression, it easily came to the second joint. He found another, confirming the size. Sometimes referred to as a dogger's heel, a few rodeo types wore that sort of heel, useful in applying the brakes when wrestling a steer to the ground in a rodeo. A second heel impression was clearly the more usual walking type.

Mohf nickered. Jake turned to look. The horse had taken a hunting dog-like stance, staring intently at the jumble of rocks twenty yards uphill from the camp. Ears lay forward like two fingers pointing at the area as he pawed the ground. Shifting the weapon back to his right hand, Jake worked through the rocks, many the size of a refrigerator. Nearing the base of the cliff, he detected a familiar odor. Behind the last boulder, next to the cliff, two bare feet protruded from behind the rock belonging to a body tossed into a small opening between boulder and cliff. Jake reached down and felt a leg, all too aware of the feel of death. After looking over the area carefully, reading the book for signs that would reveal the story, he retrieved a camera from the saddlebags and took photos before pulling the body out for a closer look. More photos.

Small welts marred the smooth skin. That was familiar. Jake was also familiar with gunshot wounds, both to himself and to others. A bullet had entered the rear of the right thigh, exiting the front. He took copious photos of every detail before turning the body over. There was one knife wound just below the sternum.

Remembering forensics lectures from Federal enforcement school, rigor mortise maxed twelve to twenty-four hours after death before dissipating from one to three days later depending on external conditions. There certainly were external factors affecting that timetable, however, coupled with the fire pit, preliminary evidence suggested the boy died about the same time as Darrel Windpipe.

Having firsthand knowledge of the culture, the boy

would be about twelve or thirteen. Jake didn't recognize him, but then he didn't know many of the younger people in the pueblo anymore. He had only returned for short visits and funerals, and hadn't been to a rodeo since turning eighteen where he would have met many of them. The pain was still close to the surface even after all these years, something he didn't care to revisit. What he did see was disturbing. The face had a hauntingly vague familiarity, but couldn't remember who.

Disliking the proximity of anything dead, Mohf shied away. Jake wasn't sure what would happen, but his four-legged friend was going have to carry it out. Before broaching that thorny problem, he studied the crime scene again with a trained eye, not only noting what was present, but also what was not. That could be as important as the physical evidence. In this case, three things were missing— the boy's moccasins, knife, and blanket. Each would have been handmade, if not family heirlooms.

Completing a careful search, making notes, and taking photos, the time came to face a difficult task. As expected Mohf was none too cooperative as Jake tried to secure the body behind the saddle. Not the usual way to transport a body, it was small enough to be done this way. He simply wasn't that interested having a decaying corpse directly under his nose for the next couple of hours, even if wrapped in a wool blanket. It took a lot of coaxing until the stallion grudgingly acquiesced and the body securely tied.

Swinging into the saddle, Jake made the radio call he had put off, using the reservation frequency to call Jays Roost. "Curt, radio the res police. See where Ken Herbert is."

The chief answered. "I've been trying to have a conversation with Sheoyeway at the mouth of Cuchillo Cortar. He's not talking, but I hear you fine, Jake. That light you saw was coming from Darrel's International."

"I'm starting up the gorge, Ken. 10-58. It will take me at least three hours. I'll need a body bag and truck with a horse trailer. My pony's going to be pretty tired when we get there."

"I'll get it myself. Need any other help?"

"If I do I should be able to reach Jay's Roost. Curt, have someone pick up my truck at the Sebastian Mine trailhead and bring it to Taylorsville tonight or early tomorrow. They can leave it at the police station. I'll be spending a day or so in that area. Let my wife know I won't be home for dinner. I'll call her tonight. Then let Carrie know she's in charge until I get back. And you better call the Forest Supervisor and let him know just to keep him happy. I'll call him tonight as well."

"Want me to call Mr. Douglass, too?" Curt answered.

"He's most likely in the field. I'll call him this evening as well, if he's available."

The Forest Service in New Mexico adopted the Albuquerque police ten-code. Hearing 10-58, referring to a dead body, was not a welcomed reference. Rarely used on the forest, Jake had now used it twice in almost as many days. The journey seemed particularly long as horse and rider made the steep assent. At one point Jake wasn't sure they would get around a large rock that had recently peeled off from somewhere above almost completely blocking the trail. It was necessary to remove both body and saddle, carry them to the other side, and then coax Mohf through the narrow gap without scrapping his sides. Fortunately, the gray cooperated and remained calm. In many ways, he was good at that. However, that calm lasted only until Jake went to put the body back on. Gentle persistence prevailed, but the discussion took nearly twenty minutes.

The climb was difficult enough; however, with an extra

hundred pounds, Mohf was showing signs of fatigue as they neared the half way mark so Jake walked, stopping often for rest and water. As wild and secluded as the canyon was, there were faint whispers that someone had passed this way, more than once, nothing concrete, just shadowy hints. Recent rains and the resulting wash had obliterated much, like an eraser cleaning a blackboard, leaving a chalky residue. Ken was waiting at the spring near the top. The trip had taken nearly four hours.

"Hello, White Bear. What have you got?" Ken said using Jake's Pueblo name while uncovering the head to look at the face. He wasn't one to swear, but it slipped out. "Shit!"

卍

Incident at Beaver Creek

Chapter
14

Despite knowing Jake was transporting a dead body, Ken's heart still skipped a couple beats when he saw the small, bare feet protruding from the blanket. He'd handled a lot of corpses over the years, repeatedly reminding himself that the taboo was nonsense, but being weaned on the old stories, they lay dormant in his mind ready to spring to the forefront on a moment's notice. That the victim was someone on a sacred quest was too close to the old ways, and this was one of those times he had to fight down the fear crawling up the back of his neck.

"Who is it?" Jake asked as he kicked his right leg over Mohf's neck and slid to the ground, watching the officer back way.

"Little Beaver, Toleshnec's youngest grandson."

Jake didn't repeat the explicative, although he mouthed

the word as it felt his heartbreak loose and fall into his gut. Now he understood why the boy looked familiar.

"What happened?" Ken asked.

"Best I can tell the boy was coming up from the river with water when someone shot him. Took out his right leg, but he managed to make it back to camp. Whoever it was, caught up to him there. Boot prints of two adults. Knifed him and threw the body in the rocks next to the cliff."

"There's going to be hell to pay."

"I'd like Doc Gardner to examine the body before I take him home. Is my uncle still at Quaking Meadows?"

"Yes. Sure you want to do that?"

"Yeah. It's been a long time. I probably should talk with him."

"And head off a full scale war party riding out of the mountains."

"Where's Darrel's pickup?"

"I brought one of my deputies and had him drive it back. I checked it out pretty thoroughly. The letter from James was on the front seat. The keys were in the ignition."

Highly relieved with the burden removed, Mohf snorted what might be considered a sarcastic thank you, and wandered over to the small pool of spring water to drink—as far from the body as possible without losing sight of his partner. He was tired enough not to care if the earth was wet and spongy. Meanwhile, the two men placed the corpse in a black, body bag prior to loading it into the back of the reservation truck. Ken had brought one of the F250, four-wheel drive rescue units with a shell, a two-horse trailer attached to the rear.

Jake remained quiet as they began the impossibly slow journey back to town. A remnant of the mining trail no longer used since abandoned. Much of it was invisible. Jake did spot where the quest trail crossed several times resurrecting flashes of when he and Henry walked it. Pulling a horse trailer over the eroded ground without pitching its occupant back and forth was nearly impossible, even going slow. Breaching a wash without bogging down in the loose sand required a lengthy detour. The trip took time and Mohf complained frequently. First having to ford an icy river, and then tolerate a stinking body strapped to his rump to haul it up a steep incline, finally getting banged around inside a noisy trailer with no oats to console the indignities. He'd had about enough of this human nonsense.

Eventually, Ken broke the silence. "When's the last time you saw your uncle?"

"At Grandfather Riley's funeral. That's when he packed up his family and followers and moved to the mountain. He couldn't get the government to keep prospectors from digging in the area, despite the law, so he decided to do it himself." Jake stared out the side window, as his mind drifted back to that first time he met Toleshnec. It hadn't been pleasant.

~ ~ ~ ~

Jake didn't remember much about his dad except that when he came home from work the two would wrestle or play games. After dinner, he would snuggle between his dad's legs as they sat on the floor listening to Tarzan or the Lone Ranger on the radio. Then one day he didn't come home. Hit by a drunk driver. His mother cried a lot. An older man, man came to help. Not much later, they moved from their big house to live in a tiny apartment.

Taking settlement money his mother went to college to earn a degree in Wildlife Management. That was not a particularly good time in his life. Left with babysitters while she attended classes, he then had to amuse himself when she was home because her time focused on study. That all changed shortly after his seventh birthday. She graduated and they left the tiny apartment to move into a big, log house in the middle of the forest.

There were a number of other boys his age living in a logging camp near the Forest Service compound, but they reflected the "Us versus Them" attitude taught by their fathers. Loggers didn't like the Forest Service. Having learned to be alone, Jake was content to spend the summer months before school started just roaming the hills behind the compound. That's where he met Henry Riley.

Henry was an Antigua Pueblo Indian, a descendant of the ancient people who originally occupied the region. The pueblo village lay a half mile north of Taylorsville and two miles east of the forest station. The same age as Jake and fatherless, too, they found a lot in common. The friendship started slowly, maturing to the point they seemed glued at the hip. At first, he knew Henry's Uncle Marshall was a member of the Raven Clan, and one of the elders of the pueblo. It was much later Jake learned the man shared supreme leadership with his father. He and Henry's mom became very fond of the "White boy," and after Grandfather Riley said something, everyone accepted him as one of them. That's where he went when his mom was called away on project fires, often spanning two to three weeks, sometimes longer.

~ ~ ~ ~

"From what I understand, you and Toleshnec didn't strike it off at first," Ken said, breaking the oppressive silence again as they headed back to town.

"Yeah. Henry and I became good friends that first

summer. Mom Riley and Uncle Marshall kind of adopted me. When I turned eight, they threw a birthday party for me. A month later, it was Henry's turn. That's when Toleshnec showed up like a spirit stepping out of smoke.

"I had no idea who he was. I just remember whenever they mentioned Toleshnec's name it was something like, 'He's been arrested again.' Being from the Raven Clan and with his position as *qaletaqua*, he was chief spokesman in those days, and it got him into a lot of trouble with people off the res.

"Like a modern Popé who united the Pueblos to oust the Spaniards in 1680, Toleshnec was good at uniting the Pueblo Nation to demonstrate unprecedented cooperation to stand against the powerful mining interests. The preservation of Sacred Mountain was at the heart of it all because of what it meant to all of The People—Pueblos, Hopi, and Zuni. Outsiders never cared to understand about the meaning of that mountain. Only the minerals mattered. Victory came with the Wilderness designation, but not without bloodshed, on both sides."

"Holding a Master's degree from the university didn't hurt," Ken said. "But that made him really unusual. Just getting our kids through high school can be a major project."

"Yeah, but the spirits told Grandfather that it was necessary. Being highly visible, aggressive, outspoken, put uncle constantly in trouble with the law, but that education stymied them. He lapped up the attention like a thirsty dog at water, leading demonstrations, nonviolent, but noisy, constantly ruffling the feathers of his opponents. On the surface, he drove the Pueblo governor nuts, but they played off one another to become very manipulative in a passive-aggressive sort of way. The other side, of course, flexed their muscles to put the uppity Indian in his place.

Toleshnec quickly lost his idealism, coming to mistrust politicians and corporate leaders. His biggest mistake was applying that judgment to Whites in general."

"So what happened? At the birthday party," Ken asked.

"He walked up to the where we had gathered and just stood there, glaring down at me. The first words out of his mouth were, "Send the White boy home where he belongs." Someone with his reputation and power in the community is obeyed without hesitation, so I got up to leave." Jake chuckled. "That's when we all learned about Mom Riley's temper. She rose up like a great thunderhead. I swore at the time lightning flew out of her hair."

The memory of that incident came to Jake's mind as clear as the wasted mesa spread outside the truck cab while relating the incident to Ken.

"'You sit down Jake,' she said so sharp it scared both Henry and me. Despite her brother being straight and tall as a war lance she put her short-barreled body between him and me and got right in his face. There was talk they heard her all the way at the back alter of the Mission church. She really ripped into him.

"'So, you get out of jail and come around here to order us around?' she said. 'Jake is Henry's friend and as much a member of this family as you. But you wouldn't know that, you who comes around here whenever it pleases. Where have you been all these months? You, who should have been here to teach Henry what he should know to be Antigua after his father died. No, you put being the big shot in Washington and Santa Fe ahead of family obligations, when you should have taken the responsibility for teaching your only nephew. We don't need your misplaced bitterness and hatred. Be Antigua or leave.'"

"Whoa! Mom Riley said that? I'd never thought that

sweet lady capable of something like that," Ken said.

"Oh, she's capable. You should have seen the shock on his face. He'd been roundly upbraided, but he didn't leave angry. Late that evening, me and Henry were sitting with Uncle Marshall listening to stories of rabbit, fox, and mouse when he returned. Didn't say a word, just sat between Henry and Uncle Marshall and stared at the fire. I was scared and started to get up, but Uncle put a hand on my leg to stop me without missing a word of the story.

"When he finished speaking, Toleshnec said, 'I have thought much on what my sister said this afternoon. I come to apologize to you, Henry, for shirking my responsibility.' Then he looked at me and said, 'I have been told much about your friendship with my nephew, Jake Bershinsky. I also come to apologize to Henry's brother.'"

"That is amazing," Ken said.

"I don't care what politicians and White folk might think Toleshnec is a thoughtful, humble man. Show him he's wrong and he'll openly repent. From that moment, he considered me family and spent more time with us both. He taught us to ride horses, to hunt, and to survive in the wilderness, and from his perspective, how to survive in the world of White men. That's also when he married and started a family. However, that certainly didn't stop him from continuing to be a royal pain in the White man's butt. If the politicians and mining execs thought having a family would temper their bitter rival, they were wrong. Toleshnec continued as fervent in his cause to protect the land and people as ever, more so, because he had a bigger stake in success."

₪

Incident at Beaver Creek

Chapter
15

Doc Gardner stepped out of the emergency entrance as the truck pulled up. "We're all set up," he said as two EMTs working the emergency room offloaded the body bag onto a gurney and wheeled it inside.

Ken arranged for a couple young men to meet them and take Mohf to a shady pasture next to the river close to his home. Locked up the night before for being drunk and disorderly, they were still battling hangovers, but happy to get out of the stark cell. Sgt. Walter accompanied them more to provide transportation than being their guard. When they saw whose horse they were providing service for, the boys were awestruck. Mohf received better than royal treatment, and for the first time since his morning oats, was satisfied.

As Jake followed the gurney inside, a nervous dread

began to spread through his body. There was something very unsettling about an autopsy room. Jake concluded it was not so much what happened within the sterile walls, but the lighting. Without shadows there was no depth perception causing a disorienting feeling. Beyond the stainless steel table dominating the center of the room, a refrigerated walk-in occupied the far end with floor to ceiling racks to hold bodies until final disposition. Normally, earthly remains didn't stay housed there long enough to get chilled, but then White men designed the facility.

The instruments spread out on a stainless steel counter were the most disturbing aspect—an assortment of tools for the destruction of the human body, some purchased from the local hardware store. Both lawmen involuntarily eyed the instruments as the EMTs opened the bag and transferred the body to the table. Jake and Ken would remain as witnesses.

A real plus was that Doc Gardner studied forensic medicine. The onset of Parkinson's several years earlier reduced his father to supervising walk-in emergencies and follow-up. Nurse Ben, one of the original nurses, continued working.

"I don't play golf, I don't like TV, and I am not about to sit in the shade listening to other old men rehash their youth," he once told Ken. For times like this, that was good. Doctor and nurse worked seamlessly together.

As the lawmen donned surgical attire, Nurse Ben removed the boy's only pieces of clothing, a kilt, and cloth headband, while Doc Gardner inquired about the specifics of the discovery. As Jake finished a narrative, the phone rang. Nurse Ben answered, and then handed it to Jake. It was the Assistant US Attorney in Santa Fe. Jake gave him a verbal report before returning the phone to Nurse Ben who answered some questions with either yes or no while writing on a yellow pad. Finished, he hung up.

"The US Attorney has given approval for the autopsy," Nurse Ben said to Doc Gardner with a snicker.

"As if I need his blessing."

"Just his money," Ken pitched in.

"Well, let's get started," Doc said reaching up to a panel suspended over the body to turn on an overhead lamp and microphone. Clearing his voice, he began speaking. "June 24, 1992, the official autopsy of Small Beaver, age about thirteen, a member of the Sacred Mountain Clan, Antigua Pueblo, grandson of Toleshnec as identified by Ken Burning Arrow Herbert, Assistant War Chief and Chief of Police, Antigua Pueblo, New Mexico. This autopsy is conducted at Wí yeh P'oe Regional Medical Center, Taylorsville, New Mexico by Gardner Ryan, MD., assisted by Benjamin Arotto, RN, witnessed by Jake White Bear Bershinsky, US Forest Service Law Enforcement, and Ken Burning Arrow. Authorization received at 3:35 P.M. this date via telephone from Frederick Pinchott, Assistant US Attorney, New Mexico Federal District who is paying for this."

The mention of Toleshnec's name put a lump in Jake's throat. It was largely because of his activism that Two Waters hospital existed. A wild-eyed idealist in youth, he became a politically savvy manipulator. Now a recluse, the name continued to strike fear in the memory of many still in power.

Doc Gardner began a minute examination starting with the feet, working up, commenting on what appeared to be insignificant marks on the body, finally taking X-rays of the leg wound and chest. There was little need for invasion of the body. Jake was glad, not because he was squeamish—he'd seen his share of mangled bodies—it would be less disturbing to the boy's family. Doc Gardner understood that as well. The autopsy's conclusion was much as Jake suspected.

Turning the body slightly on its side he continued narrating, "The leg wound was created by a small caliber weapon entering the right rear thigh, angling downward at approximately ten degrees, grazing the femur, and exiting the front." This was determined by inserting a long, glass rod a quarter of an inch in diameter into the entry wound until it emerged through the front. "The artery was missed."

Jake thought of the .243 caliber rifle casing in his jacket pocket found at the mine.

"The cause of death appears to have resulted from a knife wound to the chest. Entry just below the sternum, angled upward into the chest cavity, piercing the heart."

Using a portable fluoroscope, Doc inserted a long, flat, flexible, plastic object that resembled like a tongue depressor for a horse to explore the wound. "The weapon was about two inches wide at the hilt and ten inches long," he said. "There are bruises on both arms that look suspiciously like fingers squeezing down on the tissue. There is considerable abrading on the injured leg, right hip, and both hands with small pieces of gravel imbedded under the skin."

A twinge of anger rose up in Jake. The knife wound was not a quick stab. The boy apparently was held down and the blade inserted, suggesting he could be looking for psychopath.

"Dragged himself about fifteen yards," Jake said when the autopsy was finished. "I found the boy's water jug about thirty yards up from the river and saw what suggests crawling and pushing sign in the gravel. Also, what possibly could have been blood from that point to his camp. I suspect the location of the shooter ties to this. Found it on the mine tailings on the other side of the river. Several others down the tailing slope. I'd have to repel down to get them." Jake pulled out the bullet casing. "That he was able to crawl back to camp before being caught confirms in my mind whoever did it was on the opposite side of the river. It took them that long to cross over and catch up to him. Another thing, he must have been wearing moccasins since his feet don't show evidence of scraping. I didn't find any moccasins or a knife, which he would have had. The wound measurement would be similar to the knife he should have had."

"They killed him for his moccasins and a knife?" Doc Gardner said.

"Probably fruits of the crime. There's been suspicious activity in that area recently."

"Really? Couldn't tell by all the bodies you're hauling in here," Nurse Ben said as he wheeled the corpse to a cleaning area to wash down before placing it in cold storage.

"I can't shake the thought the boy may have seen Darrel Windpipe murdered. Time of death of both victims is certainly close enough as well as both deaths occurred in the canyon, too."

"What now, White Bear?" Ken said.

"I'll take the boy to his family in the morning."

"Need a bed?"

"Mom Riley would expect me to stay at her place. Probably should visit more."

₪

Incident at Beaver Creek

Chapter 16

Despite being energetic and robust, age wrinkles made Mom Riley appear much older than sixty-eight. Short in stature and always petite, she was a giant in other things. Except for that one explosion with her brother, she remained soft-spoken, although her words could be direct and sharp in a gentle way, like a table knife cutting soft butter. The same could not be said for Uncle Marshall. Tall and more slender than in past years, he looked and sounded frail for a man only seventy-three.

"It has been seven months since you last showed up. So what brings you here? Not a social call. You are in uniform," she said.

"I found Small Beaver's body at the vision place this morning."

Hand covering her mouth, she gasped as moisture

came to her dark brown eyes. "My brother's heart will hurt. Small Beaver was such a beautiful child. Did he fall?"

Jake avoided the question. "I'm taking the body to Uncle tomorrow. I'd like to use my old bed tonight."

"You don't have to ask."

"I should accompany you," Uncle Marshall said.

"You should remain here and take your Geritol," Mom countered.

"Our brother has suffered a great loss. I should be there."

"I can do that, Uncle," Jake said.

"So, you think I'm too old to travel?"

"I apologize for offending you Uncle, but yes."

The old man stared at Jake for a time through dulled eyes before answering. "You are probably right. I haven't been on a horse for a few years."

"A few years? More like since Jake left for the Army. You can barely walk now. How would it be after riding a horse for a couple of hours, even if we could get you in the saddle," Mom said.

"Thank you for reminding me that I have one foot on the road to the Land of the Dead, and the other on one of those infernal skateboards my grandchildren use."

After a meal of fry bread with beans, meat, and grilled green chilies, Jake sat with Uncle Marshall behind the house in the diminishing light. Leaning back in a lawn chair, eyes closed, he breathed in the aroma of burnt piñon drifting over from the outside oven, letting his thoughts drift back to less complicated, less painful days. Opening his eyes, he spotted the small, black shape of an Eagle, wings stretched out to glide lazily on heat thermals high overhead.

"What are you remembering, nephew?" Uncle Marshall said.

Jake looked at him sitting in another chair several feet

away.

"I was remembering the time I spent the summer in the mountains with Toleshnec. It wasn't long after Henry and I turned eight. "

"You and my brother became close then."

"We came to understand one another."

"Do you think that Eagle flying over us might be a guardian spirit?"

Jake startled. How could he know about that Eagle? Then he remembered and smiled. Uncle's eyes might not be as sharp as they once were, despite cataract surgery; he had other ways of seeing. Jake realized he had been looking upward, and laughed softly to himself.

"It was good you came home from the war and not go back a third time. Your guardian needed a rest."

Thankfully, the subject changed as Mom joined them and he could speak of his family in response to her many questions.

"We would like to see Katelyn and the children more often," she said.

"Jake is a very busy man with many responsibilities," Uncle Marshall said.

"I have been remiss not bringing them to visit. It's not because I am too busy . . . or ashamed," Jake said looking into Mom's eyes.

She reached out and laid a hand on top of his. "I understand. As we move on in life, some pain often moves along with us."

"I must put that aside for my children's sake. I will do better."

After the two elderly people retired to bed, early as usual, Jake strolled down to the diner for a soda before crossing the street to the police station to begin making phone calls. Davidson and Hayes were there.

"Interesting," Jake said after they filled him in about Raymond Windpipe.

"Do you think he's laying out there somewhere?" Hayes said.

"I doubt it. I didn't see any vulture activity. If whoever murdered Darrel and Small Beaver, killed him, they most likely dumped the body in the river, too. Probably swept further downstream. If so, he'll turn up sooner or later. "

"Could have buried him," Hayes said.

"Could have buried Small Beaver. I get the feeling these guys have a lazy streak."

"Chief Herbert put out a state-wide pickup and hold on Raymond, just in case he's still out there."

"Could you clear up something for me? I've noticed folks around here have several different names," Hayes said.

"Each Antigua has three names," Jake explained. "We each have a sacred spirit name known only to the individual. Then we have an Indian name. The first one we receive at birth. Girls tend to keep that name through their life. Boys who go on a spirit quest to seek a connection with a personal spirit can receive an adult name that comes from their vision. Then we have a European name. For the older folk, it is typically Spanish, but over the last couple generations, The People have opted for more Anglo names. For example, I have a sacred name that goes with me to the Land of the Dead when I die. I have the name Bershinsky from my father, and White Bear from my spirit vision. Those two names die with the body."

"Then which do we use?"

"As an outsider, if an individual accepts you as a friend he will allow you to use his Indian name, otherwise use their Anglo name. Of course, it depends where you are. Here on the reservation, you can refer to me as White Bear, but out there, in the other world, it would be more appropriate to call me Jake or Bershinsky."

"Kind of complicated."

"Sometimes."

"Well, I got to tell you these folks cook up a darn good meal. Guess we'll head back to town," Donaldson said, pushing back from the table.

"A burial detail from Albuquerque will be here in the morning. The funeral's set for nine," Hayes said. "You plan to be there?"

"Yeah. I'll visit James and Mary in the morning. Haven't seen them since running into them just before Darrel shipped out," Jake said, watching as Donaldson laid a five-dollar tip on the table. He obviously did like the food.

After making the requisite phone calls, he spoke to Katelyn. She would bring the children over for the funeral. Returning to the Riley home late, he stretched out on his old bed to mull over all that had happened, listening to Mom snore from across the room.

The nocturnal vehicle trespass, Small Beaver's murder, Darrel Windpipe's truck—a lot of things pointed to the old Sebastian Mine as the hub. He'd bet a bundle that's where Darrel had been killed, and the gorge the most likely path for bringing drugs to the pueblo. The trail was difficult, remote, and the least detectable. The only person to use it would be boys going on their vigil, and Raymond had inside information when that would happen. The exception was someone coming from Toleshnec's clan. Yes, a good setup until Darrel and Small Beaver showed up.

The next morning, after sharing his thoughts with Ken, Jake spoke with Matt Douglass.

"If it was anyone else, I'd worry, Jake," his boss said, "but frankly, with the NCIS agents, and Chief Herbert, and you on the case, I don't know of a better team to handle this case. Things are getting dicey here. The druggies are pushing back. One of our teams had a shootout yesterday afternoon. No one hurt on our side. They lost one outright. A second isn't expected to see another birthday."

Jake walked to the Windpipe home an hour before the funeral and accompanied them to the LDS chapel to honor Darrel's life, and then on to the cemetery, a grassless expanse of red dirt surrounded by a black metal fence. Many of the graves had a cement or rock border, the dirt piled into a rounded hill over the site. A headstone bore the name and requisite dates. What impressed Davidson and Hayes were the number of American flags marking the final resting place of those who had served in the military.

After most everyone left, Jim approached Jake, placing a hand on his shoulder. "Thank you, White Bear. I know coming to this place is hard for you."

Jake was standing next to a grave, looking down at its cement border freshly painted white. A new American flag next to the granite marker moved in the crisp breeze. He'd been here only one other time in nearly thirty years, when they buried Grandfather Riley in 1969. That was just before he left for Vietnam. His heart ached. His throat burned as he fought back tears. Mary hooked arms with Jake. As the three walked away together, Jake noticed Hayes huddled with the Air Force burial detail's officer and two Pueblo elders.

Katelyn and the children planned to spend the day with Mom Riley. Jake wanted to, but could no longer postpone setting out on an even harder job and returned to the hospital where the body was loaded into the box of the police pickup to begin the trip home. Rested and rejuvenated after a night in knee-high grass, Mohf seemed eager as he bumped Jake while getting into the trailer. It would not be an easy ride to where Toleshnec's clan was camped in the eastern side of the Sacred Mountains, not far from where the mining companies had operated and prospectors still tried to sneak in.

"We're not going home just yet faithful steed," Jake said, latching the butt chain and securing the door before giving him a reassuring pat on the hindquarters. The Arabian didn't care. He was too busy rooting his snout around in a pan of oats.

Driving through the pueblo to pick up the trail, he noticed the burial detail in fatigues working around the Windpipe home. Hayes was spearheading a service project repairing things Darrel would have done, and Raymond should have. The military was good at caring for their own.

Dale and Muir had ferried Jake's rig to Taylorsville that morning which he drove to within five miles of the camp. Ken followed in another vehicle with the body. Jake would go alone from that point.

At the jump-off point, Ken began assembling a travois to carry the body using poles they brought along. Jake didn't want to bring the boy home slung indignantly over a horse's rump. Mohf wouldn't be that fond of it, either. While Ken lashed the poles together, Jake stepped out of sight behind the trailer. When he next appeared, Ken stopped work. Before him stood a Native American as if he had just stepped from a history book—checkered shirt, dark blue, cloth kilt over cotton trousers, moccasins, and a headband with two Eagle feathers hanging along the right side.

"Mom Riley thought my visit to Uncle's camp would be more easily received if I wore these," Jake said.

"Last time I saw you wear something like that was . . ." Ken stopped.

"You remember? That was a long time ago. You were what, ten?"

"Eight. We younger boys looked up to you and Flying Rabbit. That was a sad day, seeing the two of you leave."

Jake felt awkward. Nothing more exchanged between the two as they attached the travois to Mohf's saddle and secured the body on it. A simple waive was enough as Jake rode into the conifer forest and the trees closed in around them, affording a quiet not present in the world except in special places like this. While peace came to the ears, there was none in his mind.

The Army seemed a long time ago. It had been good for him in many ways. That's where he earned the second feather, and others. He was not ashamed of the service like so many civilians who didn't go to war seemed to be, but that was different time. Instead of stalling life and perpetually live in the past, he continued moving forward. Yet, one's past has ways of trotting up to run alongside the present as when Katelyn and the kids fitted his Distinguished Service Cross, Silver Star, and two Purple Hearts overlaying a Presidential Unit Citation in a glass enclosed shadow box. They were mementos of the Vietnam days of his career. It was a birthday present they insisted to be hung over the fireplace.

The forest seemed unusually quiet as horse and rider made their way along the trail. Only Mohf's hoof steps, occasional snort, and the scraping sound of the poles dragged across the ground invaded the silence. Even the wind normally singing a gentle song in the pines remained still. The forest buffered the sun's heat; the sweet scent of pine mingling with the musty odor of decay had a calming effect on his feelings.

Winding over several hills and through small meadows, they crested the final hill. Below, partially hidden by the trees, Jake looked down on Toleshnec's village clustered in a long oval-shaped meadow. In the near end were a couple dozen large, stick and mud dwellings. With no wind, smoke from cooking fires rose lazily into the sky. A few people milled about the village while he could see more tending fields at the far end of the meadow. Standing like a sentinel on a knoll off by itself was a kiva partially buried in the rocky ground attended by its sweat lodge.

Dropping down the zigzag trail, the Lodgepole and Spruce-Fir forest yielded to tall, white-barked Aspens. As Mohf stepped into the meadow, a shout went out from a group of boys playing nearby. Immediately people looked up or exited their homes, gathering to follow the visitor as he passed through the camp. Jake instinctively knew where to head and stopped as Toleshnec exited his hut and stood apart from the others.

Twenty-three years had passed since they last set eyes upon one another. His uncle was now seventy-three, but looked older. His face was as lined as a Rand McNally road map of eastern New York State, yet he still stood erect, the muscling on his chest showing only a slight hint of sagging. Jake dismounted to face him. Eyes that once burned with fire now appeared dim.

"Why has White Bear caused my people to sing the song of death?"

The old warrior looked beyond Jake's broad shoulders to the travois. Walking to it, he stared down. Jake came to his side and bent over to pull back the blanket enough to reveal the face of his grandson. The boy's mother launched a heart-rending scream, the boy's father dropped to his knees, tears streaming down his brown face, hands stretching out to touch the boy until another quickly checked him with a firm hand on the shoulder.

"What happened, White Bear?" Toleshnec's voice cracked pitifully as he fought to retain control of his emotions, but could not hold back the tears as they began trickling along the crevices of his face.

"I can't say for sure. I found the boy's body beneath Maseway. He was murdered."

"It will be tomorrow before one who can handle a body returns," Toleshnec said, his eyes not leaving the boy's face. That was something they really didn't want. His spirit might return and plague the village.

"If it would please Uncle, I have already handled the body. I cannot be harmed by his spirit," Jake said.

Jake startled at those words. They sounded so distant, as if spoken in another time as his mind flashed back to another time.

Toleshnec turned toward Jake and stared into his eyes for what seemed an eternity, beholding that same vision, before saying, "Bring my grandson."

As Jake took up the body, Toleshnec directed some youth to remove the travois from Mohf and take him to water. Jake's destination was the community center also set apart from the main village, but not as far as the kiva. Its door faced east as did all doors in the village. In the middle was a small fire ring with dry tinder and grass ready for lighting. Jake knew the procedure and laid the wrapped body on the dirt floor on the east side of the fire. Outside the women raised their voices in the death chant as in the distance a solitary drum began a slow beat, a signal to those in the fields and to the spirits that something bad had taken place.

Using a flint and steel that lay next to the fire pit, Jake coaxed a small flame to life as Toleshnec positioned himself cross-legged on the opposite side of the fire. Jake then knelt alongside the body, facing the old man. The boy's father knelt off Toleshnec's left shoulder. Three other men stood behind the father. These were the four sons of Toleshnec Jake had last seen as boys. Next, Small Beaver's brothers entered. The oldest was first and laid a bowl of corn meal next to Jake's right hip before taking his place in a semicircle behind their father. The next oldest brother set a rolled mat next to the bowl. Tightly bound, it contained the boy's ceremonial clothes. Two more brothers joined the others, the four ranging in age from mid teen to early twenties, making Small Beaver the youngest son. Jake was struck by how handsome they were, reminding him of the beauty of Toleshnec's bride. Disturbing were similarities to Henry in the oldest boy's face. Jake quickly diverted his gaze, but looking at Small Beaver's father was difficult, too. His face was pale and drawn, eyes bloodshot and glazed, the expression of shock and disbelief, and pain etched deeply so that he looked much older. Outside, the women continued wailing, the mother's voice rising above them all.

With everyone present, Toleshnec began a raspy chant in the dim light. After a time, he took up a small, neatly wrapped bundle of grass and touched one end to the tiny flame. Immediately a delightful aroma filled the room, replacing the smell of death, as he waived it slowly back and forth over the body from head to foot. After a time Jake unwrapped the blanket. If Toleshnec was startled by the wounds, he made no indication, but continued chanting. The father gasped. Jake's heart felt as if being torn from his breast knowing how much the man wanted to hold his son one last time, but all he could do was to sob openly, the sound only slightly muffled by the mother's wails outside.

Turning to the bowl, Jake scooped up some cornmeal and rubbed it between his palms, sprinkling it over the body from the crown of the long, dark brown hair to the soles of the feet. The slightly musty odor mingled with the sweet herbs Toleshnec had ignited was a welcome relief from that of decay, but only intensified Jakes memories.

Finished, he leaned back on his heels and waited as Toleshnec sang more prayers.

As the chants continued, Jake turned to open the bundle on his right. The white cotton tunic was most probably woven by his father. There were also a woven belt and white, cotton trousers, and dark blue kilt, things the boy had worn in this very lodge before setting out on the vision quest with so much joy and excitement. They would have been the same worn upon his triumphant return, but now to be worn on his journey to the Land of the Dead. Jake carefully placed them on the body.

As Jake began dressing the boy, his mind continued to dwell upon that time he had struggled to forget, when he sat in a similar structure with Grandfather Riley to receive instruction as to how to prepare his brother's body.

~   ~   ~   ~

"The dead do not turn into evil ghosts," Grandfather said. "Each person has two souls. One is the name soul, the life and breath in each of us as we live on this earth. This dies with the body.

"But not the memory," Jake protested.

"No, not the memory as long as there are those alive to hold onto it," the old man replied gently before continuing, "The second is the free soul. This goes to the Land of the Dead.

"In this life we live as families which are very close. When the free soul begins its journey, it takes seven days to reach the Land of the Dead. Once arriving it finds that all live as families in a land that is sweet and good so that it does not care to return. But the journey to this beautiful land is long and frightening so the soul tries to take someone to be a companion on the journey. We living are not ready to leave this world, so it is important to shun the one we once loved until its soul gets to the Land of the Dead. If any of those who loved him were to touch the body, they would die also.

"You were more than just a friend to Flying Rabbit, White Bear. There has always been a special bond between you two as if you had been born as one. You may have been born in the White man's world, but that is not what makes you different. I have seen this in a vision. You have a special gift of protection from the Great Spirit. You need not fear touching the dead as we must."

~   ~   ~   ~

Using a bone comb, Jake carefully parted the boy's hair and laid it along each side of his face before slipping on the cloth headband. Finished, Jake leaned back and stared at the bare feet. The lad's journey was long and difficult, and he had no protection for his feet. That was more than sufficient reason for the freed soul to stay and look for the stolen moccasins.

Toleshnec looked up at Jake. "You did not find his moccasins?"

"No Uncle. I believe they were stolen along with his blanket and knife."

"This is not good." Toleshnec looked worried.

Jake would have gladly given his, but that would not help. Finding the murderers now became secondary to recovering the boy's moccasins. Without them, the free soul would roam the earth, not wanting to travel the difficult trail barefooted, and for these people that spelled trouble. Big trouble. It was imperative they were found, and that would most likely uncover the murder.

Toleshnec spent a great deal of time chanting and

imploring the freed soul to continue its journey. Nearing exhaustion, he finished. Jake wrapped the blanket neatly around the body, using the leather cords to tie it securely. He then easily lifted the light body into his arms and stepped outside into the glaring sunlight.

With Toleshnec taking the lead, he followed, the father behind him joined by a sobbing mother whom he held close. Behind them came Small Beaver's brothers, joined by three girls—older sisters. The remainder of the clan completed the procession as they made their way to the burial grounds.

Traveling what Jake judged to be about a quarter mile, the procession passed the cultivated ground and into the trees, following a small, but active stream. After a time the trees gave way to a long, rock-strewn valley. Crossing over the stream, they weaved between large, pyroclastic boulders up a steep, rocky incline to an opening in the rock cliff face. Barely wide enough for single file passage, Jake struggled to carry the body through some areas, finally entering a large, almost perfectly round, grassy valley surrounded by sheer rock walls fifty to sixty feet high. This had to have been a volcanic crater at one time. Large holes pockmarked the walls. Tattered, American flags marked three and he remembered several WW-II and Korean vets left the pueblo with Toleshnec. Their time on earth done, the clan obviously had not forsaken all modern tradition.

Proceeding to the side bathed by the rising sun, several men began removing melon-sized rocks used to seal the opening to a small cave. Meanwhile, others were gathering rocks and carrying them to a place near the other small mounds. With the opening cleared, Toleshnec stepped inside briefly, then exited.

"Another left us a year ago. Would you take the bones to her final resting place?" his uncle asked.

Jake thought this another interesting deviation from tradition. Normally, the Pueblos bury their deceased's remains almost immediately in the ground. Glancing around he noticed the valley grass was a false facade; digging the ground was impossible. By placing a body in a small cave like this, it would be safe from wild animals until only bones remained. These they moved outside and buried beneath a mound of rocks.

"I know what you are wondering," Toleshnec said. "I knew we would not always live in these mountains, and I wanted a safe place where our loved ones might rest for all time and eternity safe from prospectors and witches intent on mischief. While attending the University, I went to a lecture at the Mormon's Institute of Religion and learned how the Jews handled their dead at the time of Jesus. As we supposedly have a connection, I believed this was an appropriate way to resolve our problem."

Jake lifted the tightly bound, woven mat containing the bones. It wasn't very big, indicating it had been a small person. There was hardly any weight to it at all. Setting it aside, he placed Small Beaver's wrapped body on the rocky ledge, picked up the older remains, and carried it to where its family had prepared a spot. Like Little Beaver, the head would have been turned to face the rising sun, so he laid it on the ground with the same orientation. As the family covered their loved one with rocks, Jake returned to the cave.

Toleshnec had begun another chant to implore the boy's soul to continue its journey. Unfortunately, everyone knew that wasn't going to happen. Finished, he nodded for Little Beaver's brothers to reseal the cave.

"He will not leave on the journey. When White Bear finds Small Beaver's moccasins, then we shall return and plead for him to go on to that paradise where our great family lives."

Two men were set to guard the entrance for the next four days. After placing a protective charm on them and the entrance, Toleshnec lead the clan on a very circuitous route hoping Small Beaver's free soul would become confused and unable to follow them back to the village. Once back, Toleshnec, Little Beaver's father, and brothers gathered around a fire where they maintained heated rocks close to the sweat lodge. Toleshnec began chanting again, a different prayer.

Removing his clothes, Jake knelt on the ground as the clan's patriarch began the purification process, more for them than Jake. Once completed, they adjourned to the sweat lodge while an old woman took his clothes for washing.

Once the six sat around the central fire, someone passed in more rocks to increase the heat. Once accomplished the oldest brother asked, "I am called Runs Fast. Did you find an Eagle's feather?"

"No. Just before transporting the body, I climbed up to vision rock. There was no prayer circle.

The young man seemed comforted. "That means my brother must have received his vision. He will at least have a spirit companion . . . while he searches for his moccasins."

"Tell us what happened, White Bear."

Jake explained, beginning with the discovery of Darrel Windpipe's body, what brought him home, and finding the body.

"My heart grieves for Lone Owl's father and mother," Toleshnec said, using Darrel's Pueblo name. Despite his own grief, he could still have sympathy for another's loss. It also indicated Jake's adopted uncle was in closer contact with the outside world than he suspected.

"It was necessary to perform an autopsy, but it was not needed to violate the body, only to seek information that might help me find the murderers.

"I understand. Give my thanks to Dr. Gardner. He and his father have been good friends to The People."

The expressions of grief on the father's face began to turn to anger as the story unfolded, prompting Jake to say, "You can live apart from the world, but you are still of this world. You may live as in the old ways, but that is here. Out there, in the other world, you must live by those laws." It was a veiled admonition aimed at aggressively thwarting further violence.

"The soul of my son will wander the earth. Those who killed him must be brought to justice," the father said.

"I can promise you this, I shall do everything in my power to track down those responsible and bring them to justice," Jake said.

"White man's justice?" the youngest brother asked bitterly.

"In that, the world has changed, thanks to what your grandfather did, standing up to speaking for The People," Jake said. "Little Beaver was murdered on Federal lands. Those responsible will be tried in a Federal court, but it will be a fair trial. When it comes to that, I will have the evidence to convict them."

"They will die?" the young man asked.

"I cannot guarantee that they will receive the death penalty, but they will certainly be put in prison for a very long time, long enough they will probably die there."

"That is not good enough," the father said.

"What good will it do for you or any of you to kill them? I would have to come to arrest you and take you to jail. Then what would become of your family? What of your children."

"You will not find me."

"Do not be a fool," Toleshnec snapped. "This is White Bear you challenge, he who stands with one foot on green grass and the other on red earth. If he says he will find the murderers of Little Beaver, he will do so. If he says he will see these persons brought to justice, he will do so. He is a member of our family. He has a personal stake in this as well.

Incident at Beaver Creek

Chapter
17

As student and teacher sat by a small fire outside Toleshnec's home long shadows silently crept across the elongated valley, slowly taking away the light until total darkness gained possession of the land. Overhead, a vault of stars blazed like tiny diamonds as a three-quarter moon cast a pale, cold, bluish glow over the land. Campfires scattered about the village spread islands of warm, flickering gold light. People came to thank Jake for his kindness, many of the young men and boys stayed to take in every word as the men spoke in the Tewa language of the Antigua. Jake was a bit rusty, struggling at first, surprised how quickly it returned.

Some of what they discussed was about Small Beaver. Toleshnec obviously doted on the boy. The pain in the old man's heart was evident as he gave voice to memories. Some conversation was about what Toleshnec had been doing in the mountains and about his family. However, what kept the silent listeners' interest was hearing about their newfound family member—the battles, the career of teaching others to be soldiers.

Toleshnec knew there had been medals and awards. Getting Jake to speak about them was like wrestling a hungry wolf for a piece of deer meat. Little Beaver's oldest brother was curious why Jake seemed reluctant to speak about his victories.

"Are you ashamed of what you did?" he asked

"No, to speak of such things would be bragging. I was taught such talk should come from others."

"Then I will speak for White Bear," Toleshnec said. "The feathers and White man's medals came because he and his band of warriors did their job." Jake was a little surprised. The old man had kept track of his life. Toleshnec spoke to the eager ears of his young men at some length about Jake, at times making it sound like an obituary. Jake would have preferred he hadn't mentioned a couple pranks he and Henry pulled as teenagers. That was better left forgotten, especially to the ears of his sons who were great imitators. As a result, the next morning a solemn escort of over thirty young men, an honor guard of sorts, accompanied Jake as he rode back to the truck.

Having radioed Ken before leaving camp, the officer was waiting. The vision cantering out of the trees struck a chord deep in the police officer's breast, as if his soul remembered what it must have been like in the old days. Davidson and Hayes were standing next to him. The astonishment expressed on their faces was priceless.

"We rode to the crime scene yesterday," Ken said, removing Mohf's saddle and brushing him down.

"That explains why you two are walking funny," Jake said, going to the front tack door to change back into his uniform.

"We don't ride many horses in the Navy," Donaldson said, eyeing the escort milling about, still on their ponies.

"Find anything?"

"Eagle Eye Hayes found a pretty good heel print down by the river. Made a cast. Not much else in the way of evidence," Ken said.

"Did you find any moccasins?"

"No."

"Are they important?" Hayes asked.

"Small Beaver was wearing moccasins his grandfather made. We had to bury him without them which means his spirit will most likely stick around looking for them. Think of it as a ghost wandering around here instead of going to the other world where it belongs, and doing things because it's alone and upset. Bad news. Really bad news."

"Some of the old people in my culture still hold to silly superstitions like that," Hayes said.

Jake looked at him intently before speaking. "Don't pass something like that off too quickly. There's always basis to those kinds of stories." He stopped abruptly, remaining in silent thought a moment. "Why didn't I think of this before? Excuse me a minute," he said and walked off to be by himself.

Everyone watched with heightened curiosity as Jake stood alone, his lips moving as if in conversation with someone. A couple minutes later he returned and asked Ken, "You didn't happen to find an Eagle feather around the camp?"

"Nothing but the foot prints. Whoever it was cleaned house pretty good."

"Is there something important about an Eagle

feather?" Donaldson said.

"I'm pretty sure the boy completed his quest. A feather would prove it and he would at least have a spirit companion with him. Other than going to war, that's about the only way to earn one."

"Eagles are still protected aren't they?"

"Yes. Only Native Americans can possess them for spiritual reasons. That's why a White man, a smart one anyway, wouldn't steal something like that. It would make him stand out. In this instance, that's the last thing they'd want to happen," Ken explained as he stepped the stallion into the trailer.

"And that's why the person or persons who murdered Small Beaver may be Indian," Jake said. "As for the moccasins, blanket, and knife, they would bring a fair amount of change on the collector's market.

"Is that why they killed him?" Hayes asked.

"I don't think so," Jake said. "From that letter Jim sent to Darrell, Raymond is probably involved in drug running up to his eyebrows. I saw some things in Cuchillo Cortar to suggest it has seen more use than just the occasional passage for a quest. I think Darrel came home to stop him and stumbled onto something, and was killed. Small Beaver may have been a witness and they eliminated him. Just a guess. Whatever is going on, the Sebastian Mine seems to be the focal point."

"I'll work on this end. There may be a way to recover the items," Ken said.

"Man, that was quite a sight, you and these Indians coming out of the trees. Think I know how Custer felt," Donaldson said.

"If we don't find who killed Small Beaver, the next time you see something like that could just be the beginnings of the second Little Big Horn," Jake said as he climbed into his truck.

~ ~ ~ ~

Jake returned home well after the children's bedtime, but still went to each, kissing a sleeping head like every night that he was home. Katelyn warmed leftovers, listening in as he phoned Douglass to fill him in on the details. While eating, he called Carrie to get an update on activities during the absence. Gratefully, all had been quiet. Finally, seated on the floor before a crackling fire in the fireplace, Jake cuddled Katelyn in his arms, relating his visit with Toleshnec and getting a run down on their visit with Mom Riley.

"The boys had so much fun and Mom Riley loved being with the girls. In a way, they're her grandchildren."

"I've been wrong keeping them from her. We will visit more often, and you're absolutely right. The children need that experience, especially Henry and Peter," he said.

"I worry about the dead boy, though," Katelyn said. "It must be very frightening to be where he's at."

"He'll be okay. I asked Henry to keep him company. I just hope those two don't cook up some mischief. Henry was always good at that."

"And you just followed?"

Jake's body quaked slightly with a silent laugh before leaning forward to kiss his wife.

₪

Incident at Beaver Creek

Chapter
18

Despite being bone tired, Jake spent a fitful night, his brain continually going over all the events of the past few days, trying to sort them out, searching for some missing piece. To complicate matters, no amount of Ibuprofen was helping the ache in his body from hair roots to toe nails. With a storm approaching, his arthritis kicked in big time. Uncharacteristically, he came down to breakfast 7:30 in pajamas as if a day off.

"You look terrible," Katelyn said.

"Thanks," he grumbled, taking a swallow of orange juice. "Where are the kids?"

"In school."

"That late?"

"Sit down. There's a piece on the news about that boy you found."

"We now go to Tony Romano in Taylorsville on this breaking news."

"Lori, I'm standing outside the Antigua Pueblo Police Headquarters in Taylorsville where Police Chief Ken Herbert just told me of the brutal murder of a twelve-year old Antigua boy, the grandson of Pueblo Indian activist, Chief Toleshnec of the Sacred Mountain Clan.

"Chief Toleshnec was a driving force years ago blocking mining operations in the Sacred Mountains by successfully having the entire area designated a National Wilderness. That apparently didn't stop people from entering the area so he and a group of followers set up residence in the mountains to protect the mountains from anyone with other than recreational activities in mind.

"Chief Toleshnec and his followers chose to follow the old Pueblo traditions and about a week ago his grandson, known as Little Beaver, went alone to an area particularly sacred to the Antiguas as part of a religious experience. When he failed to return in a reasonable time a search party discovered the boy's body hidden in rocks near where he was camped.

"The bizarre aspect of this crime is that it appears the boy was murdered during a robbery attempt. Missing are a pair of moccasins, a knife, and a blanket, all of antique value to collectors. Chief Herbert speculates because boys are undertaking a religious experience at this time of year, perpetrators may have been lying in ambush. The stolen items would net sufficient money to purchase drugs, a growing problem in the area, not just on the reservations.

"An interesting side light to this crime is that in Pueblo religious belief, those items should accompany the boy's soul as he journey's to reside with his family in the great heavens. Without them, his soul will remain searching for them, and this poses a serious threat to whoever has the items in their possession as that person or persons could be taken by the boy's spirit to accompany him on that journey. Frankly, that seems a fitting punishment. This is Tony Romano for KRQE News, Taylorsville."

"How come they didn't mention you found the body while checking a wilderness violation? I wouldn't have thought Ken the type to grab all the glory to himself."

"He's not." Jake chuckled. "He's being cagey. By not mentioning me, the true reason I was there won't be known and scare the perpetrators off. Dwelling on the native religious beliefs is an attempt to get the items back. Make it too hot to keep, especially if they were Indian who stole them."

"What makes you think they were Indian?"

"A number of things, but one in particular is the dogger boot heel we found. Not many folk wear those around here except rodeo types, and those are predominately Indian."

The way his body felt, Jake decided to spend the morning typing up a detailed report, stopping often to consider how to proceed with the investigation. At the moment, there weren't any additional leads, while a pile of safety inspection reports needed review so the recreation department could fix any problems, an important necessity to maintain a safe environment for visitors. There were other reports requiring data collection for bean counters and status seekers. That required making a schedule for his compliance officers to gather that information. The only report he didn't privately grumble about were those for his boss, which helped to focus on details of the murders, focus that is, until the phone rang.

"Jake, this is Nick." It was his counterpart on the neighboring Kachina District. "I'm sorry to bother you, but I need to vent." Frustration dripped from his voice.

Nick Elam graduated from college with a criminal justice degree, and then spent nine weeks at the Federal enforcement academy in Georgia before starting work on the Zuni. Jake saw a lot of potential in the twenty-six-year-old who worked hard at his chosen profession. With three years under his gun belt, everyone still considered him a rookie.

Leaning back in his chair, Jake said, "Okay, vent."

"So far this year I've had four fires. Three of them were man-caused. In addition, I've had a half dozen timber thefts, nothing big, just small thefts from decks."

"Are they related?"

There was silence.

"I hadn't considered that. The district's timber inspector discovered some of the thefts several weeks after they obviously happened. It would be hard to correlate."

"I'm guessing you're in your office. Okay, put a red pin in your wall map for each man-caused fire with a date. Now pin each theft with a date. Let's take the most recent incident. Where was the fire in relation to where the theft occurred and where were you when the call came in?"

"I was making safety inspections on the north end of the District. Your man at Jay's Roost spotted the Horveston Fire about two in the afternoon on the south end of the District. The Timber inspector reported the theft a week later from . . . the Chipmunk Sale on the north end." Nick's voice trailed off. "A Dozen logs went missing from a deck the contractor hadn't moved, yet. The thefts might have gone undetected longer except we've got a good sale inspector who's been complaining about missing timber. Now that I think on it, that's kinda the way it went down with the other thefts. They seemed to have occurred on the north end while I'm on the south end."

"As if someone knows your location and how to pull

you away?"

"Holy cow! You don't suppose . . ."

"Might be worth thinking about. Don't change how you do things over night, but look at the way you disclose your schedule. Mix up how you travel about the district, because it's obvious someone knows where you are. Probably because you use the regular Forest radio channel a lot."

"Me and my big mouth."

"Don't be too hard yourself, Nick, just observant about your behavior. Don't always give your correct location when someone asks."

"Are you saying give a false location? That's not what we've been taught for safety reasons."

"I never let the enemy know my real position. On the Forest-wide frequency, I don't always give out my true location, but I always keep Curt at Jay's Roost updated on our private channel. That's how I often show up sooner than expected."

"And all this time you've been accused of speeding."

"Keeps folks off-balance. Even if someone has the frequency numbers, it's encrypted so they won't hear anything but static. If a fire breaks out, don't go rushing off to it. You've got competent help to take initial attack. Position yourself at a point where the timber thieves would pass. Investigate the fire later."

Two days later and still behind in work, Jake wondered if anything would ever get done when Nick reported a wild fire and requested reinforcements to stop its progress. That took most of the people on both districts. Fortunately, quick action snuffed the timber and grass fire before consuming more than fifty acres. They were lucky. Wet conditions and a thundershower helped control its spread. The day after the crews returned, Ted Grimes, head of timber sales, called to report the theft of logs from the Saw Mill Lake sale on Jake's turf.

"Half this deck is missing," the forester said to Jake as they stood next to the depleted stack. "This is the first theft we've had on our district for several years, but when they started having problems on the Kachina, I started spraying the butts with an orange paint that has special markers in it. I checked the mills. They aren't there. I even had the mill on the Pine Nut District checked. Nothing. All the logs are eight feet long, ten-inch diameter. Doesn't make sense. Too green for firewood and not enough to account for much value, even if you found a mill to take them."

Standing back from the deck Jake squat and chewed on a long blade of grass. No, it didn't make sense. No one saw any suspicious activity, no vehicles hauling logs. At least no one was admitting to seeing anything. Of course, with everyone on the fire there hadn't been any Forest personnel around to notice. The logs just disappeared.

Included in the disappearing act were Davidson and Hayes. With no further leads, they returned to San Diego until something more productive surfaced. Little did he suspect the turn of events that would take place a few days later.

While washing up for dinner, Katelyn called out, "Jake, come here." The distress in her voice was obvious leading to wonder if Osoquenada or one of his cousins had ambled onto the compound. It wouldn't be the first time.

Hurrying to the front door, he found his wife standing like a statue, staring outside, one hand on her chest, eyes wide. Their two daughters, Lora, nine, and Katherine, four, were peeking from behind her legs, terrified. On the porch stood the murdered boy's oldest brother, Runs Fast, a strapping model for a Greek statue. A lone Eagle feather with colored porcupine quills hung on the right side of his head attached to long, coal black hair held out of a deeply tanned face by a broad, cream-colored headband. His broad, deep chest was bare except for a leather strap angled across holding a quiver of arrows and bow on his back. A leather belt held a kilt to his waist with a large, lethal-looking knife hanging off the right side. Moccasin boots covered his feet. Other than when they first met at Toleshnec's village, he was the same, handsome, young man with a hint of Henry's features. The one distressing aspect? War paint.

"Grandfather sent me to inquire if White Bear has found those who killed Little Beaver." he said when Jake appeared.

Jake stepped passed his wife and onto the porch leaving her and the children to gawk, the boys having joined.

"No, I have not," he said.

"I will stay until that happens."

"That will be fine, but when I do find the murderers they belong to White man's law. I want that clearly understood or our kinship will be sorely tested." Jake spoke softly, but his voice contained a firmness that left no doubt about the message.

"Runs Fast will abide by White Bear's law. Grandfather has spoken. But if White man's law cannot punish this person, then he belongs to me," was the equally firm reply.

"Agreed," Jake said, later wondering what kind of unholy bargain he'd entered into.

He was confident his law would prevail, yet harbored thoughts that were not pleasing. If some slick lawyer wasn't successful getting them off, White man's law would be just and certainly more merciful than Toleshnec's ancient law. In some ways, he thought that too bad in this case.

Runs Fast would not come into the house, saying he

preferred to be outdoors. Over the course of several days, he built a lean-to with the help of Henry and Peter, who spent increasingly more time with the young man. Katelyn wasn't sure about the relationship, but Jake was. The boys were learning skills he had failed to teach them. In return, Runs Fast learned he wasn't a great wrestler. All of a precocious fourteen, a much lighter and shorter Henry repeatedly put the Antigua on the ground using Judo when they wrestled. A bond was forming that pleased Jake immensely. Katelyn wasn't as enthusiastic, struggling to accommodate the situation as a cumulus cloud began building on the horizon.

₪

Incident at Beaver Creek

Chapter
19

Once the District Ranger and staff lived on the area of forest they administered. Eventually they abandoned the stations for more modern homes closer to civilization. Jake was the only administrator not based in Cosa Peluda thirty miles away where the District offices were now located. The Supervisor agreed. Having people stationed in the heart of the Chivato District placed personnel closer to their work areas, reducing travel time up to three hours a day in some instances. The move potentially cut into productivity. However, because the staff were dedicated professionals on salary and not paid hourly, they frequently worked overtime. Such was the machination of Washington bureaucrats.

The Arroyo Station remained important, however, becoming a storage location for heavy construction equipment when not in use, and as field storage for the engineering, timber, range, and recreation departments. Besides being home to Jake's family, there were quarters for two of his initial attack fire teams and two dozen summer employees who worked for the various departments. It was also a refueling hub for field vehicles. Arroyo Station was a busy place with people going and coming all day. Add to that tourists stopping with questions or seeking directions. The sight of an Indian boy sitting on a picnic table in traditional garb playing a flute or playing with the children provoked a lot of questions from people who didn't live in the Southwest.

Katelyn did appreciate the extra help keeping the boys entertained and out of mischief, but frequently commented about their visitor's scanty attire. Often as not, the only thing Runs Fast wore was a cotton headband, kilt, and moccasins. He had shed the war paint much to everyone's piece of mind. When Henry and Peter began to emulate his dress using old bath towels she objected, but found no support from her husband. The thundercloud that had hovered on the horizon moved in two days after an unresolved discussion about appropriate attire. Jake sensed a problem with only one foot set in the house.

"Some tourists stopped this afternoon," she said, forcing herself to stifle welling anger. "It seems Henry, Peter, and that Indian boy were swimming in the lake this afternoon."

A crescent-shaped lake lay along the south side of the compound, wrapping around to the west, necklaced by a goodly number of trees. However, a curtain of trees were removed when the road was widened giving a clear view. It appeared as a beautiful blue and emerald, squash blossom pendant. Not more than five or six feet deep, there was a particularly good spot for diving where it began to wrap around to form the west end. Several years back seasonal engineers dredged out an oval-shaped area ten feet deep, and built a springboard in addition to a rope swing strung from an overhanging cottonwood. It was perfect for diving.

Jake saw the lightning bolt coming and, "It's a pretty warm day," didn't help deflect it.

"They were naked!" Katelyn said, raising her voice.

"Oh. I'll talk to them."

"You better. I am not going to tolerate any more of this running around naked nonsense. My children will wear clothes like civilized people."

"Queen Victoria rules?"

"What?"

"I will speak to the boys about using better judgment. There's a good swimming hole a bit further upstream below the waterfall, out of sight of the general public."

"Fine. With bathing suites."

"Bathing machines aren't optional?" he countered using the term for a bathing suit in those contradictory days of the English queen.

"Jake Bershinsky!"

"I will speak to them Katelyn, but if they wish to dress as their new brother or I did at that age, so be it. It's not going to warp their minds or turn them into perverts unless they are pushed into it by unreasonable societal expectations that have plagued these people since the invasion of the Spanish brand of Christianity."

She realized a tender subject had been touched and by Jake's soft-spoken firmness, the discussion had ended. She tried a different approach. "How long is he going to stay?"

"Until I find his brother's murderer."

"And if you don't?"

"Then I'll give Henry to his father as a replacement."

Katelyn's mouth dropped open. "Excuse me!"

"Just kidding. I've got a feeling something is going to break soon."

"Well, I hope so. I'm not giving up my son to become a primitive."

"I didn't turn out so bad." There was a twinkle in his eyes.

Jake could be infuriating, but she knew there was no point continuing.

~ ~ ~ ~

With the Fourth of July three days away, the recreation department was busy with last-minute fix-it items in the campgrounds to ready them for the influx of visitors. Jake had one last trail to check. This he reserved for himself and had had been looking forward to this opportunity.

The variety of open meadows, forests, and mountain top vistas made it one of his favorite trails. The ride was especially enjoyable with Runs Fast and their two shadows, Henry and Peter.

"When you and Grandfather spoke, I understood White Bear was a great warrior, but I did not understand where this battle was," Runs Fast said, still struggling with English, but wanting to improve with use.

"Vietnam. That's a country very far from here," Jake said, knowing Runs Fast would not have any understanding of world geography.

"You only fight in one battle?"

"No. I was there for seventeen months off and on, between trips to the hospital and rotation."

"But you only have two feathers?"

"That's all I wish to wear. Any more would be boasting."

"How many feathers did White Bear earn?"

Jake thought for a moment, reflecting on that period of his life, which now seemed so long ago. "Thirty or forty, I guess."

"So many! More than grandfather?"

"Your grandfather fought a different war. Folks don't attach a lot of glory to what he did, but in the long run, it was more important. He had a special bravery to stand before the President of the United States, the Congress, Judges, and others to challenge their treatment of The People and the land. He should have received many feathers for that, but didn't."

Their ponies carried them out of the cool over story of Lodgepole and spruce-fir into a sunbaked area of dead trees. Several years before Jake arrived, a lightning strike blasted a lone snag creating a Roman candle that shot embers into the air to be carried fifty yards on the wind into denser growth where they started a fire. Fortunately, rain held it in check until the crews were able to jump on it, containing the destruction to less than fifteen acres, but the stark, gray and black spires of the burned tress remained as mute testimony of what can happen. He'd been this way last fall and noticed that several of the dead trees had fallen. Today, one lay across the trail, much too heavy to lift, but by tying ropes to the top end, they were able to use their four horses to drag it aside.

Finished, they were coiling lariats when a nervous voice said over the radio on his hip, "Bershinsky this is Jay's Roost." The call was coming over the enforcement only channel.

"I'm about a mile west of Granite Peak trail head. Go ahead Curt."

"Carrie has a 10-58 at Pickaroon Campground."

"I'll be there in thirty minutes." Turning to his sons, he said, "Boys, I want you to return to the house."

"Why can't we come?" Peter said, picking up on the urgency and suspecting some real excitement afoot.

Jake knelt on one knee before both boys and put a hand on each shoulder. "10-58 means Carrie has found a dead body. I'd like you to go back to the house and stand by the radio. I may need you to get someone to bring my truck to the campground. It's important, okay?" Somewhat appeased, the brothers mounted and sped back toward the compound. Then to Runs Fast he said, "Let's see what's going on."

Pickaroon lay on a knoll overlooking a sweeping bend in the White Tail River three miles west and a bit north of Beaver Creek. To get to the river where Carrie was parked they had to cut through the campground proper which gave the campers a real eyeful—two horsemen, one a forest ranger, the other a Native American out of a grade-B western bursting from the forest at a full gallop and coming to a sliding stop in the river side parking area. For an instant, his mind flashed back to Agent Harris' remark. They must have looked like The Lone Ranger and Tonto.

Carrie sat on the edge of her truck seat, feet out the door as the two approached. Jake was out of the saddle the instant Mohf slid to a stop. Holding his pony's mane, Runs Fast swung both legs to be parallel with the neck, and then stepped to the ground as she stopped.

"It's caught in the rocks," Carrie said, pointing toward a cluster of large boulders in the river about fifty feet from shore. "That gentleman over there spotted it while fishing."

"Not a good year for fishermen, they keep coming up with bodies instead of trout?" Jake said.

From shore, it appeared to be debris lodged in a cluster of boulders not unlike how they found Darrel Windpipe. Binoculars made it possible to make out one arm and the head protruding from the jumble of sticks and rocks. Given the binoculars, Runs Fast quickly became fascinated by what he could see and began looking everywhere after seeing the body, jumping backward into the river as he leveled on a fire truck pulling into the parking area. Dale and Muir happened to be returning from checking a lightning strike further north and heard the call. Jake quickly filled the fire guards in before using the radio to call the Ranger Station to make sure the boys got home alright and to arrange for his truck and trailer to be brought over. Unfortunately, he had to use the Forest-wide channel as McAfee was waiting on a part to fix the station's enforcement receiver.

"Hi, dad. Did you find the dead guy?" Peter asked.

"So much for keeping a lid on this," Jake thought, and then said, "Yes. For all you who just heard that, I'd appreciate you stay clear. Got all the help I need." The last thing he needed was an influx of gawkers. "Is there anyone at the station, Peter?"

"Mom's here," he answered.

"Ah, yes, kids." Jake muttered, shaking his head. "Anyone else there who drives a green truck?"

After a pause, Peter responded, "Mr. Diebert is here working on the road grader, and Mr. Petersen is looking over his shoulder giving him instructions." Petersen was the grader operator and when the two Dutchmen were together one never knew what to expect—volcanic eruptions or pranks. Fortunately, a mouthful of sunflower seeds helped minimize verbal exchanges and reducing disagreements.

"Would you ask Mr. Diebert and Mr. Petersen to bring my truck to Pickaroon, please?"

"Sure thing, dad. Can I come?"

"No."

With that exchange, Jake was about to remove his boots when he noticed Bill Muir nearly undressed.

"I know the routine," Muir said.

"We flipped a coin. He won," Dale said with a sly grin.

"I go, too," Runs Fast said, quickly shucking his moccasins and trousers. "Water is strong. You will need help."

Jake stood with hands on hips. One time and everyone claimed to know the drill. Dale fetched a rope from the fire truck. With one end tied around his chest, Muir waded into the river behind Runs Fast, stopping as the water came over his knees.

"Damn! Next time I flip a coin with Dale, somebody kick me," he yelled.

"Muir complains a lot. His way of joking," Dale said with a sheepish smile.

"Probably has good reason," Jake said. "The water temp was still in the fifties."

Muir repeatedly muttered curses as the water inched higher up his legs. When it hit the groin a pitiful squeal didn't assuage the curse that carried up to the crowd watching from the campground, and some distance beyond.

"Just a low tolerance to pain," Dale said.

"And doesn't know about flipping coins," Jake responded to which Dale shrugged.

The main current whipped along their side of the river so that the waist-deep water was particularly strong at this point, and as usual, the bottom rocks were like glazed ice. Apparently, Muir's foot slipped off one those basketball-shaped rocks. Thrown off balance the current finished the job. Arms flew up as he let out a surprised yelp and disappeared from view for couple of seconds, his head reappearing to bob like a beach ball on the surface as the current carried him downstream a few yards until he regained his footing in shallower water. Working upstream, he made it back to the rocks where Runs Fast stretched out a hand and pulled him onto a large, mostly flat boulder. They stood for a time looking over the situation, discussing how to best proceed.

Muir re-entered the water to work the rope around the body, the waist-high current deflected enough by other rocks so not to pin him against the debris. Runs Fast bent over to help, appearing to suddenly slip off the rock and into the water. Watching through binoculars, Jake knew better. The boy had jumped causing his foot to slip on the wet rock. Muir grabbed his arm, preventing him from being swept away. The speed in which he recovered the rock was amazing, like a cork held under water and released to pop above the surface.

Finally, Muir gave the signal for Jake and Dale to reel the rope in. Once the body was ashore, Jake quickly removed the rope from the body—a lifeline if needed, but wasn't as the two rescuers came ashore where Carrie had blankets waiting. Jake noticed how she tossed Muir one while laying the other over Runs Fast's shoulders. A thank you wasn't voiced, but Runs Fast did give her a faint smile.

Everyone was surprised when Jake began to slip off his cowboy boots.

"Where you going?" Muir said through teeth chattering like a machine gun.

"I noticed something in that debris pile closer to shore. Just want to check it out."

"Oh, hell! I'm already wet. What is it?"

"A log."

"A log?"

"My turn," Dale said, starting to unlace his boots.

"Never mind. You need to warm up, Bill, and I'll be back before you're ready, Mike," Jake said, and taking the rope, waded in. It was only mid-calf deep, but definitely cold and the rocks slippery. Nothing ever changed with mountain streams, yet this was a pleasant feeling, harking back to more youthful days when he was impervious to such things—almost. Slipping the noose over the log, he cinched it up and signaled for Dale to pull it ashore as he followed.

"Sure, you get all the easy jobs," Muir said.

"Age and wisdom always prevails over youthful exuberance," Jake flipped back.

After a visual inspection of the body, which was lying face down, Jake turned it over and motioned for Runs Fast to come over. He approached with great hesitation. "You know him?"

"No," he said, being sure to stand back some distance. The boy was shivering, but not from the cold.

The victim was a Native American male, Jake guessed to be about the same age as Runs Fast. One might surmise the cause of death to be drowning except the body was missing its genitals and the face was hamburger, along with a host of other injuries. It was difficult to know for sure, but he had a good guess who this was.

₪

Incident at Beaver Creek

Chapter
20

By taking using the private bridge over the White Tail at McKenna's ranch not only shaved off driving time, but it was also the most discrete and direct route to where he needed to go. The ranch owner, Miles McKenna, was amenable to Jake or his people using it to access Federal lands on the opposite side of the river for emergencies. That had not always been the case. A lot of friction had developed over the years between the older McKennas and the government. Two years behind Jake in school, Miles was one of those little kids the bullies liked to pick on until Jake and Henry put a stop to it. It was quite a brawl as the two boys took on five. Only adult intervention cut it short, keeping the bullies from being totally annihilated. That was the start of the feud between Jake and Clyde Barker; however, Miles and the others weren't bothered again.

That wasn't all. Nine years later Miles found himself down to counting ammo when the Viet Cong attacked his unit and had them pinned down. The situation was not good, and then a bullet grazed Miles' helmet. Disoriented, the next thing he knew was a series of loud explosions, wild yelling, and massive gunfire like a fireworks stand full of ladyfingers going up. When it was over, there was someone standing over him.

"Hi, Miles. I didn't know you were joining our picnic in these woods. Looks like you're gonna need a new helmet." It was Jake. Granting something as simple as right-of-way access fell far short of what he owed him.

Carrie was concerned as she frequently glanced toward the Indian boy. Since stepping out of the water, he seemed persistently cold. The blanket and warm sun quickly abated any effect the icy water would have had; still, he periodically broke into shivers. Also, his expression changed from excitement to one of fear.

A gate across the bridge entrance had two locks, one belonging to the McKenna Ranch, and one to the Forest Service. After passing over the bridge, Jake and Runs Fast headed south with the body in the back of the truck, the young man sitting as if a convicted criminal on the ride to prison, staring blankly out the window.

"Did you touch the body?" Jake asked quietly as they drove through a huge meadow along the western end of Sacred Mountain, kicking up a thick cloud of dust that hung in the windless air.

"He reached up to take me with him. He will try again."

"The dead guy's arm flipped up and he jumped like it was a rattlesnake," Muir explained earlier in private, confirming what Jake had seen.

The road entered the south end of the pueblo, skirting

the newest section, modern adobe homes built to look like every other home on a curbed, asphalt street with two trees planted in the front yard. It was the BIA's attempt to give the Indians a place to live just like every urban American tract setting. Before reaching the old ruins turned tourist stop, they came to the older section of the community set among tall deciduous trees. Here, Jake followed a narrow, uncurbed asphalt street that wound around the rolling contours upon which the homes sat to accommodate rather than bend the land to The People's needs. Stopping at one, nondescript home, Runs Fast watched closely as Jake spoke to an old man for several minutes.

"Runs Fast, this is your grandfather's brother. He is the cacique. He'll help you," Jake said, then continued on to the hospital, leaving him standing in the yard.

"White Bear says you touched the dead man," Uncle Marshall said.

"He grabbed for me. The White man called Muir was tying a rope around the body. I was standing on the rock trying to help when the dead one's hand reached up. His free soul grabbed at me, knocking me into the water. It held me under to take my life so that I would accompany him to the Land of the Dead. I would be traveling that path now if the White man had not helped me break free and escape the water." Pure panic sharply etched in the young man's voice.

"Come with me. We shall see about breaking the hold he has on your living soul."

"Why can White Bear touch the dead and they not come for him. Is it because he is White?"

"White Bear is only part white. No, it is because he has the protection of one who has died and refuses to leave his side until it is time for him to make the journey. When that time comes for him to travel to the Land of the Dead, then the two will walk together as they did in life. The White preachers call such a guardian angel. Jake's guardian is very strong."

"The one who is dead and White Bear must have been very close."

"Close? Yes. Very close. They were brothers."

~ ~ ~ ~

Ken and Nurse Ben came out of the emergency entrance as Jake drove into the driveway.

"This is getting to be a habit you could break," Nurse Ben said as they moved the body from the back of Jake's pickup onto a gurney.

"It's Raymond Windpipe," Ken said, taking look at the body.

"I was afraid of that," Jake replied. "I saw him only briefly five or six years ago. Couldn't be positive with the facial damage, but he's the only one I expected to show up in the river."

"I'm all too familiar with the boy," Ken said, "but I recognize the tattoo above his left breast. Sort of a one-of-a-kind, at least around here."

"Somebody sure took a disliking to the kid. Worked him over good," Nurse Ben said. "Which of you is staying to witness?"

Each officer pointed at the other.

"I guess you both stay."

"Do I have time to get something to eat before you start?" Jake asked.

"These things make you hungry?" Ken said.

"Not especially, but I've seen a lot worse. At some point in time, a person gets desensitized to the gore, I guess. It's been a long time since breakfast."

"It will take us about twenty minutes to get things in order and notify the US Attorney. Special today is chili dogs," Nurse Ben said with an almost imperceptible smile.

"You two are gross," Ken complained, to which both men laughed.

Most people would be appalled at the levity surrounding such morbid circumstances, but that was a way for each to combat an oppressive situation. In no way did it affect their professionalism. Instead, it actually kept their minds clear and focused on the work at hand.

An hour and a half later Doc Gardner turned the body over to an intern who had just arrived to work at the hospital. While he cleaned up, the two officers departed for the doctor's lounge. When Doc Gardner joined them, he was reading something attached to a clipboard.

"I'll have a complete report when the State lab gets back to me, but that will be a couple weeks at bests," he said. "For your needs, the victim has rope burns to both wrists and ankles just like his brother Darrel. Most of his ribs are broken. More like shattered. The ones not broken are cracked. We're not looking at injuries caused by a flush downstream. My guess is whoever did it used something like a baseball bat. He has perforated lungs, a ruptured spleen, lacerated kidneys and liver . . ."

"Sounds like you're saying he was beaten to death," Ken said.

"Good guess. Death could have been the result of the castration with attending shock and loss of blood, but the amount of internal damage could be the cause of death, too. Pick something and you will probably be right, except drowning. There's no water in the lungs, just blood. No trace of alcohol this time so I doubt he wasn't drunk at the time, but we'll see what the blood tests return."

"What about time of death?"

"Hard to say for sure until I get the State report. Considering the amount of decomposition and water temperature, I'd guess about a two weeks."

Jake and Ken looked at one another.

"Most likely killed up by the old mine," Jake said.

"One other thing," Doc Gardner said. "There's evidence he was in the early stages of HSV2."

"What the devil is that? Norwegian?" Ken asked. The two had a long-standing joke about each other's accent— Gardner's slight Scottish brogue contracted while studying in Scotland, and Ken's Pueblo-tainted English.

"Herpes simplex virus. Most likely type two. Blood tests will confirm that, but I saw it more than a few times during residency. Incubation is usually three to fourteen days. I'd say he contracted it not long before dying."

"That may explain the sexual overtones to this murder. Finding the donor may lead us to the killer or killers," Jake said.

"I'll nose around on this side," Ken said.

"Let me know, too," Doc said. "We need to track down the donor's other victims . . ."

"That don't end up being flushed down your river," Nurse Ben piped in as he entered the lounge and headed to the coffeepot to refill his badly stained cup.

"I'll put out the word to physicians and clinics in the area to see who they've treated in the last while. State Health will throw out a bigger net."

In the privacy of Ken's office, Jake called Matt Douglass to apprise him of the initial findings.

"You've got a bad situation, but I can't be of much help," Douglass said. "This drug case in Gallup is bigger than we thought. There's a sizeable drug lab somewhere in the area, but we don't have any leads on it, yet. We're calling in extra help. As for your situation, frankly you're in a better position to handle this with your background and connections anyway, but if you need help I can see what's available."

"Not right now. If this all ties together, the boys from NCIS will be back, and Nick hasn't been called on any project fires, yet."

"Thanks for reminding me. I'll put a flag on both of your names. What with his arsonist and your murders, neither of you should be called out unless the world comes to an end.

₪

Incident at Beaver Creek

Chapter 21

Prior to transporting Raymond Windpipe's body to Taylorsville, Jake radioed Ted Grimes in Forestry to "take a look at something at Pickaroon." Transmitting on the open Forest channel, Jake was intentionally vague, but Grimes understood. Carrie was to wait until the Forester arrived and show him the log retrieved from the river. He also radioed his sons to come to the campground and take Mohf and Runs Fast's pony back home. When Jake awoke the next morning, Grimes was sitting in his pickup in the station parking lot waiting for him. Like a number of Forest Service personnel, he often started work early and finished late.

"You were right. That log you found yesterday is from the Saw Mill Lake timber sale."

"Let's take a look at the map," Jake said, going to the

wall, still in his pajamas. "Okay, there was a fire on the Kachina District here. That effectively pulled everyone from our area to fight it. That log disappears with some of its buddies and ends up in the White Tail about twenty-five miles downstream."

"The north fork cuts the southern boundary of the sale," Grimes said.

"What about the other thefts?"

Jake put a pin into the map at two other locations Grimes ticked off in addition to those on the kachina district.

"Everyone is adjacent or close to the river," Jake said when he finished.

"You mean they're floating the logs downstream? Where to? There's only one mill and that's way down downriver. Someone would surely see a bunch of logs floating downstream. I'll check the catch boom above the dam to see if any have shown up there."

"Maybe they weren't supposed to go that far. Maybe they are only to go as far as the Sebastian Mine."

"Why?"

"For mine timbers."

"Doesn't make sense. You can buy them cheap enough. Why steal them? Besides, I thought that place has been sealed up."

"You'd steal them if you don't want people to know you've re-opened the mine. Besides, there's no other way to get them there," Jake stepped to the desktop radio and keyed the mike. "Van this is Bershinsky. What's your location?"

"At the gas pump."

Jake looked out the window. The man was standing next to a green Dodge 4X4, waving. The two walked over to speak to him.

Van's eyes flashed a perpetual smile despite the hardships faced at home with a chronically ill wife. Resigned to the problem, he coped with a dry wit. "New uniform?"

"Casual Friday," Jake responded in kind. "What can you tell me about the Sebastian mine?"

"The place was closed down before our fathers were even a twinkle in someone's eye. About 1914," Van said. "Played out, at least as a commercial operation. There are probably pockets of ore here and there, but it's dangerous. Still, there are crazies who want to strike it big and sneak in. About a year before you arrived a father and his thirty-something son were reported missing after going there. Never did find them. The place is a honeycomb of tunnels. When Congress allocated restoration funds, I installed a gate. That was about six years ago. Still have the nagging notion I should've dynamited it shut."

"What kind of lock did you use?" Jake asked.

"A special issue Master Lock. It uses a different key than our generic. Why do you ask?"

"I'm not sure, yet. Where do you keep the key?"

"In the key cabinet on the wall behind my desk."

"So anybody could have access to it,"

"Well, yeah, and the District Ranger has a copy of every key used on the District. That's in a box on his wall, too."

Just before noon Jake, Runs Fast, and Van arrived at the old mine on horseback. After inspecting the lock on the heavy, steel gate closing the tunnel, the engineer said, "This is the lock I put on."

"Suppose you don't have the key with you."

"Sorry. It's not something I use every day."

"Let's look around a bit," Jake said to Runs Fast who hadn't dismounted, yet.

"What do we look for?" the young man asked.

"Anything that doesn't belong at an old mine site that hasn't been used since, way before your grandfather was born."

Jake then checked the tunnel opening, but didn't find anything to indicate activity. His flashlight couldn't penetrate very far inside, but there wasn't anything out of place there either. It appeared just as dark and ominously evil as any abandoned tunnel. Rain showers had fallen the last couple days obliterating any sign on the tailings plateau.

The Sebastian penetrated a ridge on the south side of the White Tail some fifty feet above and several hundred feet back from the bank. Tailings formed a yellowish plateau filling in the steep decline to the water. It had been at the edge overlooking the river that Jake found the rifle casings. The near-petrified remnants of a tower stood ghostlike, the old, dark wood rising up out of the tailings thirty feet from the drop-off. Consisting of two sets of eighteen-inch poles, each set formed an inverted "V" sixteen feet high with the base spread twelve feet apart and buried in the ground. These two "V" supports were about ten feet apart and connected by an equally large crosspiece at the top and middle. A badly rusted pulley hung from the lower cross bar.

"From the history I've read, they originally took the ore out on wagons across the river and up the gorge to the smelter at Taylorsville," Van said, "until the spring runoff made it impossible to ford the river for six weeks, so they built a bucket conveyor. There would have been a tower like this on the other side. Fill a bucket, cable it over the river, and load the wagon there. Simple enough."

Jake walked to the right pole set, looked up at the cross member and pulley, then back down. Kneeling, he began inspecting the weather-blackened wood closely. Using a four-inch, collapsible Buck Knife, he chiseled something from one of the many fissures near the base.

"What you got?" Van asked as he bent over Jake's shoulder.

"I'd say rope fiber. Scuff marks on the weathering patina of the pole, too." After retrieving an evidence bag from his saddlebags and securing the wood piece inside, he walked over to look at the companion pole. "Same here," he said, removing another sample and placing it in a separate bag.

Removing a lariat from Mohf's saddle, Jake tossed the loop end over the upper cross member and tied the free end to the saddle horn. Winding his right calf around the hanging end, he slipped the toe of his boot into the loop, and gripped the rope.

"You're not going to? . . . Van started to say, obviously surprised.

"Trick I learned in Nam from the Hmong, only they used elephants." Jake whistled and said to Mohf, "Back."

The Arabian backed slowly lifting Jake to the lower beam where he said, "Whoa." The horse stopped and Jake stepped onto the beam.

"Well, I'll be darn. A cowboy elevator," Van said, patting the gray on the neck. "You two continue to amaze me. What other tricks does this fella do?"

"Pass gas if walk behind him," Jake called down as Runs Fast sauntered up behind the horse. "Scuff marks and fiber here, too." Carving out more samples, he stepped back into the rope, swung off the beam, whistled, and said, "Forward." Mohf walked ahead until Jake reached the ground.

"Both Windpipe boys had rope burns on wrists and ankles. I'd say they were stretched out between these poles and worked over before being tossed into the river." He looked out toward the other side. "Just a theory, but your brother might have seen what was going on. They spotted him and shot him from this side, then crossed over to finish him off. At least one of them knew the value of his knife, moccasins, and blanket and stole them to pick up some extra money."

But who would do something like that?" Van said.

"I don't know, but I hope a little virus may tell us."

A clap of thunder lifted their heads skyward. The scattered cumulus were uniting, turning the sky a menacing, dark gray.

"No cover here. Think your horse is up to a run?"

"Well, let's find out. Last one to the truck gets wet."

As the thunder rolled and lightning began to close, the three raced back to the trailhead. At least Mohf and Runs Fast's pony were in the mood for a spirited race. The engineer's American Saddlebred at seventeen hands had the legs, but not the heart from too many days lounging at pasture, until a close lightning strike changed his mood. As he streaked passed, the two heard Van yelling, "O-o-o," which was either yahoo or whoa. It was hard to tell mingled with the rumbling thunder.

ꄓ

Incident at Beaver Creek

Chapter
22

One of the first things Jake learned that first summer he lived in the mountains was that showers could be fickle and difficult to predict, dumping on one spot while fifty feet away the rain can be a light mist or nothing at all. Jake, Van, and Runs Fast missed the deluge that hit the old mine thus narrowly missing a cold soaking, a dangerous proposition at any time in the high country where hypothermia silently stalks every traveler. Pulling up to the Arroyo Station horse barn, they managed to get their mounts inside just as another black thunderhead boiled in overhead.

"Get in your truck, Van. I'll unhitch the trailer," Jake said as the first half dollar-sized drops splattered on the truck's windshield.

"You'll get soaked."

"You want to drive back to town wet? I got a change of clothes in that warm house."

Henry and Peter were in the barn practicing Judo when the men arrived and quickly pitched in to unsaddle and put a blanket over each of the horses' backs, and then see to feed and fresh water. As Jake struggled to break the connection between trailer hitch and ball, the storm unloaded a deluge of baseball-size raindrops and slush. Van had to wait in the truck cab until the worst of the storm tapered off, but Jake got soaked to the bone.

Runs Fast wrapped a horse blanket over Jake's shoulders in an attempt to stave off more serious shivering as men and boys stood just inside the barn door. Ten, and then fifteen minutes passed as the rain continued making it obvious the storm had embedded over the mountain and not moving on. When the downpour eased up momentarily Van honked and drove off. Using the blanket as cover the four squeezed together and made for the house where Katelyn was waiting on the porch. The warmth from the antique, wood stove she used to bake bread radiated onto the screened porch.

"Leave those wet things out there. I'll take care of them."

"What would the Queen say?" Jake asked struggling to unbutton the wet shirt with uncooperative fingers.

"You're pushing it, Bershinsky," Katelyn said, stepping into help him undress. "Now off with you to a hot shower," she countered, sounding like the red headed, Irish drill instructor she could be. To Henry and Peter she said, "Leave your Judo uniforms outside. You definitely can do with a shower, too."

"Did Queen Victoria let kids run around the house in their underwear?" Henry asked. Her glare sent the brothers in full flight to the second bathroom.

"Does Katelyn want Runs Fast to leave his clothes on the porch, too," the young man asked with the hint of a mischievous grin.

"You don't wear enough to worry about, but you could leave your muddy moccasins outside," she said, handing him a warm blanket as he readily slipped them off.

The relationship between Katelyn and the Pueblo boy started out strained because of his attire and the growing influence on her sons, which she initially viewed negatively. However, things improved over the weeks to the point they could tease one another. Wrapped into another blanket she'd prepared, he stepped into the kitchen, savoring the aroma of fresh bread and chili. They were having Jalapeno soup, perfect on a cold night.

Sitting cross-legged on the floor before the family room fireplace, Runs Fast patiently waited while Jake and the boys showered. The Bershinsky's tolerated his refusal to enter the White man's house for only a couple days. Following a long talk with Jake, the young man came in for meals and family evening time, the stays becoming longer.

When both sons returned to the kitchen, they were wearing flannel pajama bottoms, but no T-shirt. Katelyn had a rule, no bare chests at the dinner table. As toddlers, Henry and Peter quickly learned how to shed their diaper. There was just something about them and clothes that didn't seem to mesh as they constantly pushed the limits. With Runs Fast's arrival, she felt fortunate they acquiesced at least to wear swimming shorts with the kilt they adopted. A lesser person might have given in as a lost cause, but Katelyn marched them back upstairs for T-shirts. Runs Fast followed. When they all returned the he was wearing a pair of Jake's flannel PJ's, a T-shirt, and a pair of commercially made moccasin slippers. He had been the only exception to her no shirt, no service rule and he was obviously showing her respect. She quickly busied herself at the stove so he didn't see the misting in her eyes.

The first time Runs Fast was convinced to come inside and join them for dinner, it was awkward. He'd never used a chair before.

"Think of it as sitting on a log," Peter suggested.

He eased onto the chair, holding the edges with both hands while testing its sturdiness. With a bit of a smile he said, "More comfortable than a log," and carefully leaned back to test it further.

Their guest had never used western utensils before, either. Fortunately, Katelyn had made fried chicken that first time. Jake picked up a drumstick and tore off a chunk. That was a signal for Henry and Peter to use their fingers, too. Runs Fast took a bite and chewed, checking out the different flavor.

"This is good," he finally said, taking another huge bite.

Over the course of the next few meals, Henry and Peter flanked him at the table, demonstrating how to use a fork and knife. She was a little concerned how his digestive system would adjust to the different spices. It went better than hoped, but there was another concern. Would her boys eat this much when they reached Runs Fasts' age? Her husband was reassuring with, "Most likely." He consumed two to three servings at every meal. This evening Katelyn inwardly beamed as the family devoured her labor, the spicy meal chasing out the last vestiges of cold from her men folks' bodies. Despite the usual table banter, Jake sensed something afoot. During desert, Katelyn broached the issue.

"Alright, Henry, are you going to just sit there and drive me crazy, or are you going to tell your father?"

Sitting next to Runs Fast, Henry glanced at his mom

before turning to address his father. Biting a lower lip, he was obviously nervous. "Dad, there's going to be a Judo tournament in Phoenix just before school starts. They are having a special section on *kata*. It's for unfil . . . unaff . . ."

"Unaffiliated," Katelyn helped.

"Yeah. That kind of judoka." He gave up struggling with the word, intent on the whole message. "It's the only way I can move up in rank."

"Other than demonstrating proficiency in *randori*," Jake corrected.

"What is this . . . kata?" Runs Fast asked.

"In Judo, the kind of Japanese fighting the boys practice, there are two forms. One is randori, contact fighting like you three do, and kata, a kind of dance using a series of fifteen throwing techniques to demonstrate knowing them without being in actual combat. It's called *Nage no kata*. I've taught the boys Judo, but since we aren't part of a recognized club, and it's too far to drive to town twice a week, it is very hard for them to advance in rank," Jake explained to Runs Fast, and then to Henry he said, "So, you want to enter kata?" He was surprised.

"I know, I know, but I've been thinking about what you said a while back when I lost that match and wanted to quit. Well, I know I can compete in matches, but getting advanced that way is . . ., well, this is tougher and probably the only way it can happen."

"What about you Peter?" Jake asked. He had not yet competed.

"We've been working really hard. I'd like to try randori," he said, obviously apprehensive about the commitment, "but Henry needs my help to pass the kata, and since I'd be there . . ."

"I told him this is a bad time for you," Katelyn said.

"When is it?"

"Two weeks before school starts," Katelyn said.

"I suppose we could put them on a bus. They could stay with one of your sisters there, but why don't you go with them? You haven't seen either of them for a while. It would be a good visit."

"But, but . . .,"

"And, maybe, well, depending on what's going on . . . if these murders are cleared up and there aren't any fires, I might go, too. I haven't participated in a match for a while."

Katelyn was so surprised to be speechless, a rare malady.

"Yeah!" Henry said, jumping up to show his dad a brochure that had been on the buffet table.

"You could fight, too. They got stuff for old people."

Jake's left eyebrow shot to the hairline.

"I mean, well, ah, they got a master's division," the boy quickly said, trying to smooth over a major mistake.

"They *have* a master's division for older people," his mother corrected quietly with the hint of a devilish grin.

"Kata?" Jake said, stifling a laugh.

"Yes, sir. I've been working on it real hard and I think . . . I know I can be ready by then."

"What about fighting?"

"I've been working out with Runs Fast. He doesn't know Judo, but he's a good wrestler, and faster than a coiled snake, but I can beat him most of the time." Henry realized he might have said something to offend his big brother.

"Small Warrior with Pale Coat is very good," Runs Fast said, shoveling down a third helping of tacos, not offended by any unintentional slight.

"Small who?" Katelyn asked.

"That's the name he's given me because of my Judo uniform. Small Warrior for short," Henry said.

"I'm Little Cricket, because the way my voice keeps changing," Peter added.

"And never stops?" Jake teased. "Well, let's leave it this way. Small Warrior continues to practice. I'll evaluate his performance from time to time. If it looks good, then okay, we'll find a way for you to go. That goes for Cricket, too."

Henry and Peter sprang from their seats, flying into their father's hug. Jake was pretty sure his sons would be going. Henry was entering a difficult age, caught in that cultural limbo of being a boy and a man. Katelyn saw the transition smoothed with Runs Fast's arrival and Jake's handling of the spirited colt. Still, she was concerned when the boys and Runs Fast retired to the hut for the night.

"They'll freeze out there tonight," she moaned.

"They'll be as warm as if right here in the kitchen. Runs Fast started a nice fire inside while we bedded the horses down so it should be quite toasty by now. You'd be surprised how comfortable a stick and mud house can be, even in the middle of a winter storm," Jake said, who had spent a lot of his youth in one he and Henry built in the mountains—their private retreat.

₪

Incident at Beaver Creek

Chapter
23

Lying in bed, Jake stared at the ceiling as Katelyn purred like a contented kitten next to him. He found it difficult to sleep as his mind kept mulling over the events centering around the old Sebastian Mine. He wanted resolution to the murders. He had made a promise, the fulfillment of which seemed to be slipping out of his grasp with the passage of time. Worse yet, elements of the case had also dredged up memories he could no longer push down.

The incident started innocently enough at a local rodeo the month after graduation from high school. Throats hoarse from shouting encouragement and laugher as comrades succeeded or failed in Herculean efforts to master spirited beasts, the cowboys finally retreated from their perches along the top rail around the arena.

Congregating in small groups to drink and talk, the beat of a drum signaled the beginning of dancing near the circle of tents and travel trailers.

Henry drew two rank horses, scoring low on the first, and then dumped by the second. He took a lot of pride in his ability to stay on a horse. Being unseated was rare, which was cause for a lot of good-natured kidding from his peers. Despite appearing to take it in stride, he didn't take it well. Not well at all. Wandering through the camp he needed a friend—a particular friend to help console his ego, but wasn't finding him. Not finding him, that is, until passing near one of the unused horse barns where no small number of rodeo riders tried a different kind of bucking bronc. In the dim light from a small overhead light above the center door, he spotted Jake emerge from the shadowy interior to lean over a metal hitching post. By the sounds of things, he was suffering a bout of the dry heaves. Henry shook his head. Jake couldn't handle booze, but had been drinking more lately. On top of that, he was clad only in brown briefs.

Total surprise came when Sally Morton, the school's voluptuous, centerfold candidate, appeared out of the barn to lose a string of epithets at Jake. Culminating a flurry of deriding filth, she kicked Jake with a bare foot and stomped away. Once she disappeared, Henry walked up to Jake and put a hand on a quaking shoulder.

"You okay, brother?'

Jake didn't respond.

"What'd she mean drunk or sober? Have you been getting it on with her?"

Jake had long hair, so being bent over the rail it completely covered his face; however, the answer was understood as the mangled mess of hair embedded with straw bobbed up and down to indicate, yes.

"Geez! Every guy in school's wanted that, but she's Clyde Barker's one and only. He's threatened to kill anyone that even looks at her wrong. So what'd you do to tick off the biggest whore in town?"

Silence was the only response to the question, a silence broken only by the soft, staccato of a sob choked off. Then a terrible feeling came over Henry as he suddenly realized what might have happened.

"Oh, Jake! I'm sorry," he said, reaching an arm around his brother's shoulders. "Let's go talk to Uncle Marshall."

"No! No one must know!"

"Oh, hell, Sally's big mouth'll have it all over town by morning. Doc Ryan said there could be problems. Come on. Uncle Marshall will know what to do."

Jake stood motionless, eyes glazed, looking pathetic and lost. Leading him back inside, Henry found his clothes and helped dress him like when he lay with a broken leg. Taking his comatose-like brother by the hand, they slipped through the shadows around to the far end of the campground. The party was just beginning so they were able to go undetected to a particular dome tent on the fringe of activity. No one was home.

"Sit here. I'll go find Uncle."

Jake slumped down, pulling his knees up to burying his head on them while Henry headed for the drum. On the way, he passed some Zuni girls standing apart from the dance, watching the boys and comparing notes. Several turned their eyes toward him. The overtures were silent, but obvious. He cursed to himself. Any other guy his age would return the look, walk quietly into the darkness, and see what followed. Expelling a deep breath, he continued on, finding Uncle Marshall seated in his favorite spot near the drum where he could watch the dancers. Henry knelt behind him and whispered at some length into his ear.

In the meantime, Uncle Marshall's wife, Naoma, found Jake curled up by their tent. He scrambled to stand, but his head spun causing him to sway like a tall Lodgepole in a high wind. He'd had less than half a bottle of beer, but that was enough. It never agreed with him despite trying to adapt over the past couple months. He grabbed a tall pole stuck in the ground from which Uncle Marshall had hung a talisman to keep from falling down.

"It's been a long time since you visited," she said, her words crisp with reproving sarcasm. "Only time you or that nephew of ours visit is when one of you need medicine. What is it this time?"

Jake hung his head, saying nothing. She sniffed his breath.

"Too much liquor? Your stomach hurt from too many tacos? You don't appear to have been in another fight."

Typically, others practiced the healing arts, leaving the cacique to tend to larger issues, but until replacing the previous Squash Kiva cacique, healing had been his responsibility for many years. During that time, Naoma acted as Uncle's receptionist, screening out the hypochondriacs, but her penetrating eyes caught the pain in Jake's expression even if partially hidden by hair. Stretching forth a wrinkled hand, she gently touched his cheek. At that moment, Henry and Uncle Marshall arrived and quietly explained to her what had happened.

Her voice softening, Naoma said to Jake, "Go inside and put off your clothes, then wrap in a blanket, and come out here. Both of you."

"There's nothing wrong with me," Henry whined.

"You two have traveled the same path for many years. All of a sudden you would let your brother travel this one alone?" she said.

Henry lead Jake inside the large dome tent where they

stripped to their briefs, emerging wrapped in wool blankets. Walking behind the tent, Naoma lead them to a small campfire ring where the two stood while she quickly added more logs to the fire. Presently Uncle Marshall appeared, also encased in a somewhat older and worn blanket.

Moving to a sweat lodge next to the fire ring, Uncle Marshall stood before the door. Naoma came from behind and grasped the top of the blanket. When she removed it, he was gone, having passed through the door cover into the lodge. Jake was next, followed by Henry. When all three were inside, she began passing in hot rocks from the fire pit. Henry placed each in the small, ring inside. As the temperature rose, Uncle Marshall sprinkled more water on the rocks. Steam sprung up to begin the purging process.

The silence was broken when Uncle's deep, resonating voice said, "What ails a strong, healthy-looking warrior?"

He knew the answer, but it must come from the afflicted person. Jake kept his head bowed and remained silent. It was not for Henry to answer. Uncle waited patiently until Jake began speaking, the words weak and difficult to hear.

"I . . ., I . . ., I tried to be with a woman tonight. Nothing happened. Nothing does any more."

Uncle Marshall began a chant. Breathing became difficult with the increased volume of steam. Uncle added small bits of herbs to the rocks. As the smoke rose and encircled Jake's head, the edges of the dim shadows that were his brother and Uncle blurred.

"Tell me what has been happening . . . in detail," Uncle Marshall said.

Jake started slowly, halting often until all the sordid details spilled from his lips. "A couple weeks ago I went to a party out by the lake. I don't know why I went. Guess I just wanted to get drunk. I had a beer. It was getting dark, and I had to take a leak so went off a ways in the trees. I just finished and turned to go back when this girl from school came up. Her name's Sally Morton. She didn't say nothin', just gave me the damnedest kiss ever, and then began rubbing her hands all over my body while she kissed me.

"She's really built and sometimes in class I'd dream what it would be like to have sex with her. I think a lot of guys have had that dream. She's, well, loose. I really liked what she was doing and wanted her. Next thing I know she's got me flat on my back with my shorts around my knees. Like I said, nothin' happened. I was kinda drunk and she teased me because of that. Geez! I'd only had half a beer 'cause I really can't handle booze."

Henry silently agreed. When it came to liquor, Jake was pathetic. He was okay sipping one bottle of beer over a long period of time, but if he chug-a-lugged or had more than one his body revolted. But then, he had to watch the stuff, too. There was just something about alcohol and his genetics precluding coexistence.

"So, tonight I see her here. I was just starting my first beer when she coaxes me over to the horse barn and starts all that kissing and pawing again. In no time, she's got me skinned. As much as she tries I just can't do nothin', then I get the heaves. One lousy beer and I get the heaves. What's wrong with me, Uncle Marshall?"

"Yep, he chugged it," Henry thought.

The old man listened intently to the words and heard the desperation in the boy's voice. "You said you wanted her. How did you feel that?"

"It hurt, right here," Jake said, poking a finger into his stomach just below the navel.

"And she touched you."

"Yeah, but I just couldn't get it up. I haven't been able

to since, you know, the accident."

"That's been a while."

Seven months earlier Jake had been working some colts. Familiarity breeds carelessness. He stepped into firing range and a yearling's kick struck him in the groin. Slung over the shoulder, Henry carried his unconscious brother nearly a half mile to the hospital where he lay for several painful days. At the time, Doc Ryan was fearful there might be testicular damage considering the swelling, and warned Jake.

Uncle Marshall sprinkled more herbs on the fire and began to invoke specific spirits with chants before taking up a flute and playing a happy, bouncy tune. Listening to the music, Jake felt as if another had entered the lodge and was gently stroking the back of his head. By closing his eyes, he could envision the visitor, a tall, lean figure dressed in a kilt, holding a flute this time, not playing it as he usually did when visiting. Kokopelli had come.

Jake felt Kokopelli's fingers run down his spine. When it reached the small of his back, a warm glow entered his body, centering behind the naval and radiating to the tip of his toes then upward. When it reached his head, it felt as if he was floating off the ground. Opening his eyes to be sure he was still glued to the earth, the vision vanished, but not the warm sensation.

After a time the three went outside. Instead of Naoma there were three, metal buckets of water from the nearby lake. Stepping off to the side, Uncle Marshall hefted one bucket and slowly poured water over Jake's head and another over Henry. After the heat of the lodge, the night air felt cold, the water like ice recently imported from Antarctica. Henry reciprocated and poured water over Uncle Marshall. Returning to the tent, they toweled off and dressed.

Clothed, Uncle Marshall's last instruction was, "Take this powder before going to sleep and come back tomorrow."

As instructed, Jake returned late the following morning. The old man was sitting on a Cottonwood bolt whittling a piece of wood. Saying nothing, he folded the knife, slipped it into a sheath on his hip, and stuck the small carving in his front shirt pocket. Remaining silent, he handed Jake a fishing pole and started walking down to the lake. There, beneath an old, ragged Cottonwood they watched their bobbers float on the glassy surface of the water and talked. Mostly Uncle Marshall talked and Jake listened.

"See that rabbit over there? It takes a mate whenever the opportunity presents itself then moves on. On the other hand, the dove finds a mate and they are together for life. In the winter, the rabbit has only itself to keep warm. He is cold, but the doves snuggle together and help keep one another warm. Man is to be like the doves. He looks for a mate and when each knows it is right their hearts unite as one."

"Doesn't the Great Spirit expect us to have children?" Jake asked.

"He expects all his creations to multiply and replenish the earth . . . when it is right."

"And how can I do that? I'm a cripple."

"You took the powder last night?"

"Yes."

"And you slept?"

"Yes."

"Did you dream?" There was a faint smile in the old man's eyes.

"Yes," Jake said, hesitating. "I dreamed I was lying on a bed, beneath sheets. There was a woman beside me. She was a White woman with long, reddish brown hair. We were both naked. I think we just had sex. I felt warm in my chest and my body felt as if floating in the air. Kokopelli was sitting on top of a dresser near the bed, playing his flute. When I awoke I had . . . What'd you give me?"

"When men get old, many times they are unable to act like the stallion they were when young. The powder I gave you helps them revisit their youth. There is nothing wrong with you."

"Then why can't I get it on with that girl?"

"Man has four sacred obligations, White Bear—to develop a strong body, a clear mind, and a pure spirit with a devotion to the wellbeing of The People. You try too much, White Bear. You try to drink like the others. You try to be like the rabbit. You're companion spirit knows it is not right and tells you it is not time. Count that a blessing. Listen to your spirit, not what others try to put into your mind."

Several days after that incident, Jake and Henry went to the movie house. About to enter, they encountered Sally Morton and Clyde Barker coming out. Sally was wearing dark glasses, but they didn't hide the discoloration around her left eye. The four stood facing each other. Barker's face turned crimson. He obviously had been drinking giving him the backbone to engage his big mouth.

"Morton's mine, half-breed. I ever catch you alone with her, you bastard, I'll cut your useless balls off and shove them down your throat."

Henry's hand snapped like a Mojave green rattlesnake's strike as he grabbed the town bully by the shirt and jerked him nose to nose.

"You scumbag. *Toowhdydeh!*"

Jake winced. His brother just unleashed a seriously derisive insult in Tewa.

"You only got guts for beating up women and little kids. How about doing something now 'cause I'm in the mood to hang your slimy scalp from my belt."

Barker had no stomach to take on Henry even with his usual entourage of wanna-be misfits in tow. Once had been enough, then a year ago some big city bikers passed through town looking for trouble and found it. Henry took their pro wrestler-like enforcer and methodically dismantled him until he was a pile of rubbish. When a couple of buddies stepped in, Jake laid two out with one hit each and mauled another. A dozen Indian friends held the rest at bay. Henry had a temper more dangerous than a powder keg next to a sparkler. Normally passive, Jake was unpredictable and could be even more volatile. It didn't take much to ignite a super nova. Barker was scared of them.

"I ain't got a fight with you. Lemme go," Barker whined, trying to wiggle free from Henry's one-handed grip.

"Morton ain't no one's property. Don't you ever think otherwise." Henry's voice was low with a contemptuous rumble as he pushed Barker backward against the brick, movie house wall ready to unleash a clenched fist.

Jake touched his friend's arm lightly, a signal to calm down. Sally Morton tried to come between the two.

"Please, Henry, don't. I'm sorry. Please, let him alone. He didn't mean anything. He's just had a bad day."

"You'll think bad day, Whitie. I see any more bruises on her, I'll come after you and make Geronimo's war look like a church picnic," Henry said. Barker clearly understood that was no idle threat.

Several months later, the two brothers stopped at the 7-Eleven on the edge of town after returning from Albuquerque. Henry had an irrepressible sweet tooth. He liked Snickers. Sally Morton was there filling her mom's car with gas. Continuing to avoid her, Jake took the trail across the highway that lead to the Forest Service compound leaving Henry and Morton to talk.

₪

Incident at Beaver Creek

Chapter
24

As Jake sat at the kitchen table sipping a steaming cup of hot chocolate, Katelyn softly hummed an Irish tune while frying up a mess of bacon. The hickory aroma started his stomach to rumble in anticipation. It was Wednesday, the beginning of his weekend, but his eyes kept wondering toward the door to his office.

"Henry's hit a growth spurt. His socks are showing when he wears his Sunday trousers," she said. "The girls could use new dresses, too, and the collar on your white shirt is getting frayed."

"It's okay," Jake said.

"I'll not have my husband going to church or court looking like a bum."

"I wear my uniform to court."

"And a couple of those could be replaced. It's been

two years since you had a new uniform."

"That long?"

"I asked Patti at the office to order you a couple new sets. Heavens knows you have enough in your allowance."

"Thanks," he said his mind really not on the conversation.

Glancing over, Katelyn saw him staring at the door to the office. Taking a day off from work was always mentally difficult, not because he didn't have competent help. There was just so much to do. The murder investigations only added to the workload and frustration.

"I also ordered a box of polkadot shorts for you to wear in court, too."

"Thank you."

"Jake!"

"What?"

"Get you mind off work this instant. This is our weekend."

"Sorry. There's just so much . . ."

"And it will be there when we get back from town tomorrow."

There was a soft, rustling noise at the kitchen, screen door. A moment later Runs Fast was standing barefooted on the inside carpet having removed his moccasins so not to track dirt into Katelyn's kitchen.

"Hungry?" she asked, swiping an errant curl dangling over one eye.

With a huge grin, he said, "Yes."

"Didn't know a growing boy who wasn't. Where are the other two?"

"Sleeping."

"Well, wash up and sit down."

Unaccustomed to using western table service at first, Runs Fast quickly mastered their use with the boy's help.

He could now shovel food into his mouth almost as fast as she filled the plate, secretly amazed at how much he put away, but did like seeing someone enjoy her cooking.

"I will return to my village while you are gone," he said.

"We'll be back tomorrow . . . late," Katelyn said before Jake could commit to returning sooner.

Jake's main problem was that he wasn't looking forward to following Katelyn like a leashed puppy as she methodically sorted through the sale racks.

~ ~ ~ ~

Stepping from the Sear's store, Jake looked up at Sandia Mountain and took in a deep breath of air, feeling freed despite the burden of packages. The next stop was a Subway and then off to the park.

More resigned to taking a day off now that they were totally away from any association with work, Jake played with the children, chasing, climbing, swinging as if a child again. Katelyn's loud whistle was the signal to pack up and head for the theater and *Honey, I Blew Up the Kid*. Following the movie with several buckets of popcorn came more shopping before picking up Grandma Bershinsky and going to a nice restaurant for dinner.

They stayed the night at her home as usual. Despite the opportunity, he couldn't sleep in. Neither could his mother, both conditioned to rising early. This gave them the rare opportunity to sit at the kitchen table sipping hot chocolate and talk privately. Naturally, she'd heard of the death of Toleshnec's grandson and inquired of him. If awake, Katelyn probably would not have allowed the conversation, she was that jealous to see her husband rest from work once in a while.

"I feel so bad for Toleshnec," Samantha said.

"You two had a thing for one another, didn't you?" This was the first time he broached the subject.

She didn't answer right away; instead, her eyes seemed to glaze over, obviously thinking back in time. Finally, she answered. "In a way, but he had his career and I had mine."

"Dad wasn't Californios, was he?"

She stared at him silently for a long moment. "No. That's what your father's foster parents came up with."

"Foster parents?"

She had never discussed Jake's heritage with him. After what happened, it didn't seem that important. She took a deep breath and let it out slowly. "Your father was adopted through welfare. His step-grandfather had prejudices against Native Americans, so they told everyone his family was original Californians, Spanish dons, and that's how they raised him. When Niles' stepfather passed away shortly after we were married, his stepmother told him the truth that he was Native American, but didn't know what tribe. Abandoned in Phoenix, they guessed he was from one of the local tribes, but with so many, there was no way to know which one. He planned to track down his parents or at least where he truly came from, but a drunk driver ended that."

"How come you never said anything?"

"I was going to tell you when you got older and would understand. Strange how things worked out. With him gone, I was totally lost. I had no idea what to do, but that night I had a dream. You and I were sitting by your father's grave when he walked up and sat with us. He took my hand and told me everything was going to be all right, but I should go to school to become a forester, and accept a job near Taylorsville. His family and mine pressured me to move closer to them, but I trusted Niles completely. Of course, if I had told anyone that story I would have been locked up.

"The man who owned the company where Niles and I worked came by early the morning after the accident and literally took charge. He made the funeral arrangements, put up a reward to catch the driver, and arranged for a lawyer to negotiate a generous settlement with the driver's family. The kid was underage from a prominent family. That allowed me to attend college, then some."

"A woman forester in those days? That must have been rough."

"Hazing and prejudice? You bet. I was invading a male bastion. They just never dealt with a Kansas farm kid." They laughed. "I didn't understand at the time why your father was so specific about Taylorsville until we moved there and almost immediately you met Henry. Your heart found its home, and I knew everything was going to be just fine."

"I remember the first time I met Grandfather Riley he held my face in his hands and smiled, then kissed my forehead, and said welcome home. I thought he was just dear old man who was super friendly."

"He knew you were Pueblo just by looking into your eyes. He could see more than normal men."

"Did he know my parents?"

"I think he had a strong suspicion, but he asked Toleshnec to help me with the welfare folk. They weren't going to reveal anything about your father until he leaned on them. Your uncle has a way of doing that. They didn't have a clue to who his parents were. They found him in a hospital waiting room. I'm sorry for never telling you. I guess I just felt that your spirit had come home and that was all that was important."

Jake reached out to hold his mother's hands. "It all

worked out. I really couldn't have been luckier. I remember little things about father, but wish I could remember what he looked like."

"Funny you should say that. We didn't have a Brownie so I never had a picture of him to show you, but last week I received a letter in the mail from the man who helped me after your father died. He and his wife have kept in touch, mostly Christmas cards." She stepped to the kitchen counter to retrieve an envelope and handed a photo to Jake. "His wife found this while going thru an old album."

Jake stared at the black and white as his heart nearly stopped.

"What's wrong, Jake?"

"This is my father?"

"Yes. It was taken at a company party about a month before . . ."

"Now, I understand. In my vision, a bear changed into a man. This man. He was dressed exactly like this, too."

"Your father loved us beyond words. I shouldn't be surprised."

"He's my Kachina. Now I understand why someone from the spirit world always seems ready to help me."

Jake and the boys worked in the yard, and repaired a couple things in the house that morning until called in to face a heaping platter of Samantha's fried chicken for lunch. No matter how carefully Katelyn followed directions, she just couldn't seem to capture that same taste. Of course, the three menfolk made pigs of themselves with extra helpings of chicken, Colcannon potatoes, and Reno green beans. That was Jakes personal favorite vegetable, a mixture of French-cut green beans, asparagus, onions, and Portobello mushrooms simmered in real butter. The creator, Chef William, fixed the dish special when Katelyn and Jake were on their honeymoon in Reno, Nevada.

By late afternoon, the little ones napped as the older boys became engrossed in a VHS, providing time for grocery shopping, another burden for Jake. Pushing a shopping cart down the narrow isles reminded him of driving the 236 during rush hour between Annandale, where his family lived and work at the Pentagon, marginally patient and hopelessly jammed.

The evening shadows had devoured their mountain home by the time the van pulled into the yard. Runs Fast rode up as the last of the groceries were put away. Now came the time Jake liked most, adjourning to the lake to sit by a small campfire and enjoy S'mores—something the young Pueblo took a definite liking to. Carrie joined them a half hour later.

"Chief Herbert called for you on the radio this morning," she said. Jake hadn't looked at the telephone messages, not ready to ruin a good weekend. "I told him you wouldn't likely be back until late. Said it could wait. Call him in the morning." She sat next to Runs Fast to join the S'mores assembly line.

Peter brought down his guitar so they could sing a few songs while gathered around the small, golden fire, which seemed to crackle in rhythm. After a time, Katelyn took the girls back to the house for bed while they could still walk. By nine, Jake watched the heads of his two oldest beginning to nod and shuttled them off to the house, leaving the two young people sitting by the glowing embers, talking.

Jake was on the phone to Ken by six and on the road to Taylorsville by seven-thirty with Toleshnec's unusually sleepy-eyed grandson seated in the truck cab. He still had no idea what Ken had on his mind except for both to bring their horses. The Chief flashed a big grin as the two entered his office. Jake guessed there had been a break in the case.

"I had hoped my story about Little Beaver's spirit

looking for the stolen things might get some results, but when nothing happened, I figured it hadn't worked. Then someone left a present on our doorstep the other night," Ken said, opening a bottom drawer of his desk. "Thought you would want these, Runs Fast."

He pulled out a pair of moccasins and an obsidian knife and laid them in the middle of the desk. Runs Fast slowly stretched out his hand to touch the moccasins then jerked it back before making contact.

"Are those your brother's moccasins?' Jake asked.

"Yes. And the knife."

"When I went to leave the other night there was a paper grocery sack on the hood of my car. These were inside. I grabbed a quick bite to eat and drove straight to the crime lab in Albuquerque. They confirmed that traces of blood on the knife belong to your brother. Whoever had it wiped any prints clean. The bag is another story. All sorts of fingerprints."

Ken reached into the drawer again and pulled out a vanilla file folder, pushing it across the desk. Jake opened it. It was an arrest record and picture.

"Wallace Humphreys?" Jake said.

"Sioux Nation, Pine Ridge, South Dakota. Works for the Mountain Home Timber Company over your way. I made a discreet inquiry. He's a sawyer on the Saw Mill Lake sale."

Jake stood up. Runs Fast continued to stare at the moccasins. "I'll have a word with this Humphreys, but we need to take care of this, first." Jake picked up the dead boy's things.

"That's why I said to bring your horses. Oh, there's something else." Ken again reached into his desk drawer to pull out the feather of a Golden Eagle and handed it to Jake. A single tear sprung from Runs Fast's eye to trickle down his smooth cheek.

"Thank you Chief Burning Arrow," the young man said, his voice cracking with emotion. He started to reach for the feather, again checking himself inches from contact.

"The blanket was not returned," Ken said as he accompanied the two men outside.

Arriving at the trailhead leading to Toleshnec's camp, the two saddled up and rode into the forest. This time Jake remained in uniform. A group of boys working horses near the Aspens first spotted the two emerging from the trees. One of the older boys swung astride his mount and raced into camp. Toleshnec was standing in front of his home as they approached. Stepping out of the saddle, one of Runs Fast's cousins held Mohf's reins as Jake stepped up to the old warrior.

"I have good news," Jake said.

"White Bear has found those who killed my grandson?"

"Not yet. We're getting close. Burning Arrow recovered Small Beaver's moccasins and knife."

"Small Beaver has a feather," Runs Fast quickly added.

A sudden flash of relief flickered in the old man's dark eyes. The boy would have a spirit companion. Jake hoped it was mature enough to keep Small Beaver and Henry in check.

"Let us prepare ourselves to return these to my grandson," he said.

"Would my uncle have something I could change into," Jake asked, knowing what was about to transpire might not make him welcome in civilized society, and Katelyn might not be too receptive that he burned a new uniform. Runs Fast was quick to respond, gathering up a shirt, trousers, belt, kilt, moccasins, and headband.

Once changed, Jake and Toleshnec sat as they had the

first time, across a fire from one another, except this time in the kiva. Toleshnec began singing, a mournful prayer. After a time they went to where the body lay in the cave. Unwrapping the decomposing body was not a pleasant task, yet Jake felt a sense of peace as he slipped the moccasins on the boy's feet, and placed the knife in the empty sheath. Reverently, he attached the feather to Little Beaver's headband and re-positioned the head so that it would always face the rising sun.

~ ~ ~ ~

Again, the procession took a torturous route back to the village so Little Beaver's spirit would get confused if it tried to follow. Arriving at the village Jake cleansed both ceremonially and with a visit to a sweat lodge to expel the last visages of death's smell embedded in his nostrils.

Once seated in Toleshnec's home, he was asked the burning question. "You have a suspect?"

"I have someone to talk to," Jake said. "Did Grandfather Riley know my real parents?"

The chief was startled by the sudden shift in the conversation and by this question in particular. There was a moment of silence before answering, "Yes, but father was not positive until after we learned things from the welfare people."

"Were they Antigua?"

"Your grandmother was white."

"Then my grandfather?"

"Yes."

"Can you tell me about him?"

Toleshnec was silent. Finally, he said, "I will not speak of one who cannot defend himself."

"Why was my father abandoned?"

"Your grandfather went to live with your grand-mother's people. In those days, it was difficult for a Native American to integrate into White society. A friend in the Phoenix Sheriff's Office helped me find arrest records. Your grandfather . . . he was killed in a car accident."

"Drunk?" Jake didn't need an answer, the old man's eyes spoke. "It would seem I am plagued by drunk drivers."

"We can only guess, but we think your father was born shortly after his father died. She left him at a hospital. We do not know what happened to her after that. She disappeared even to her own family. The welfare people took your father and placed him with White people."

"The Pueblo didn't want a half-breed?"

"If we had known, he would have been accepted among the Antigua as a son and cared for. The child was not known to us, and the welfare people conveniently did not mention it." A hint of bitterness edged the comment. "When my father, Charging Buffalo, saw Antigua in your eyes, he spoke discussed this with your mother. She and I approached the welfare people and learned what happened. Their records said, 'Abandoned by person or persons unknown.' They always take the easiest way out.

"Charging Buffalo felt certain you came from a family that no longer exists. Neither does their clan. It was because of the mark on your shoulder, the one you covered over with that tattoo. The elders decided to adopt you into the Raven Clan. My sister pushed that over some objections from the Corn Clan. As you know, she can be very persuasive. So, the lost was found and your spirit had returned home."

Jake thought on what he had learned and silently shook his head in agreement, then turning to Runs Fast, asked, "Are you returning with me?"

"I will stay with my family for a time."

"My sons will miss their big brother. Maybe another?"

Runs Fast didn't answer, but flashed a worried glance toward his father. It was not noticed except by Toleshnec.

Jake returned to Arroyo Station well past dinner and immediately put in a call to his boss' cell phone. "Chief Herbert recovered the murder weapon and got the State lab to lift some prints. I'll head over to the Mill Creek sale in the morning to talk to the suspect. Name's Wallace Humphreys, a sawyer for Mountain Home."

"No good, Jake. Sorry to tell you, but you won't be able to talk to him. There was an accident while you were gone. A deck of logs Humphreys was working next to broke loose. He was crushed to death. Elam drove over from the Kachina District to help with the investigation since you weren't available. The Sheriff's office moved in and sent him packing so I don't have many details. When Chief Herbert called to tell me what he had found, I passed the info on to Davidson at NCIS. He'll be here by morning. Humphreys' death sure seems to be a coincidence, or maybe I'm just getting paranoid in my old age, but something smells bad in the timber business over your way."

Jake slumped deeper into the old, swivel, desk chair. Katelyn recognized the signs of disappointment and came to rub his shoulders. The next morning he called Pinchott's office to discuss obtaining a search warrant for Humphrey's lodging.

"Agents Davidson and Hayes were camped on my door when I got here. They have a copy of Elam's report, such as it is. I want to see of the Sheriff's report."

"Don't expect much," Jake said.

"How's that?"

"Barker owns the mill that hired Humphreys."

"OSHA will conduct their own investigation."

"Seen that routine before. Mountain Home had some incidents a couple years back, clearly OSHA violations. Got a token fine. A couple thousand dollars. Anywhere else, it would have been a lot more. Five months later a tree faller died when a tree barber chaired. Those things can happen, but I noted some serious safety violations. Nothing happened. Nothing. Nothing ever happens. Barker married into the political system," Jake said. "I expect him to throw all sorts of interference in our way."

"Do you suspect he's involved in these murders?"

Jake was silent for a moment. "I've got nothing against Barker except an old grudge from when we were kids. Actually, he has the grudge. My brother and I caused him all kinds of grief while we were growing up. I don't think he's forgotten."

"Tell you what, I'll see to it he's too busy to notice what you guys are up to until after the fact. The State Police should legitimately investigate this because of his conflict of interest. Now that I think of it, his department is afoul of jail certification requirements. He also has a lawsuit pending from an inmate. I'll put my ladle in the pot and see if I can stir things up. A phone call to OSHA in Washington should prompt the assignment of a different investigator. Even if he plays the political card that should be enough smoke screen for you to nose around underneath."

"Remind me not to get crosswise of you. How about a search warrant for Humphrey's lodging?

"Davidson has it in hand and a radio. They are headed your way."

"I'll radio them to meet me at the mill."

₪

Incident at Beaver Creek

Chapter
25

Jake met Davidson and Hayes in a campground just off state highway 41 a mile north of the tiny logging community of Mountain Home where the sawmill was located. Reading over Elam's report, he winced.

". . . the victim was working next to a log deck when three pieces apparently came loose, knocking him to the ground, and rolling over the body. Death was instantaneous."

"I guess so," Jake mumbled out loud. Each log would have weighed in the neighborhood of 1,500 pounds. Looking up from the report he said to the agents, "Had breakfast?"

"Grabbed some fast food before driving up."

"Then how about some Tums?"

Davidson flicked his eyebrows in agreement. Hayes

quietly belched. They spent the next hour discussing the case over a thermos of peppermint-spiked hot chocolate and fresh cinnamon rolls from Katelyn's oven.

"After we take a look at Humphrey's cabin, I want to head over to the logging site and interview Humphrey's co-workers. Doubt we'll get much."

"Why's that?" Hayes asked.

"Loggers tend to be tight-lipped around us. Don't have much use for Forest Service people, especially Forest cops."

Humphrey's room was at the end of a long series of one-room apartments fashioned like a one-story motel, part of the company's crew quarters. Opening the door, Jake took one-step inside and stopped.

"Something wrong?" Hayes said, standing off his left shoulder.

"Just getting an overall picture of the room in mind before starting out. Either Humphreys was a total slob, or someone else has rifled through here."

Armed with the search warrant, they began a methodical search of the decease's overturned room. There was nothing useful for a lead until Jake checked the man's cowboy boots setting innocently in a corner next to a bedside table. They had a standard, low heel, but he tipped them over to look anyway. A tightly folded piece of paper fell out of the left boot. Opening it, Jake stared at a series of numbers and symbols, the others looking over his shoulder.

"Lottery numbers?" Hayes asked.

Jake shook his head from side to side before refolding the paper and sticking it in his shirt pocket and resume the search. There was a small table stuck in one corner of the room where porn magazine apparently had been stacked, but were now scattered on the floor. Opening the small drawer, he pulled out a well-used compass. Holding it in one hand, he retrieved the folded paper.

"I think this compass is a clue," Jake said. "These numbers could be coordinates and distances."

"Okay," Donaldson said, sounding skeptical. "Where does it start?"

"This first series looks a lot like latitude and longitude. I've got topographic maps in my truck. Opening a small-scale map that covered a large area, he quickly zeroed in on the beginning spot. "Right here in Mountain Home."

"So what's that funny thing at the end of the numbers?" Hayes asked.

Jake stepped outside and walked around to the back, obviously looking for something. "I'm guessing this symbol represents the starting point," he said, referring to a rectangle setting on its small end with a ragged top.

The long, bunkhouse-style structure gave way to ever increasingly dense forest. Twenty feet behind Humphreys' room was the stump of an old tree, broken off hip high. They looked at each other and smiled.

"Which number is the compass heading?" Hayes asked.

"150 degrees would put us in those piles of timbers. 285 degrees heads toward the forest," Jake said.

Using Humphrey's compass, Jake took a bearing of 285 degrees and stepped off 150 paces. At the end of the code was a half-round symbol. Jake looked around. Two feet to the right, a rounded rock about eighteen inches in diameter lay buried in the ground. The next entry lead them 305 paces on a course of 265 degrees and deep into the forest. There were three more sets of directions. Each time they found something that matched the symbol. Their excitement grew.

"This is the symbol for a survey marker," Jake said

about the picture at the end of the second to last line.

Straight ahead was a tree bearing a small, weathered, yellow sign noting a section corner. The last bearing took them down to the north fork of the White Tail. At the end was another vertical rectangle with ragged top. Ten yards up from the bank, they spotted the charred remains of a tree. Humphreys had placed a small "X" inside this rectangle at the bottom. A fire had hollowed out the eight-foot spear creating a cozy home for a ground squirrel. Jake knelt, reached in with a gloved hand, and extracted a pot of gold—a plastic coffee can containing $10,000 in hundred dollar bills, and a savings account book showing $170,000 on deposit. There was also another slip of paper—a signed I.O.U.

True to his word, Pinchott had the Sheriff's Office tied in knots that morning; however, someone obviously made a phone call alerting him that Jake was nosing around Mountain Home. Unbeknown to the sheriff, the US Attorney had the Marshall's office acquire a listing of all his "private" radio channels, which Forest radio tech McAfee programed into a hand-held scanner. That was on Hayes' belt.

Within fifteen minutes of beginning the search, they heard the call to Deputy Putnam sending him to Mountain Home. However, from where Putnam was in the county, it would take over an hour to arrive, even at the excessive way he drove. That was more than enough time for the search. When the deputy roared into the small community, red lights, and sirens as usual, Jake smiled and waved as they drove out.

That was the day from hell for Barker's Office. Putnam no sooner arrived at Mountain Home than he had to hustle back to town to answer questions by an investigator from the State Attorney General's office concerning the lawsuits.

From the direction Jake and the Navy investigators took upon leaving the logging camp, Putnam could see they were head for the logging site, and unable to do anything about it. The Sheriff dispatched a different deputy. Not seeing the need for an emergency response, he took longer to arrive, pulling into the area as Davidson and Hayes finished questioning the equipment operators working in the area of the deck where Humphreys died.

"Hi," Deputy Bradley said as he walked up to where Jake was chatting with two investigators from OSHA. "Sheriff Barker wants me to stick my nose in to find out what you're doing up here."

Frank Bradley was in his mid-thirties, ex-military police, and not as dumb as Barker thought. Jake and he had meet several times informally and struck a cordial friendship. Stepping aside, they talked privately.

"The OSHA folk are skeptical that this was an accident," Jake said, testing the waters with the relatively new deputy.

"Putnam conducted the investigation. Concluded it was an accident, in his words, "Pure and simple." Bradley made a fair imitation of Putnam's high, nasal voice. Jake had to wipe his nose to hide a giggle. "The man's an idiot. Wouldn't recognize a homicide if it happened in front of him." Anyone with common sense saw Putnam for the fraud he was. Bradley kept glancing in the direction of the NCIS agents.

"Humphreys was a prime suspect in a murder investigation."

"The guys you pulled out of the river?"

"Maybe. For now, we're focusing on Chief Toleshnec's grandson, but there may be a tie in there. Some items stolen from the murdered boy turned up in a grocery sack with Humphreys' fingerprints all over it. He had a partner.

Someone wearing dogger-heel boots."

"You think the partner iced him because he was getting cold feet?"

Jake silently nodded his head, yes.

"Any way I can help?"

"I'm going to pay the Mountain Home tavern a visit this evening. Can you arrange to be there? Just between the four of us?"

"I can do that. Sure."

After parting, Jake listened to Bradley's report on one of the Sheriff's private channels. "Ranger Bershinsky is talking to the OSHA folk to see what they found out. He's completing some routine paperwork about the accident."

That evening Jake walked through the front door of the Mountain Home tavern and into a dimly lit, smoke-filled room smelling of stale beer and body odor. Davidson and Hayes had arrived twenty minutes earlier taking a table off to one side to eat dinner where they could see the entire room. Jake smiled inwardly. Between himself, Muir, and Dale, they had been able to find enough old clothes so that the agents looked like a couple of fishermen at the end of a long day. Dale had the most fun erasing Marine from Hayes' posture, but managed. Muir went so far as to produce a fish to give them the appropriate aroma. Jake didn't ask how he had come up with the meal-size trout that appeared headed for their cabin when they finished with the disguises. Jake was dressed in civilian clothes to reduce any visual tension that a uniform would create.

Most of the dozen or so men in the bar were talking or watching a baseball game on the television when Jake walked in and went to the back end of the bar to chat with the owner. Known to stop occasionally for a soda, they paid him little notice. Three men seated at a center table did, frequently turning their heads slightly to glimpse what he was doing. Sipping a Diet Coke while talking to the owner, Jake's eyes moved from one patron to the next. The three who had noted his entry tried to resume their conversation, but one in particular couldn't seem to keep from glancing up to see what the Ranger was doing.

As if on cue, Deputy Bradley walked into the bar. Everyone noted his arrival. Jake set his half-full glass down and moved to where the three men were seated.

"Hi," Jake said, sounding casual. The men looked up. The room fell silent as all eyes were now on the ranger. "What's your name?" he said to one of the three in particular, a large hulk with two braids who had trouble keeping his eyes off Jake.

The man glanced at his table friends, then at the deputy, and grinned.

"What's it to ya?"

"I just like to know the name of the man with dogger heeled boots I'm asking to step outside. I've got some questions regarding a couple incidents that have happened in these parts recently."

"Ain't interested in no conversations."

"That may have sounded like a polite invitation, but it wasn't, Fulton," Bradley said, approaching the table.

"Whose side you on, deputy?"

"Stand up."

Bradley knew Red Wing as a brawler who used his 300 plus pounds of muscle on more than one occasion to put people in the hospital and himself in jail. The Sioux slid his chair back slowly and stood, a big smile creasing his pock-marked face. Jake saw him wink at his buddies just before clenching a right paw. So did Bradley who slipped a nightstick out of its ring with incredible speed to deflect the swing with a stinging block. Tables and chairs overturned as the other loggers cleared the playing field. The behemoth immediately found himself in a chokehold, but unfortunately, Bradley's 190 pounds was no match for the bigger man who threw him aside as if a spent matchstick, and then turned to come face to face with the Ranger.

Loggers perpetuate an animosity toward the Forest Service who repeatedly reined in their attempts to circumnavigate rules. Red Wing was no exception. Jake deflected his roundhouse swing, countering with a straight-arm punch to the diaphragm losing the stale stench of beer. The next thing Red Wing or anyone else knew all 300 pounds lifted into the air. When it slammed on the wood floor, the deafening roar sounded like a dynamite blast. In that instant, Bradley and Jake were on his back applying double-cuffs.

The two who had been sitting with Red Wing thought to aid their friend while he was down. One went as far as grab a beer bottle to use in club fashion. Davidson stepped close, slid a hand along his belt to draw his coattail back revealing a gold badge while resting a hand on the butt of a firearm.

"Want to join your friend?" Davidson said. The man quickly changed his mind and dropped the bottle.

"Geez, Fulton, you have got to be the most stupid idiot on the planet. Assaulting a deputy . . . and a Federal officer? Let's go," Bradley said.

The two officers helped a dazed Red Wing up, but while escorted out of the bar he managed another grin and said, "See you boys in the morning."

Outside in the cool, fresh air they met two men in a white SUV with government plates.

"Fulton Red Wing, you are under arrest for assaulting a Federal officer," Jake said. "Sounds like you've been here before, but just to refresh your memory, you have the right to remain silent. You have the right to an attorney before answering any questions. If you cannot afford an attorney, you can petition the courts to appoint one. Do you understand these rights?"

"Yeah, yeah. I ain't answerin' no questions. Go screw yourself. I'll be headin' back here before you walk out of the jail."

"These gentlemen are from the US Marshal's office. You're going to a different facility this time. Don't count on getting back to work any time soon."

As Jake followed the Marshals to town, he listened as Bradley reported to his office. "Fulton Red Wing tried to assault Ranger Bershinsky."

"Did he get a piece of him?" Jake clearly recognized Barker's voice. He sounded pleased, obviously picturing a lopsided fight.

"Yeah. Bershinsky laid him out pretty good. US Marshals are transporting Red Wing to town now."

"Why didn't you stop him?" Barker fired back.

"I used my nightstick to put him in a choke hold, but Red Wing threw me off."

"You were supposed to stop Bershinsky you idiot!"

"Oh."

₪

Incident at Beaver Creek

Chapter
26

Red Wing, a Pine Ridge Sioux like Humphreys, began waging war on the world with the onset of puberty. For his twelfth birthday, he got drunk on his butt and picked three fights that night. Big for his age, he only lost one of those. Actually, it was a draw, but to his notion, anything short of winning was a loss. Seated alone in a small interrogation room he kept mentally rehearsing how a puny Forest ranger could put him down, not only down, but so quickly. He had hardly started drinking, really drinking, so was sober. It was still a blur. When Davidson entered the interrogation room Red Wing snorted. He'd been here before and outlasted the best cops at the interrogation game. He was in for another surprise.

Jake attended a Federal Enforcement course several years earlier covering interview techniques, read several books, and attended mini-refresher classes, but really had little need for hardcore tactics. That's where Davidson picked up the ball. Jake watched through the one-way glass and listened closely. Some of what the agent did was interesting and borderline legal. Red Wing initially denied any association with Humphreys other than working with him and an occasional beer, however recanted when Davidson produced the I.O.U. bearing his name. When Pinchott arrived at eight that morning the evidence was still too meager to charge him with anyone's murder.

"The guy's a pathological liar. He shifts from one story to another like an Olympic slalom skier without blinking an eye. He wouldn't recognize the truth if it was a train about to run him down," Hayes said, coming out of the room. "I can tell you one thing; he displays some classic indicators of a psychopath. This guy is scary."

"I'd like a search warrant for Red Wing's cabin," Jake said to the attorney.

"Can't be carte blanch. What are you looking for?"

"The victim's blanket for starters and a .243 caliber rifle."

"That should appease the Magistrate. I'll have my secretary draw one up. He's is in a hearing until ten. Go get some breakfast."

"Mr. Pinchott. There's a woman inquiring about posting bail for Fulton," his secretary said after coming into the office and closing the door behind her.

Jake reopened the door just enough to peek outside. What he saw was an older woman, whose double chin sagged and wobbled like a turkey's neck. Dressed in a thrift shop reject dress, she was haggard, unkempt, and dumpy. There had been an attempt to comb the dirty blond hair, with little success. It was a ball of errant frizz as if she had stuck a finger in a light socket. He wondered how someone so obviously dirt poor could come up with bail money.

"I think I've seen her somewhere before, but not sure where," he said after closing the door.

"Her name is Jenkins," the secretary said. The name meant nothing to Jake.

"Tell her the judge hasn't set bail yet. It may be awhile." Then to Jake, Pinchott said, "How much time do you need to execute a warrant?"

"Including travel time, a couple hours."

"I'll talk to the Magistrate. I'm sure he'll wait until his regular court session at two o'clock to arraign this joker. Until you bring me some meat to go with the potatoes, all we've got is assault."

Like Humphreys, Red Wing had a room in a second long bunkhouse across from where Humphreys lived. As before, Jake opened the door and stood barely inside to survey the interior. It was a pigsty, but no one had contributed to the mess by ransacking it. Davidson followed him in while Hayes stood point guard outside. Donaldson might know a thing or two about interrogations, but marveled at the eyes for detail the Ranger had. Fifteen minutes into the search, an approaching siren whistled through the trees.

"Putnam," Jake muttered while turning over the mattress. The pickup's sliding stop and ensuing cloud of white dust confirmed his arrival.

"Here comes Wyatt Earp," Hayes said more than ready to intercept him.

Putnam's cock-of-the-walk strut faltered a moment upon seeing the agent baring his path, arms folded across their chest. Hitching up his gun belt and courage, he walked up to the cabin.

"Hello, Deputy Fife." The insult went over the man's head.

"The name is Deputy Putnam, Fredericks County Chief Deputy Sheriff Bertram Putnam," he said, pointing to his gold nametag with large black lettering. "What's going on here?"

"Police business," Hayes said.

"This is private property."

"Do tell."

"Got a complaint y'all's trespassin' on private property."

Hayes stepped off the porch.

"Do tell, Chief Deputy Sheriff Putnam. This is a Federal investigation," Hayes replied, slapping the search warrant in Putnam's chest. "Read and weep."

Jake and Donaldson snickered quietly while listening to the exchange. Hayes was short compared to Putnam, but the muscling on his chest and arms stretched the tan polo shirt, coupled with a daunting stare, and textbook, Marine attitude stalled Putnam who stammered, read the search warrant, sputtered some more, and tried to crane his long neck around Hayes to see what was going on, but was effectively blocked.

"Now listen here Mr. Federal . . ."

"I don't believe you want to interfere with an official, Federal investigations, so don't trip on the way back to your vehicle. Over . . . and . . . out."

Putnam withdrew to his patrol car and radioed the office. Donaldson turned up the volume on the scanner to listen."

"Sheriff, they got a search warrant for Red Wing's place. What do you want me to do?"

"Pull back and keep an eye on them."

Seconds later the sheriff's main frequency came on. There was a blaring siren. "This is Bradley. I'm in pursuit of a possible DUI west on 41, ten miles east of Mountain

Home. Request backup."

"Putnam, give the kid a hand," Sheriff Barker's voice came back.

"Bring 'em on kid. I'm ready and waitin'."

"They're turning north on Columbine Pass Road."

"You get a license plate?" Barker asked.

"It's mudded over. It's a newer, green, Toyota pickup. Looks to be a couple kids in it."

A long silence ensued while Barker obviously struggled with what to do, until Bradley made the choice for him.

"I hit a wash boarded curve. I'm off the road. They're gone."

"Is the truck alright?"

"No damage, but I'm going to need an assist back on the road."

"It's a four-wheel drive pickup. Use it," Barker snapped.

"I'm dug into soft dirt, Sheriff. The only way it wants to move is down."

"Putnam, help the idiot out."

"What about these Feds?"

"Forget them for now. Get the kid back on the road so he can look for them kids. The truck is probably stolen. Catch up to the Feds later."

With Putnam off their back, the officers took a more leisurely stroll through the cabin. Red Wing didn't have much in the way of personal belongings except a few changes of work clothes—plaid shirts, and jeans. There were a couple items of interest. One item was another pair of cowboy boots with a higher than normal heel. A second was an ax handle leaning against one corner of the tiny, room next to the bed. Examining it in the meager sunlight filtering through the filthy widow, Jake noted dark stains. The last item was a large, Buck hunting knife. They photographed these items in place before placing them into individual, brown paper bags, labeled, and recorded. Hayes carefully rolled the ax handle in a couple of paper, grocery sacks split apart and secured with string. They didn't find the rifle or anything relating to it.

As the trio drove back to town, they listened to Putnam call his office. "I got the kid out. Wasn't stuck that bad. Just doesn't know how to drive a four-wheel."

"That's interesting," Jake thought, remembering that Bradley mentioned during one of their conversations how he and his brothers four-wheeled in the mountains all the time as teenagers." He had a pleasant suspicion he owed the deputy a favor.

.

₪

Incident at Beaver Creek

Chapter
27

Three people influenced Jake's developing years—his mother, Uncle Marshall, and Toleshnec—and the one thing they stressed was to keep things simple. He took that to war and drove both the Viet Cong and his superiors crazy. "It's too simple. It won't work." It did, time and again. During his military career, he lived by that rule, taught it, and carried it over into his work with the Forest Service. It was no surprise that he would simplify the chain of evidence and deliver the items from Fulton's cabin directly to the crime lab in Albuquerque. The lab supervisor agreed. The fewer people to handle evidence, the easier to testify in court. By signing for the articles and logging them in, only he and Jake would have handled the evidence, and only he and Jake would be required to testify about them in court.

Once received, the lab supervisor launched into a close, visual inspection of each item with a hand-held magnifying glass. That was to size up the evidence and decide how best to proceed with the many tests and examination procedures available.

A strange, little man, the top of the supervisor's reddish-brown head barely skimmed Jake's shoulders. Obviously not someone who went outdoors, his skin was a sickly, pale white. Jake initially guessed him to be in the mid-fifties. He wasn't often wrong. He was this time. The man was barely forty-three, a part of Generation Y with traces of earlier times. Large, round, horn-rimmed glasses perched mid-way on a long, slender nose projecting from between bushy eyebrows. A small, round earring dangled from each lobe. Gray etched the hair moussed into spikes that gave him the appearance of a porcupine on the defensive.

As punkish as the man appeared, he was professional and all business. Extracting the blade from the sheath, he eyeballed it while issuing an annoying clucking noise that sounded like, "Tut-tut." The tag on his jacket read, "Tuttleman," but the nickname, "Tut," was a dig at the noise he unconsciously made when in thought and not because of this name. Something he was oblivious to.

After examining the boots, Jake handed him a small box. "Chief Herbert at Taylorsville took a plaster cast of this heel near the crime scene," he said. The supervisor carefully undid the bubble wrap.

"Nice job. I might be able to work with this. Tut-tut." The ax handle seemed of greater interest as he went over it methodically. "Tut-tut. Might be bloodstains on the wood fibers and, tut-tut, something embedded in the crevices. Looks like I'll be running some DNA comparisons. Tut-tut. Can't promise anything at this point."

The more Tuttleman spoke, the more Jake detected remnants of a northeastern accent. Having lived in that area for a while, he guessed Massachusetts.

"This will be the first case I've had DNA done. Never quite understood how that works?"

"Are you familiar with genetic strings?"

"From a science class in college a long time back."

Tuttleman's desire to share knowledge appeared to excite him. "With the PCR-based tests we use, samples don't need to be large, and that's what it appears we have here . . . not much. The process is pretty good at replicating small samples, though. Tut-tut. What happens is that the original is copied, and then copies are made of the copies. Kind of a chain reaction. There can be a problem with the technique, though. Tut-tut, one stray molecule can contaminate the sample and cause a significant error."

"How long will it take?"

"A week. Maybe longer. Depends."

After stopping at Pinchott's office to appraise him of what had transpired and return the search warrant as executed, he called Douglass who met him at a truck stop on the edge of town.

"Had dinner yet?" his boss asked as Jake joined him at a quiet, corner table.

"No."

"I live a half mile from here. It's handy. Don't do that home cooking routine so eat here when in town. The chef salad is the best. At least it isn't fried."

"Wondered how you traveled so much and managed to keep your weight down," Jake quipped.

"Chef Salad and house dressing," he said to the waitress, then to Jake, "You like raspberry vinaigrette? Good. Double up. Coffee?"

"Don't drink it. Diet Coke will be fine."

"We got Pepsi."

"Water will do."

"Picky," Douglass said.

"Must not serve many Native Americans here if all they got is Pepsi."

"Okay, fill me in."

For the next hour, the two discussed the case and consumed the huge salads.

As the two prepared to part company, Douglass said, "I'm heading back to Gallup in the morning. If you need anything give me a call, but it looks like you guys have everything under control. Oh, by the way, from what I hear, you've got Sheriff Barker tied in knots. Well, you and Pinchott. Wish I could be around more to enjoy it."

The children had gone to bed long before he arrived home, but still he visited each one, tucking in blankets, and kissing each on the forehead, all except Henry and Peter camped outside with Runs Fast.

Mid-morning the following day Frank Hererra, Pinchott's assistant prosecutor called as Jake prepared to head into the field for the day.

"Red Wing posted bond despite our argument that he was a flight risk. Unfortunately, the evidence from the cabin is too tentative, and the assault charge isn't that severe. He also had Mountain Home's lawyer."

The young attorney did not say anything directly, but the dislike of his opposing colleague was evident in the tone of his youthful voice."

With no further leads until the crime lab reported back, Jake busied himself trying to finish some reports a bean counter absolutely needed. At mid-afternoon two days later, he was ten miles from Arroyo Station when Curt called to say that the US Attorney wanted to speak with him, ASAP. Tossing the clipboard with data forms on the passenger seat, he hurried home.

"The State Lab called with preliminary results," Hererra said. "They found blood on the knife similar to the second victim from the river. Problem is that Red Wing's got the same blood type. They are running more tests to separate them out better. As for the boots, they really didn't hold out much hope of making a match with your cast. The size and shape are very close, but nothing defining. An interesting development is the ax handle. They discovered skin tissue embedded in the cracks in the wood. They are running DNA on that."

₪

Incident at Beaver Creek

Chapter 28

For a person like Jake who loved the outdoors, the Forest Service was about the best job around. The downside was the constant clamor for reports. He'd rather pull nose hairs than sit in front of a computer screen filling out forms. A reprieve came when Ken, Davidson, and Hayes converged on his office to revisit the evidence and brainstorm their next move.

Absorbed in scouring the evidence they were startled when shortly before noon a cry went up that echoed throughout the old house. "Papa! Papa!" The urgent voice of Jake's youngest daughter, Kathlene, destroyed whatever he had formulated in his mind before reaching the keypad. "Papa!" He was amazed how much noise the four-year-old's small feet made as she roared through the house like a spooked buffalo while screaming as if being chased by her brothers with a garter snake before sliding to a squealing stop next to his chair.

"Indians, daddy! More Indians!" she said.

"Jake," Katelyn called from the living room. "Some Native Americans just rode up to Runs Fast's hut. There appears to be an argument."

The officers nearly collided as they converged on the exit door. At the picnic table near Runs Fast's hut stood the young man, Carrie, Runs Fast's father, several uncles, and someone Jake couldn't believe had left the mountains. Toleshnec stood listening to a heated exchange of words between father and son.

"Is there a problem?" Jake said.

The young man's father rounded on him. "What have you taught my son, to disobey his father?"

"I'm not sure what you're talking about," Jake said trying to cool down the situation by projecting calm.

"He has taught me no such thing," Runs Fast said, his voice raised to match his father. "Grandfather has said we cannot marry the girls of our clan. The blood is too close."

"Yes, marry, but among our people, not the Whites," the father said, trying to be heard in the next ranger district.

"Shouting in anger will resolve nothing and only upset the spirits," Jake said. "Let's sit down and discuss this."

"There is nothing to discuss. He will not marry a White girl, and that is final."

Toleshnec had been quiet during the face-off. Before either could say anything more, the old chief put a hand on each one's shoulder and said quietly, "I believe White Bear's invitation is appropriate."

Runs Fast's father stared at Toleshnec, mouth open as if to say something, but thought better, closing his mouth to just glare.

Jake sat cross-legged on the ground where he stood.

Toleshnec followed suit, as did Runs Fast and Carrie who continued to hold hands tightly. Burning Arrow sat between the father and Jake as the latter dropped roughly as a truculent child might do. The Uncles, Davidson, and Hayes sat, forming a loose circle behind them. Jake had seen the two young people spending more and more time together. He had said nothing. Now he wished he had.

"Do I understand that you two want to marry?" Jake said, cutting straight to the apparent problem.

"Yes," Runs Fast said. His response had the firmness of negating further discussion.

"No," his father said, equally set.

"What has been done so far?" Jake asked Runs Fast.

"I made the bundle of clothes and left them at Carrie's door. She took them."

"Carrie, did you know that the bundle meant a proposal of marriage?"

"No. I knew they came from Runs Fast, but I didn't know what they meant. They are beautiful."

"It is not a proposal," Runs Fast's father said, trying to sound triumphant.

"I showed them to Katelyn the next morning, and she called Mrs. Riley. She explained their meaning and purpose. I wanted them more than ever."

"No," Runs Fast's father shouted. This turn wasn't going his way.

"That you do not want this girl as a daughter because she is White is understandable," Jake said. "Your mind has been prejudiced against Whites by your grandfather because of his dislike for the people of my White half."

Toleshnec's eyes widened with surprise. Being chastised was something he was unaccustomed to, except from his sister, and began thinking that his former student had been too influenced by her.

Jake didn't give him time to respond. "I am against such a union as well."

"Jake Bershinsky, how could you say such a thing?" Katelyn said. She was standing a few feet to one side and behind Agent Hayes.

"This is for the men to decide," Toleshnec said. The last thing he wanted was a woman getting involved, especially in all likelihood someone like his own wife and sister.

"And you'll screw this up just like men screw up everything else in the world when it comes to matters of love. You have forgotten its meaning." Katelyn was undaunted when her Irish became aroused.

"Your woman does not know her place," he said to Jake.

"Does Toleshnec's wife keep quiet about important decisions?" Jake said. "Neither does mine, only she is more public about it. Katelyn, you might as well join us."

"I will not sit in council with a woman," Runs Fast's father said, starting to rise.

"Sit down," was Toleshnec's sharp command, then spoke in Tewa, "I do not want my wife and your wife joining with White Bear's wife as they would surely do. You heard White Bear. He does not agree with this, either."

Jake's smile was imperceptible. His uncle had apparently married someone influenced by the same spirit that Mom Riley had.

As Katelyn settled between her husband and Carrie, Jake began speaking, "I don't agree with these two becoming husband and wife, but not because of one is Pueblo and one is White. It is because of the way each has been raised. Runs Fast grew up as a 16th Century Native American. He cannot read. He cannot write. To provide for his family all he can do is farm and hunt. If he were to move to Carrie's home or even to the pueblo according to custom, the people in this world would make fun of him because they will think he is ignorant. Other than his wife, he would have no friends. He would become bored. He would drink and die young. Carrie grew up in this century. She has no skills for living in your world. She would eventually become frustrated and leave."

The truth of White Bear's words weighed heavy on father and grandfather. Tears began to trickle down Carrie's cheeks. Runs Fast looked devastated.

"I feel pain in my heart," Toleshnec said, breaking a long silence. "I remember the story written by William Shakespeare of a young man and woman who were denied marriage by their fathers. I do not wish to lose another grandson."

"Our house is large enough," Katelyn said. "They could live here with us until he understands how to live in our world. Surely he has useful skills."

"That would undo all that Toleshnec has attempted to do with his people—escape from the Whites," Ken said.

"Perhaps I was wrong." Toleshnec startled everyone with the confession. "I believe my anger with the Whites continues to be founded. To leave and live as my ancestors was right for me, but not my grandsons. I have done them a wrong. I have lost one to murder. I am about to lose another to love. Eventually, I will lose them all as they marry and move to the home of their wife's family. I had not thought of the things White Bear speaks of. They have no future."

"There is always a way. There is always hope," Katelyn said.

"Burning Arrow would speak," Ken said. "There may be a solution to this. White Bear mentioned a few weeks ago of the need for someone to do trail work, and asked if anyone from the pueblo might be interested. Could Runs Fast fill that position?"

"It is a year-round job—patrol, inspection, and maintenance. He'd have to learn to read and write, but yes."

"I can teach him those things. I am to student teach in the Consolidated Pueblo School District, and will have my teaching certificate next spring," Carrie said. "I am sure to find a teaching job in the area."

"Oh, really," Ken said. "This is looking better. Now, where to live. Here at Arroyo, for a while for a short time, but I am thinking of a place between their worlds. The old Miller Resort that burned down has been an eyesore along the highway for years. It is actually on reservation lands. I understand that all the legal stuff has ended and it can now be clean it up. There's about thirty acres between the highway and river. These two could locate there and help restore it back to nature, with a little help, of course. That would put Runs Fast close to his work.

"Now, Toleshnec, let's address your problem. You've been squatting on Federal lands for years. No one has bothered you because of your reputation, and frankly, it would be too much trouble to move you off. Besides, out of sight, out of mind, out of hair. You can stay there, but how do you help your grandsons or their children? Perhaps it is time to come back."

"To die ignorant and full of whiskey and drugs?" Runs Fast's father said.

"Your father made a great impact on how we are treated, and we have new industries to provide employment. I don't lie. Alcohol and drugs are a problem, but I feel we have come a long ways to addressing those issues. I'm thinking of a meadow at the western end of the Sacred Mountain. It's probably three or four hundred acres with a good stream and spring."

"But that would put them on Wilderness lands. I don't think Congress would go for that," Jake said.

"It's not on Wilderness lands. It's reservation land. I have studied on this some lately. Let me show you. This is the White Tail River," he began, making a weaving line in the soft dirt with a twig. "On the north side is Forest lands and that piece of wilderness called Taylor Flats. On the south side is the Sacred Mountain Wilderness. The western end of the wilderness is across the river from where Beaver Creek comes in. West from there is the private land belonging to the McKenna's, except for a strip of reservation land that runs between the Wilderness and McKenna property."

Everyone followed Ken's tracings closely, those in back standing to move closer so to see.

"The McKenna's were granted a perpetual right-of-way on this piece of reservation land south of Beaver Creek because it was the only reasonable place along the White Tail he could build a bridge for year-round access to his other lands. That happened back in the early thirties with the understanding we had use of the bridge. That is why there is a fence along the east side of the trail road connected to the bridge from the south. Our ancestors crossed the river at that point to hunt the forests as they did for hundreds of years. We stopped going there in the late 40's when the government changed regulations on hunting. Then some White men sweet-talked the elders into letting them build that resort. As you see, it's cut off from the res by the river. Just a little piece of land we had no use for. They paid a little money each year, but that place is gone and the land is available to us again. If Toleshnec relocated to Round-Top Meadow a mile and a half south of the river, he would occupy the land legally. That would give him easy access to Taylorsville, the Pueblo, and to Sacred Mountain.

He would also have access to that piece of land where the old resort was built."

"Why would we want access to that land?" Toleshnec asked.

"A school has been needed to serve the children in this area because of the influx of more people. With the Sacred Mountain Clan living in the area, that need will be even greater. The problem is that the White community school board doesn't have the funds to build one. My sister and my wife's uncle are members of the Pueblo school board. They can get Federal monies to build a school on that piece of property. I am suggesting these two kids occupy this piece of land. Carrie could be the teacher."

"Could our children attend that school?" Katelyn said.

"Like the hospital, it would be open to all the people in the area. I'm sure we could work a deal with the White school board and obtain money for a school bus and driver, too.

"We left to live in the mountains to keep the miners away," Toleshnec said.

"And you managed to scare the devil out of more than a few. They don't dare come to mine commercially anymore," Jake said.

The old man thought for a time then said, "Your proposal sounds too easy. I would see this place."

"What about my son marrying this White girl?" the father said, drawing the conversation back to the original problem.

"That has been settled," Toleshnec said. "This is interesting. In this way they may live between two worlds, one on green grass, and the other on red earth." He looked straight at Jake.

Runs Fast wrapped his arm around Carrie as a beam of sunshine fell upon the circle like a blessing from the spirits.

The boy's father still wasn't happy, and continued to grumble until Toleshnec cut him off short. Happy or not, his new daughter was going to be White.

"And what will I tell my wife?" he whined.

"Tell her she is going to have a daughter," Katelyn said.

Providing food for three extra guests wasn't a problem, but Katelyn felt a bit stressed to appease the appetites of four more, especially not knowing how to match their diet. The first few days Runs Fast had eaten with them had been a challenge for his digestive system. She solved the dilemma by fixing tuna fish sandwiches as if feeding all the Forest crews on the compound, and these weren't finger food sized portions. Meanwhile, Toleshnec sat with his grandson and bride-to-be wanting to know her better. That she had made an effort to learn some of the Tewa dialect and customs pleased him. The same could not be said of Runs Fast's father. He remained quiet and sullen, mostly from shock. Ken borrowed a Forest Service horse and accompanied Toleshnec's party to the meadow that afternoon with the promise they would return in time for dinner.

Before she could feel overwhelmed, Ken added, "I'll have my wife come over and help prepare a meal. I think Navajo tacos would work best and I'll have her bring some venison."

Toleshnec was pleased with Round Top, and Jake was glad his uncle stayed an extra day providing an opportunity to become better acquainted with Carrie and with his family. Of course, the elderly patriarch chastised him.

"You should spend more time with your sons as I did with you. Perhaps I should come here and teach them."

"I couldn't think of a better teacher."

"Except it is your responsibility."

~ ~ ~ ~

Roving fireguard teams like Dale and Muir patrolled assigned sections of the forest as first responders to limit the spread of fires. Nature had them running hard early on in the spring with lightning strikes, often in the hardest to reach areas. Arrival of the June monsoon dampened the threat allowing them to concentrate on contacting people camping outside designated areas and insisting on having a campfire and not tending them properly. Through education and public relations, they greatly reduce problems caused by man. Unfortunately, the only means of educating some people came down to issuing a citation, which meant they had law enforcement authority similar to compliance officers like Carrie. Because of severe budget cuts, the Regional Enforcement Agent and the Forest Supervisor agreed that it only made sense to have the fire guards come under the supervision of the District Law Enforcement Officer, in this case, Jake. And, just to keep things tidy, he supervised the fire tower in keeping with Jake's philosophy of simplicity.

In order to maintain a sense that everyone on Jake's team were on the same page necessitated weekly meetings. He disliked formal sit-downs that took valuable time from patrols. The solution was to wander over to the bunkhouse area each Friday evening where his people billeted and invariably gathered around a campfire, drinking sodas, toasting marshmallows, and talking. The informal meetings were productive. That he brought a batch of Katelyn's fresh-baked cookies was an incentive to attendance. As Jake said, "These kids have their priorities."

The night following Toleshnec's departure and the announcement that Carrie and Runs Fast were to be married made public, he walked over to the campfire with a large bag of raisin-oatmeal cookies. His people had already gathered about a fire as usual, the topic seeming to be a Dale roast.

"You might have done better if Carrie had seen a little more skin like that Indian boy," one of the other fireguards, Jensen, teased.

"How much more did she need to see?" Muir defended his partner. "I mean, he took everything off but his skivvies when he pulled that body from the river."

"And you still lost?" Jensen said.

"Thanks." Mike started to stand, not in the mood for ribbing.

"Hey, do I smell cookies?" Jake said in a loud voice, stepping from the shadows, and placing a hand on Mike's shoulder to hold him down while sitting on the log next to him. "I didn't know you had an interest in Carrie."

"It was nothing."

"Nothing? You guys went to the movies and a nice restaurant just about every weekend. You were always together talking, at least until the Indian boy showed up. Should've done less talking and gone for a moonlight swim," Jensen continued, shaking the topic like a dog with a new chew toy.

"You are obsessed with taking your clothes off," Mike snapped.

"That's probably the worst approach to courting a girl I know," Jake said. "A relationship needs to be built on mutual respect and that sure ain't the path. As it is, Mike may not have had a snowball's chance in hell.

"When I was young and frisky, my Uncle Marshall set me down and said some marriages are made before we came to earth. We believe there is a world where our spirits lived before coming into this life and we knew each other.

Some of us made pledges there that if we met on earth we'd become husband and wife."

"Well, how do we know if we've met that person?" Muir asked.

"I can only go by my experience, I guess. I was a hot-blooded stallion like you guys, once. Yeah, I know. There may be snow on the roof now, but it wasn't always there. I chased the girls. Got chased, too. I tried the bed routine. It was a disaster. Not having two spirits, like gay men, I sought release by partying as if there'd be no tomorrow.

"In Nam, no tomorrow was a distinct possibility. The second time I was in the hospital in Japan I made my share of immature passes at the nurses, then one day this girl with auburn hair steps into the room to scold me for something I said that was out of line. The minute our eyes met, well, it was like we'd known each other forever. We spent a lot of time talking while I recuperated. After I returned to Nam, we wrote each other. When my tour ended, I went back to Japan to visit. Whenever I was with her, there was this peaceful feeling in my chest. Honestly, from the first time we met, marriage was a foregone conclusion, because it just felt right.

"I think that's exactly what happened here. No matter what Mike would have done, he'd lost from the first Carrie and Runs Fast met. The thing is, Mike and Carrie could have been good friends. Marriage might have worked, but going by what my uncle said, there is another girl out there, somewhere, and when Mike meets her, he'll know, this is it."

 וש

Incident at Beaver Creek

Chapter
29

An unusual nervousness pervaded the Sacred Mountain clan as Toleshnec and the others rode into their mountain village. Perhaps it was the expression on the riders' faces, a muted solemnness. Tension escalated as everyone assembled in the community building. Typically, there were always small, private conversations before a meeting started, but this time no one spoke. Even the smallest children sensed something and generally remained quiet. Once the last person arrived and stood against the back wall, Toleshnec laid out all that had happened during his journey and of the relocation plan.

He left nothing out—the good, the bad, the challenges, and the advantages— explaining everything and answering questions. Following discussion, the move was agreed upon. A few men and boys would remain behind to finish the harvest while the rest began preparations to move. Centuries of traditions came into play so that by the second, following morning entire households were loaded onto travois. Although their brothers in Taylorsville volunteered trucks, the Sacred Mountain clan desired to continue pursuing the traditional way.

The journey would take two days. To help, a dozen men from the pueblo arrived with additional horses for the elderly, pregnant women, and young children. Another group from town joined those men from Toleshnec's group sent ahead to begin building forked stick dwellings. These would serve as temporary homes until permanent adobe structures were completed. Had outsiders observed the event they would have been more than impressed with the cooperation and camaraderie. But then, these people were a close-knit family despite the distance they lived apart—physically and in time.

"Relocating is nothing new to us," their old leader said. "This is not the first time in our history The People have picked up and moved. Our ancestors were doing it even before stepping out of Sipapu onto the earth." Then with a wry twinkle in his eyes, Toleshnec added, "Blame Moses."

With the Sacred Mountain clan settling into their new location by Friday, the next order of business was to clean up the old resort land. Burning Arrow contacted a church in Taylorsville who wanted a service project for their youth. Early Saturday morning cars and pickups arrived at the site.

Van arranged for several dump trucks from Engineering and a place to haul the debris as the charred and broken cabins came down. The District Ranger authorized drivers from the Senior Citizens crew. A dozen District summer and permanent personnel pitched in as well. Miles brought over a dozer and frontend loader with people to operate them. Year-round residents from Tipton showed up, too.

The project started early Saturday morning. By evening, the eyesore had disappeared. As a celebration reward, Katelyn organized the Taylorsville church mothers and Forest Service wives in preparing a barbecue at the Arroyo compound. Chief cook was the Forest Supervisor with help from the District Ranger. Dale and Muir assisted using squirt bottles to keep the flames down.

On Monday, Van's people seeded the now bare ground with native grasses and wildflowers, and planted a pickup load of seedling conifers donated by the Forest Service. The former main lodge was in decent condition. A spacious log structure, tucked well back in the trees, it only needed some shingle repair and interior work. Carrie and her new sisters began cleaning it and some Pueblo carpenters and electricians came to make upgrades. This would be the school until replaced by a new building, and then it would become the newlywed's permanent home.

Jake wasn't able to participate much because of the increase in campers and inevitable problems which kept him going from early morning until late at night. All the time the murder investigations lay just under the surface, festering like an old wood splinter.

Davidson and Hayes continued the investigation; however, their call to Jake late Wednesday afternoon was the most startling.

After summarizing their work Davidson said, "Oh, by the way, you remember that woman who posted Red Wing's $50,000 bond?"

"The Jenkins woman."

"Yes. Her real name is Sally Morton."

"You said what?"

"Sally Morton."

"You've got to be kidding."

"Do you know here?"

"Oh-h, yes. That was Sally Morton? I haven't seen her in years, but geez! She's changed."

"Deputy Bradley says she lives in an old motel on the edge of Santa Fe. Poor as a church mouse. If she has any spare change, it goes for booze. Obviously, the money didn't come from any coffee can she had salted away. By going through her instead of a bail bondsman, whoever is fronting the money can remain anonymous. This case gets more and more interesting. Hayes and I are going to pay her a visit and see what shakes out."

"Any word on the lab results?"

"Not yet. I'm hoping they are able to develop something soon because what we have on Red Wing right now is thinner than a pair of Magic Johnson's old sneakers."

Late the next morning an elated NCIS agent called. "The Jenkins-Morton woman was of no help. Acts like her brains are fried by booze and drugs. Claims she doesn't even remember posting bail, but she is hiding something.

"However, we got some good news while driving back to town. The lab made a preliminary DNA match with tissue found on the ax handle. Most belong to Raymond Windpipe, but they found traces of tissue belonging to his brother Darrel. The US Attorney has filed two First Degree murder complaints on Red Wing. The Magistrate issued an arrest warrant and ordered the Marshals to pick him up."

Just before noon Friday, Jake received another call from Davidson. "Guess this should be no surprise. Red Wing appears to have skipped. Your counterpart, Nick Ewen, is on his way to your place. We're coming up as well. Let's see if we can get anything out of his logging buddies. Wear your armor."

Katelyn was singing softly while doing the laundry, but

her perky attitude vanished as she glanced through the office door. Her husband, stripped to his T-shirt, had just removed a Kevlar vest from a closet and was slipping it on.

"Something serious?" she said, an unmistakable quiver in her voice. She had never seen him use the vest except for training.

"Red Wing's our murderer. He's run, but I have a feeling he hasn't gone far. Nick, Davidson, Hayes, and I are going to shake some trees and see what falls out," he said, re-buttoning his shirt.

A lot of years had gone away since he last prepared for battle. This was something Katelyn dreaded would happen as any law enforcement wife. He loaded a shotgun and put additional shells in a leather pouch that hung off one shoulder as Nick pulled into the visitor parking lot in front of the house. The NCIS agents appeared ten minutes later. Bent over a forest map spread out on Nick's truck hood, the lawmen discussed a plan to find Red Wing, starting with his cabin.

"Looks like he left everything behind," Nick said as he stepped out of the cabin into the sunlight. "Not that there's much to leave."

"Like he is planning to come back," Hayes said.

"Let's talk to the bar owner," Jake said, heading straight for the rectangular, log building next to the highway as he spoke, then stopped suddenly.

Off to the side of the cabins, a pair of T-shaped, metal poles held up four sagging lines to which a woman was pinning laundry. Making a detour, he approached the stout woman in jeans and T-shirt and asked, "Where did that Indian blanket come from?"

"Fulton Red Wing sold it to me a few days ago. Said he didn't have no use for it."

Jake looked the blanket over carefully, almost positive

it was the one Small Beaver had, recognizing the colors and pattern as similar to one he had used during his spirit quest. They were clan specific.

"Did you wash this?" he asked.

"Oh, no, dear. It's wool. Can't wash it like dirty underwear. I'm just airing it out. I plan to have it dry cleaned this weekend when I get to town."

"How much did you give him?" Davidson asked.

"Twenty bucks. Don't tell me. It's stolen."

"I think so," Jake said to which she unloaded a string of words hot enough to light one of Davidson's after dinner cigars.

"Here," Hayes said, digging into his wallet. "I'll give you forty dollars for it."

Not needing to be clairvoyant to see she could lose the blanket and be out twenty bucks, she said, "Sold," snapping the bills from his fingers so fast Hayes was lucky to have retained all five digits.

"That was generous," Jake said as they walked away.

"Expense account. I'll just eat salads for a while."

The barman, Reg Carpenter, had been a sawyer until an accident eleven years earlier gimped his leg. Working the trees or dancing heavy equipment with a prosthesis was nigh on to impossible so Clyde Barker set him up with the bar, "To help out." The generosity surprised Jake until learning latter the offer was a way to keep Reg quiet when the OSHA folk nosed around. Buying him off with a bar was a lot cheaper than paying the fines or being shut down.

"Hey, Reg," Jake called out as they entered and didn't see anyone about.

The barman stepped from a back room wearing a soiled apron. His limp was noticeable.

"Come to apologize for the ruckus the other night."

"No problem. If anything got broke I'd send ya a bill,"

Reg replied with a big grin. "Not really. Warmed my ticker to see that jerk go down. Whew! Did he ever." Reg had a big, rolling laugh that nearly rattled the bottles lined up behind the bar.

"We're looking for him again. You see him?"

"Yeah. He was in here yesterday afternoon. Had a couple beers. Asked him when he was goin' back to work. Said he had a better offer. He kept lookin' out the door, then I hear this car or truck pull up. Musta been going fast. Folks are always doing that, you know, sliding their tires. Anyways, he left. Be drinks on the house when I know he's gone permanent."

"Why's that?" Nick said.

"The gorilla is a moron. Cross him and he reaches for that ax handle he keeps handy. Had to step between him and Randy Gardner, then he had the balls to threaten me, but I know his kind. Wouldn't do nothin' right then or have the whole crew on his back. His kind jumps you in a dark alley. The idiot actually tried that a couple days later."

"What happened," Nick said.

"Ax handles don't fare so well with a .38," the barman said, reaching under the bar and bringing up a snub-nosed revolver. "We had a understanding."

"Did you see what kind of vehicle it was or which way they went?" Davidson asked.

"Naw. Was busy stockin' the bar for when the guys come in after work. One thing, though. I'd like to get my hands on the jerk who was drivin'. Spun his tires and kicked gravel at my windows. I know the place ain't much, but those puppies are pricey to replace."

"Reg's right about that," Jake thought to himself, often wondering how the place managed to avoid a Health Department closure. The windows were small, circular affairs providing a little light, but certainly no view.

"This Randy Gardner still around?" Hayes asked, feeling they had a lead worth pursuing.

"Oh, yeah. Nice guy. Runs a skidder. Ain't much more than a light breeze, but he's a real good hand with heavy equipment.

"Short, skinny, full, red beard, works on the Thompson sale?" Jake said.

"Yep, that's Randy."

"Okay, I know who you're talking about. Helped some forest visitors a couple weeks back who got lost and had a flat. Changed it for them then lead them back to the highway."

"Yep, that's Randy."

They planned a visit to that timber sale next anyway, now there was someone to focus on. The crew was just finishing lunch as the officers pulled up. Rough men like these were already edgy having had more lawmen hovering around than they'd seen in years. That the two rangers were working together, and in company of two others wearing jackets with Federal Agent emblazoned on the back was a tip off something had definitely gone south. Any dolt could put two and two together and figure Fulton Red Wing was the magnet. Gardner wasn't difficult to spot. Seeing them heading his direction, he dumped his lunch pail and bolted, Hayes and Nick in pursuit, Jake and Donaldson close behind. The two younger men seemed about to catch Gardner when they slowed down.

"Run out of steam, guys?" Jake said as he caught up. They were less than thirty feet behind the fleeing man.

"He hollered back, 'Not here. Don't catch me here. Talk behind the hill,'" Nick said.

"Think it's a trap?"

"We're about to find out," Hayes said as Gardner disappeared over the crest of a hill and into a small gully.

When they arrive, guns drawn, he had stopped at the bottom, hands on knees, breathing hard.

Hayes and Nick slid down to him while Jake and Donaldson stayed on the crest, Jake using his senses to detect anything unusual. The change in altitude had come down hard on the sea level dwellers, judging by their gasping for breath.

"I knew ya guys wanted to talk to me about Fulton, but I couldn't let the others see me talkin' to ya," Gardner said between gulps of air.

"Okay, so what about him?" Donaldson said as he slid down to join them. Jake remained above, continuing to watch for anything that might be an ambush.

"I saw him murder Humphreys. They was arguin' behind the deck where no one could see 'em, exceptin' I did. Was takin' a leak in the bushes. Fulton hit him with his fist and knocked him down, then levers a log loose from the deck. Couple more went along. Rolled over the poor bastard like a D-9 Cat. Then Fulton slips away and acts all innocent like."

"How come you didn't come forward?" Hayes asked.

"Are you kiddin'. With that maniac walkin' free. If he didn't slit your throat while you were asleep, one of his buddies would."

"Alright, guess you're going into the witness protection program," Donaldson said. "We'll need a signed statement about what you saw."

Satisfied there was no one else around, Jake slid down the hill. "Cuff him so it looks like we are arresting him. If anyone asks, he's being taken in for questioning about . . . where'd you work before coming here?"

"Pagosa District, on the San Jaun in Colordao."

"Okay. We're taking you in for questioning about missing timber on the Pagosa Ranger District."

Coming out of the draw, they saw red lights flashing. Deputy Putnam was parked next to their vehicles, standing in front of his pickup, arms crossed, waiting.

"Harassing the loggers, ranger?" Jake disliked just about everything about the man, probably the most irritating was that he was a disgrace to a good profession. He said nothing as Gardner was placed in the back seat of the agents' SUV. "So what's he done?" Jake just looked at Putnam, saying nothing. "Hey! You answer when I talk to you, half breed."

Putnam grabbed Jake's arm to turn him around. He had a habit of putting his hands on people unnecessarily. Bad mistake this time. The bevy of onlookers later tried to recall what they had seen over a beer at the Mountain Home bar that evening. One instant the deputy reached out to touch Jake, and the next he was face down on the hood of his own patrol car in a hammerlock.

"I told you when we were kids, don't touch me. Well, this is official. Don't ever touch a Federal officer in the performance of his official duties like that, especially this Federal officer, or we'll revisit Lincoln schoolyard. You got that?" Jake's voice was low enough so as not heard by the loggers standing some distance away, but Putnam got the message. A slight tweak of the arm acted like an exclamation point.

Putnam quickly gained his truck and sat there a moment, shaking, becoming aware he had wet his pants. He still had nightmares about the school brawl when he was on the wrong side of Jake's Krakatoan temper.

ⴖ

Incident at Beaver Creek

Chapter
30

The bundle Runs Fast laid at Carrie's door contained a long, cloth belt, two all-white wedding robes, one white wedding robe with red stripes at the top and bottom, white buckskin leggings and moccasins, and a string for tying her long hair. This he wrapped in a reed mat after spending several months weaving the cloth using cotton gathered from the clan's field and assembling the garments. The buckskins he made from a deer hide he hunted and painstakingly tanned. He did all this as tradition dictated the preceding summer in anticipation of the day he found a girl to propose marriage to.

With Mom Riley's help, Carrie followed through with more of the pre-wedding tradition. She already knew how to bake bread and made a loaf in Katelyn's kitchen. Normally, Carrie would deliver this to Blue Flower, Runs Fast's mother; however, Mom Riley sent a message to the woman, inviting her to the Bershinsky home. Escorted to the ranger station by her next two oldest sons, the woman was eager to meet the girl Runs Fast found favor with. The first minutes were tense and nervous, but Katelyn quickly set everyone at ease and Blue Flower became delighted with her son's choice and accepted the bread. As Mom Riley, Katelyn, Carrie, and Blue Flower spent the day together, the three brothers and Jake's sons wrestled, swam, and bonded as well.

That Wednesday morning, before Jake received word that an arrest warrant had been issued for Red Wing, Carrie loaded Runs Fast into her car for a trip to Taylorsville. Sgt. Walter was waiting to help them secure a marriage license. Afterward, they visited Uncle Marshall who spent several hours counseling the young people about the sacredness of marriage, problems they would encounter, and ways to make their union solid and lasting.

Toleshnec sat quietly to one side during that discussion, saying nothing until the very end. "May I make a suggestion? When the two of you are alone and talking over what my brother has counseled, consider making a commitment that during your lifetime together you will not speak of separation, and even though you may retire for the night angry with one another, do not sleep any other place except next to each another."

Neither was under any delusions that they faced some cultural mountains to navigate in the years ahead, but with people like Uncle Marshall, Jake and Katelyn, Mom Riley, Runs Fasts' mother, and Toleshnec, there was little doubt their devotion and love would prevail. Even Runs Fasts' father began showing signs of softening and contemplating becoming a grandfather.

In the early morning darkness of the following Saturday everyone from Toleshnec's camp and most of the Antigua Pueblo gathered at the site of the new school for the wedding. Runs Fast's brothers gathered hand-sized rocks from the river the night before to construct a large circle in an open area overlooking the river. At the appointed time, the young couple stepped into the circle.

Katelyn stood next to Runs Fast's mother and Mom Riley, each woman dabbing at a joyful tears. They had helped Carrie dress and everyone couldn't help but notice how the couple seemed to glow in their white garments as the sun began to lighten the sky.

Katelyn looked on proudly as Henry and Peter helped Uncle Marshall tread the uneven ground and step into the circle to join the nervous couple. Jake smiled inwardly because his boys were dressed much as he had at that age, cotton shirt, trousers, kilt, and moccasins. Grandmother Bershinsky resurrected some old photos of their dad when their age during the family's last trip into town. The revelation left little chance Katelyn would prevail about their dress until school started. The boys even wore a bright blue headband just as their dad did.

"Now join hands and face toward the rising sun," Uncle Marshall said softly and began chanting the prayers to unit them as one. As the sun's golden disk began peeking over the top of Sacred Mountain the chants swelled in volume.

When the sun's full orb rose above the mountain, Uncle Marshall received the small wedding pot with its two spouts from Naoma and handed it to Carrie. She took a sip of the herbal tea from one spout and handed it to Runs Fast. He took a sip from the other spout. Next, she took a sip from the spout he had used, and he drank from her side. The two then stood close, side-by-side. Tipping the pot, they drank the tea each catching it from the spout on their side.

"Not a drop spilled. This will be a good marriage," Naoma announced loudly when her husband concluded the prayers.

With that, the party began, something that would last all day—food, games, dancing, camaraderie. There hadn't been time to speak with his uncle and Little Beaver's father prior to this gathering, so after a time Jake took them aside to apprise them of what happened. He concluded by saying, "Red Wing's on the run, but every lawman in the west is looking for him."

"If we find him, we will turn him over to you," Toleshnec said.

"Alive and in one piece would be nice," Jake said, although deep down he didn't care what condition Small Beaver's family might return the Sioux, and both men knew the ranger's feelings by the reflection in his eyes. The party took Jake back to better days in his youth, and for the moment, he was able to take his mind off work and renew old acquaintances. He was still recuperating from the celebration when a 6:30 A.M. phone call Monday from Jay's Roost and Katelyn's persistent elbow brought him awake.

~ ~ ~ ~

When Curt landed the fire tower job, Jake told him to "Bring plenty of reading material." He did. The second and third summers on the job he signed up for distance learning classes. It was the perfect situation, even if he didn't receive the hazard pay like those actively involved in fire suppression.

Working for Jake Bershinsky only intensified his love

for the job. Every few days Katelyn sent fresh-baked treats with the fireguards or a compliance officer. On days off, he would drive to the compound to do laundry and use a computer in the office to submit course assignments. There was always the invitation to stay for supper. Those were more than enough reasons for him to be so conscientious about the job.

Most tower personnel quit after dark during calm weather. He'd go to his cabin and prepare a meal, but often slept in the tower when late afternoon storms rumbled through, setting his alarm to make a careful sweep of everything in his visual range at midnight, 3 A.M., and at dawn. Of prime concern were those areas he recorded as receiving lightning strikes within the last twenty-four hours. That conscientious effort was responsible for sounding early alerts on several "sleeper" fires before they got a running start.

After spotting a vehicle on the flats weeks earlier, Curt also kept a close eye for further activity. Using surplus Navy, high-powered binoculars, he scoped the area just before sacking out for a couple hours. That's when he thought to see a light in the area of the Sebastian Mine. A brief flicker, he eventually passed it off as a reflection of moon light or his imagination; however, as the sun began rising over the horizon he saw a low layer of dust hanging along the old trail.

"I'm positive a vehicle was out there, Mr. Bershinsky. It's not low-hanging fog, and I can see a dust cloud coming up off Road 547 heading toward highway 41. The vehicle is going at a pretty good clip. The cloud starts in the vicinity of the trailhead."

After the first vehicle trespass, Jake scratched a line in the dirt across the old entrance road next to the trailhead. Carrie checked it daily and kept it fresh. Looking down at the soft ground much of the line was missing. Crouching, he ran a finger over the dirt. Drag marks. Someone had used the pine bough to erase the evidence. He walked out onto the road. Whoever it had been wiped the trail clean all the way to the road. The mistake was that they forgot their tracks would show up on the main road. Any vehicle traveling along the road left an imprint in the loose dirt. What Jake found was the imprint of two rear tires starting in the middle of the road and going east. What his trained eye also noticed was an abnormal wear pattern on the inside of the right tread. For this, he loved the new digital camera received from the Army for civilian testing. He still had friends in the military who remembered him. It was a Nikon F-3 equipped with a Kodak 1.3 megapixel sensor and a couple advanced features not available to the photojournalists for whom it was intended. It allowed him to take multiple shots at different angles until positive the abnormality showed clearly.

Returning to his office, Jake called Curt on the phone to let him know it wasn't his imagination, and then casually ate breakfast, but Katelyn saw her husband repeatedly check the clock. After a second glass of orange juice, he went into the office and unlocked the gun case. Standing in front of the opened door, he obviously debated on what to take until withdrawing a Browning shotgun. The American Oak stock was customized with a silver plate handcrafted with Pueblo motifs and particular Antigua designs. A single, black feather hung from the muzzle. It was nothing short of 12-gauge, 3-1/2 inch chamber, hand-held howitzer. The only time she had seen him handle the weapon was to clean it.

"You're expecting trouble, aren't you," she said.

"Not necessarily. Appears whoever was up at the old mine has left."

"That Red Wing guy could be there."

"Possibility," Jake said as he unlocked the cartridge drawer in the lower part of the cabinet. "I sure hope so," he thought to himself.

"Are you taking someone along?"

He looked out the window and nodded toward it. A green Forest Service truck with horse trailer was entering the parking lot. Nick Ewen. Davidson and Hayes pulled up behind him.

"I am," he said, dumping a box of shells into a leather pouch slung over his shoulder. Katelyn glanced at one of the boxes. She and Jake often shot clay targets and was familiar with guns. He was taking Remington 12gauge Expander slugs.

"You expecting an elephant?" she said.

"If Red Wing is up there the best defense against someone with his mentality is more fire power than needed. This should be persuasive enough."

"I've never seen you use that weapon before," Katelyn said.

"It belonged to Henry. Toleshnec gave it to him on his sixteenth birthday." Jake chuckled softly. "Knocked him on his butt first time he fired it. It shoots a four-inch pattern at seventy-five yards. Used it to hunt elk. Never needed more than one shot."

"What have we got?" Nick said as the three men entered the office.

"Curt up at the Roost thought he spotted someone at the old mine last night and leave early this morning. I drove up to the trailhead and confirmed entry. Just a hunch, but I'm guessing Red Wing was, or is up there. I want you and Hayes to ride in from Taylor Flats, but don't come closer than 500 yards. Davidson and I'll come in along the river."

"You want us to be a decoy?"

"Sorry. Just mosey along. If he's up there that will keep him distracted and won't see us coming up from behind. Use our private radio channel."

Again reaching into the gun cabinet, he withdrew two rifles, handing Davidson and Hayes each one.

"A 45-70! Are you kidding? My grandpa had one of these. We'd go to the shooting range and blow up milk cartons. I loved it," Davidson crowed as his hands lovingly slid over the weapon.

Hayes was happy with a .243. The lever action rifles were good choices for what they needed.

Altogether, Jake emptied twenty-five shot into a leather pouch, and slipped extra magazines into other pouches on his gun belt for the Ruger. Each clip held seventeen .38 caliber rounds. The firepower of that weapon was more than impressive.

Years before, the Secret Service had commissioned a special round that would bring down the bad guy without going all the way through and taking out innocent bystanders in the background. At police conferences, her husband was often the brunt of numerous bards about his "toy pistol." He only smiled and shrugged. She knew her husband had been a weapons specialist during the Vietnam War and knew exactly what worked and what didn't. The Ruger Company also knew Jake and gave him the PX38S, a prototype that never went into production because of caliber bias. The serial number on his pistol was 00002.

"Be careful, Jake," she said, rising up on bare toes to kiss him.

"Do I get one of those?" Nick asked.

"I'll make you a bumble berry pie when you get back."

"That's a deal! Start baking. This won't take long."

"Just watch your backs," she said. Katelyn was smiling, but her eyes betrayed the nervous fear of every woman watching her man go off to war.

Only two families were using the Beaver Creek campground as the lawmen rode through, the shotgun with a feather dangling from the barrel's end laid over his lap. The campers wondered why black feathers hung from behind the floppy, military hat, but didn't have the opportunity for photos as the horsemen loped passed.

"Was that a Forest Ranger, daddy?" a little girl said as they watched the strange-looking man ride over to a Forest Service fire truck in the parking lot before disappearing into the trees and head upstream. With him was another who looked totally out of place on a horse.

"I don't know, Bri. He had a uniform shirt like the lady who comes around here, but I've never seen one look quite like that."

"Maybe he's looking for the man that rode his motorcycle that way last night."

凹

Incident at Beaver Creek

Chapter
31

From Beaver Creek to a point nine miles east of Sebastian Mine, the White Tail was restricted to a narrow canyon. Along the south side were the near vertical walls of the Sacred Mountains. On the north, the ground rose at an impossibly steep grade with a narrow, one lane trail carved out alongside the river. That meant once in this canyon, radio transmissions were trapped except along its length. That's why Jake had Dale and Muir station their truck in the Beaver Creek parking lot. They would act as a radio relay to Jays Roost and the outside world.

Before setting out, Jake was giving them a quick briefing when Dale pointed to the river. "What the heck! Look at that."

A number of long logs were floating out of the canyon, bouncing along the current, and bumping boulders protruding from the water. The loud thuds echoing off the rocks produced an eerie sound.

"Think those are some of the stolen logs you told us about?" Muir asked.

"No. Too long. That's curious." Triggering the portable radio, he called Nick. "What's your location?"

"In the parking lot. Ready to move?"

"Hold up. Something's not right. We just had some long logs float out of the canyon. We're going in to take a look." Turning to Davidson he said, "Let's ride."

What they initially observed were five logs, each about twenty feet long. They encountered a fourth log at the waterfall, a sizeable portion of its length projecting into the air over the drop off like a giant boom. Several hundred yards above the falls, they rounded a bend in the trail into a slightly wider area. More logs stretched out from the bank partially blocking the river. Altogether, fourteen logs had plummeted off the hill and across the trail. Looking uphill Jake could see the stump tops glisten a yellowish white. Recent cuts. Logging was not permitted in this area and he instantly recognizing what had happened as his mind leaped back to a place 8,000 miles away and twenty-two years earlier, just before meeting Katelyn.

~ ~ ~ ~

Orphaned, like so many kids during war in Vietnam, Vhin was not much older than Jake's Henry when Delta Platoon made him their mascot. Despite seeing the death of his parents, and siblings, and so many more, Vhin maintained a happy demeanor on the outside. Desperately wanting to attach to something or someone to compensate for the loss, he worked overtime to please. From the moment he arrived, his very presence lifted the men's spirits.

Lt. Bershinsky's platoon consisted of three squads of twelve to thirteen each, thirty-eight men in all, a bit short of the normal forty-two due to injuries. Two squads carried the Colt Commando, a shortened M16 with telescoping stock. The third squad was a special weapons unit equipped with two M60 machine guns, two M203 automatic rifle/grenade launchers, and the rest with Browning 12-gauge shotguns using double-ought buck. Everyone carried his favorite weapon, a twelve-inch KaBar knife.

What set this platoon apart was that every member was Native American at his request, which proved extremely effective. Despite tribal differences back home, they worked as a cohesive whole, using their tracking, hunting, and fighting skills to the consternation of the enemy.

On the most heart-breaking mission he would experience, a squad of fifteen Hmong soldiers had joined his platoon. They were to find and eliminate a Vietnamese regular army unit launching attacks north of Tay Ninh then retreating into Cambodia.

Col. Barnston's orders were, "Lose the border. Get those . . ." Barnston had a vocabulary that would curl the edges of any report, even after sanitizing.

Following in the NVA's wake of brutalized villages, his unit arrived at a small farming village close to the border where they discovered one of the worst crimes. After tying the headman to a post, he was forced to watch as his two teenage sons had their intestines pulled out through a slit by the naval. It was a slow, agonizingly brutal death, mirrored on the victim's faces. Following more atrocities, they blinded the man.

From survivors who hid in the jungle, Charlie's Chinese commander was looking for American collaborators. Despite assurances there were none, the soldiers methodically raped the women and killed the village chief and sons as a warning.

As they buried the last victim, Jake was surprised to see Vhin walk into the village, carrying a message from Col. Barnston. Sending Vhin back, they left shortly after noon, his unit working along a trail that wiggled between dense forest, fields, and a river toward a village in the path of the marauding enemy.

The forward scouts discovered the log debris a couple hours into the move. The trap had rolled off a steep hillside, obliterating the trail to embed in the muddy riverbank thirty feet below. The men immediately spread out checking for snipers and more traps. Once the area was determined clear, Jake focused on the logjam. That it had been a trap was obvious. Something had triggered the booby trap preventing Jake's unit from being seriously crippled.

Standing on the trail above the tangled debris, he spotted a discolored, brown branch protruding from the entangled logs. If not for how observant Toleshnec had taught him to be, it would have remained just an odd-looking branch. A wave of shock rolled through the unit as two men retrieved Vhin's mangled body and laid it on the trail. What was he doing here?

"He was pretty upset about what happened back at that village," Jake's radioman said. He and the boy hung together a lot. "He said the animals had to be stopped. Said he could find them for us. I really thought I'd talked him out of it."

Touching a dead body wasn't a problem for any of his men in Vietnam. Everyone had done that at one time or another, but it was First Sergeant Hunts Elk, a Wyoming Arapaho, who took their little friend in his arms and wept as they buried him in a temporary grave on the hillside before continuing on. He had buried a son the same age just before deployment to Vietnam. The memory was still close to the surface.

As the unit neared the next village, Jack and Eddie, the Wolf brothers from the Blackfoot Confederacy in Montana, returned from scouting ahead. The NVA unit was there. No one had any doubts they were responsible for setting the trap their little friend unwittingly triggered.

The North Vietnam regulars felt confident of detecting the bumbling American soldiers who weren't supposed to cross over into Cambodia. They had no experience with the lethal stealth of Native American warriors. Neither the terrorized villagers nor the arrogant soldiers had an inkling when a deadly snake slithered into their midst, not until dawn when Col. Cao stepped from his hut to see his men laid out neatly before him, those still alive bound and gagged. His astonishment was brief as he reflexively turned to re-enter the hut to escape only to bounce off Sgt. Elk Hunter's broad chest.

Bound hand and foot, they left the commander in the village clearing, moving some distance away to prepare a proper grave for their friend. Temporarily leaving had been a deliberate act on Jake's part. The villagers tossed the VC bodies into a common grave after taking revenge on the survivors for the atrocities they and their neighbors had endured. Col. Cao had a front row seat as hoes and knives dismembered the bodies of his soldiers, before visiting him.

~ ~ ~ ~

Davidson tethered his horse to a sturdy-looking bush as directed. Jake draped Mohf's reins around the pommel as the horse's small ears pointed like two fingers while staring intently at the logjam.

"Wait here. I'm going down. There's something down there."

"Is it safe?"

"No."

Jake picked a way down the mud and rock slope, an ungraceful, slalom-like decent, clumsily gaining the first log to begin working out onto what appeared to be the most stable log. Two-thirds the way across he stopped and knelt. The next thing Donaldson heard was Jake's voice on the radio.

"Dale this is Bershinsky. I've got an injured hiker about three hundred yards above the waterfall. Get a rescue unit out of Tipton. Donaldson, get down here. I need your help. The guy's pinned under this log."

Sliding out of control, the agent banged into a log preventing him from going into the drink. Feeling like a drunken tightrope walker, he wondered how Jake seemed to travel the slippery log so easily while he wobbled and skidded across its damp surface. Reaching Jake, he saw a forearm and hand sticking out of the crevice between two logs. Jake was holding the hand. The fingers moved.

"Okay, son, I've got some help now. I gotta let go of your hand for a minute. Donaldson, go back about twenty feet or so, sit on this log and put your feet against the next one. When I give the word, push."

The agent was good at following orders, but the log wasn't. No matter how much they pushed, it wouldn't budge. A half-buried rock held it in place. Jake retrieved a large limb and tried using it as a lever. There was some movement, but not enough. Moments later, Dale appeared, breathing hard from the uphill sprint.

"Bill's got the radio. The rescue unit is en route. What can I do?"

"Use this pole in the middle. I'll take the end by the

kid. Donaldson, move closer to the other end. We only need to move that sucker a foot or so to get him out."

Jake went back to where the trapped man was located, sat on the log and put his feet against the next one.

"Okay, move you dirty . . ."

Each man strained and grunted. Slowly, grudgingly, the log began to move until Jake could slip into the abyss. Brushing long hair from the young man's face he began checking for injuries; a compound fracture of the right leg below the knee and broken right wrist were obvious. He didn't like the blood slowly oozing from his nose and ears.

"I can't see, man. I can't see."

"Okay, okay. Relax."

"Where's Angie? Have you found Angie?"

A lump leaped into Jake's throat. Of course, the hiker wouldn't be alone.

"Not yet," he told him. "Mike, there's another somewhere in this mess. Take a look."

"The paramedics are on their way up," Muir radioed.

When they broke into the open Jake said, "Okay, son, I've got to move so the paramedics can get you out. I'll look for your friend, okay? Stay with us."

Jake pulled out as a paramedic took his place. Dale came up from the river.

"No good, Jake. The girl's pinned face down in the water," He kept his voice low so the injured man didn't hear.

The paramedics worked on the survivor, a twenty-year-old college student, for some time trying to stabilize him. Finally, one of them stood up.

"Hand down the backboard, Mr. Bershinsky," then whispering, "I think he's got a broken back and some serious head injuries. This is going to be tough. No working space."

"Give me a minute. Mike, Donaldson, they need room. Let's shove these downside logs into the water."

One by one, they pushed and levered the lower logs into the water until there was room to move the last one clear, giving the paramedics plenty of room to shift the victim onto the backboard. By this time, three more Forest personnel arrived in time to help carry the stretcher out to the rescue unit. They were also able to retrieve the body of the hiker's girlfriend during the process.

"Want to call off our trip?" Donaldson asked quietly.

"No. Whoever did this don't give a damn about human life. It could just as well have been one of those families with kids back at the campground. Climb up to that rock outcrop. You should be able to reach Nick on the radio. Tell them what's happened here. Have them stay put, then just make yourself comfortable. Once we get the other victim headed down, I'll waive, then tell them to start the operation."

When he looked up, Muir was coming into view with two more people.

"Carrie's got the radio," Muir said.

"Okay. Find a couple poles and use the blanket off the back of my saddle to make a stretcher to take the body out."

Jake then radioed Carrie, "They're bringing out the dead hiker. Load the body into your truck and transport to Taylorsville. Use McKenna's bridge and let the Taylorsville police know so they can alert the hospital. Mike and Bill are returning to that location to resume radio relay. We're continuing on."

"Okay. The medevac helicopter from Taylorsville is just taking the injured guy aboard," she responded. "They think the injuries are too serious so they are flying him directly to Albuquerque."

"That was quick. Who called them?"

"Curt."

Jake appreciated someone who took the initiative to make a judgment call like that.

A half hour later Jake's waive brought Donaldson down from his perch to round up their horses. The Saddlebred was still tethered, but Mohf had wandered further up the trail to avoid the sudden influx of people and find more grass. A whistle brought him back.

~ ~ ~ ~

Donaldson had been reassured his horse was trail smart. He sure hoped so as the terrain on this side of the river rose so steeply to be a hand-over-hand climb to the top. The narrow slip of bare ground they followed was the cap of a very narrow ledge with a very precarious plunge into the rock-lined river below. It was only a twenty-foot drop, but looked a whole lot further from the back of his tall horse.

Ahead, Jake was moving slower than before, scanning the trail, occasionally looking up the side of the mountain. Donaldson was a city boy who knew how to spot danger on the streets. This had been a great assignment, trucking around the wilds, but he was way out of his element, grateful to follow someone who knew the mountains.

After a time, Jake stopped and raised his left hand. The agent's heart missed a beat. When Jake swung out of the saddle, stepped ahead a few feet, and squatted to inspect the trail, he instinctively looked up the overhanging cliff, but didn't see anything dangerous except an outcrop of rock and trees. Of course, that didn't mean anything.

"What is it?" Donaldson said, speaking softly.

Jake stood and returned to Mohf. "Bear."

"Where?" Donaldson was really looking over the terrain now.

"Up ahead. Maybe a half hour. No problem. It's a black. They tend to keep their distance."

"What if it decides to come back this way?"

"We negotiate," Jake said with a matter-of-fact air as he remounted.

"Yeah, negotiate with a wild bear. Sure." Donaldson grumbled to himself. The trail was too narrow to turn a horse around.

As the two continued, Donaldson began to reconsider this assignment and how many things could kill him—trees, rocks, bears, falling off a cliff into a raging river twenty-foot below and drown, what else?—wishing he were back in the city, or better yet, back aboard ship where it was safe.

"How are you doin'?"

Donaldson rose up in the saddle. His butt was sore, but more so the insides of his thighs. He winced.

"Sorry. I forget about first time riders." Jake keyed the radio. "Dale this is Bershinsky." Muir answered. "Call Nick and remind him to have his sidekick stretch his legs or he won't be worth kindlin'."

The two listened as Muir relayed the message. There was a chuckle in the young man's voice. Unintelligible static responded then Muir said, "Nick says gotcha. They're about a half mile from the mine."

"Advise him to hold up about fifteen minutes, then proceed as planned. Have his partner walk around. If they are being watched the delay should be obvious."

Muir relayed the message, heard the static return, and received confirmation.

"Ah-h, Jake. We got a problem," Donaldson said. The color in his copper-colored face disappearing as eyes became big as radar dishes.

Jake looked up the trail to see a two-year old bear stopped on the trail, staring at them. Stepping in front of his gray, Jake raised his right arm to the square as the creature stood on his hind legs."

"Hello, Brother Bear. We've got important business up ahead and would appreciate it if you would let us pass."

"Yeah, sweet talk a bear," Donaldson thought to himself while easing his rifle from the scabbard. To his amazement, the bear dropped to all fours, turned, and trotted up the trail, away from them.

"He understood you?"

"The bear is my totem. Blacks are okay. Grizzlies have a different outlook on life, my way, or the highway. Sometimes you have to take a tougher approach with them."

In truth, the youngster didn't want anything to do with humans accompanied by two Moose-sized creatures and naturally beat a hasty withdrawal. Jake just happen not mentioning that to the city boy.

"There's a spot just ahead where you can stretch."

"I think that's the problem. Too much stretch."

Jake smiled, swung into the saddle without using the stirrups, and moved forward to a place wide enough for Donaldson to painfully dismount and walk around. He was sore, but trying to comprehend what had just happened helped distract his mind some from the pain. After a time the discomfort worked out to a reasonable degree.

Break over, Donaldson stood looking at his horse. The creature stood seventeen hands at the top of its shoulder. One hand equaling four inches made the saddle sixty-eight inches off the ground, and the stirrup needed for a boost up was higher than his leg would reach at the moment.

"Use that rock," Jake said casually.

At this point, the agent wasn't proud. He climbed up

on a rock several feet high and used it like a ladder to reach the saddle. Another ten minutes or so the ground on their left became less steep.

"The mine is less than a quarter mile ahead," Jake said, studying the mountainside. "There's a spot up there. We'll leave the horses and go in on foot."

"Jake, this is Dale."

"Go ahead, Mike," Jake answered on the radio.

"Got a problem. Curt just reported a smoke eight miles north of here. Pretty good column."

"Jay's Roost, can you hear me?" Jake said.

"Scratchy, but I hear you, Mr. Bershinsky."

"Okay, Mike, go for it. We're in radio contact with the Curt."

At that moment, a loud boom echoed off the canyon walls and reverberated down the canyon. There was no doubt it was a gunshot.

"Rifle. Small caliber," Jake said, leaving the agent to wonder how he could tell. It sounded like a ship's five incher. "Loosen your reins and follow me."

Reining Mohf left, he goosed the horse smartly in the side with his heels and leaned forward as the animal began climbing, its back legs digging into the soil and rocks to propel upward in a lurching motion. Donaldson followed suit. He wasn't expecting what happened next.

The Saddlebred was docile on the trail, something he thoroughly appreciated, but as it turned and responded to a kick, the beast shift into granny—extra low gear. It was like riding a bucking personnel carrier up the side of the hill, and the only thing to hold onto was a little thing on the front of the saddle—a horn that didn't work.

Jake continued beyond where he initially intended to leave the horses, instead heading straight for the top. The Saddlebred followed, probably thinking it was in a race because he was catching up with the smaller Arabian as they neared the summit. Meanwhile, more rifle shots thundered out.

At the ridge top, Jake dismounted, flipped his stirrup up, and released the cinch. "They need to breathe," he called out quietly as Donaldson pulled up alongside. Once dismounted, Jake slung the shotgun over his right shoulder, looped the Saddlebred's reins around the pommel, and released the cinch. Both horses were heaving heavily from the climb, foam slathering from the corners of their mouths. Donaldson pulled the .45-70 from the scabbard as more shots pounded against the canyon walls.

"Nick," Jake said into the transmitter. Silence. "Nick, you better be answering me." More silence, then another shot. "Damn it, Nick, answer me," Jake said.

"Geez, Jake. Give me time to get this thing out of the holster."

"What's going on?"

"Some clown's shooting at us from the rocks off to our right. Killed Hayes' horse with the first shot and spooked my horse. Tossed me off. Hayes might have a broken ankle. We're pinned down. Hayes is behind his horse and I'm in some rocks."

"You alright?"

"Banged my knee, but nothing's broke. We ain't got our rifles. My stupid nag is half way back to the trailer with it, and Hayes' can't get his out from under his horse."

"Forgot to mention, always carry it at the ready when going into battle. I'm closing in on foot. How far is the target from you?"

"Too far for a good pistol shot."

"Stay put and stay alert. Just give him something to worry about. Watch in case he tries to move in."

Jake and Donaldson left their horses, working along

the ridge until reaching a point overlooking the mine tailings. The rifle shots now came with a cracking noise followed by the echoing boom. It was obvious from the sound when Nick and Hayes returned fire, spraying the general area where they determined the sniper was located.

Not seeing anyone move about below their position, the two continued downhill, keeping well in the trees until level with the tailings. Another shot rang out from where the ridge dipped to form a saddle. It was there the Taylor Flats trail crossed over to plunge toward the river in a series of zigzags. Staggered pistol shots answered the rifle, then a very different sound.

"I'd say Hayes got his rifle out," Donaldson said as the .243 rang out a series of volleys. "That should flush our shooter. He's got a damn good eye."

Following another exchange Nick said over the radio, "He's comin' your way, Jake. Big guy. Pretty sure it's Red Wing."

"Okay," Jake said.

When another rifle shot rang out, Nick answered with six pistol shots in a deliberately slow cadence. Hayes' rifle added to the exchange. Immediately following that, Jake saw someone career downhill in a straight descent, cutting the switchbacks. Crouching in tree cover on the west side of the tailings, the lawmen spread out and waited. Red wing stopped on the opposite side of the barren plateau about thirty yards distant, crouching behind a boulder with his back to Jake and Donaldson.

Mountain echoes give pistols a popping noise, rifles a loud bang, but a 12-gauge firing a three-inch magnum shell sounds like a ten-inch naval gun. Red wing must have believed that when a sizable chunk of tree next to where he had hunkered down was blown away three feet overhead and toppled over.

Diving for cover on the other side of the rock the Sioux was obviously trying to see where the shot came from. Jake obliged, felling another six-inch pine to the man's left, dropping it on him. Red Wing answered with a flurry of wild shots from a semiautomatic rifle that came nowhere near.

"Federal Officers. Give it up Red Wing. Put the weapon down and come out with your hands on your head." Jake's voice echoed off the cliffs, clearly repeating the order.

Red Wing hesitated, then must have thought to see the ranger and fired off another burst. His weapon was now set on automatic. The bullets passed high and well to Jake's right. With that exchange, the big man ran with surprising speed toward the mine, firing wildly, several shots actually coming close.

Wanting to take Red Wing alive, if possible, Donaldson opened fire, the rounds kicking up dirt in front of the running felon, intending as a warning to stop, but it wasn't working. Jake took aim and laid a mortar shell in the man's path. Red Wing practically went vertical, but ran through it as well. Donaldson intended for his next round to take out the man's foot. Nicking the boot heel, the fugitive stumbled sideways and fell, sending his weapon sliding several feet ahead. As he reached to recover it, Jake's shot split the weapon in half, sending pieces flying toward the mine tunnel.

"Don't shoot! Don't shoot! I give up!" Red Wing yelled, putting his hands on top of his head and remaining in a kneeling position.

"Cross your ankles and make like a rock," Davidson's voice rang out.

At that point the agent sprang from the trees, rifle slung over his back, ran up behind Red Wing, locking the man's hands and a clump of hair with one hand while training a pistol on him with the other. Jake moved in.

"Cuff him, Dave-o," Jake said, parodying an old TV cop show.

Davidson holstered his weapon, removed a set of cuffs from a rear pouch on his belt, and snapped one end on Red Wing's right wrist.

"Okay, Red Wing, other hand behind your back."

"Lucky for you, my next round is double-ought buck. Makes a hell of a mess out of the body," Jake said, keeping his shotgun trained on the big man who was actually trembling.

At that moment, a horrific roar sounded from the mine tunnel as if they had awakened a dragon. The next they knew the beast shot from the opening aimed straight at them. A motorbike. They were too close to the entrance to react as a helmeted biker careened between the prisoner and Jake, knocking the ranger to the ground. Red Wing fell against Davidson knocking him off balance. The lumberjack took the opportunity to lay a fist against the lawman's jaw and sprint for the mine.

Shaking off the hit, Davidson took aim with his pistol. Still not wanting to kill Red Wing, he sighted in on the lower leg and fired, but missed. Before getting off another round Red Wing disappeared into the tunnel. From his prone position Jake rolled onto his belly, leveled the shotgun, and fired at the biker, attempting to hit the back tire. The shot clearly ripped rocks, trees and ground in that area.

"I think you hit him," Nick said as he came limping up.

Jake thought so, too. The bike appeared to go out of control for a split second before careening around a big rock to disappear into the dense timber.

"Watch the entrance, but be careful. He probably has more weapons inside. Really would like to ask him some questions, out of sight of lawyers. I'll see if I hit whoever that biker was."

Jake trotted to where the trail paralleled the river back toward Beaver Creek Campground. Bending down, he picked up a piece of plastic while listening to the faint throttling of a bike moving away. The best he could hope for was Brother Bear taking exception to the noisy intrusion. He couldn't think of anything better than a frightened bear on a one-lane trail. Jake chastised himself for not asking his brother to guard the route, and wondered if semi-retirement had dulled him somewhat. He was not thinking ahead as in the old days.

₪

Incident at Beaver Creek

Chapter
32

"Lt. Bershinsky. Sgt. Elk Hunter. Come in," the Company Captain said, standing at a large map spread out over a table in the center of the tent. Lieutenants Granger and Thornton were with him along with a native. "You know Quan. He just brought news about a VC movement headed for our area. Guess you boys really ticked them off with what happened to Col. Cao. They've dispatched a company of regulars to wipe you out or make it too hot for you stay around."

"Where are they?" Jake said.

Quan was a Hmong spotter for the American forces. Using a long, slender finger, he pointed to the trail coming out of Laos through Cambodia north of Tay Ninh. It was here Jake's Native American platoon successfully disrupted the movement of enemy men and supplies, but the major coup was eliminating Col. Cao and his bloodlust company of eight-seven soldiers without firing a shot.

"Battalion suggested I pull you out until things cool down."

"So they get a victory without firing a shot? That will give them a big advantage, pump their morale, and wipe out most of what we've accomplished."

"I can't disagree. What do you suggest?"

"We'll go out and give Charlie a big howdy."

"I counted 164 soldiers," Quan said, the concern obvious on his face.

"I have thirty-one healthy. That's what, about five to one? Doesn't hardly seem fair to them," Jake said.

He wasn't boasting and Captain Harrison wasn't about to dispute that assessment. "I agree, but Granger and Thornton are in on this. I want to send a clear message we aren't about to be intimidated. They'll go with you. I'll also send a platoon of Hmong. That'll give you 140 men."

"Okay."

"And you'll be in charge . . . Capt. Bershinsky."

The announcement took Jake off guard as the two platoon leaders smiled.

"Your promotion came through this morning. You'll take over the Company when you get back." Everyone knew Capt. Harrison was about to rotate out, it just occurred sooner than expected.

Two days later, a heavy mist hung over an elongated open area in the forest just over the Cambodian border. Lt. Granger's Echo platoon waited for the advancing soldiers at the eastern end. The VC advance scouts had just signaled the all clear before disappearing into the forest—permanently.

These were North Vietnamese regulars, disciplined, trained, and well-armed that passed along the narrow trail in single file. The commander must have said something funny to the noncom next to him because they both laughed. The whole line was relaxed and in good spirits. They had traveled a long way without detection by the American Air Force. Granger's men took careful aim, each rifleman picking a specific part of the line by previous assignment. Thornton's Delta platoon waited for them to pass, cutting off their western flank, similarly taking careful aim on the column. The American ambush was simultaneous. As Echo and Delta Platoons open fire, the Hmong platoon rose up from the ground on the meadow side of the trail.

Discipline broke down as the Vietnamese were caught in a crossfire from hell. With no place to hide, survivors made for the forest—right into Jake's men. In a matter of fifteen minutes, only two soldiers remained alive in what units quietly called the Cái Chết or High Death Massacre. For reporters constantly hovering around the base, the official report called it Operation Howdy with a fictitious casualty count. They were miffed not having been aware of what was going down or allowed to tag along.

As they set the trap, Jake told Sgt. Miles he wanted two prisoners. As soon as the shooting was over, he called for a casualty count for his troops. Please to hear there was nothing more than a twisted ankle he called for the prisoners. In their late teens fresh from rice farms, they were terrified.

"Lt. Xiong, please translate for me. Tell these men that they live to take a message back north. I am Lieutenant, correct that, Captain Jake Bershinsky, known among his people as White Bear. I am the man they came to kill, but as you see, I remain standing while your comrades join Col. Cao as will any others they send here. We wait for them. Do they understand the message I wish them to take back?"

Lt. Xiong carefully rehearsed the message until the prisoners had it correct, then said, "They understand."

"Very good. Sgt. Elk Hunter, escort them back up the trail and send them on their way. Lt. Xiong, let them understand that they are to start running back to the north with this message and if they look back, the sergeant will shoot them."

~ ~ ~ ~

Switching to the general Forest radio channel, Jake called Curt. "Alert anyone on this end of the forest, there's a newer, black Suzuki dirt bike headed toward Beaver Creek on the Sebastian Mine River Trail. The rider is wearing black leather and full, black helmet. Observe only. Do not stop. Armed and dangerous." Jake had seen a pistol on the rider's belt. He waited as an obviously nervous Curt made the broadcast. When he finished Jake continued, "Now call my boss at the phone number I gave you. Tell him I'd sure like some serious backup. We've got our murder suspect trapped inside the mine. Perhaps the National Guard has a chopper that can bring backup in. Call the Forest Supervisor and advise him what's going down and we'll need authorization for a chopper to land here. Also, see if someone can come in on the meadow trail and take care of Agent Hayes."

"I'll try," Curt said, "But everyone has responded to the fire."

He'd forgotten about that. Jake looked back toward the mine.

"Hayes, here. I'm fine. Nick helped me into pretty good shade, and I got plenty of water, and his radio."

Feeling better about the NCIS agent, Jake watched as

Nick joined Davidson to take up a position on the east side of the tunnel. Working along the tree line along the west side of the tailings, he settled next to a sizable boulder.

"What's are move, Jake?" Nick called out.

"Wait for backup."

Donaldson was a patient man, but for the less experienced Nick, waiting was the hardest thing he'd done except for proposing to the girl he fell in love with in a forensics class. Patience was something Jake learned as a boy tracking mountain lions, just for something to do. It was an invaluable skill in Vietnam on more than a few occasions and helped his Native American unit repeatedly catch the wily VC flat-footed.

~ ~ ~ ~

It didn't take Curt long to come back with the news that Supervisor Todd was personally arranging for backup. Jake wasn't sure if that meant he was sending the secretarial pool or state police. An hour later the measured, thumping beat reverberated off the cliff walls of Sacred Mountain. Jake knew that sound well; the sweet song of a helicopter, but this sound was from no lightweight chopper as the sound grew to deafening intensity. Minutes later a Sikorsky Sea Stallion crossed over the saddle like a giant gnat from a B-grade, sci-fi flick. He wasn't expecting something that large and it seemed a bit of overkill to bring in the five or six US Marshals or State Police officers he was expecting to respond. This elephant could carry a full military platoon of forty. As it circled the tailings, he got a good look and could not have felt better as lines dropped from both sides of the chopper before disgorging its occupants, a heavily armed Marine platoon who took defensive positions as soon as they hit the ground. Once in place, their lieutenant trotted over to Jake, but there was yet another pleasant surprise. When the Sea Stallion lifted off to fly back over the saddle, the noise faded as it landed somewhere on the flats above to be replaced by the lighter thump of chopper blades. Almost immediately, a Little Bird helicopter swung in and landed, pointing its guns at the mine entrance as directed by the lieutenant. Aptly named, this was a small support craft carrying some big hurt with missile launchers and .50 cal. guns.

"Col. Bershinsky? Lt. Grossman, 1ˢᵗ Battalion, 23ʳᵈ Marines. What have we got?" the Lieutenant asked as he crouched behind the boulder with Jake.

"One individual as far as I know hold up in the mine. Left a AR-15 with us. I'm guessing he's re-armed himself. You guys are a surprise."

"We were just getting ready to head out on a mountain training exercise when a request came in saying some Federal agents needed backup. When our CO heard it was you, he thought this would be a good warm up. Two more platoons are standing by if you want them."

"Who's your CO?"

"Col. Dudley."

"Do-right Dudley?"

"Yes, sir."

The two met when Jake was assigned to the 75ᵗʰ Battle Command Training Division in Houston. Col. Dudley was one of Jake's better Judo competitors.

"I got a man down north of here on the flats."

"Saw him as we came in. That's where the first chopper went. One of my medics is looking after him. Made any contact with the guy inside?"

"Nope."

"Not a good deal."

"Been thinking on it. Bring any tear gas?"

"Sure did."

"Let's try that. Put it far back in as possible then use the chopper rotors to push it in."

"Sounds like a plan," the lieutenant said before radioing his sergeants to set the operation in motion.

Standing on the western side of the mine tailings next to the tree line, Jake waited, noticing the hairs on the back of his neck begin to tingle. Experience told him danger was on the prowl. He suspected that once the gas reached him, Red Wing would charge out shooting. A suicide stunt, but apt to get someone else hurt.

Jake moved closer as the young officer trotted over to the chopper and explain what the plan. In seconds, four Marines took position either side of the shaft in preparation to fire the gas. The chopper began revving up, creating a whirlwind. Across the way, Nick and Donaldson were not taking appropriate cover. Jake tried to alert them, but the chopper's whine drowned him out. Suddenly a sizable piece of bark was ripped from the tree a foot off his left shoulder. Jake's old Vietnam reflexes kicked in as he dove behind a suitcase-sized rock, tucking his head and rolling onto his back. His body had just flattened when he heard a bullet ricochet off the rock, throwing up a cloud of powder.

Taking a quick peek, he tried to see where the bullets were coming from, chastising himself for not considering the biker might come back. The chopper's rotors were making too much noise for anyone to hear either the shots or his warning. Another shot tore up the ground inches from his right leg. He needed better cover. There wasn't any. He had moved too far from the big boulder, so tried to make the most of what little was available and position the shooter. A fourth shot hit the rock just above his head. The bullets had to be coming from slightly to his right. When a fifth bullet hit the ground between his outstretched feet, it was time to return the favor. Jake fired off three quick shots of double-ought buck, spraying that area. That did two things. One was the cessation of being shot at for the moment. The other was to alert the soldiers that war had broken out on their left flank.

Quickly reloading, Jake tensed his muscles, ready to change position. A larger boulder and several trees stood twenty feet ahead and to his left. Another quick peek still didn't reveal his attacker's exact position. Rolling left brought him upright. Sprinting to new cover, he fired five rounds cross hip as he ran. The chopper whine began subsiding, but he wasn't sure if he had been shot at again. He made new cover in Olympic sprinting time. Meanwhile, the soldiers, Nick, and Donaldson realized what was happening and began to move into position. With silence returning, Jake heard the crack of a stick being broken. He glanced over his shoulder. Incredibly, Red Wing was standing thirty feet away, a rifle pointed at him with a clear shot.

There was little chance of drawing down on the Sioux let alone find cover as the fugitive brought the rifle to his cheek and with smug deliberateness, aimed at Jake's chest. He didn't shoot. Instead, Fulton's head jerked as eyes and mouth opened wide in frozen surprise. Jake leaped aside, bringing his shotgun muzzle around, ready to shoot, but checked himself as the big man dropped to his knees in slow motion.

Detecting movement further back in the trees, Jake held fire, uncertain if the unseen person was friend or foe. The answer came as Red Wing toppled face down in the rocky duff, a feathered shaft protruding from his back. Looking beyond, into the woods, Jake saw Runs Fast standing next to a conifer, an arrow notched and ready in his bow. It wouldn't be needed.

Straightening up, Jake stared at the body, then at Small Beaver's brother, smiled, and waived a weak thank you. Meanwhile, the soldiers formed a security perimeter as their lieutenant trotted over to Jake, stared first at the body, and then at the 16th Century apparition standing back in the trees.

"Is that him?" the lieutenant asked, nodding toward the man lying face down.

"Yes."

"He do that?"

"Red Wing killed his little brother. Native justice," Jake explained.

"I thought you said this guy was in the mine."

"He was. Obviously there is another way out."

With the arrow shaft broken off, they wrapped Red Wing's body in a tarp and lashed it in a basket attached to the chopper's skids preparatory for the flight to town.

"Before you boys head back I sure'd like to know what's so important about that old mine, and how he managed to go in and end up at my back."

"Let a couple of my men check it out in case it's been booby-trapped," the lieutenant said.

"Thanks. My confidence is a little shaky right now. That's the first time anyone's got behind me like that. Damn! I hate getting old," Jake grumbled. "Any word on my guy above?"

"The medics report he's okay. We'll fly him out when we leave."

A demolition specialist and two riflemen entered the mine. After what seemed an eternity they reappeared and signaling the all clear.

"One trip wire hooked to a bundle of dynamite. It's deactivated. You're not going to believe what's in there," the specialist reported.

Still shaken, Jake entered the tunnel. The horizontal adit went into the mountain about twenty yards before slopping downward at a five-degree angle. Equipped with a headlamp provided by the Marines, he continually scanned for any trap the Guardsman might have missed. Well into the tunnel, Jake stroked a mine support. It was new.

"So this is where the stolen timber went, to replace the shoring," he said to himself.

Further in, he began picking up the sound of an engine. Several hundred feet more the narrow adit opened into a large, natural cavern. From here, four tunnels bored deeper into the mountain, radiating like wheel spokes. Six pallets of cocaine were stacked in one tunnel while sufficient cutter was stored in another. They used the cavern room to process and repackage the drug for distribution, and then stored it in another tunnel, ready for shipment. The mystery was how the materials were brought in and removed without being seen. If through the gorge, it would take a lot more people than one person like Raymond Windpipe and they would have left obvious sign of passing through the defile.

"Quite the setup," Jake said.

"And another way out," Davidson said, pointing to a small tunnel that angled up from the cave with daylight showing at the end. An air shaft.

"Camera time," Jake said, and for the next twenty minutes took copious photos of the operation.

"What about the guy that got away?" Donaldson asked as they wrapped up the documentation.

"We'll deal with that when we get back."

Jake and the Marine demolition specialist were the last to leave.

"It's all yours," Jake said as they came out into the glaring sunlight.

With the flick of a button on a small, black box the size of a cigarette case, a rumble deep within the mine shook the ground followed by a chalky dust cloud spewing from the opening like a heavy smoker exhaling. When the dust settled, the demolitions specialist inspected his work. It was sealed. A check of the airshaft confirmed it had also caved in. The explosives had been set to collapse the cave room as well.

"Thanks for your help, gentlemen," Jake said. "I'll have an ambulance meet you at the airport to haul the body and Agent Hayes to the Albuquerque hospital. We sure appreciate your service."

"No problem. I'll have Tweety Bird take them. We can sling the dead horse out with ours as well," the lieutenant said.

"Thanks. Just drop it off by the truck out by the road. I'll have the road crew bury it."

"Any chance I can hook a ride? Need to round up my horse before he roams too far. He's probably at the truck," Nick said.

"No problem."

"Extend my thanks to Col. Dudley. Donaldson here'll buy you all a beer at the base. He's got one of those bottomless, government expense accounts." The agent winced and gave a pained smile, mentally calculating the cost of beers for the platoon and helicopter crews.

With the choppers gone, Jake locked the steel gate, stood back, took aim with his pistol, and fired a round into the padlock. Van would be pleased. One less abandoned mine and key to worry about.

₪

Incident at Beaver Creek

Chapter 33

"I don't know how you missed the biker with that cannon of yours," Davidson said. He was ahead of Jake as Runs Fast lead them along the river trail back to the campground.

"I didn't. That was buckshot I threw at him. I hit the tail end of the bike. That's what helped him turn the corner so fast."

"Aiding the escape of a felon? Not a good move," Donaldson teased.

Jake smiled weakly.

As they rode to Beaver Creek, Jake was disappointed no one had been able to intercept the biker. He kept checking the river for remains of a bike in the water. That would have meant an encounter with Brother Bear. He again mentally kicked himself again for not asking the bear to stand guard until they got back. He was obviously becoming soft.

Passing where the remnants of the log trap lay, he made a mental note to have the timber department send some folks to cut the pieces up and move them downstream. The last thing needed was a dam holding back the summer monsoon rains. It wouldn't hurt anything upstream, but a sudden release of water could harm unsuspecting people playing or fishing downstream. The problem was that the job would put the Timber Department behind in their planned work, and their boss was a veteran complainer.

"So be it. People are more important than targets designed to enhance work evaluations, budgets, and pay raises. They can work overtime like the rest of us," he thought.

Breaking out of the canyon into the flatter, grassy area, Jake wanted to give the horses a water break before heading up the trail back to the station. It was then a camper brought his daughter to where they were standing. She appeared to be seven or eight.

"My daughter wanted to see your horses. We're from Chicago. She's never seen a horse up close."

"Are you a Indian?" she said to Runs Fast.

He looked at the girl, a bit startled. Jake hid a chuckle behind his hand. Headband, feather, leggings, kilt, and moccasins, all he lacked was war paint only because he hadn't had time.

"I am terribly sorry," the father began to apologize, but the young man held up his hand and squatted in front of her.

"Yes, I am. I am Antigua Pueblo of the Sacred Mountain Clan," he said.

"What kind of feather is that?"

"It is the feather of the Golden Eagle."

Nick was impressed with the young man's patience and willingness to speak with children.

"You don't wear very many clothes," she said.

"That's not very nice, Margaret," her father said.

"That is alright. For children to learn they must ask questions, and we must give our best answer. My Clan is very different from the others on the reservation. We live the old way. This is how my grandfathers dressed before the White man came. I live in a house made of sticks and mud, and I farm and hunt for food for my family."

"Can I pet your horse?"

"Yes," he said. Taking her small hand, they stepped over to his pony. "To pet a horse, place your hand on her shoulder and then rub the neck. If she wants more she will lower her head so you can pet the nose."

Margaret followed the instructions. The mare turned her head to present its nose to be rubbed.

"It's soft. What's her name?"

"Pink Flower. Would you like to sit on her?"

"Oh, can I daddy?"

"Is it safe?" her father asked.

"Yes," Jake said. "My youngest is four and has ridden her many times."

With the girl seated on the horse's back, Runs Fast led her around the parking area as the mother took copious photos from the road. Easterners were still dubious about how civilized it was beyond the Mississippi River. Those pictures weren't going to help dispel such notions.

"I guess you are looking for the guy on the motorcycle that came down the trail," the father said.

"Yes. He was riding in a wilderness area. You saw him?"

"Yes. He, well it could have been a woman I suppose,"

the man said, casting a furtive glance at a blocky woman who joined them. "Anyway, *the person* stopped here a couple minutes then went on down the trail along the river. I watched . . . the person . . . through my binoculars. Went across the bridge and disappeared in those trees on the other side, came out, and went behind that hill."

"What about how was the person acting," the woman said.

"Yeah. What my wife means is that when the *rider* stopped, he or she rubbed his or her right leg," the father said.

"Like the person had a cramp," his wife said.

"HE was scratching his butt, Irene."

"SHE must'av scratched pretty hard, Rudolph. She had to wrap one of those big, cowgirl hankies around the leg just above the knee."

Jake turned away so they didn't see his eyes roll upward while keying his radio. "Jay's Roost this is Bershinsky. Would you call Miles McKenna and see if he could meet me at Beaver Creek Campground? It's urgent."

A few minutes later Curt said, "He'll be there in ten minutes."

When Miles arrived, the man from Chicago repeated what he had seen.

"There's an old bone yard back there. It's where grandpa and dad tossed broken machinery. I haven't been back there since I was a teenager. Gave some thought to selling it off as scrap a few years back, but never got around to it."

"I'd like to take a look," Jake said.

"Absolutely. I'd be interested knowing what a biker's doing back there anyway."

Miles unlocked the gate and drove his pickup over the bridge ahead of the three horsemen. That didn't pass

Davidson's attention.

"The biker must have had a key," he said.

"Yeah. That's a Forest Service generic lock. Hardly know why we bother sometimes with all the unaccounted keys in circulation, except of the cost to replace them," Jake answered.

A three-strand barbed wire fence ran parallel along the east side of the old road separating McKenna property from the reservation. A hundred feet from the river, a wire gate hung hidden in a stand of Aspen trees.

"Single track. Motorcycle. Been in and out of here several times," Jake said, pointing to a damp patch of ground as Miles lay the fence aside.

The two partially overgrown tracks the width of a vehicle followed the river several hundred yards before a faint trail turned off and uphill through a small saddle between two knolls. That the bike used this spur was obvious. On the other side of the hill the ground dipped into a football-sized bowl littered with old farm machinery and the rusting remains of a couple cars and trucks. Following the tire tracks through the tall grass was easy enough, even for Davidson. The dirt bike lay on its side behind an old, rusted truck, the right, rear fender area clearly damaged by Jake's shot.

As Jake matched the piece of plastic found at the mine, Miles said, "Well, where the heck do you suppose the rider got off to?"

"Any other way out of here?" Donaldson asked.

"The trail road continues west a ways then circles to the south where we have a couple windmills that pump water for the cattle. I only drive up there now and then to check the herd and pumps, or put out salt."

"Footprints go that way," Runs Fast said, pointing in a westerly direction.

"Nothing beyond except pasture until you come to the highway that runs from Tipton to Taylorsville. That's about four miles out. It'd be quite a hike," Miles said.

Runs Fast began following the track from horseback.

"Davidson, go with him, if you can still sit a horse."

"Doesn't matter. Hurts whether I sit or stand," he said.

"Well, I'll be," Miles said. "How'd that get here?"

"What?" Jake said.

"That '57 International pickup. Dad blew the engine and dumped it here. I fell in love with it as a kid and had dreams of fixing it up."

Jake and Miles walked over to the rusting, dark green pickup. Standing in front of the old binder Jake stared at it without speaking.

₪

Incident at Beaver Creek

Chapter
34

A spark of excitement and trepidation edged their voices as Jake and Henry walked from the bus stop to the 7-Eleven a couple blocks down the highway. They had just returned from a daylong trip to the Military Entrance Processing Site in Albuquerque. To beat the inevitable draft, Henry enlisted in the Army while Jake was there to fulfill the draft registration required of all eighteen-year old males. For the first time since meeting eleven years before, the inseparable brothers would take different paths—Henry to Ft. Leonard Wood, Missouri, and Jake to the University of New Mexico.

Henry bought a Snickers bar while Jake used the restroom. When they stepped outside Sally Morton was pumping gas in her mom's well-used '73 Ford Bronco with as many miles under the hood as Sally had under men.

"I'll see you tomorrow," Jake said, heading across the highway to take the shortcut trail home.

Ever since the rodeo incident, he dodged meeting her whenever possible. On the other hand, Henry didn't and went over to the pumps, a bit of a swagger in his step. About to enter the trees, Jake looked back. The two were standing together, talking, Morton playing a finger inside Henry's partially open shirt. Although his brother hadn't said it in so many words, he knew the two had been meeting. It looked as if Henry would be getting home later than planned.

There was no warm, welcoming glow in any of the windows as he approached the old ranger's house. Of course that only meant his mom wasn't in the kitchen or office. Drawing closer, a sinking feeling crept over him. Stepping inside he flipped on the light and called out, "Mom, I'm back."

The only response was the dull thud of a timber settling somewhere in another part of the house.

Stepping to the fridge he looked at the message board tacked on the side. "Hope everything went well. Called to fire in northern Colorado. I'll phone. Love, Mom."

He surveyed the empty house. Tending to be dark and cold anyway, when his mom wasn't there the thing became a depressing cave. No telling how long a fire assignment might last, at least a week, usually longer. With no desire to stay alone in a place that made creepy sounds and passed creepy smells like an old man, Jake decided to stay with Henry, as had become custom. That's where she'd call when the situation permitted, anyway.

As Jake came back down through the trees to the highway, he heard a car engine winding up some distance down the road, shifting gears clumsily. Someone was definitely torqueing the engine and putting on speed and didn't have a clue as to how. As he broke clear of the trees and climbed over the wood rail, right-of-way fence he saw the northbound headlights of the noisy vehicle come around the curve. It was going far too fast and swerved onto the shoulder. In that instant, the near-blinding lights illuminated something in its erratic path. A sickening thump merged with a crunch as the passenger side headlight went out. Partially blinded by the single headlamp Jake could see something fly into the air and hit the ground as the vehicle swung back onto the road, speed pass in a blur, and disappear up the road. All he could tell was that it was an old, dark-colored pickup.

When the truck hit the object on the side of the highway, something in Jake's chest screamed out. It looked like a deer. There were a lot of them hanging close to town this year, one in particular, which he and Henry's sisters unabashedly pampered. He loved wild animals, and it sickened him when one was killed in such a wasteful manner. That it could be the adopted orphan deer tore at his heart. Worse yet, it had landed in the middle of the northbound lane. A vehicle coming around the bend from the south wouldn't see it in time causing another accident. Running toward the dark lump in the road his heart began beating viciously. The closer he came the more he could see it was not a deer.

He never remembered the next minutes. When a car did come around the curve its headlights illuminated a young man seated on the shoulder of the road holding a body in his arms, rocking back and forth.

A State Trooper met an old pickup with a missing headlight several miles north of town. Normally, he pulled such vehicles over to issue a fix-it ticket, but this had been a long day starting when a truck jackknifed and overturned, blocking the highway. It took nearly ten hours of traffic control to clear the mess. No sooner had that been resolved, dispatch sent him into overtime working another accident, followed by a request to back up a fellow Trooper with a drunk driver. He had missed breakfast, lunch was a cold, pre-made, deli sandwich the investigating insurance agent generously brought, and dinner should have been hours ago. It would be cold, too. He didn't recognize the vehicle outright, but judged it to be a local. He'd get them next time.

Henry lay cradled in the arms of his brother, until with a gasp and shudder his life spirit left the mangled body. The impact had been so violent Henry's boots lay where he had been walking on the edge of the road, 150 feet away.

~ ~ ~ ~

"Something wrong, Jake?" Miles asked.

"I think this is the truck that ran Henry down," he said so softly to be almost inaudible.

"What?" He looked the truck over more carefully. "I don't know, Jake. I remember dad saying he sold it. I'd been saving money to fix it up and was so upset I never asked who he sold it to, and never came up here again."

Jake ran his fingers over the crumpled right fender. The windshield was shattered. Halting, he squat in front of the broken headlight and studied the hood.

"What does that look like, Miles?"

"I don't know. It's like a picture stamped into the hood."

"I want to take it to the crime lab, if that's alright. I can get a warrant if you want."

"Geez, Jake! That's not necessary. There are tools in the truck. We can remove it now."

At that moment, the beat of horse hooves averted their

attention. Davidson was coming up hard in an awkward sort of way, leading Runs Fast's pony.

"What's wrong? Where's the kid?"

"He followed the tracks to a cable strung across the river downstream."

"That's the water gauging station," Miles said.

"It appears whoever dumped the bike crossed over there. Runs Fast said to come get you. He's following on foot. You better hurry, though. That storm's moving in."

Since leaving the canyon, cumulus clouds silently maturing on the horizon now poised to unload on them. The dark area beneath where rain was already drenching the earth lay several miles away, but the lightening wasn't, as a volley streaked overhead.

"Go for it Jake. I'll get this hood off and meet you at my place," Miles said.

Jake swung into the saddle. "Take the horses to the school and hold up there. We'll meet there when this thing passes," he called to Davidson before racing off. The agent admired how horse and rider seemed to blend into one, hoping he could walk again once off his . . . if he could get off. Mohf's hooves sounded like the approaching storm as he thundered across the wood bridge before cutting cross-country along the north side of the White Tail.

The gauging station was no more than a cable strung across the river where the watermaster could ride a little platform over the river to check the depth and speed. Runs Fast was trotting along the service road toward the highway, head bent toward the ground, obviously following a track. Jake caught up to him as he crossed the highway and disappeared into the trees a moment before backing out.

"Footprints go into the trees, tire marks come out," he said as Jake dismounted.

An old, abandoned logging trail lay behind bushes. Although overgrown, a vehicle had backed in breaking off saplings and brush sprouting between the ruts.

"A boot print," Jake said, squatting to look at the tracks in the soft dirt. He then concentrated on the tire marks. The inside tread of the right rear was smooth, just like the tread observed on the road at the Taylor Flats trail head. He could get a good cast of both imprints except he'd never get back with the necessary plaster equipment before the storm hit. That's when he noticed a filtered cigarette butt in the grass a few feet from where the footprints ended. The burnt end was still warm. He carefully wrapped it in his kerchief.

"I sent Davidson to your place, but we'll never make it there before the storm hits. Let's try for McKenna's house," Jake said as the two swung up on Mohf's back, the horse snorting disapproval with the added weight.

Late afternoon thunderstorms were common during the summer, part of the monsoon weather pattern. Although generally scattered, one had to be constantly alert for their development because getting wet easily lead down the road to hypothermia. Lightning was something else to contend with. Every season, the hospital treated at least one hiker for one or the other despite repeated warnings. Fortunately, no one had died in nearly eight years.

Miles arrived with the International pickup hood in the back of his truck, pulling into a an adjacent vehicle shed just as a bolt of lightning struck nearby with a hissing roar as if ordering the rolling, black clouds to opened up. Forced to wait there, Runs Fast and Jake took refuge in the long barn with Mohf, both men reassuring the animal who was upset by the explosive thunder and sound of rain and hail pellets on the metal roof. Forty-five minutes later the storm moved on and the sun emerged.

Riding to the old lodge, they found the agent hunkered on the covered porch, his horse standing in the door looking out, a pleased smirk on its face while Pink Flower's muzzle busied a clump of grass nearby.

"I know Carrie will scream at me, but I didn't want him and the saddle getting soaked," he said sheepishly. "Your horse was happy standing on the porch until the rain stopped."

"She has never been inside a building. I will talk with Carry," Runs Fast said. "There is only a little mud to clean up. No harm done. I will clean it up and all will be okay."

Miles volunteered to take Donaldson and the hood to the Arroyo station, and then he would transport the evidence to Albuquerque. Riding home, leading the Saddlebred, Jake stopped at the campground to talk with the family there.

While the little girl nuzzled Runs Fast's mare again, Jake asked her father, "After you saw the biker drive into those hills, did you notice any vehicles drive pass here?"

"I really wasn't paying much attention. The fish started biting really well before the storm hit. The only one I remember was one of your green trucks, that big one with the red lights and hoses. It was going pretty fast. You should tell them to slow down through here."

₪

Incident at Beaver Creek

Chapter
35

When the first shot rang out felling Hayes' horse, Nick's horse dumped his rider and didn't stop running until reaching the Forest Service truck. It was standing there patiently waiting instead of continuing into Cosa Peluda. The chopper spooked him, but he didn't run far, quickly returning after the noisy thing left and Nick started shaking a metal pan of oats. Still, Nick got soaked before catching and loading him into the trailer as a shower swept through the area, and again as he unloaded the animal at the station. Katelyn met him on the porch as he staggered up the steps, shivering.

"Henry, see to Mr. Ewen's horse. Peter, show him the spare room, and get some towels so he can take a hot shower, and then bring me his wet clothes. I'll run them through the dryer."

Henry threw on a raincoat and hunched against the downpour, ran to the barn where Nick's horse got some oat hay, excess water scrapped off, and then a warm blanket draped over its steaming back. He was about to return to the house when his father and Runs Fast arrived. The rain had stopped so they stayed dry, but the storm dropped the temperature so all three were thoroughly chilled after putting their horses in the barn. Pink Flower was hesitant about entering the dark, cavern-like barn, but quickly acquiesced with a warming blanket, hay, and oats. Like her friend, Mohf in the next stall, she would make good use of the deep pile of straw, circling several times as if fluffing a pillow before lying down. It had been a long day.

Two helpings of beef stew tossed off everyone's post storm chill as a fire crackled in the fireplace. While she and Carrie cleaned up, Runs Fast sat by the fire so that Katherine could "read" some of her picture books to him. Lora helped them both. The boys were busy washing dishes.

The mutual decision was that Nick would stay overnight so the two officers could begin writing their account of the shooting. Wearing one of Jake's bathrobes while his clothes finished a run through the dryer, Nick beat Malachi to a chair and occupied the desk facing Jake. In retaliation, the feline lay between the keyboard and computer screen to glare at the intruder as Nick started filling out an electronic report. Before starting, Jake made some phone calls, the first to Curt.

"Curt, thanks for the heads-up call with the medevac helicopter. Great call. How's the fire up north?"

"A shower dumped on the area containing it to fifteen acres. Van is fire boss. Says not to worry, it was lightning caused."

That was a relief. The last thing Jake needed right now

was an arson fire investigation. After giving Curt a few more Atta boys, Jake answered a call from Davidson.

"I checked the hood in at the crime lab. That lab guy is s-t-r-a-n-g-e. Red Wing's on ice at the morgue. I'm now with Hayes at the hospital. The ankle is going to be tender for a while. Just a bad sprain, but they found a hairline fracture in the left wrist. Other than that, he looks ugly as ever. With Red Wing dead it looks like we're back to square one."

Jake filled him in on what they found.

"You think your fire guards are involved?" Davidson asked.

"No. They wear work boots with a heavy tread. The one I saw was a cowboy boot, no tread. Besides, their truck has dual rear tires, and neither of them smokes. They were on the way to La Posada canyon to check on a lightning strike. That's why they were driving so fast. Nope, not so easy."

"What about that pickup hood?"

"An issue from a long time ago."

The two rangers and Donaldson were in Pinchott's office by nine the next morning filing their reports and giving depositions regarding Red Wing's death. Nick was a bit gimpy from being tossed, but still serviceable. Donaldson was walking bow-legged and moving as if he had eggs in his pockets. Ibuprophen had Jake feeling reasonably good

"Nick, why don't you and Davidson go out to where we left the bike," Jake said as they left the attorney's office. "Maybe you can pick up on something else. We were kinda in a hurry last night. Run a check on the vehicle number and take it to the crime lab. Hopefully, they can find something to link it to a person. There's a trailer in the vehicle storage area. If Gus Diebert isn't around, ask the boys. They know where everything is hidden. Also, have Curt give Miles a heads up so he knows you're in there. I'm going to mosey over to the lab."

"So long as I don't have to ride a horse," Donaldson said, moving with the speed of an old man and making pained grimaces causing the secretary to hide a giggle.

~ ~ ~ ~

"That Navy guy didn't say what you wanted done with that car ornament," the lab supervisor said, laying a half-eaten donut aside on his desk as Jake walked in.

"I believe the vehicle it came from may have been involved in a hit and run death. An old State case. It appeared to me there was an imprint on it."

"Tut-tut. Looks like an imprint alright, maybe."

"Any chance you can lift it?"

"Probably. Tut-tut. I'll have someone take a look when they have some spare time."

Jake glanced around. The place looked like an ant's nest on caffeine.

"Tut-tut. By the way, the county sheriff over your way says he wants a copy of our reports on all your murder cases."

"Oh?"

"Says it's part of his investigation."

"He should get them from the US Attorney," Jake said.

"Yeah. Tut-tut. That's what I told him. Volatile sort. Tut-tut. Pushy, too. Got a call from State Attorney General asking why we aren't cooperating with him. Then some clown shows up with a court order demanding the info."

"A court order?"

"Yeah. From a county judge. Tut-tut. Arrived just

before you got here. Kind of extreme. I called Pinchott. He's dealing with it. Tut-tut. Anyways, there's a deputy camped in the lobby waiting for us to turn it over."

Jake peeked out the door leading to the lobby. It was Putnam. He called Pinchott.

"Any idea what's going on?" the attorney asked.

"No."

"The Sheriff's acting like a total jerk, of course, nothing new there. Anyway, the Magistrate issued an injunction on his court order until I can get this sorted out. It's being delivered to the lab."

"I think it just walked in the door with your secretary. Thanks."

Putnam watched with heightened curiosity as a tall brunette walked through the lobby to the receptionist's thick, glass window. Escorted inside, she handed the order to the lab director who read it and smiled. After burning a copy on the Xerox, Jake walked into the waiting room.

"Hi, Putnam. Heard you were camped out here."

The deputy said nothing. Remaining seated, one long leg crossed over the other. Anger was obvious as his face turned crimson, eyebrows narrowed, and one corner of his upper lip arched in a tiny sneer.

Jake looked down at his cowboy boots then said, "Might as well go home. Nothing here for you," and handed him a copy of the judicial order.

"Sheriff Barker ain't gonna be happy about this at all. Not at all. You boys are trying to cover up something."

"You tell Clyde Barker there are proper ways to stick his nose into a Federal investigation and that's to contact the US Attorney."

"Yeah? Well, we'll see what our Congressman has to say about this." He started to storm out of the room.

"You hurt your leg, Putnam?" Jake called after him,

noting a slight limp.

"Went to sleep sitting there, if it's any of your business, which it ain't."

"That guy's the biggest jerk I've ever encountered," the receptionist said. "Got all huffy when I told him to take his smokes outside. He knows the law."

Jake borrowed an envelope and went out to the covered entry. After watching Putnam's pickup peel out of the parking lot, he looked at the trashcan, one of those with a tray on top for cigarette butts. There were a half dozen remnants sticking upright out of the black sand. Using a pen, he herded each into the envelope.

₪

Incident at Beaver Creek

Chapter
36

Once overcoming a volatile temper, patience became one of Jake's strong points; however, a subtle, nervous twinge began to roam around inside his gut with discovery of the old International. Every day, whenever the phone rang or Curt called on the radio, he expected to hear something about the case, but the calls only concerned routine matters. When the phone rang at 6:05 A.M. a week later, he was in the shower. Covered with soap he knew he'd never make it before they gave up. Katelyn had been up most of the night with Katherine who had the flu. Having just fallen asleep, she'd sleep through a train wreck. Whoever it was continued ringing so he shut the water off preparing to get out before the rest of the house was awaken. Then it stopped.

"Dad," Peter said sleepily, poking his head into the

bathroom. "That attorney guy in Santa Fe is on the phone. I told him you were in the shower, but he said you are to grab a towel and speak to him."

Wrapped and dripping, Jake skidded toward the bedroom, the wood floor cold and slippery from the water he was dripping. After listening he said, "I'll be there soon as I can."

He never made a trip to town with lights and siren, but did this time. Upon arriving at the Federal Building, four Marshals circling the secretary's desk voiced a greeting as she hustled him through the outer office. The State Attorney General was huddled with Pinchott.

"Jake," Pinchott said. His expression was grim, "What does that truck hood have to do with these murder cases. You didn't say anything about it in your report."

"An old hit and run from a long time back. It's a State case. Why?"

"The lab was able to lift this imprint from it," he said, handing over a photo. It was hard for Jake to look at it without his heart feeling as if breaking. "Recognize it?"

"It's from a belt buckle. My brother won it at the last rodeo he attended. He was wearing it the night he was run down by a hit and run driver."

"Any evidence to tie a driver to the vehicle?"

"I doubt it. I asked Miles McKenna. He said his father sold it to some kid, but doesn't know who."

"I might be able to help with that," Davidson said, entering the office to join them. "Was up that way again yesterday and had a talk with Mr. McKenna. We went through his dad's files and found this."

Pinchott looked at the yellowed, hand-written document before handing it to the Attorney General, then said, "The cigarette butts you collected at the lab match the one you found on the forest. They found some blood on the motorcycle, too. It all points at Deputy Putnam. I rousted the Magistrate on the second tee this morning. He didn't hesitate signing an arrest warrant for him right then and there. The Marshals will be serving it. They have a search warrant, too. I wanted you and Donaldson along. It's your case."

"Okay," the AG said after reading McKenna's document, "this has gotten pretty sticky. Let me call the State Police, and then we will all go together."

Deputy Putnam's usual cocky demeanor flushed the color of a toilet bowel as Jake walked into the Sheriff's office followed by a train of suited individuals and two uniformed State Police. Barker saw them, too, and stormed out of his office.

"You get your Federal ass out of here, Bershinsky," he said.

"Chill, Sheriff," the AG said, stepping forward to stand between them. "We're here on official business."

Donaldson handed Barker a tri-folded paper. "This is a search warrant, Sheriff Barker. We'll be taking a look at Deputy Putnam's truck, specifically the rear tires. Oh, by the way, Deputy, Officer Bershinsky has something for you."

"Bertram Putnam, you are under arrest for operating a motorized vehicle in a wilderness . . ." The deputy sneered as Jake deliberately paused, "And for suspicion of manufacture and trafficking of a controlled substance, and for the murder of Darrell and Raymond Windpipe, and Little Beaver. You'll remove your side arm and place it on the desk."

Putnam wobbled slightly as his knees buckled, hesitating a moment to look at Sheriff Barker, and then at the small army fanning out behind Bershinsky. With utmost caution, he removed his service belt and laid it on the desk, his hands visibly shaking as the last color drained from his narrow face.

"What kind of lies have you trumped up this time, Bershinsky?" Barker shouted. "Don't worry Bert. He ain't got nothing my attorney can't beat down."

"You have your own worries, Barker," the AG said.

Barker's tongue started wagging trash, but before he could work up a good run the AG said, "Step into your office, Mr. Barker. There's a little matter of a hit and run from thirty years ago I want to discuss." A State Trooper at each shoulder, the four men retired to his office, where the attorney took a seat behind the big desk, opened a top drawer against Barker's objections, and removed a revolver. The AG started his career as a cop.

Meanwhile, Jake was busy removing the right rear tire from Putnam's patrol pickup, a tire with a smooth, inside tread. As it was marked as evidence, the County Attorney arrived. A large man, both in height and breadth, and seriously out of condition, he was panting heavily and sweating.

"I got a call there was a problem over here," he said, between heavy gasps for air.

"The Attorney General is with the Sheriff. I think they want to talk to you," Jake said.

As the Marshals started to lead Putnam out in cuffs, Jake stopped them. "How come you're limping, Putnam? Leg asleep again? I think you should take a look, Marshal Scott, so he can't say he was hurt during transport."

Removed to a side office, the Marshal dropped Putnam's trousers. The right thigh was wrapped with a bloody gauze bandage.

"I'll just bet when we have a doctor examine that we'll find that wound was caused by buckshot," Jake said, realizing he was gloating. It felt good.

~ ~ ~ ~

Friday afternoon Curt radioed that Pinchott wanted to speak with Jake on the phone at his convenience. It took over an hour to reach the Roost, the nearest phone.

"Thought you'd like to know, the lab was able to recover more evidence tying Sheriff Barker to the truck. He's being held without bail. Deputy Bradley's taken over with assistance from the State Police. Best news, though, I struck a deal with Putnam and he opened up implicating his boss in the drug trafficking. Barker didn't authorize the murders of Darrel Windpipe or the Little Beaver boy, but he knew about them and didn't object. That was the doing of Red Wing, Humphreys, and Chandler."

"Chandler? Who's Chandler?" Jake said.

"Apparently he's the contact between Barker and the cocaine cartel in Columbia, South America where the drugs originated. The boys from DEA have been trying to corner him for several years with no luck. He ordered the two boys murdered and participated in Darrel Windpipe's execution. According to Putnam, Chandler was in the mine when you showed up."

"We didn't see him. Probably escaped through the trees when Red Wing and I squared off."

"According to Putnam he had just gotten there with a shipment and went way back into one of the tunnels to sleep where the generator didn't bother him."

"Then we better tell DEA where he's at so they can reopen the mine."

"From what you said about sealing it, that would be expensive. I know there's nothing in their budget for something like that. They'll have to seek a special funding request from Congress, and the way they're acting right now, that could take . . . oh, a year or so." Pinchott chuckled, revealing for the first time in their relationship that he had a sense of humor, too.

"Did Putnam shed any light on how the stuff was brought in and taken out?"

"Helicopter. Sandia Tours, the aerial sightseeing outfit in Albuquerque."

"Sweet. Always there and never seen. They routinely fly the canyon low to give the tourists a view. They could come in from the west and Curt wouldn't see them land, and when they took off it looked as if they were just flying as usual. We never paid them any attention."

"Anyway, as for Raymond Windpipe, Putnam says that he watched Barker beat him using Red Wing's club," Pinchott continued. "Red Wing did the surgery. Seems Barker caught the younger Windpipe and his daughter in bed. She's in juvenile custody and quarantined by order of the Health Department with a venereal infection. A Grand Jury is to hear drug trafficking and murder charges against Barker next Wednesday morning at ten. Be in my office by three Tuesday afternoon. I want to go over your testimony. My secretary will be in touch as to what hotel you'll stay at."

"If it's alright with you, I'll stay at my mother's house."

~ ~ ~ ~

"This is Jim Colburn, KFSM Channel 64 news at the Federal Courthouse in Santa Fe. Problems continue for former Fredericks County Sheriff Clyde Barker who is under indictment by a Grand Jury on several Federal charges including the manufacture and trafficking of illegal drugs and the brutal murder of Raymond Windpipe. He is also charged with complicity in the murders of Navy Seaman Darrel Windpipe and Small Beaver, the grandson of well-known Native American activist, Chief Toleshnec of the Antigua Pueblo tribe. To complicate things for Barker, the Grand Jury also determined that the hit and run death of a Native American in 1964, thought to be a State case, is actually a Federal case, and they issued an indictment accusing Barker of that death as well.

"We have been told that in the interest of justice, a decision was made to hold separate trials. The murder and accessory to murder trial of the three Antigua Pueblo members began an hour ago. A trial on the hit and run charge is scheduled for the middle of next month, and the trail on drug charges is scheduled three months from now. 1992 is going to be a busy year for the former Sheriff of Fredericks County.

"Hold on. John, turn your camera up the street. I can't believe this, but there is a large group of Native Americans approaching on horseback. I've never seen anything like this outside the rodeo arena. It looks like a . . . a war party. What? Who? I've just been told the man riding in front is Chief Toleshnec, the radical Indian rights movement leader. I'm going to try to work my way toward him for an interview, but police are lining up between us."

The young woman was not quiet as she charged into the courtroom to whisper in Pinchott's ear.

"Mind sharing with this court the cause of the interruption, Mr. Pinchott?" the judge said, scowling from his lofty perch.

"Your Honor, there's a disturbance outside. May we have a short recess?"

"What kind of disturbance?"

"It's Toleshnec, Your Honor. He's outside the courthouse with a lot of his warriors, and it's not looking at all friendly."

The judge's eyebrows shot into his white hairline, well

aware of that name. As a prosecutor, he had been involved more than once with trials involving the man. He quickly granted a recess to disappear into his chambers, locking the doors securely behind him.

When Jake stepped out of the courthouse, he saw the old man and his warriors still on horseback waiting behind a hastily prepared barricade, ignoring the shouts of news people wanting to speak with him. The situation didn't look good, not good at all, like crystallized dynamite ready for a bump. Jake walked through the human cordon.

"Hello, Uncle."

"You have said White man's justice has changed. I have come to see this for myself," Toleshnec said, seated straight in the saddle and looking very stern.

"There isn't a lot of space in the court room, but you and Small Beaver's father have a right to be there. The others can wait in the park across the street."

The two Antigua dismounted and followed Jake into the courthouse as the others moved across the street, city officers joining the State Police and Marshals to keep them from being bothered. Entering the courtroom, Toleshnec and his son stood with their backs against the rear wall, arms folded. When the judge re-entered he stopped mid-step on the riser to his bench and stared. Re-collecting himself, he resumed his chair, continuing to stare at the two men. Finally he said, "Can we get on with this?"

"Your Honor, I object," the defense attorney said, pointing at the two men. "Those men cast a pall over this court room denying my client the possibility of a fair trial."

"Would the court deny the father and grandfather of one of the victims their right to peacefully watch?" the prosecutor rebutted.

"This is an open trial, Mr. Jennings. Even if these proceedings were closed to the public, I would not have entertained an objection to their peaceful observance. Objection over ruled. Present your case, Mr. Herrera." The judge secretly hoped that gesture would help toward patching a couple bridges the two had damaged long ago.

Toleshnec was concerned when he saw no Native Americans seated in the jury box. Pinchott assisted Herrera, a young Hispanic, dark, eyes flashing with excitement. Despite appearing nervously eager, he presented the government's case with a methodical and detailed train of evidence, each piece like a nail driven into the lid sealing a box—possibly for Barker, a pine box.

Carrie testified, as did Dale and Muir, about the discovery and recovery of the Windpipe brothers' bodies. Doc Ryan testified about the autopsies. Ken gave testimony as to the recovery of Little Beaver's personal effects, which led to Red Wing and subsequently to Putnam. Jake was on the stand for nearly two hours tying all the information together. It was his testimony the defense had to attack and weaken.

"Officer Bershinsky," the defense lawyer began, "is it true that you and my client have known one another since childhood?"

"We first met when my mother moved to Taylorsville to work for the Forest Service. I was seven."

"You two have not been on the best of terms during all these years, is that correct?"

"That is correct."

"In fact, on several occasions you physically attacked him."

"Barker had a habit of bullying younger kids. My brother and I addressed that issue with him and his friends on a couple occasions. We were in sixth and seventh grade at the time."

Hererra gathered himself to leap to his feet to object

until Pinchott placed a hand on the young attorney's arm, smiling faintly as he shook his head to say, no.

"Isn't it a fact that you have held a long-standing and deep seeded animosity toward my client?"

Jake paused, appearing to be thinking about that, finally answering, "If you are asking if I like the man, in a word, no, but deep seeded animosity? When I returned from Vietnam, I could care less about what he did. I only came back to visit my mother and family before moving on to my military assignment. After leaving Taylorsville to attend college, I had no contact with him until returning to take the ranger position with the Forest Service."

"When you assumed law enforcement duties in this area, was not my client involved in the commercial lumber business on your forest?"

"It's not my forest, but yes, he operated a business that dealt with my employer."

The answer seemed to break the attorney's thoughts, and he cleared his throat to collect himself. "Did you at any time use your authority and animosity to cause problems for my client?"

"Did I go out of my way to harass Barker? No. Whenever there was a question or concern regarding logging procedures, the timber people on the District or in the Supervisor's Office handled that. They were contractual problems, not criminal."

"What about an incident that occurred in 1985 when a man was killed while felling timber? A man who was employed by my client's lumber company?"

"That was investigated by OSHA."

"Did you also conduct an investigation?"

"I filed a report as first responder to the incident."

"Were your findings in agreement with that of the OSHA investigators?"

"No."

"What was your response to the . . . *official* . . . OSHA findings?"

"I told the Forest Supervisor my concerns and why. The final determination was his. He chose not to pursue my findings, and that was the end of it."

"Didn't that happened more than once, regarding supposed problems with my client's lumber business?"

"Yes."

"Haven't you been secretly gunning for my client, just waiting to pin something on him because you felt he was responsible for the murder of your brother?"

Again, Pinchott held Hererra in check as Jake stared at the attorney for quite a while, daggers of anger firing from his eyes like .50 cal. machine gun bullets. Finally he said, with a clear, calm, but very firm voice, "Mr. Harper, let's get something very clear. Until the evidence surfaced implicating Clyde Barker, I had no idea he was responsible for the death of my brother. Witnesses at the time put him a long ways from the scene of the crime. If I had entertained such a thought, I would have spent every ounce of energy to bring him to justice, and he wouldn't be sitting at that table right now, and the Windpipe brothers and Small Beaver would be alive today."

Barker's attorney glanced at the jury, instantly realizing the attempt to discredit Jake had backfired.

The defense felt better upon cross-examination of the crime lab director concerning DNA tests and the susceptibility to error, even though the lab had conducted four separate tests. That left a hint of doubt in the jurors' minds. Mr. Hererra then played an ace.

"The government calls Brian Fields."

"Objection!" Harper shouted, leaping out of his chair, nearly upsetting it backwards. "Mr. Fields is a defense witness."

"Your honor, Mr. Fields is a DNA specialist who defense commissioned to conduct independent tests on the instrument used to beat both Darrel and Raymond Windpipe to death; however it will be noted that the defense has chosen to not use Mr. Fields' findings. I believe the jury has the right to hear all the evidence and decide if there are any discrepancies."

"Over ruled. Mr. Fields, take the stand."

The coloring in Harper's face gave new meaning to "White man," as he sat down slowly.

The jury, almost to the person, leaned forward in their chairs as Fields detailed how his company used slower, more accurate DNA testing.

"I found the ax handle to be impregnated with tissue from both of the Windpipe brothers," he said. What he said next was the final nail in Barker's box.

"While conducting tests, I also examined what would be the end used to hold the instrument and found traces of tissue belonging to two individuals. One sample belonged to Fulton Red Wing, deceased, and the second sample belonging to the defendant, Clyde Barker."

The judge looked over his glasses at the defense table. "Mr. Fields, did you report this to the defense attorney?"

"Yes, your honor, both orally and in writing. When I learned that he did not plan to divulge those findings, I felt compelled to contact the US Attorney."

"Mr. Harper, I want to see you and the prosecution in my chambers . . . now! This court stands adjourned until 10 A.M. tomorrow." The judge nearly broke the gavel when he slammed it down.

Up to this time, the trial had lasted four days during which Sheriff Bradley arranged for Toleshnec and his warriors to lodge at the fairgrounds. Each morning the group rode to the courthouse and waited in the park as the two elders went inside the building. The Parks and Rec Department sent someone to keep the horse droppings picked up while stewing over the amount of grass the horses were consuming with great zeal. Each night the Antigua sat around a campfire, listening intently as Toleshnec explained in detail what happened that day. Jake was there, too, helping them to understand the strange sounding procedures, but it was Pinchott who came to explain what had happened that afternoon, Toleshnec translated his words into Tewa.

"Barker's attorney attempted to cover up evidence directly connecting Barker to the murders. He will be disbarred. That means he will no longer be an attorney, but that is the least of his troubles. He's going to need a very good attorney to keep from serving time in jail. The judge declared a miss-trial and scheduled a new hearing in ninety days to give Barker's new attorney time to prepare. However, Barker took it upon himself to contact me to broker a deal. He will plead guilty to second-degree murder if we take the death penalty off the plate. I've agreed to that.

"Putnam has agreed to turn over the names of all the couriers and distributors, but more importantly, from who and how they obtained the drugs. Jake's boss will be happy because that directly effects the investigation in Gallup. In exchange, we won't pursue the drug charges, give him a new identity, and see that he's placed in a facility where the prisoners don't know him. As for the hit and run, Barker's pleading innocent. He's acting very strange about that. We will proceed with that trial as scheduled. That's the best we can do about the murder of your grandson."

"Thank you, Mr. Pinchott, for coming to speak with us," Toleshnec said. "Our hearts are heavy, but my grandson's death has been avenged. The one who killed him is dead. I came only to see if what my nephew has said, that The People can find justice in White man's law is really true. Not that White Bear would ever lie to us, but after all the years and all the battles, it was hard to understand."

The next morning Barker appeared before the judge where Hererra laid out the deal. The guilty plea was accepted. As Jake and Toleshnec stepped from the courthouse, side-by-side, cameras and reporters again vied for an interview. Toleshnec stopped. He had been here before. He secretly enjoyed the spotlight.

"I will speak to them, now" he said, and walked up to the battery of microphones aimed in his direction as cameras flashed. "It has taken many years, and there are still many miles remaining on our trail to equality, but I have learned that our people can find justice in White man's courts." With that, he turned to Jake and placed a firm hand on his shoulder. "Thank you, White Bear. Now it is time we return home, and go on living."

"There is still one matter to be settled before a certain spirit can begin his final journey," Jake said.

~ ~ ~ ~

Barker displayed a smug expression as his trial began for the hit and run murder of Henry Riley. He knew conviction was a forgone conclusion when Sally Morton's name appeared on the prosecution's witness list. He was obviously going through with this trial for another purpose.

A very different-appearing person stepped to the witness stand when they called Sally's name. Pinchott's secretary supervised her clean up, inside and out; her hair was done, and a bit of makeup applied, and put in a modest dress. That was probably the first new thing she'd had since

Henry's death.

"Miss Morton, how long have you known the defendant?" Hererra asked.

"Since we were little kids."

"Were you intimate with the defendant?"

"Objection," the defense spoke out loudly. "Such a relationship has no bearing here."

"On the contrary, Your Honor," Hererra argued. "The relationship between Miss Morton and the defendant is important to understand what transpired at the time of the crime in question . . . and why."

"Over ruled. Proceed."

"If you mean, did we have sex, you bet. A lot of times. At least for a while."

"For a while? Then it ended?"

"Yes, thank God."

"Did you end the relationship?"

"No. He did. I prayed for years he'd find someone else. He finally did and left me alone."

"Why did you desire the relationship to end?"

"He began using me for a punching bag. If something didn't go his way, he'd take it out on me. Then something happened and he threatened to kill me. He meant it, too."

"What prompted him to threaten to kill you?"

"After taking my mom to work at the all night truck stop, I stopped to put a couple dollars' worth of gas in the Bronco. Henry was at the station and we talked. He'd just come from some tests or something with the Army. He was pretty excited. He'd joined up.

"I liked Henry. He was a sweet kid. He always showed me respect. I tried to get him to come to my house for a while, but he said it had been a really long day and he was too tired to be any good. That was Henry. When it came to having sex, he was going to get satisfaction, but not at the expense of not giving pleasure back. He once said, 'The more you give the more you get back.' That's what made him one hell of a bed partner."

The judge coughed, several women on the jury blushed, and a couple of the men and women giggled. Hererra, knowing that statement was coming, waited for the effect to settle through the courtroom.

"Anyway, we sat in the car and kinda talked. After a while he went inside to use the bathroom and I left. I had just crashed on the sofa to watch TV when I heard a vehicle pull into the driveway that ran alongside the house. I was hoping it wasn't Clyde Barker, but nobody else would show up that time of night. I hated everything about him. Clyde had this attitude that he was the master and I was his slave. I could only go out with him. If he wanted sex, I was his wall plug. I couldn't speak to any other boys. If I did, he'd beat them up. Of course, he was scared shitless of Henry and Jake, so I would talk to them. Well, I talked to Henry. Jake avoided me after that time at the rodeo a couple years before."

"If you knew the defendant would assault boys who talked to you, why did you pursue conversations with Henry Riley?" the prosecutor asked.

"I hoped Clyde would pick a fight with Henry and get his ass kicked good, then he'd have to leave me alone. I had no idea Clyde would murder him."

"How do you know the defendant murdered Henry Riley?" Hererra quickly asked as defense opened his mouth to object. The question stopped him cold.

"He told me what he'd done. When I heard that vehicle come into the drive I looked out the window and saw this old pickup. I didn't recognize it, but Clyde climbed out of it. He walked in through the back door without knocking as usual. He acted like he owned the place. He was laughing. Not one of those happy sounds. It's was the sound he made after hurting someone.

"I asked him whose pickup that was 'cause he didn't own a car. He said it was his. He just bought from old man McKenna for a special occasion. He was prancing around the kitchen like he couldn't stay in one place more than a few seconds. All the time he was laughing and giggling. He was scaring the hell outta me.

"I saw the windshield was broke and asked if he was in a accident? His laugh grew louder as he said, 'It was no accident, baby doll.'"

"So I said, 'Geez, Clyde! What'd ya hit?'"

"'Oh, just a rabbit,' he says and laughs again. 'Just a dirty, brown rabbit. Should 'a seen him fly. Yeah. A real flying rabbit.'"

"How could a rabbit cause this much damage?" I said, then I realized what Clyde was babbling about and kinda screamed Henry's name."

"'Yeah, Henry, the flying rabbit,'" he says and laughed real hard.

"Flying Rabbit was Henry's Indian name. Then Clyde stopped laughing. There was a real, crazy evil in his eyes as he said, 'Yeah, that filthy Injun, Henry Riley. Sent him a hundred feet in the air.' Then Clyde grabbed my throat, jerked me close to his face, and said, 'I told you what'd happen to anyone that got frisky with you. But no, you had to egg him on. Did you like that brown meat? Did it taste like chicken? I warned you what'd happen, so it's your fault he got killed. And that half-breed Bershinsky is next. Yeah, I'll put 'ol Whitie Bear right next to his buddy. And if you so much as whisper anything about this you'll go right next to them. You got that, bitch?'"

"Then you are saying Clyde Barker admitted to you that he killed Henry Riley?" Hererra said to emphasize the testimony.

"He bragged about it. I saw the truck. I saw the broken windshield and the blood all over the front. I never could get that out of my mind except when I drank. He really would have killed me if I said anything to anyone, and Jake Bershinsky was next, but he went off to college."

When the jury foreman stood and delivered the guilty verdict Jake's whole body sighed as a great weight seemed lifted from his shoulders.

As Barker was about to be taken away, he turned to Jake and said, "Hope you enjoyed that." His whole intent had been to cause Jake to relive the details of Henry's death and stir up as much pain as possible.

Jake looked at him and smiled. "I have lived with that in my heart all these years, but what you did has set the pain free. I feel a great joy now, knowing my brother's spirit is free go to the Land of the Dead and be with his family. Thank you."

At least Jake hoped Henry would go on ahead of him, while realizing he would miss the companionship they had shared over the years.

וֹ

Incident at Beaver Creek

Chapter 37

The celebration barbecue to welcome the Sacred Mountain Clan to their new home brought the entire Pueblo to the new school site. Other Pueblo chiefs and the governor came as well. Toleshnec's brood of grandchildren joined others their age, noisily engaging in eating and games. White Warrior was demonstrating the Judo katas used to bring home a promotion to green belt. Little Cricket was wrestling with boys his age. Those matches were more or less a draw, but earned him respect. Girls from the Antigua Pueblo were busy comparing observations about the eligible bachelors added to the selection pool. Runs Fast jumped between dancing and drumming. Carrie was getting to know her new extended family. Katelyn was having a great time with the other women as they turned out a continuous stream of tacos and conversation. Toleshnec, Burning Arrow, the Pueblos' governor, Council president, and clan chiefs were ensconced in a circle discussing how to overcome the drug problem in light of a new Federal grant Pinchott had helped them to secure. Toleshnec's participation ended, however, when Jake's mom arrived and the two friends removed to quiet spot to talk.

Jake was retrieving a bag of flour from Miles' truck when Mike Dale drove up. When Carrie returned to school with plans to assume full-time teaching upon graduation, Douglass appointed Dale as Jake's new assistant.

"Hey, Boss," he called out from his truck window. "Family disturbance at Long Lake Campground."

Jake waived, finished taking the flour to his wife, whispered in her ear, gave her a kiss, and retrieved a weapon from his truck. Strapping on the .38 he climbed in beside Mike and said, "Well, hi ho Silver, Kemo Sabe."

₪   ₪   ₪

Sean Patrick O'Mordha

A retired police officer, Sean melds first-hand knowledge of police procedures, the US Forest Service, and Native Americans of the Southwest in this adventure. An award-winning and prolific writer, he authored numerous short stories and police articles before turning to novels. Incident at Beaver Creek begins the saga of Jake White Bear Bershinsky, a man with a foot in two worlds.

Visit Sean at

oldguey.webs.com
and
celtic-publications.xipherzero.net